STAR SCOUTS

THE

INVASION

OF THE

SCUTTLEBOTS

STAR SCOUTS
THE INVASION OF THE SCUTTLEBOTS

MIKE LAWRENCE

Color by Norm Grock

First Second
New York

TO MY BOYS, HANK AND GUS,
WHO ALWAYS THINK MY JOKES ARE FUNNY.
MOST OF THE TIME.

PART
1

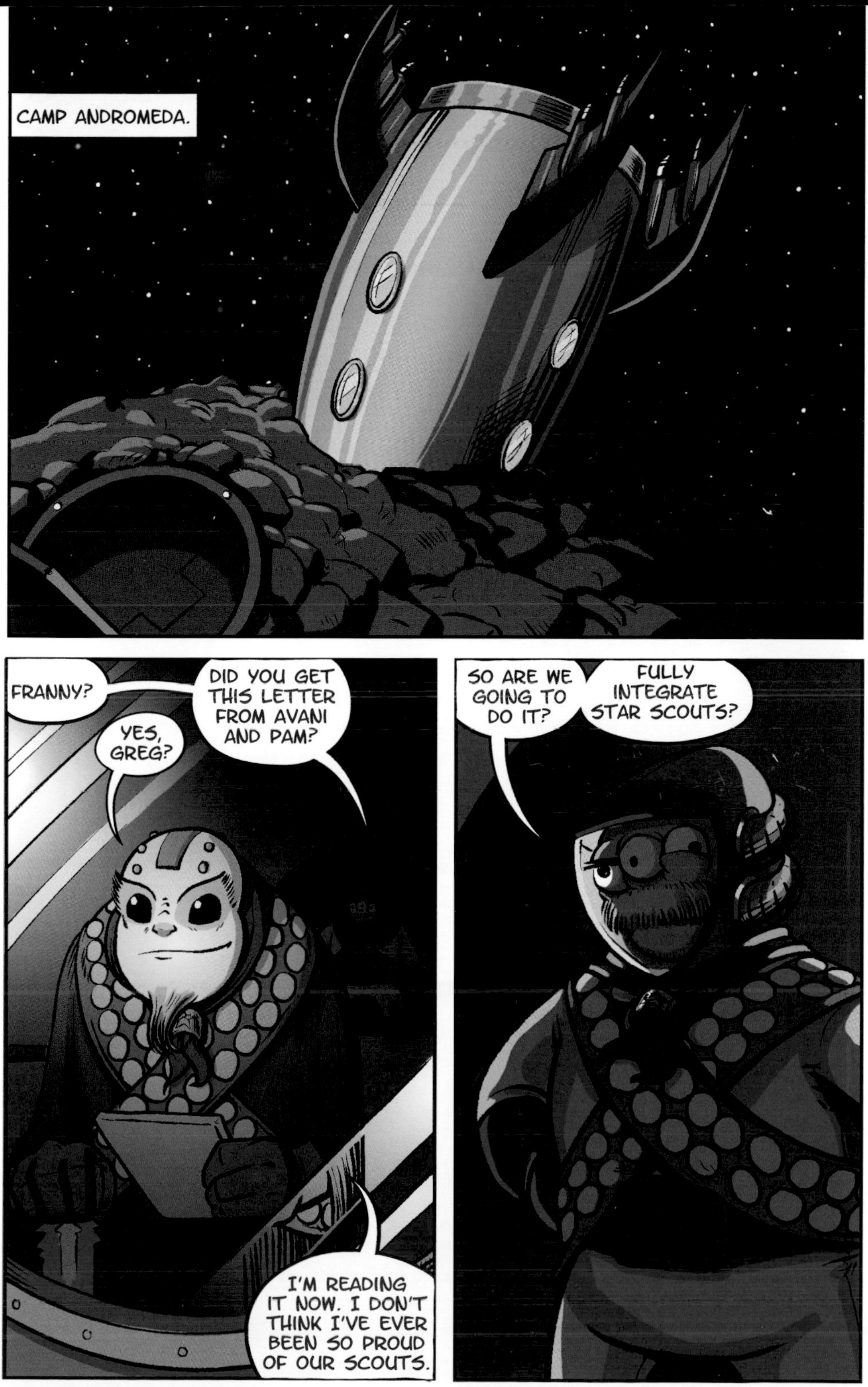
CAMP ANDROMEDA.
FRANNY?
YES, GREG?
DID YOU GET THIS LETTER FROM AVANI AND PAM?
I'M READING IT NOW. I DON'T THINK I'VE EVER BEEN SO PROUD OF OUR SCOUTS.
SO ARE WE GOING TO DO IT?
FULLY INTEGRATE STAR SCOUTS?

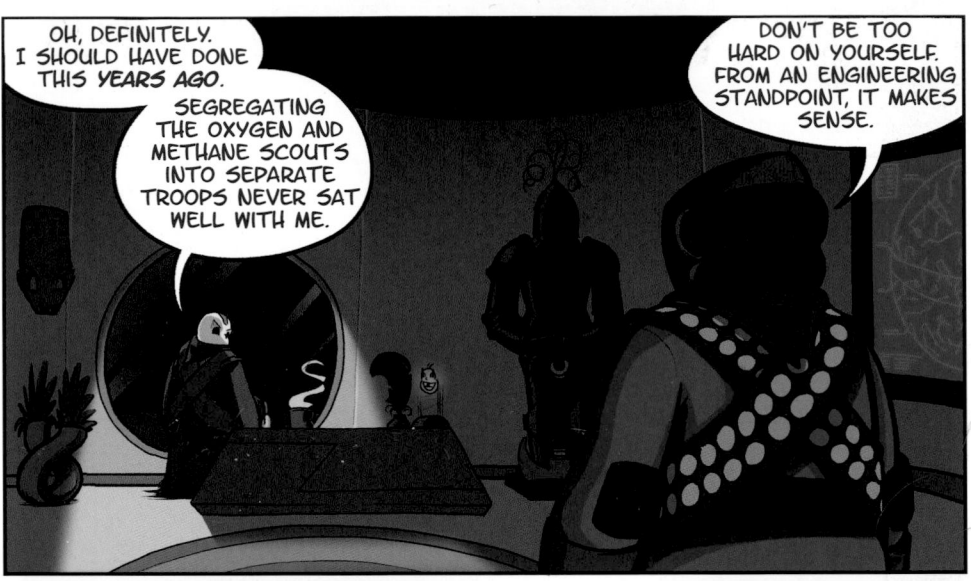

OH, DEFINITELY. I SHOULD HAVE DONE THIS *YEARS AGO*.

SEGREGATING THE OXYGEN AND METHANE SCOUTS INTO SEPARATE TROOPS NEVER SAT WELL WITH ME.

DON'T BE TOO HARD ON YOURSELF. FROM AN ENGINEERING STANDPOINT, IT MAKES SENSE.

YES, BUT CHILDREN AREN'T *MACHINES*. WE COULD HAVE FIGURED OUT A WAY TO MAKE IT WORK.

THE REAL QUESTION IS *HOW* TO MANAGE IT.

AVANI AND PAM HAVE ACCOMPLISHED SOME AMAZING THINGS TOGETHER.

I THINK WE SHOULD LET *THEM* LEAD THE WAY.

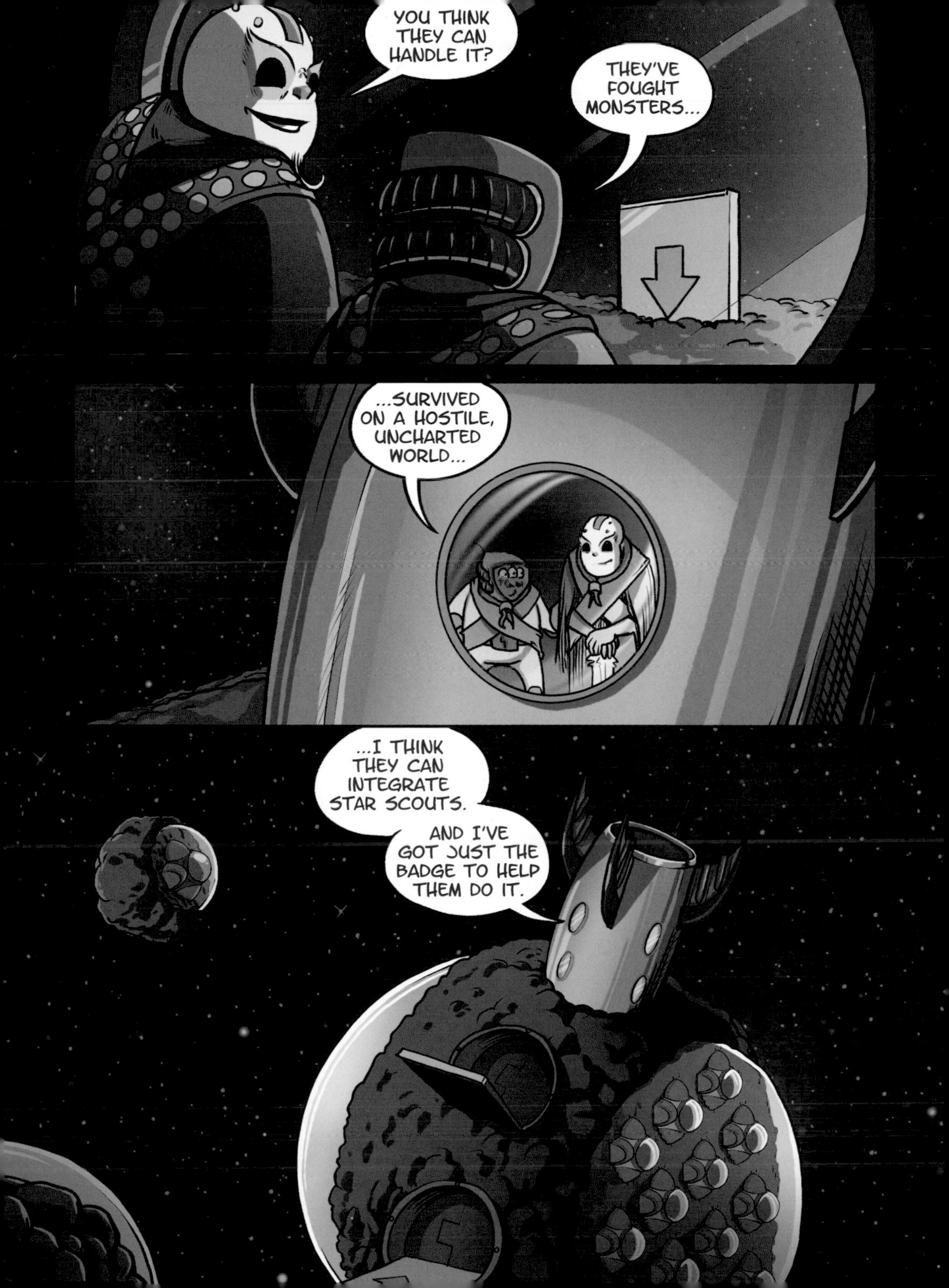
YOU THINK THEY CAN HANDLE IT?
THEY'VE FOUGHT MONSTERS...
...SURVIVED ON A HOSTILE, UNCHARTED WORLD...
...I THINK THEY CAN INTEGRATE STAR SCOUTS.
AND I'VE GOT JUST THE BADGE TO HELP THEM DO IT.

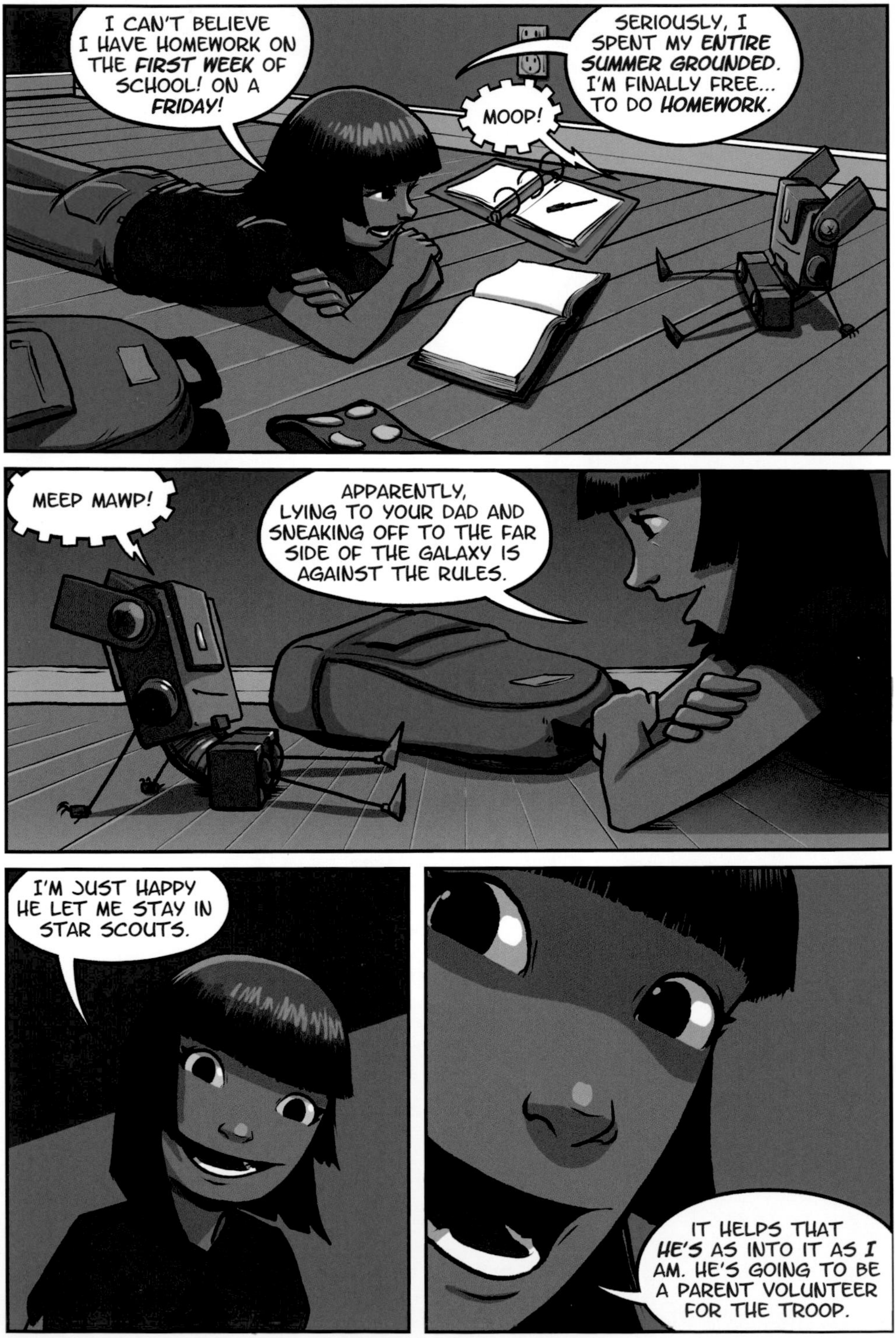
I CAN'T BELIEVE I HAVE HOMEWORK ON THE FIRST WEEK OF SCHOOL! ON A FRIDAY!
MOOP!
SERIOUSLY, I SPENT MY ENTIRE SUMMER GROUNDED. I'M FINALLY FREE... TO DO HOMEWORK.
MEEP MAWP!
APPARENTLY, LYING TO YOUR DAD AND SNEAKING OFF TO THE FAR SIDE OF THE GALAXY IS AGAINST THE RULES.
I'M JUST HAPPY HE LET ME STAY IN STAR SCOUTS.
IT HELPS THAT HE'S AS INTO IT AS I AM. HE'S GOING TO BE A PARENT VOLUNTEER FOR THE TROOP.

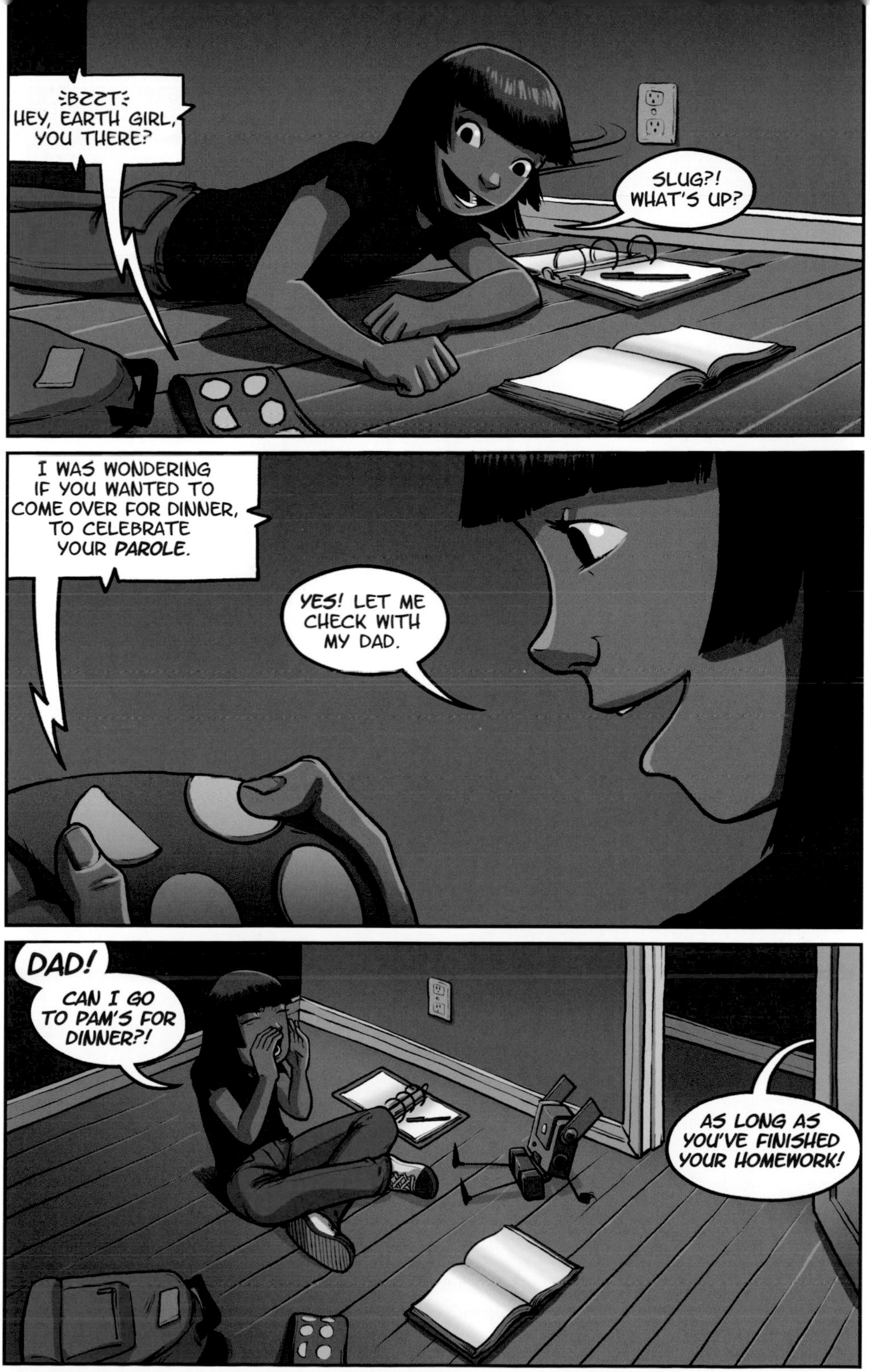

:BZZT:
HEY, EARTH GIRL, YOU THERE?
SLUG?! WHAT'S UP?
I WAS WONDERING IF YOU WANTED TO COME OVER FOR DINNER, TO CELEBRATE YOUR PAROLE.
YES! LET ME CHECK WITH MY DAD.
DAD!
CAN I GO TO PAM'S FOR DINNER?!
AS LONG AS YOU'VE FINISHED YOUR HOMEWORK!

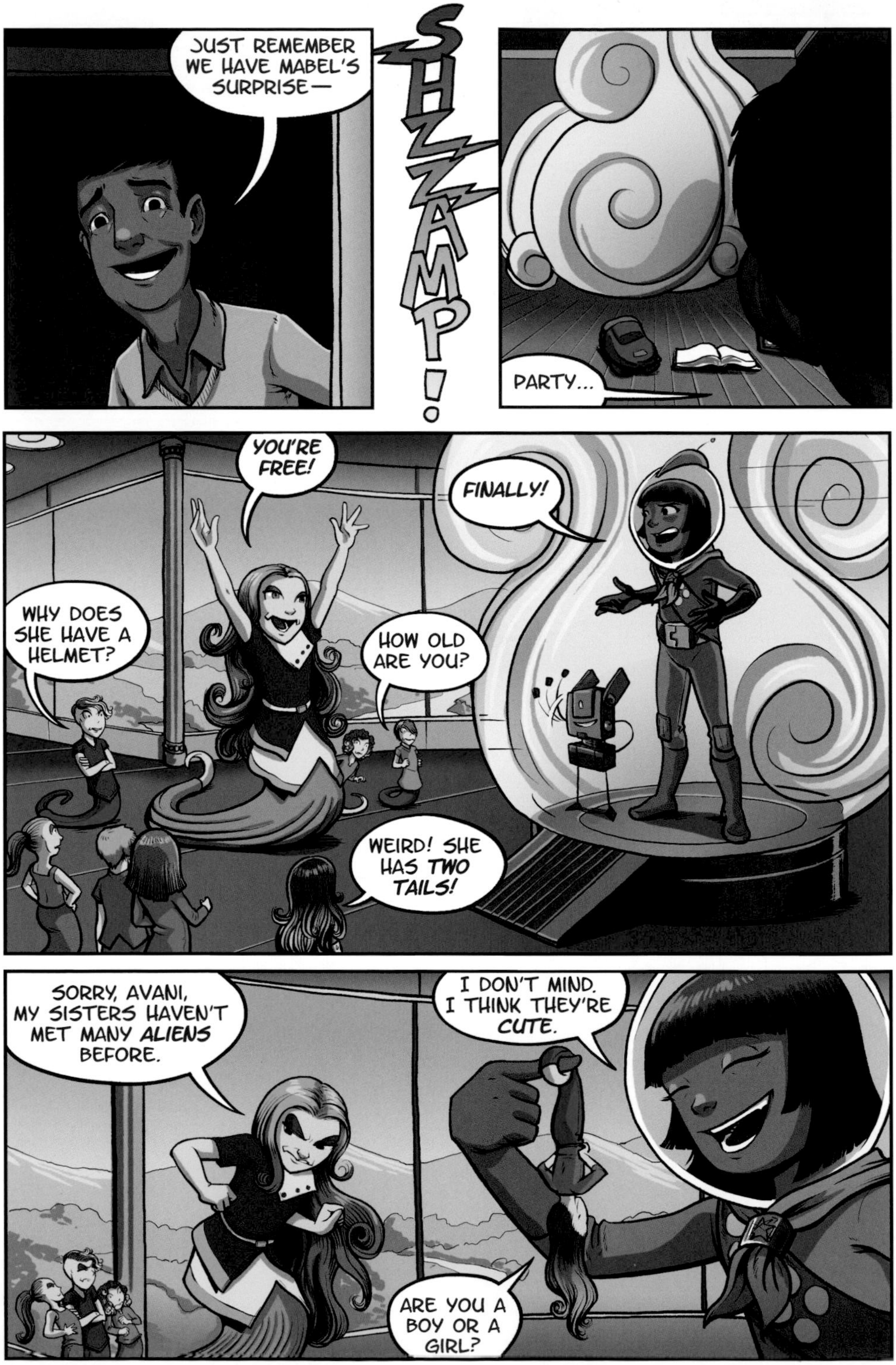
JUST REMEMBER WE HAVE MABEL'S SURPRISE—
SHZZAMP!
PARTY...
YOU'RE FREE!
FINALLY!
WHY DOES SHE HAVE A HELMET?
HOW OLD ARE YOU?
WEIRD! SHE HAS TWO TAILS!
SORRY, AVANI, MY SISTERS HAVEN'T MET MANY ALIENS BEFORE.
I DON'T MIND. I THINK THEY'RE CUTE.
ARE YOU A BOY OR A GIRL?

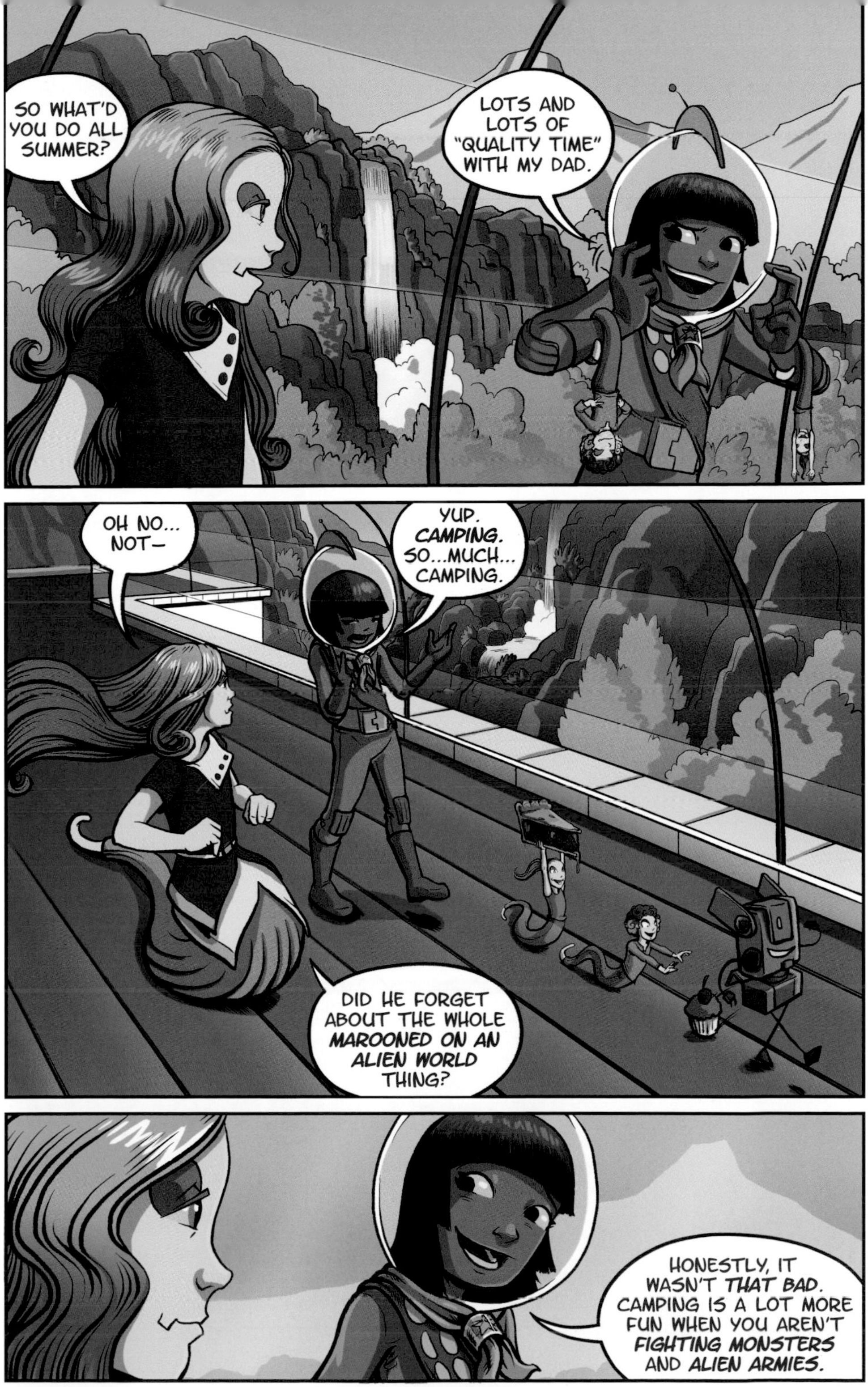
SO WHAT'D YOU DO ALL SUMMER?
LOTS AND LOTS OF "QUALITY TIME" WITH MY DAD.
OH NO... NOT—
YUP. CAMPING. SO...MUCH... CAMPING.
DID HE FORGET ABOUT THE WHOLE MAROONED ON AN ALIEN WORLD THING?
HONESTLY, IT WASN'T THAT BAD. CAMPING IS A LOT MORE FUN WHEN YOU AREN'T FIGHTING MONSTERS AND ALIEN ARMIES.

HAVE YOU HEARD ANYTHING FROM FRANNY ABOUT OUR LETTER?
NOPE. NOTHING YET.
BUT WHY WOULDN'T SHE GO FOR IT? SEPARATING SCOUTS BY THE AIR THEY BREATHE JUST ISN'T RIGHT.
I THINK IT'S SO GREAT YOU GIRLS ARE BRINGING THE SCOUTS TOGETHER.
DID YOU GET ENOUGH TO EAT, AVANI?
YES, I'M STUFFED. I DON'T KNOW WHAT I'M EATING BUT IT'S AMAZING!
THANKS. I JUST FRIED UP SOME GR'ZONKS AND TOSSED THEM WITH SOME SPLUMPS.

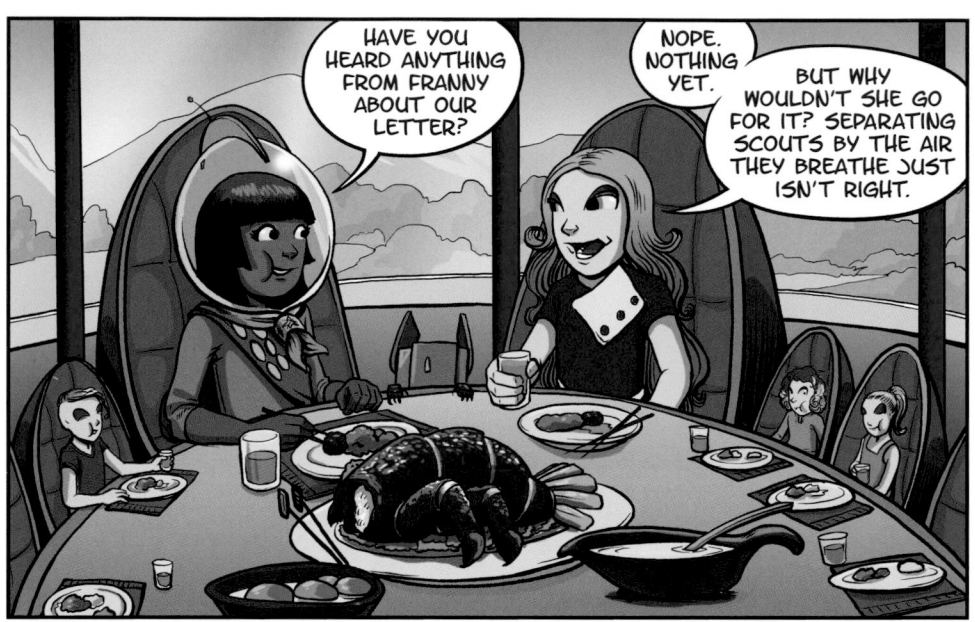

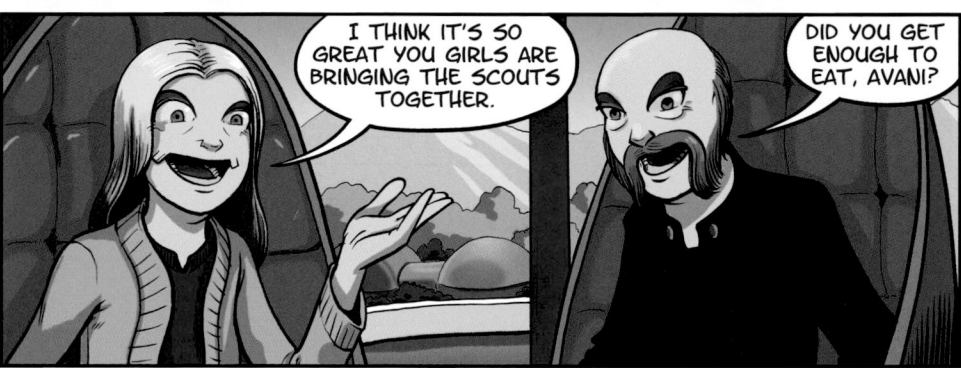

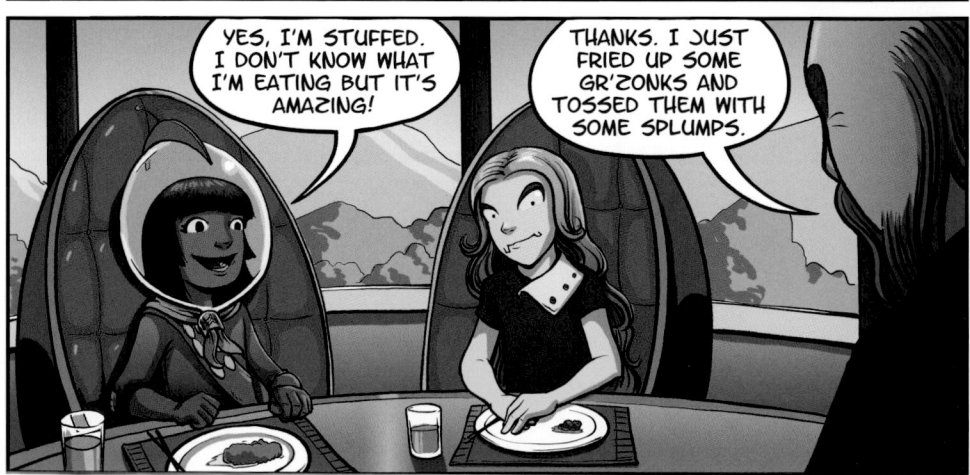

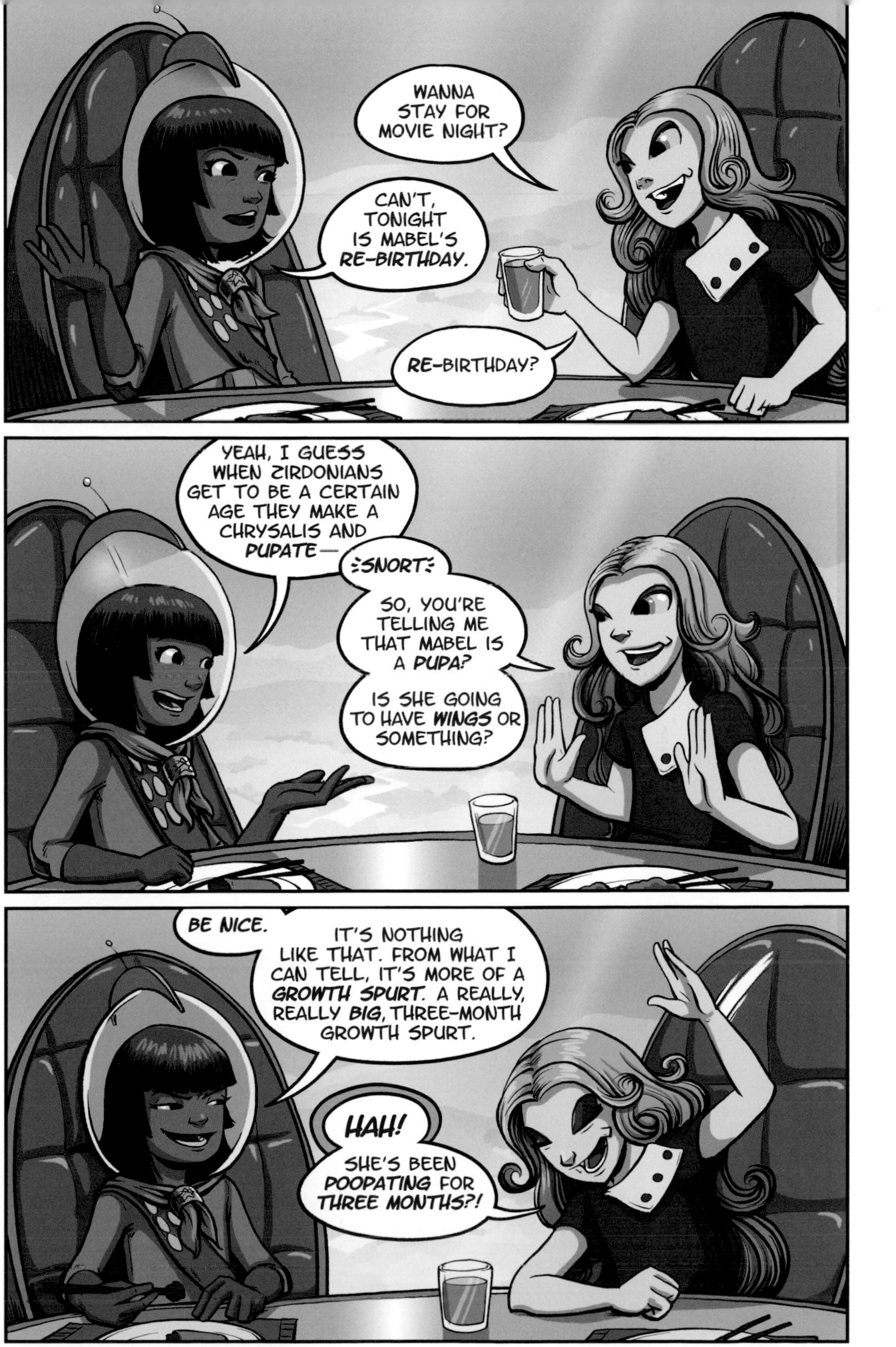
WANNA STAY FOR MOVIE NIGHT?
CAN'T, TONIGHT IS MABEL'S RE-BIRTHDAY.
RE-BIRTHDAY?
YEAH, I GUESS WHEN ZIRDONIANS GET TO BE A CERTAIN AGE THEY MAKE A CHRYSALIS AND PUPATE—
SNORT
SO, YOU'RE TELLING ME THAT MABEL IS A PUPA?
IS SHE GOING TO HAVE WINGS OR SOMETHING?
BE NICE.
IT'S NOTHING LIKE THAT. FROM WHAT I CAN TELL, IT'S MORE OF A GROWTH SPURT. A REALLY, REALLY BIG, THREE-MONTH GROWTH SPURT.
HAH!
SHE'S BEEN POOPATING FOR THREE MONTHS?!

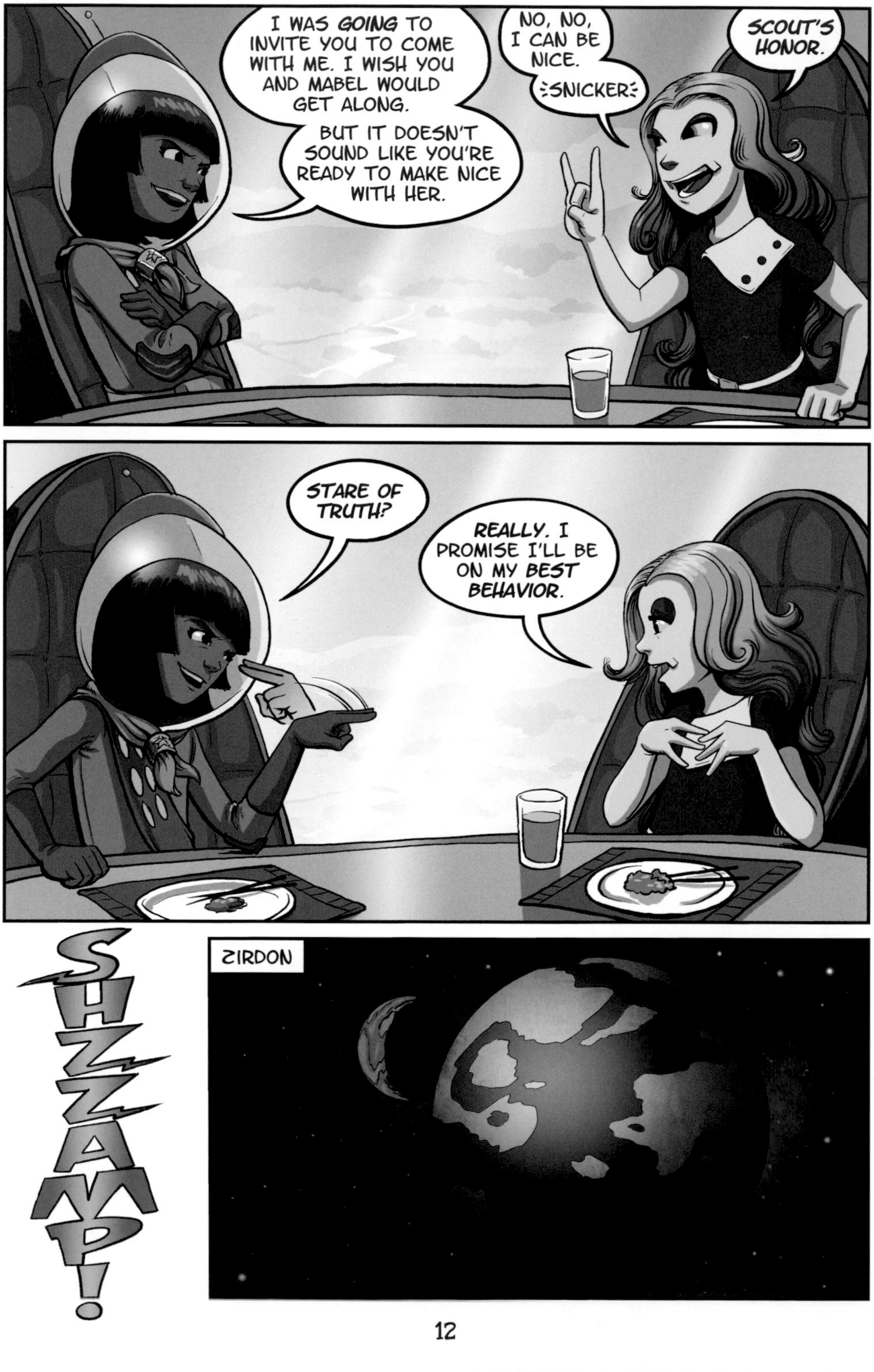
I WAS GOING TO INVITE YOU TO COME WITH ME. I WISH YOU AND MABEL WOULD GET ALONG.
BUT IT DOESN'T SOUND LIKE YOU'RE READY TO MAKE NICE WITH HER.
NO, NO, I CAN BE NICE.
SNICKER
SCOUT'S HONOR.
STARE OF TRUTH?
REALLY. I PROMISE I'LL BE ON MY BEST BEHAVIOR.
SHZZAMP!
ZIRDON

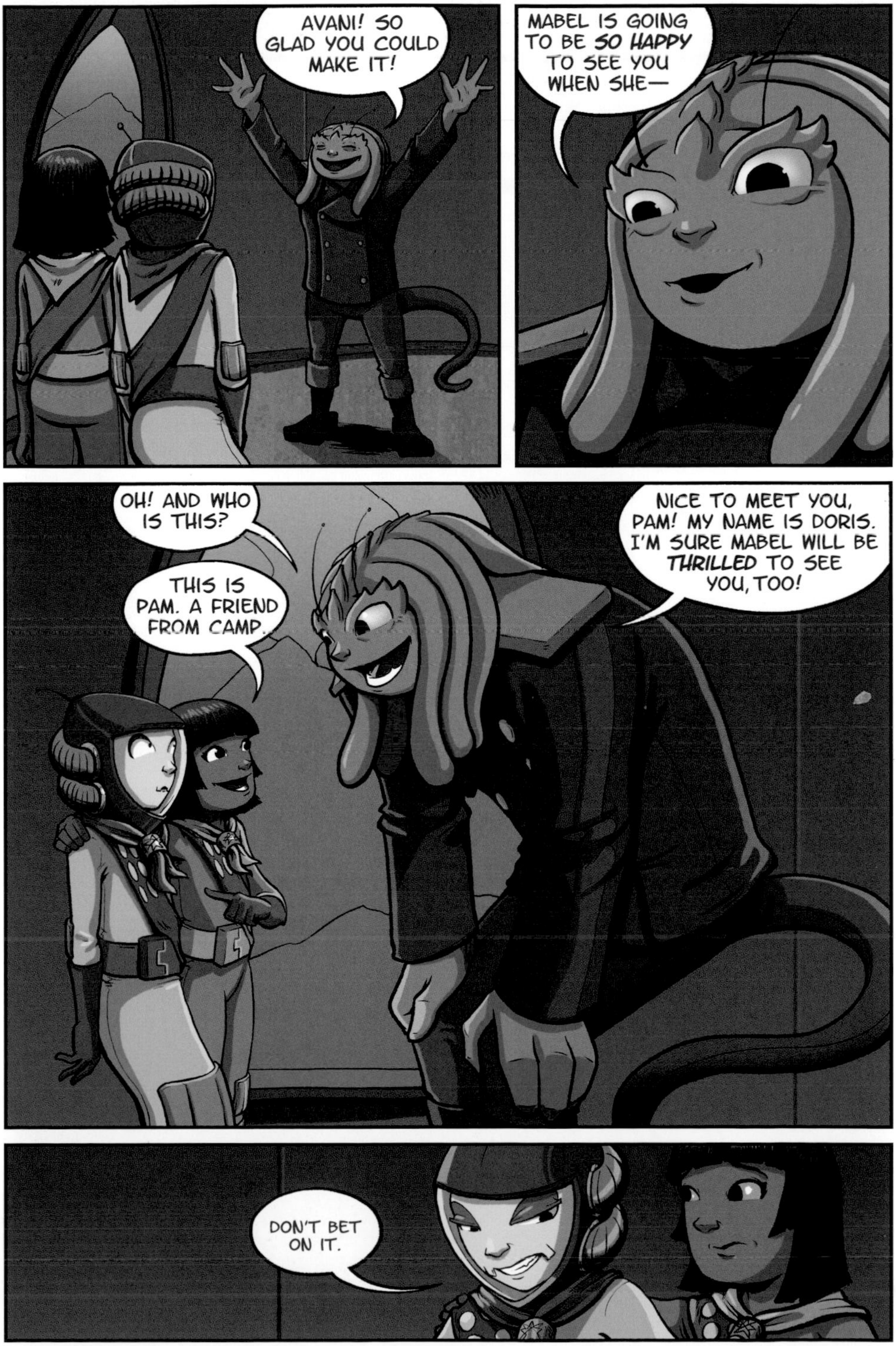
AVANI! SO GLAD YOU COULD MAKE IT!
MABEL IS GOING TO BE **SO HAPPY** TO SEE YOU WHEN SHE—
OH! AND WHO IS THIS?
THIS IS PAM. A FRIEND FROM CAMP.
NICE TO MEET YOU, PAM! MY NAME IS DORIS. I'M SURE MABEL WILL BE **THRILLED** TO SEE YOU, TOO!
DON'T BET ON IT.

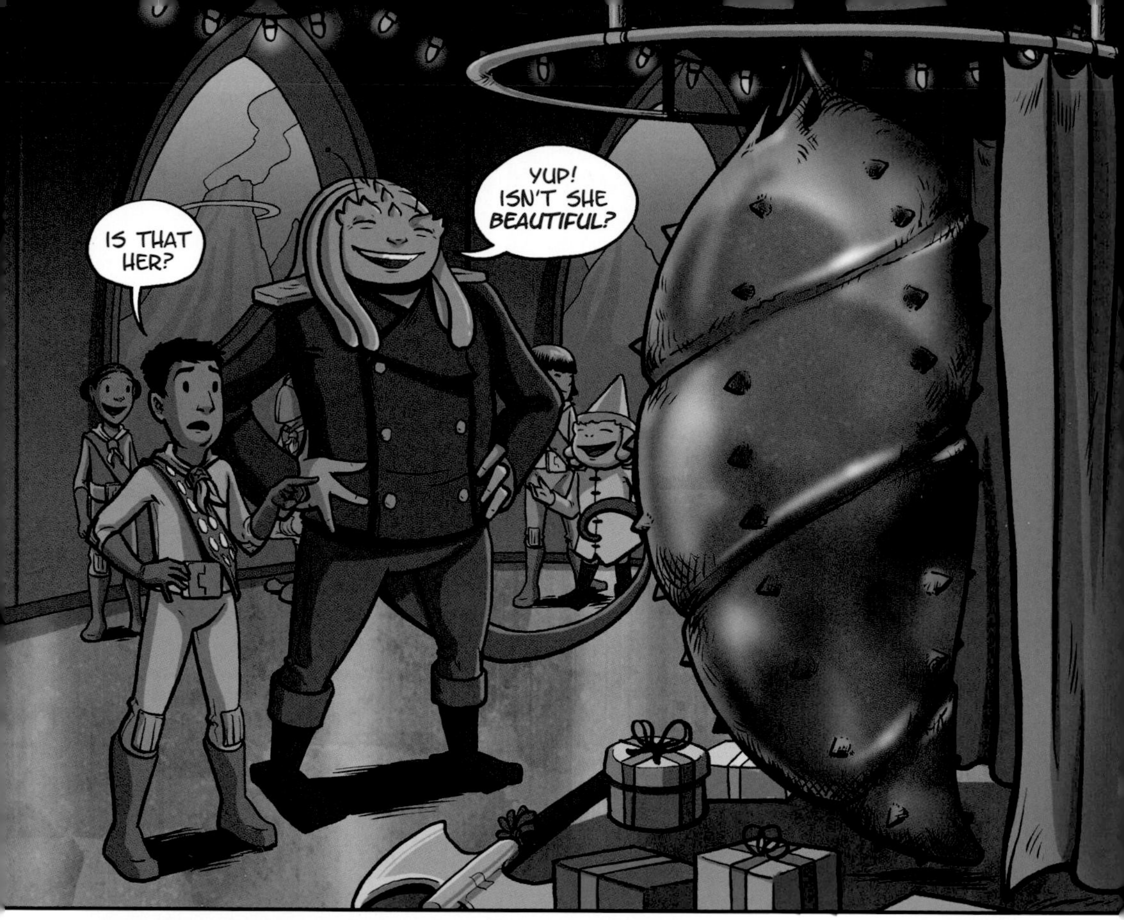
IS THAT HER?
YUP! ISN'T SHE BEAUTIFUL?

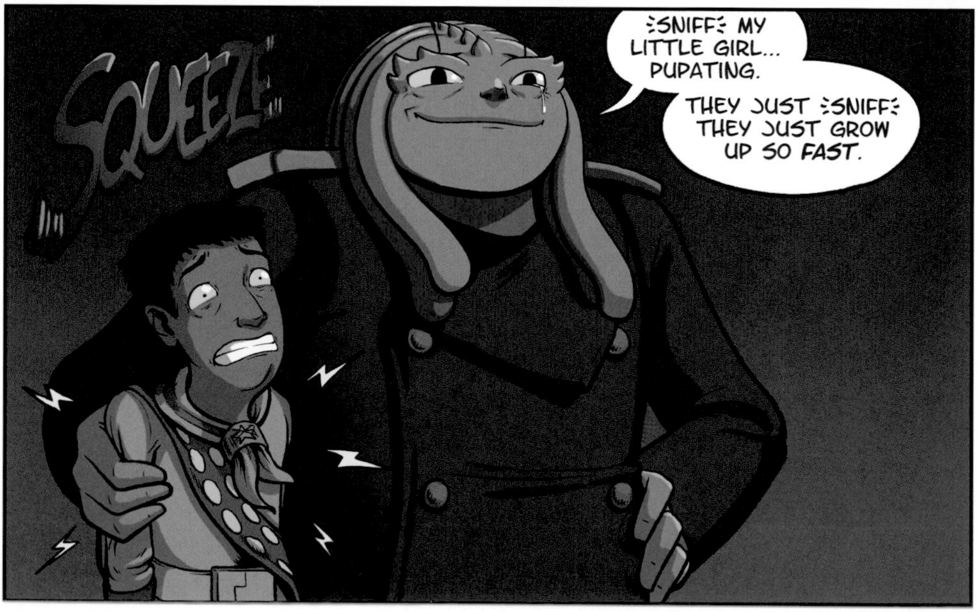
SQUEEZE
:SNIFF: MY LITTLE GIRL... PUPATING.
THEY JUST :SNIFF: THEY JUST GROW UP SO FAST.

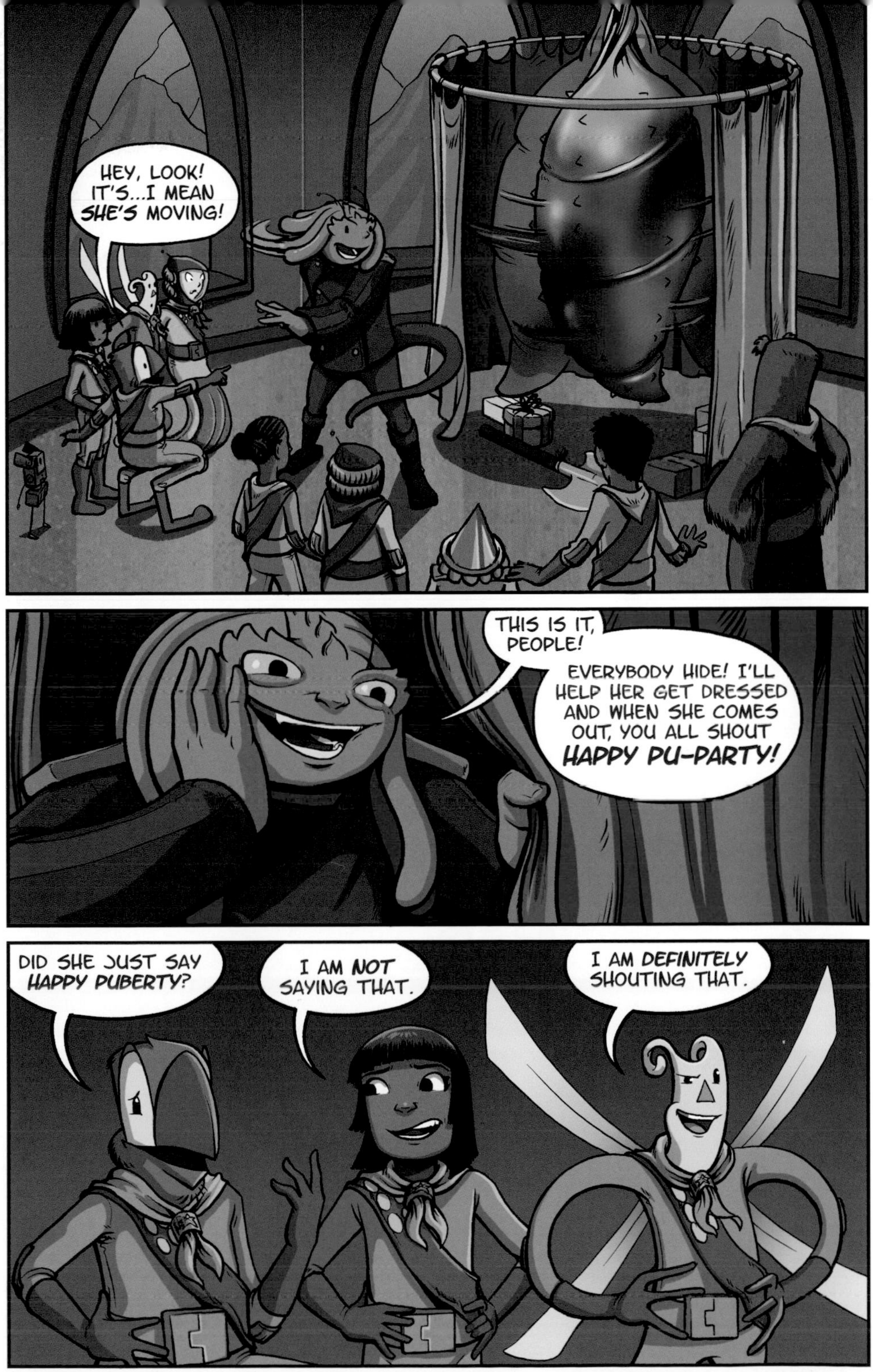
HEY, LOOK! IT'S...I MEAN SHE'S MOVING!
THIS IS IT, PEOPLE!
EVERYBODY HIDE! I'LL HELP HER GET DRESSED AND WHEN SHE COMES OUT, YOU ALL SHOUT HAPPY PU-PARTY!
DID SHE JUST SAY HAPPY PUBERTY?
I AM NOT SAYING THAT.
I AM DEFINITELY SHOUTING THAT.

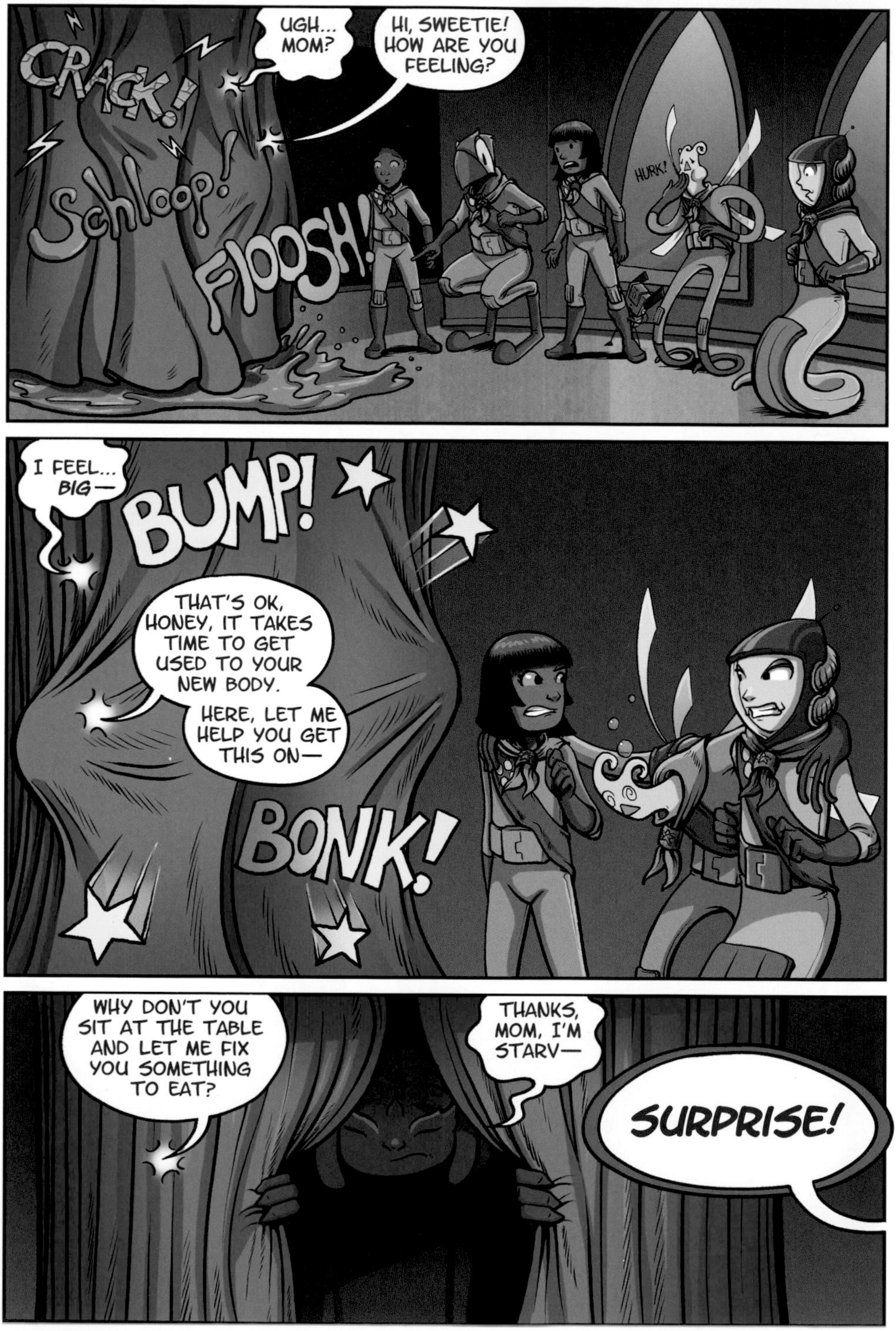
CRACK!
UGH... MOM?
HI, SWEETIE! HOW ARE YOU FEELING?
Schloop!
FLOOSH!
HURK!
I FEEL... BIG—
BUMP!
THAT'S OK, HONEY, IT TAKES TIME TO GET USED TO YOUR NEW BODY.
HERE, LET ME HELP YOU GET THIS ON—
BONK!
WHY DON'T YOU SIT AT THE TABLE AND LET ME FIX YOU SOMETHING TO EAT?
THANKS, MOM, I'M STARV—
SURPRISE!

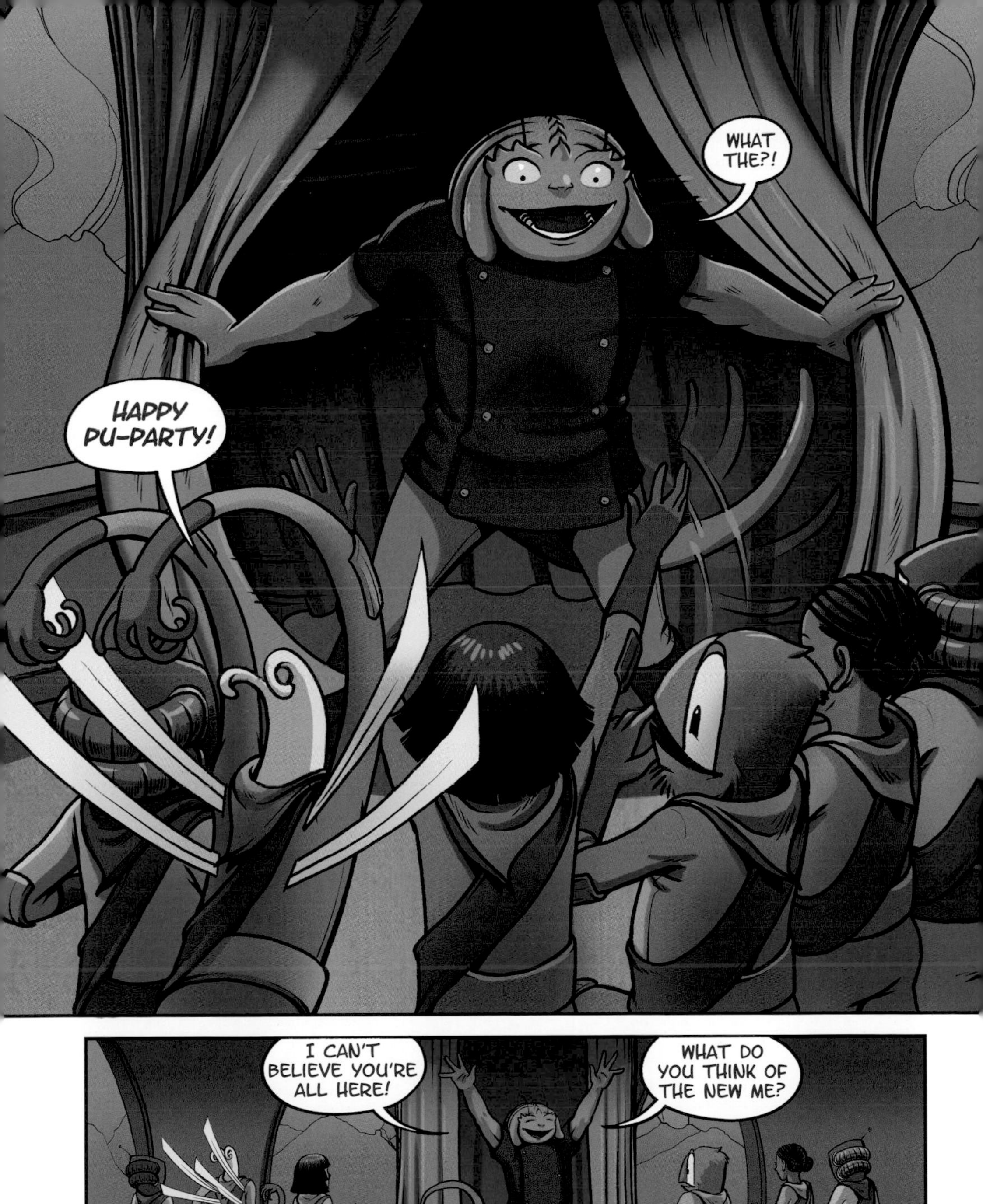
WHAT THE?!
HAPPY PU-PARTY!
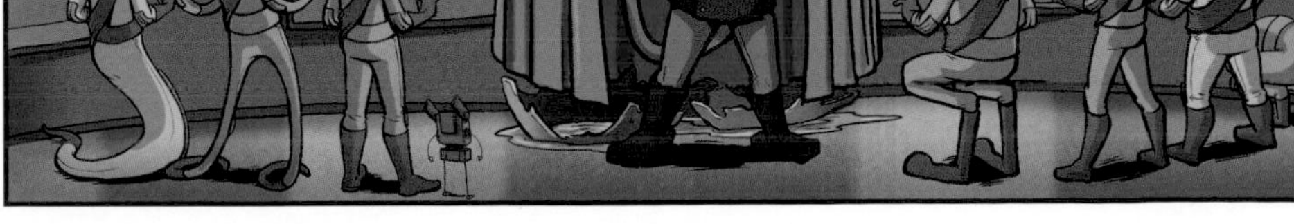
I CAN'T BELIEVE YOU'RE ALL HERE!
WHAT DO YOU THINK OF THE NEW ME?

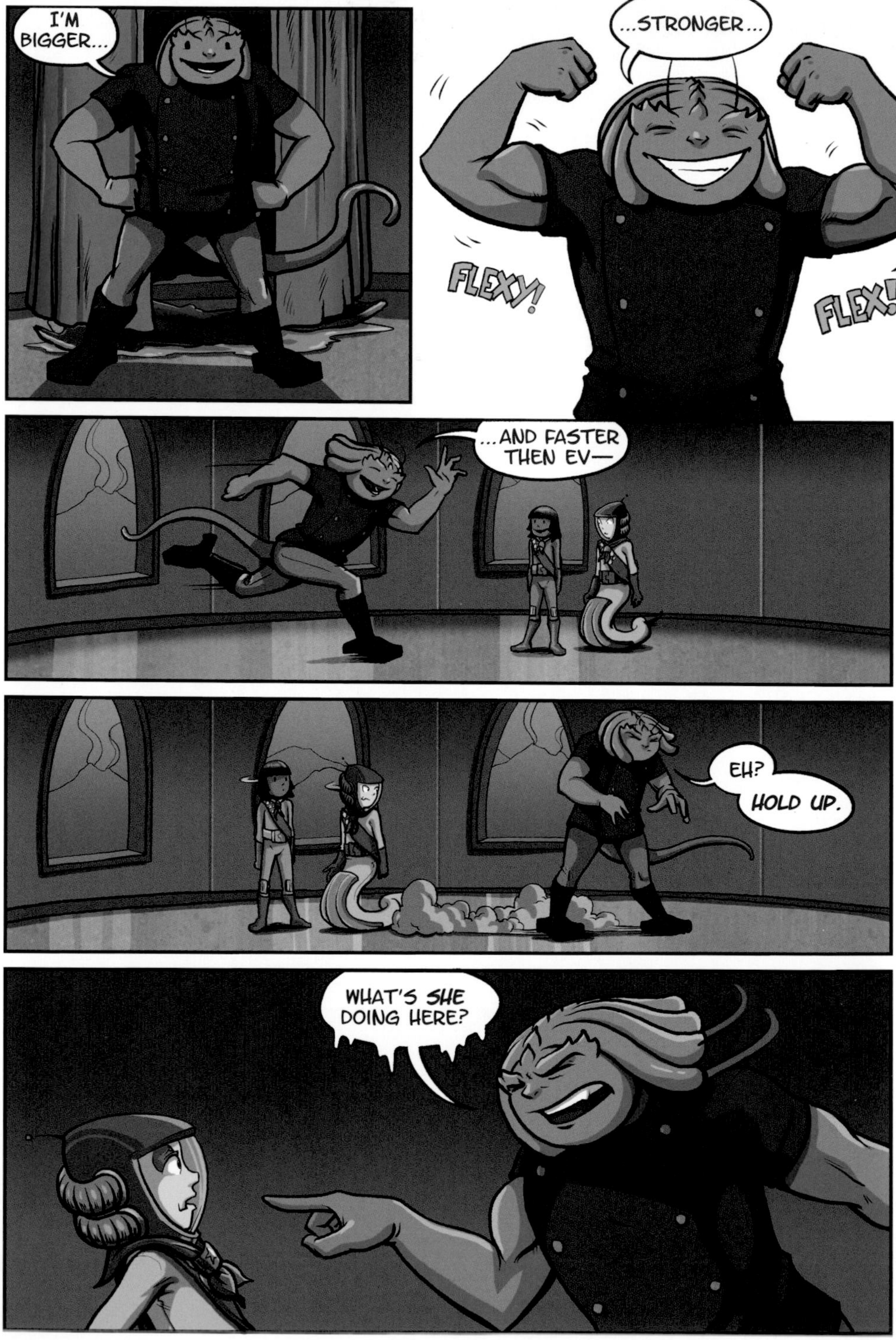
I'M BIGGER...
...STRONGER...
FLEXY!
FLEX!
...AND FASTER THEN EV—
EH?
HOLD UP.
WHAT'S SHE DOING HERE?

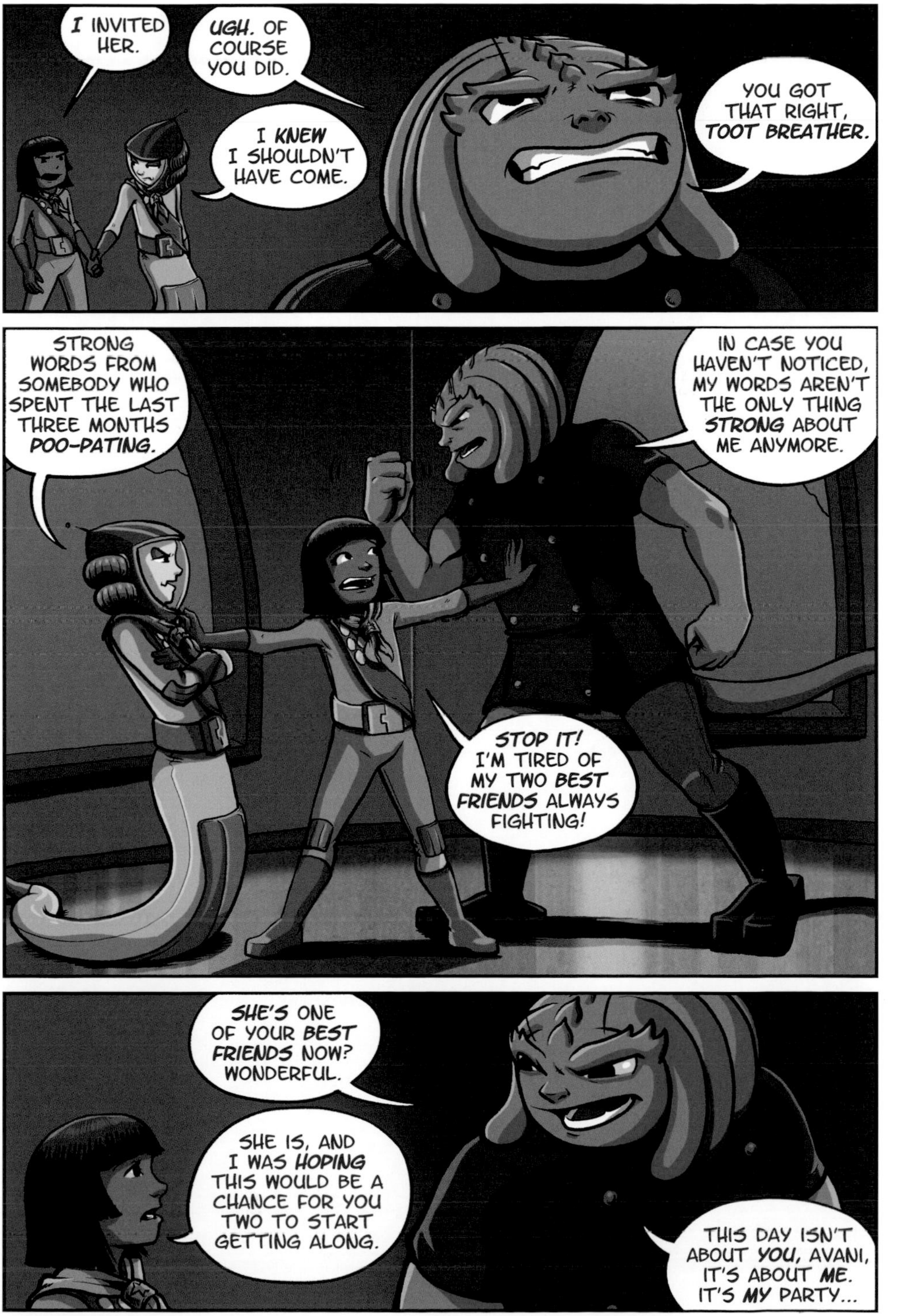
I INVITED HER.
UGH. OF COURSE YOU DID.
I KNEW I SHOULDN'T HAVE COME.
YOU GOT THAT RIGHT, TOOT BREATHER.
STRONG WORDS FROM SOMEBODY WHO SPENT THE LAST THREE MONTHS POO-PATING.
IN CASE YOU HAVEN'T NOTICED, MY WORDS AREN'T THE ONLY THING STRONG ABOUT ME ANYMORE.
STOP IT! I'M TIRED OF MY TWO BEST FRIENDS ALWAYS FIGHTING!
SHE'S ONE OF YOUR BEST FRIENDS NOW? WONDERFUL.
SHE IS, AND I WAS HOPING THIS WOULD BE A CHANCE FOR YOU TWO TO START GETTING ALONG.
THIS DAY ISN'T ABOUT YOU, AVANI, IT'S ABOUT ME. IT'S MY PARTY...

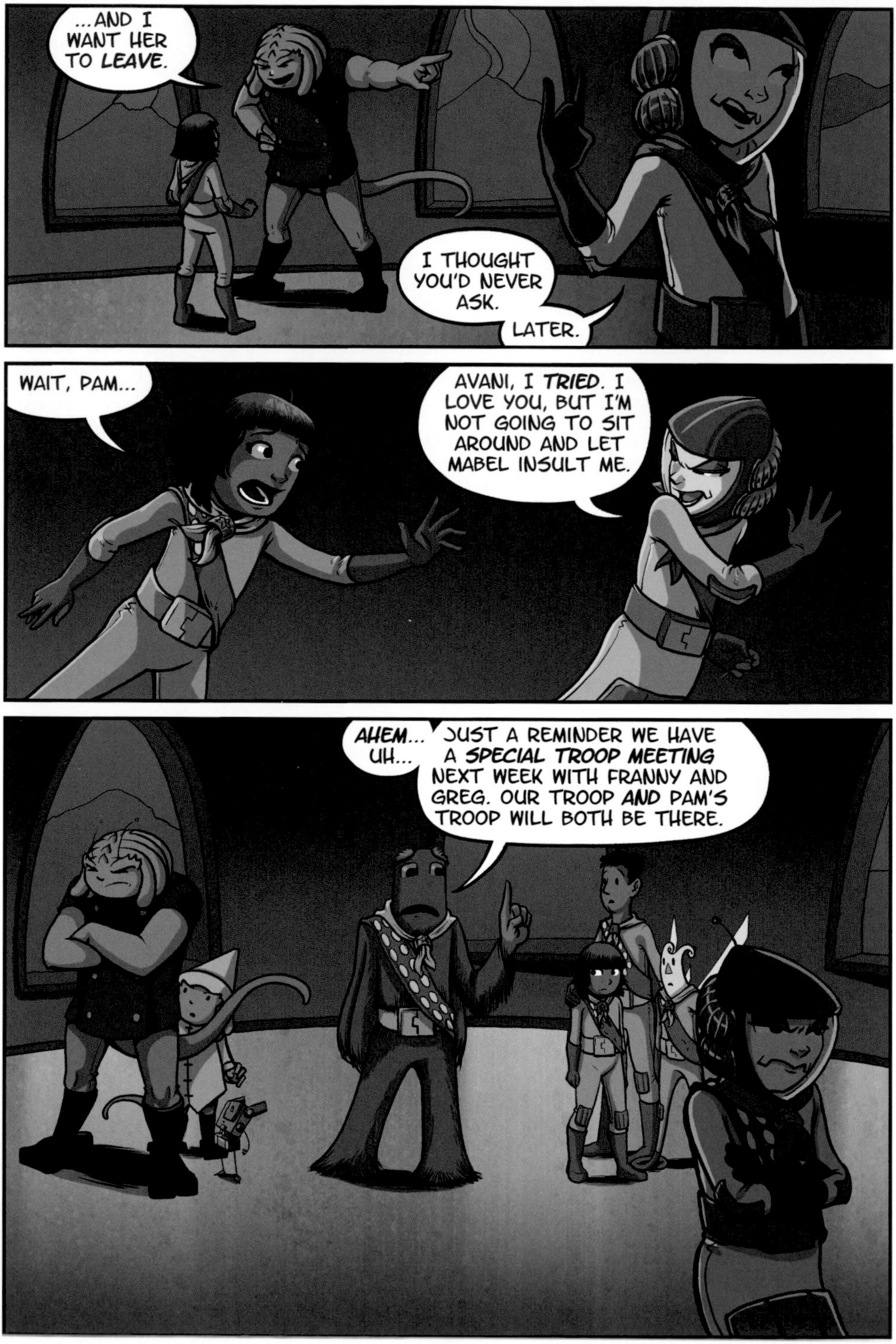
...AND I WANT HER TO *LEAVE*.
I THOUGHT YOU'D NEVER ASK.
LATER.
WAIT, PAM...
AVANI, I *TRIED*. I LOVE YOU, BUT I'M NOT GOING TO SIT AROUND AND LET MABEL INSULT ME.
AHEM... UH...
JUST A REMINDER WE HAVE A *SPECIAL TROOP MEETING* NEXT WEEK WITH FRANNY AND GREG. OUR TROOP *AND* PAM'S TROOP WILL BOTH BE THERE.

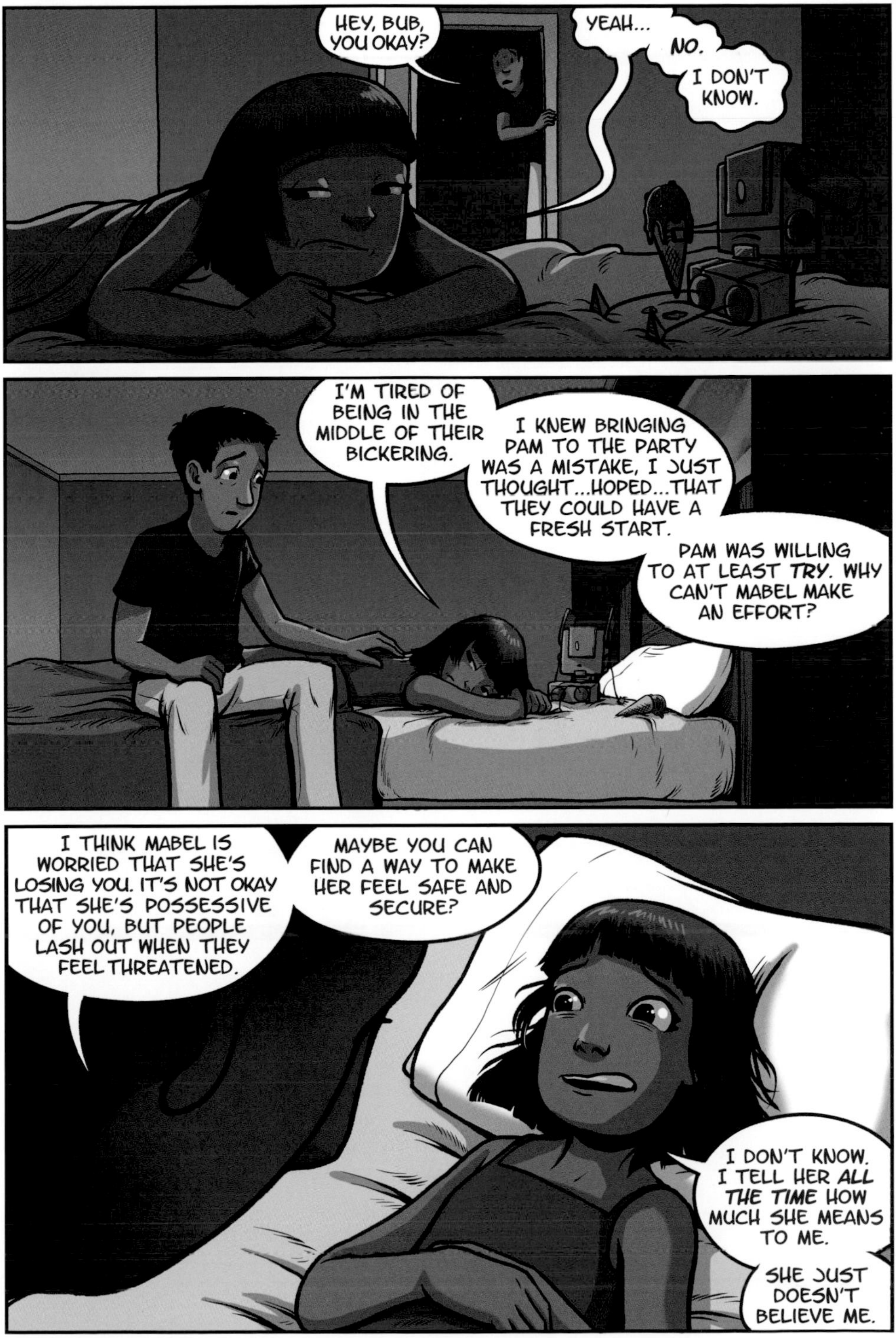
HEY, BUB, YOU OKAY?
YEAH...
NO.
I DON'T KNOW.
I'M TIRED OF BEING IN THE MIDDLE OF THEIR BICKERING.
I KNEW BRINGING PAM TO THE PARTY WAS A MISTAKE, I JUST THOUGHT...HOPED...THAT THEY COULD HAVE A FRESH START.
PAM WAS WILLING TO AT LEAST *TRY*. WHY CAN'T MABEL MAKE AN EFFORT?
I THINK MABEL IS WORRIED THAT SHE'S LOSING YOU. IT'S NOT OKAY THAT SHE'S POSSESSIVE OF YOU, BUT PEOPLE LASH OUT WHEN THEY FEEL THREATENED.
MAYBE YOU CAN FIND A WAY TO MAKE HER FEEL SAFE AND SECURE?
I DON'T KNOW. I TELL HER *ALL THE TIME* HOW MUCH SHE MEANS TO ME.
SHE JUST DOESN'T BELIEVE ME.

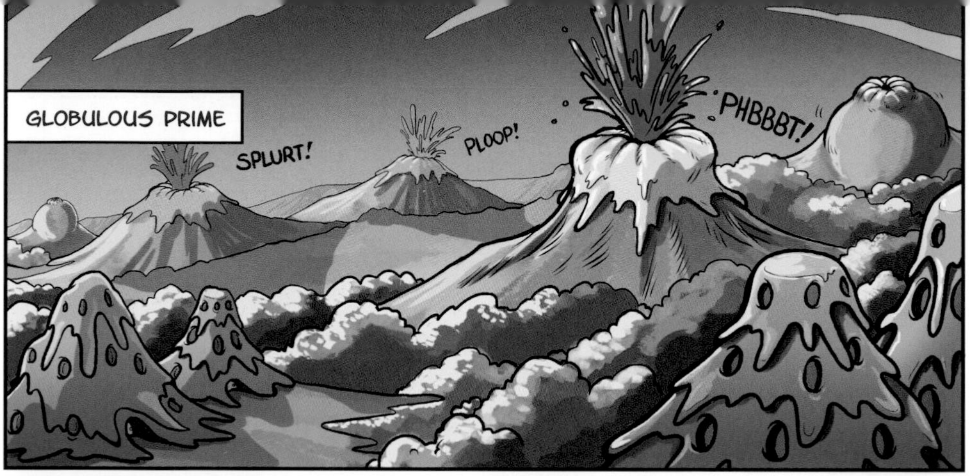
GLOBULOUS PRIME
SPLURT!
PLOOP!
PHBBBT!

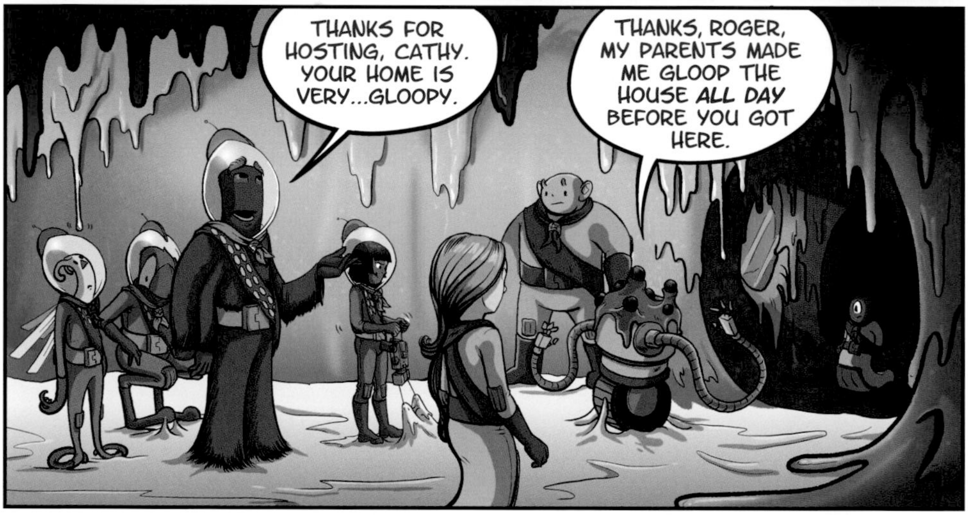
THANKS FOR HOSTING, CATHY. YOUR HOME IS VERY...GLOOPY.
THANKS, ROGER, MY PARENTS MADE ME GLOOP THE HOUSE ALL DAY BEFORE YOU GOT HERE.

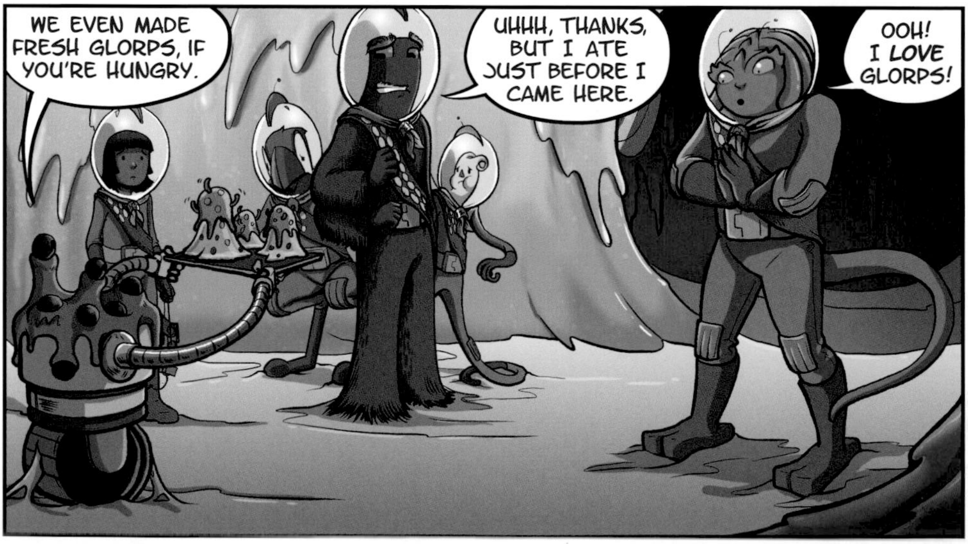
WE EVEN MADE FRESH GLORPS, IF YOU'RE HUNGRY.
UHHH, THANKS, BUT I ATE JUST BEFORE I CAME HERE.
OOH! I LOVE GLORPS!

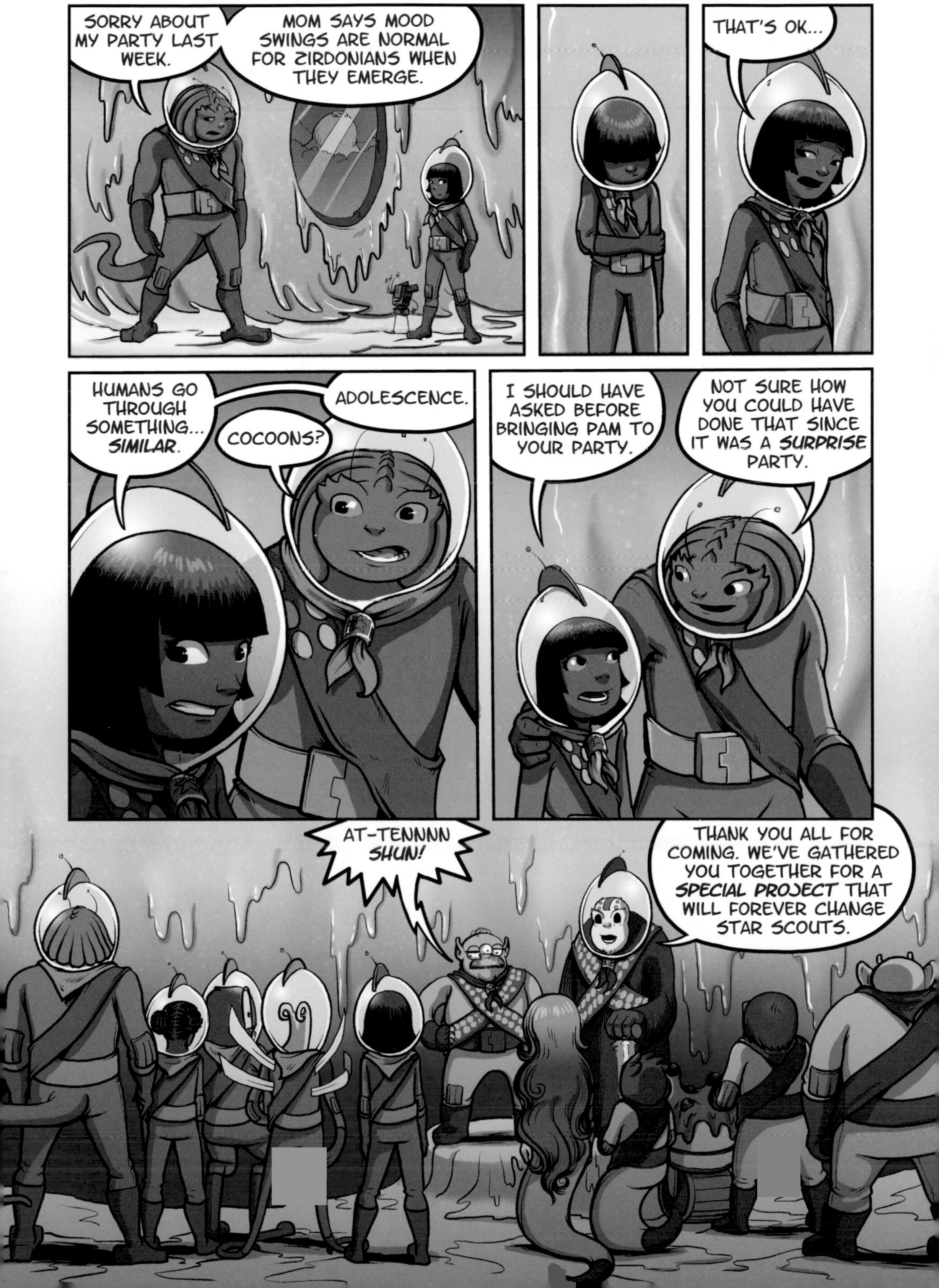
SORRY ABOUT MY PARTY LAST WEEK.
MOM SAYS MOOD SWINGS ARE NORMAL FOR ZIRDONIANS WHEN THEY EMERGE.
THAT'S OK...
HUMANS GO THROUGH SOMETHING... *SIMILAR*.
COCOONS?
ADOLESCENCE.
I SHOULD HAVE ASKED BEFORE BRINGING PAM TO YOUR PARTY.
NOT SURE HOW YOU COULD HAVE DONE THAT SINCE IT WAS A *SURPRISE* PARTY.
AT-TENNNN *SHUN!*
THANK YOU ALL FOR COMING. WE'VE GATHERED YOU TOGETHER FOR A *SPECIAL PROJECT* THAT WILL FOREVER CHANGE STAR SCOUTS.

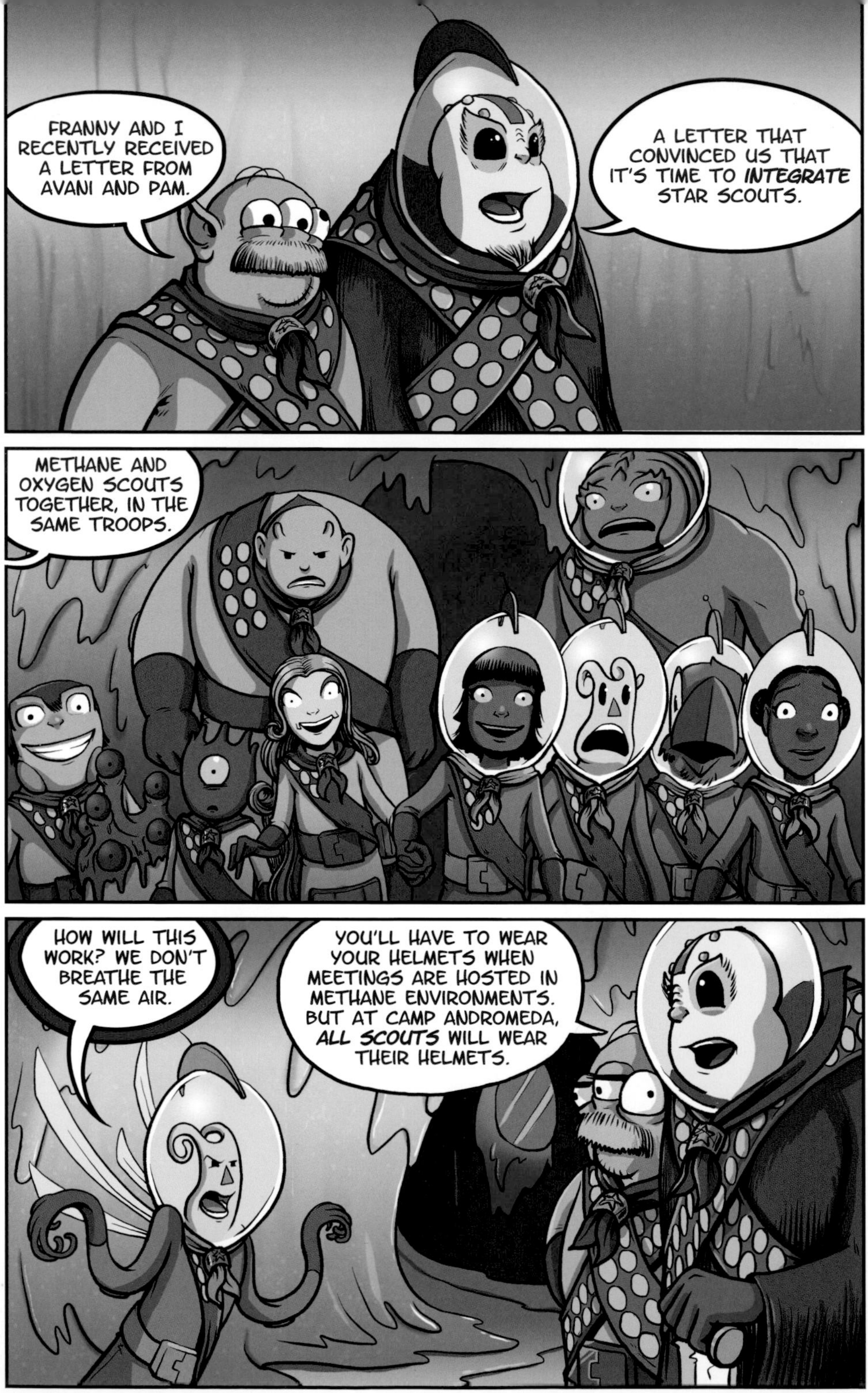
FRANNY AND I RECENTLY RECEIVED A LETTER FROM AVANI AND PAM.
A LETTER THAT CONVINCED US THAT IT'S TIME TO *INTEGRATE* STAR SCOUTS.
METHANE AND OXYGEN SCOUTS TOGETHER, IN THE SAME TROOPS.
HOW WILL THIS WORK? WE DON'T BREATHE THE SAME AIR.
YOU'LL HAVE TO WEAR YOUR HELMETS WHEN MEETINGS ARE HOSTED IN METHANE ENVIRONMENTS. BUT AT CAMP ANDROMEDA, ***ALL SCOUTS*** WILL WEAR THEIR HELMETS.

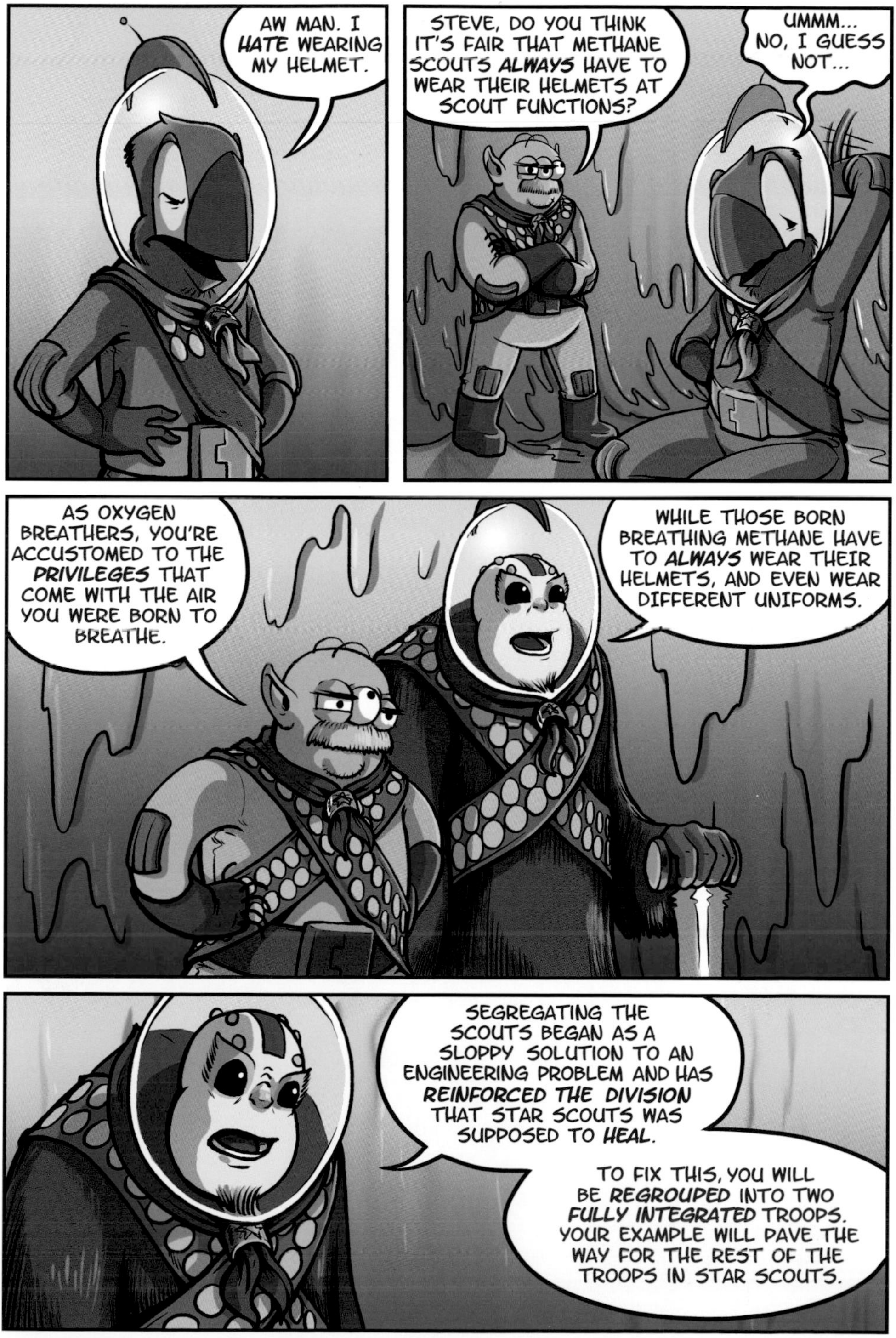
AW MAN. I *HATE* WEARING MY HELMET.
STEVE, DO YOU THINK IT'S FAIR THAT METHANE SCOUTS *ALWAYS* HAVE TO WEAR THEIR HELMETS AT SCOUT FUNCTIONS?
UMMM... NO, I GUESS NOT...
AS OXYGEN BREATHERS, YOU'RE ACCUSTOMED TO THE *PRIVILEGES* THAT COME WITH THE AIR YOU WERE BORN TO BREATHE.
WHILE THOSE BORN BREATHING METHANE HAVE TO *ALWAYS* WEAR THEIR HELMETS, AND EVEN WEAR DIFFERENT UNIFORMS.
SEGREGATING THE SCOUTS BEGAN AS A SLOPPY SOLUTION TO AN ENGINEERING PROBLEM AND HAS *REINFORCED THE DIVISION* THAT STAR SCOUTS WAS SUPPOSED TO *HEAL*.
TO FIX THIS, YOU WILL BE *REGROUPED* INTO TWO *FULLY INTEGRATED* TROOPS. YOUR EXAMPLE WILL PAVE THE WAY FOR THE REST OF THE TROOPS IN STAR SCOUTS.

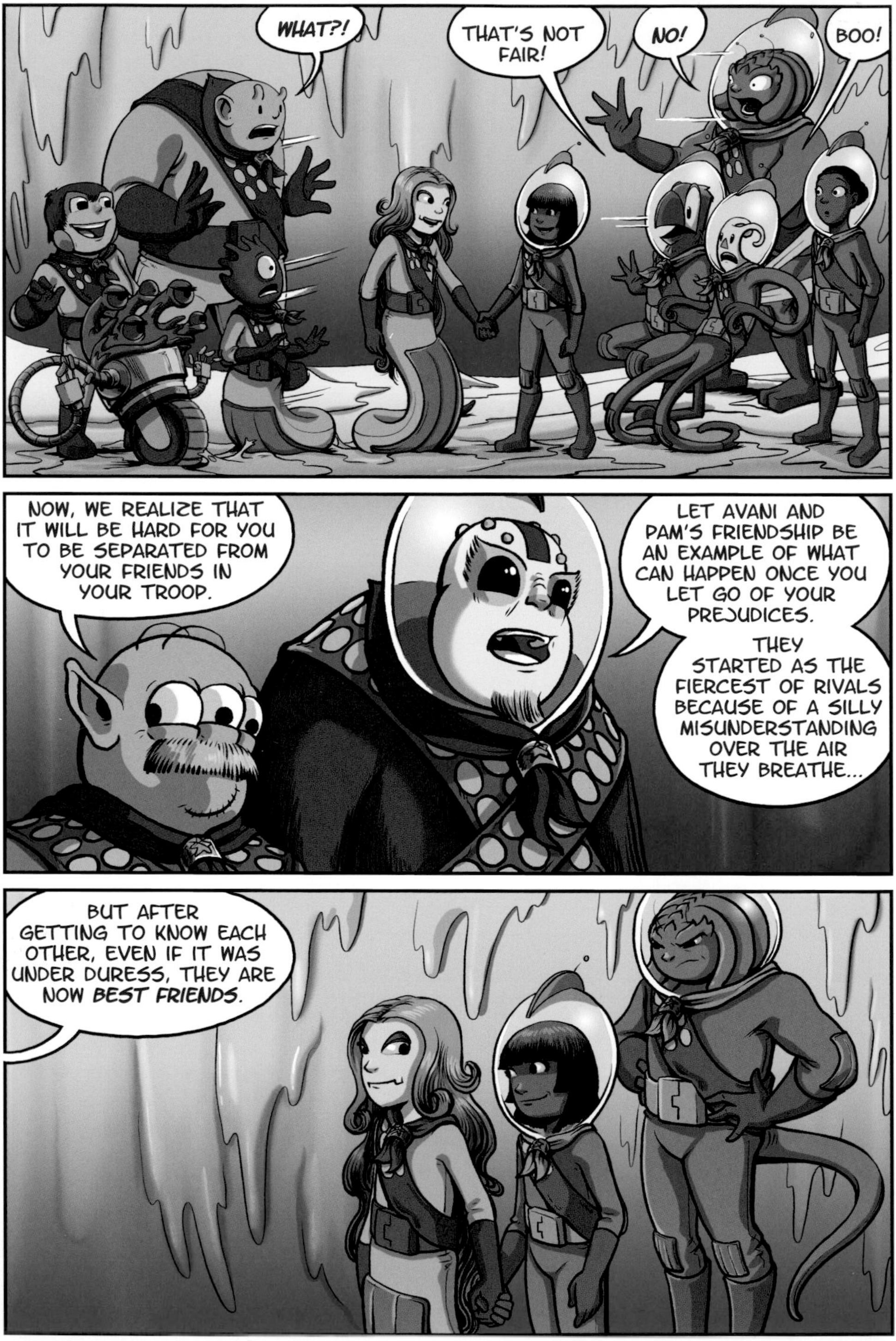
WHAT?!
THAT'S NOT FAIR!
NO!
BOO!
NOW, WE REALIZE THAT IT WILL BE HARD FOR YOU TO BE SEPARATED FROM YOUR FRIENDS IN YOUR TROOP.
LET AVANI AND PAM'S FRIENDSHIP BE AN EXAMPLE OF WHAT CAN HAPPEN ONCE YOU LET GO OF YOUR PREJUDICES.
THEY STARTED AS THE FIERCEST OF RIVALS BECAUSE OF A SILLY MISUNDERSTANDING OVER THE AIR THEY BREATHE...
BUT AFTER GETTING TO KNOW EACH OTHER, EVEN IF IT WAS UNDER DURESS, THEY ARE NOW *BEST FRIENDS*.

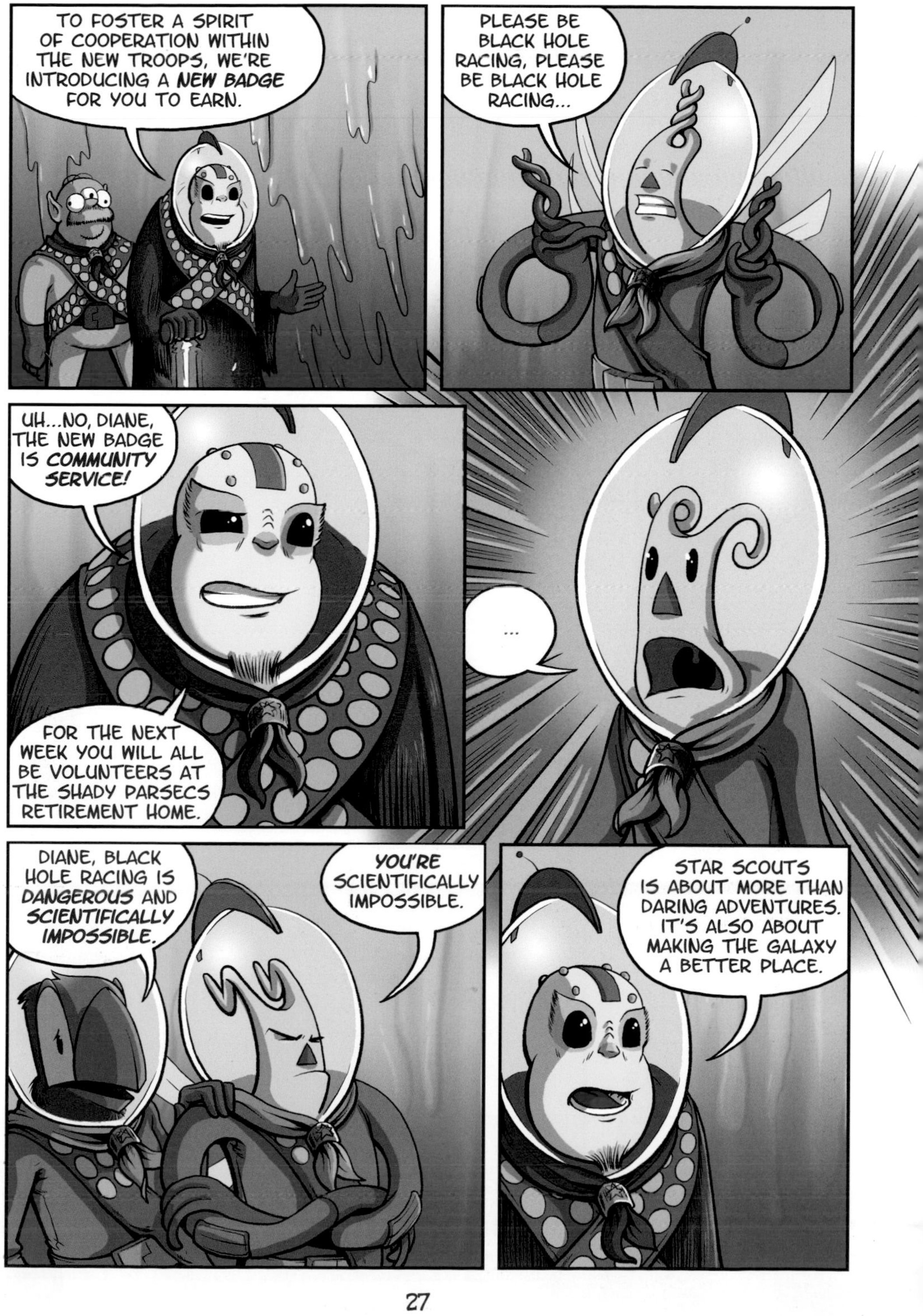
TO FOSTER A SPIRIT OF COOPERATION WITHIN THE NEW TROOPS, WE'RE INTRODUCING A ***NEW BADGE*** FOR YOU TO EARN.
PLEASE BE BLACK HOLE RACING, PLEASE BE BLACK HOLE RACING...
UH...NO, DIANE, THE NEW BADGE IS ***COMMUNITY SERVICE!***
FOR THE NEXT WEEK YOU WILL ALL BE VOLUNTEERS AT THE SHADY PARSECS RETIREMENT HOME.
...
DIANE, BLACK HOLE RACING IS ***DANGEROUS*** AND ***SCIENTIFICALLY IMPOSSIBLE.***
YOU'RE SCIENTIFICALLY IMPOSSIBLE.
STAR SCOUTS IS ABOUT MORE THAN DARING ADVENTURES. IT'S ALSO ABOUT MAKING THE GALAXY A BETTER PLACE.

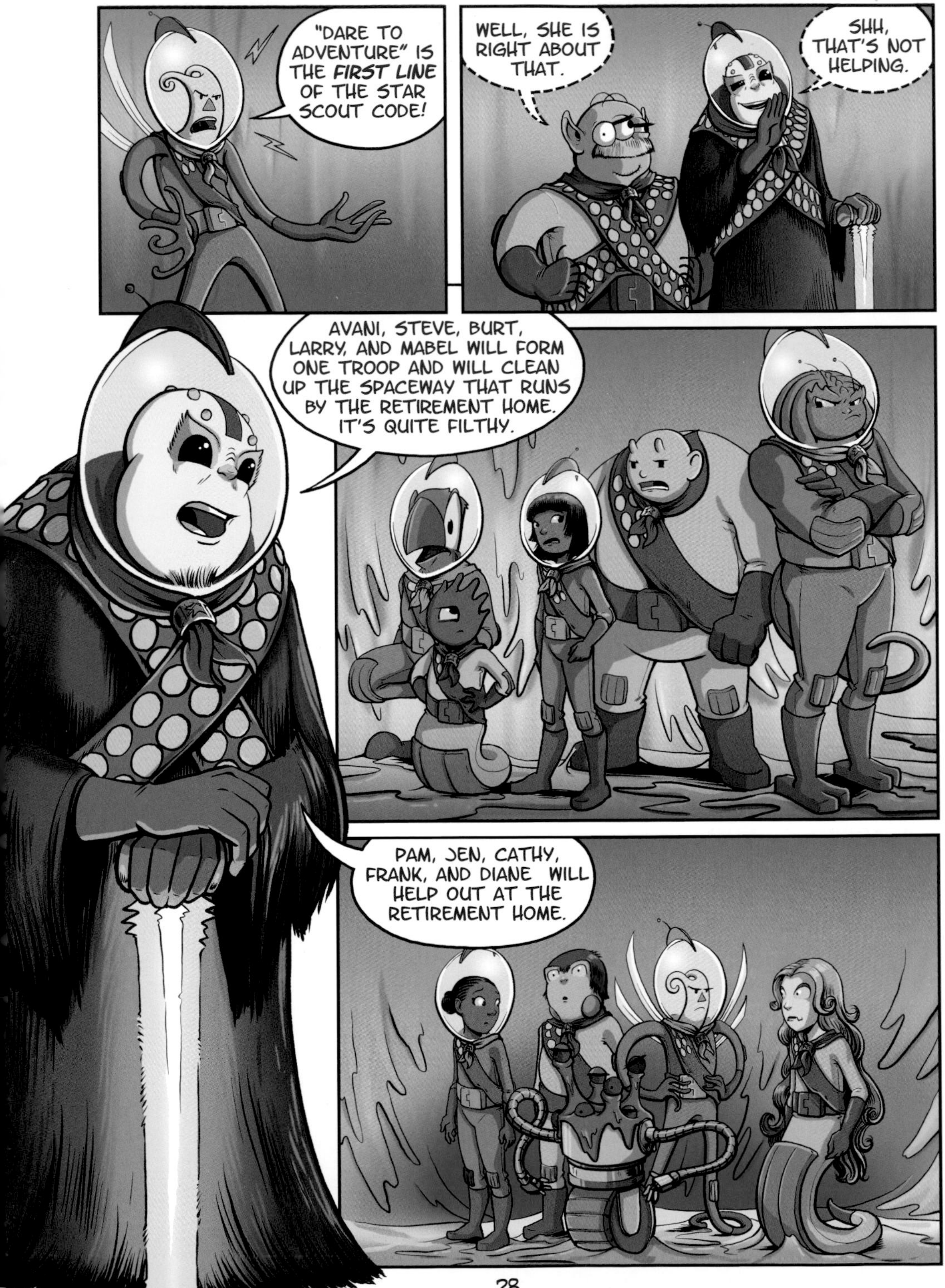
"DARE TO ADVENTURE" IS THE *FIRST LINE* OF THE STAR SCOUT CODE!
WELL, SHE IS RIGHT ABOUT THAT.
SHH, THAT'S NOT HELPING.
AVANI, STEVE, BURT, LARRY, AND MABEL WILL FORM ONE TROOP AND WILL CLEAN UP THE SPACEWAY THAT RUNS BY THE RETIREMENT HOME. IT'S QUITE FILTHY.
PAM, JEN, CATHY, FRANK, AND DIANE WILL HELP OUT AT THE RETIREMENT HOME.

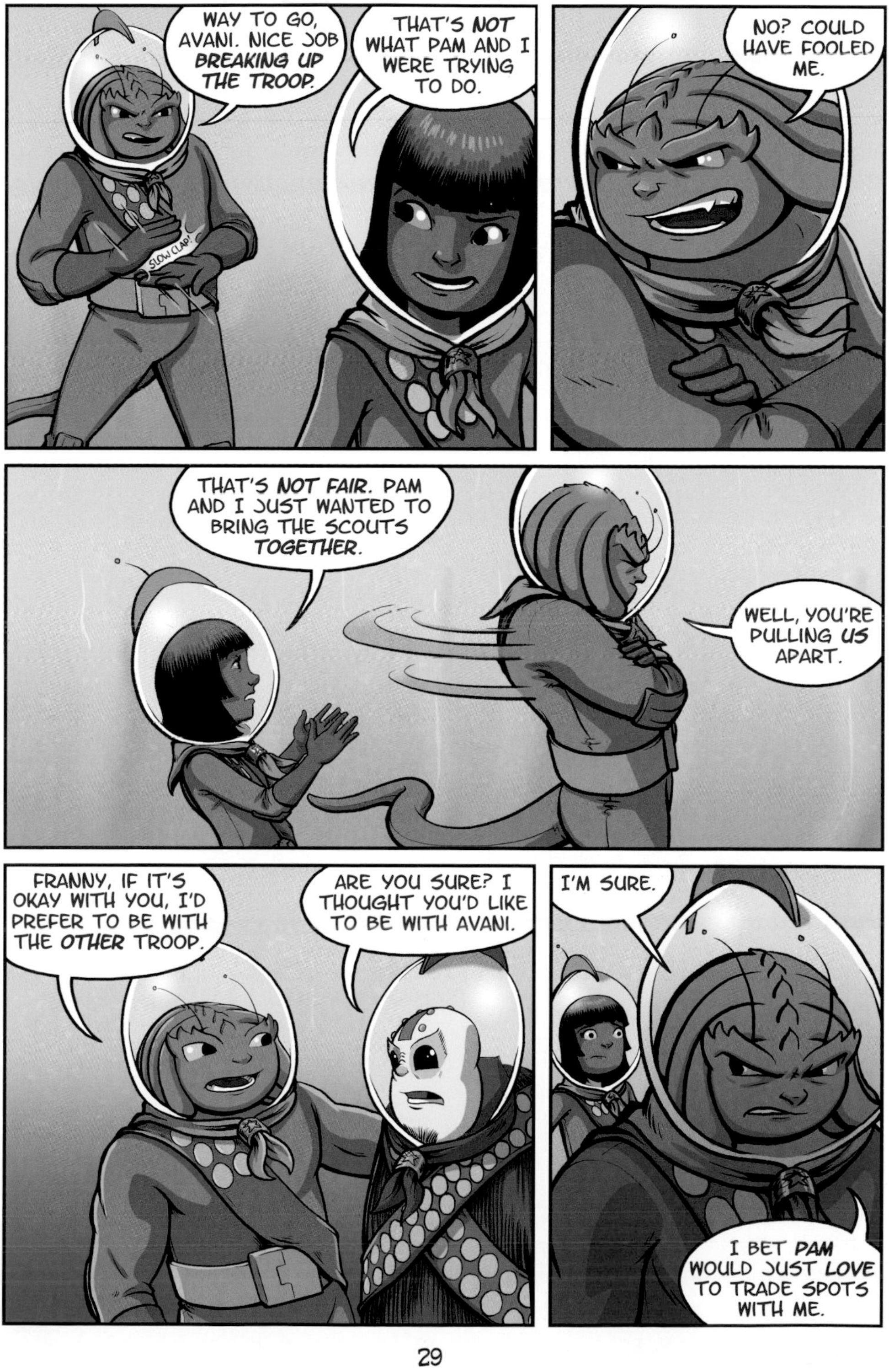
WAY TO GO, AVANI. NICE JOB BREAKING UP THE TROOP.
SLOW CLAP!
THAT'S NOT WHAT PAM AND I WERE TRYING TO DO.
NO? COULD HAVE FOOLED ME.
THAT'S NOT FAIR. PAM AND I JUST WANTED TO BRING THE SCOUTS TOGETHER.
WELL, YOU'RE PULLING US APART.
FRANNY, IF IT'S OKAY WITH YOU, I'D PREFER TO BE WITH THE OTHER TROOP.
ARE YOU SURE? I THOUGHT YOU'D LIKE TO BE WITH AVANI.
I'M SURE.
I BET PAM WOULD JUST LOVE TO TRADE SPOTS WITH ME.

PART
2

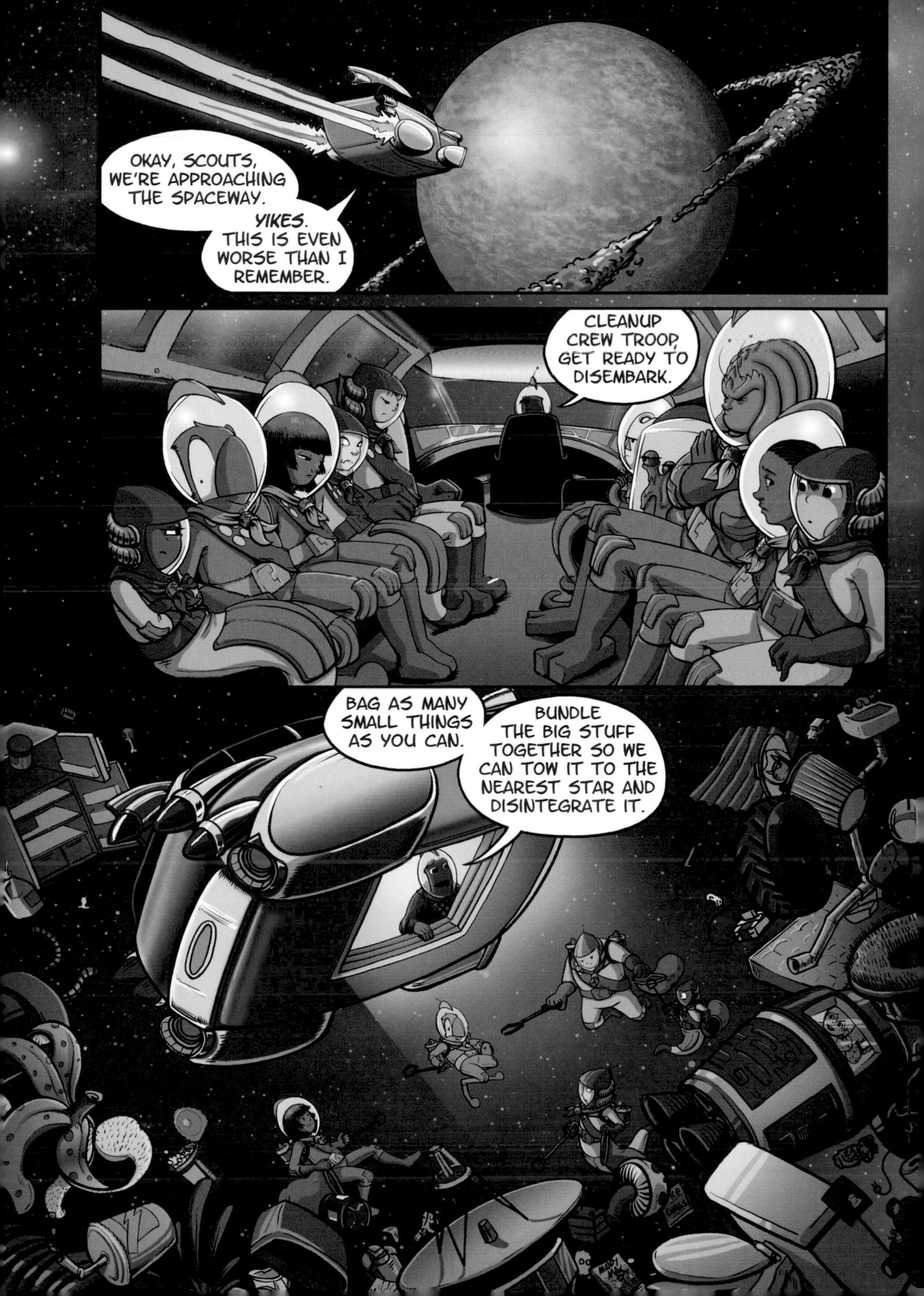

OKAY, SCOUTS, WE'RE APPROACHING THE SPACEWAY.
YIKES. THIS IS EVEN WORSE THAN I REMEMBER.
CLEANUP CREW TROOP, GET READY TO DISEMBARK.
BAG AS MANY SMALL THINGS AS YOU CAN.
BUNDLE THE BIG STUFF TOGETHER SO WE CAN TOW IT TO THE NEAREST STAR AND DISINTEGRATE IT.

I CAN'T BELIEVE FRANNY BROKE UP OUR TROOP.

YEAH, SORRY. THIS ISN'T WHAT I HAD IN MIND FOR INTEGRATING STAR SCOUTS.

'S'OKAY.

AT LEAST WE'RE NOT THE ONLY ONES WHO HAVE TO WEAR THEIR HELMETS.

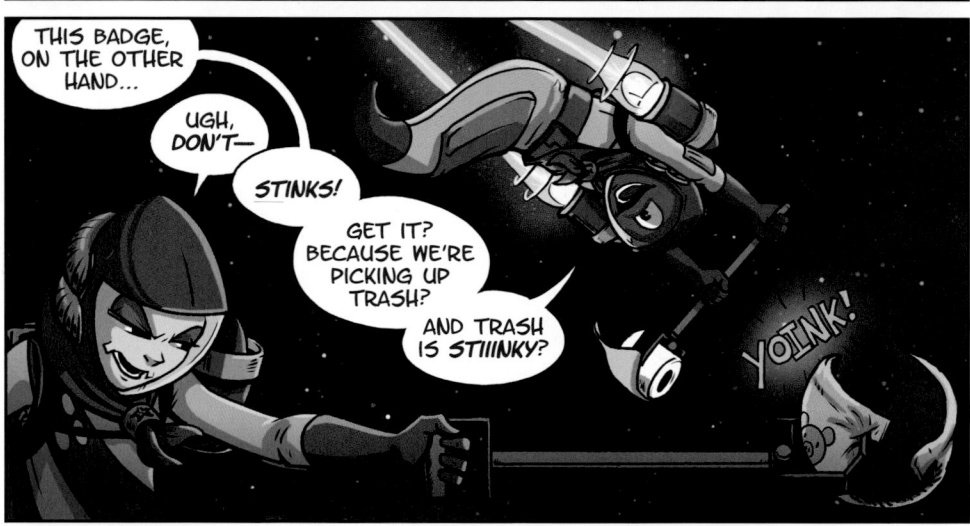

THIS BADGE, ON THE OTHER HAND...

UGH, DON'T—

STINKS!

GET IT? BECAUSE WE'RE PICKING UP TRASH?

AND TRASH IS STIIINKY?

YOINK!

EXPLAINING A JOKE DOESN'T MAKE IT MORE FUNNY.

WE CAN AGREE TO DISAGREE.

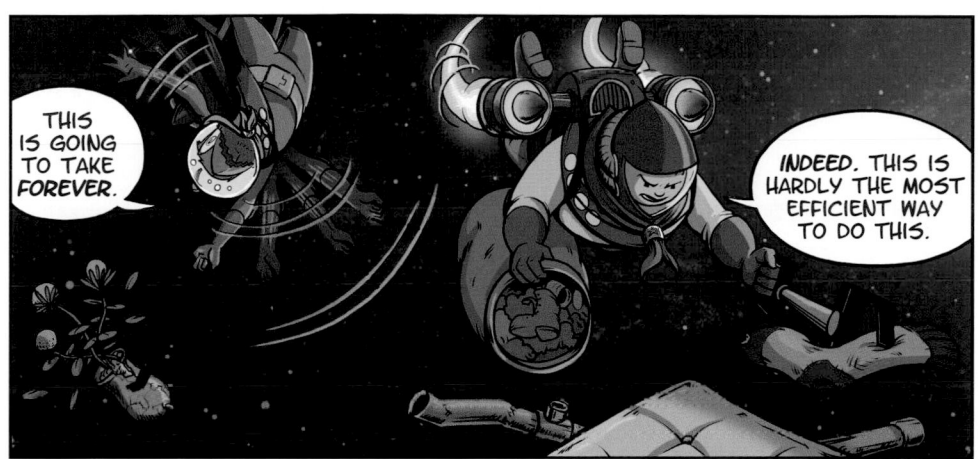

THIS IS GOING TO TAKE FOREVER.

INDEED. THIS IS HARDLY THE MOST EFFICIENT WAY TO DO THIS.

HELLOOO... WHAT HAVE WE HERE?

IS THAT THE HEAD OF A MAIM-O-TRON 4000?

BACK OFF. I SAW IT FIRST.

TAKE IT EASY— I JUST WANTED A LOOK.

BESIDES, WHAT ARE *YOU* GOING TO DO WITH IT?

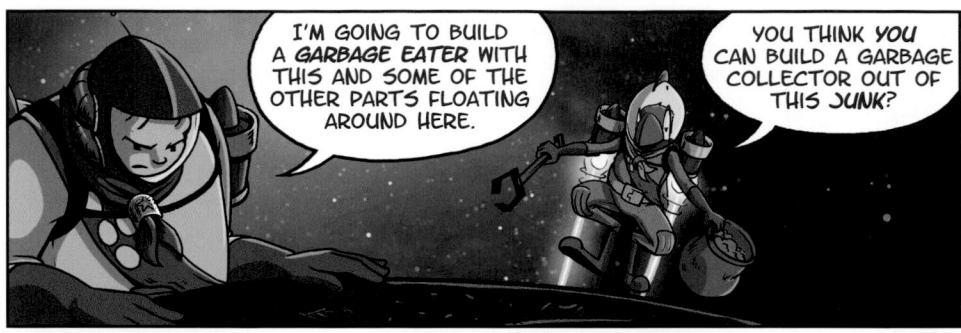

I'M GOING TO BUILD A *GARBAGE EATER* WITH THIS AND SOME OF THE OTHER PARTS FLOATING AROUND HERE.

YOU THINK *YOU* CAN BUILD A GARBAGE COLLECTOR OUT OF THIS *JUNK*?

YOU HAVE A PROBLEM WITH THAT?

I GUESS YOU'D RATHER PICK THIS MESS UP BY *HAND*?

I JUST THINK YOU MIGHT BE OUT OF YOUR LEAGUE.

OH, AND I SUPPOSE *YOU* KNOW A THING OR TWO ABOUT ROBOTICS?

I DABBLE.

YOU WANT TO HELP?

NO OFFENSE, BUT I THINK YOU'D JUST SLOW ME DOWN.

OH, REALLY? HOW ABOUT YOU GO WORK ON YOUR *OWN* PROJECT, AND I'LL WORK ON *MINE*. WE'LL SEE WHO'S THE *SLOW* ONE.

PAH-LEASE... EAT MY ENGINEERING DUST.

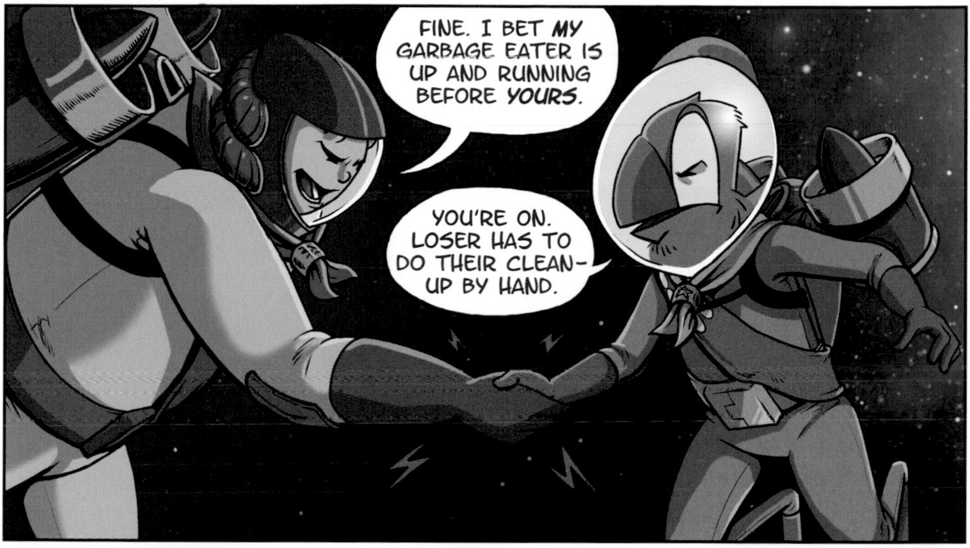
FINE. I BET MY GARBAGE EATER IS UP AND RUNNING BEFORE YOURS.
YOU'RE ON. LOSER HAS TO DO THEIR CLEAN-UP BY HAND.

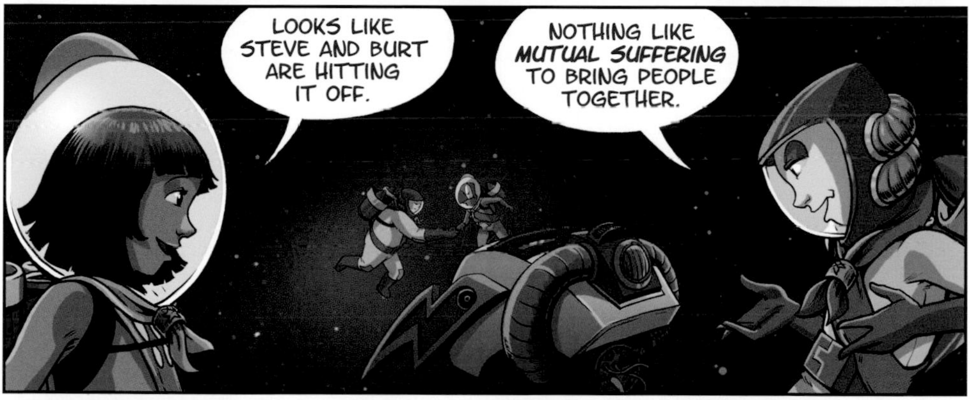
LOOKS LIKE STEVE AND BURT ARE HITTING IT OFF.
NOTHING LIKE MUTUAL SUFFERING TO BRING PEOPLE TOGETHER.

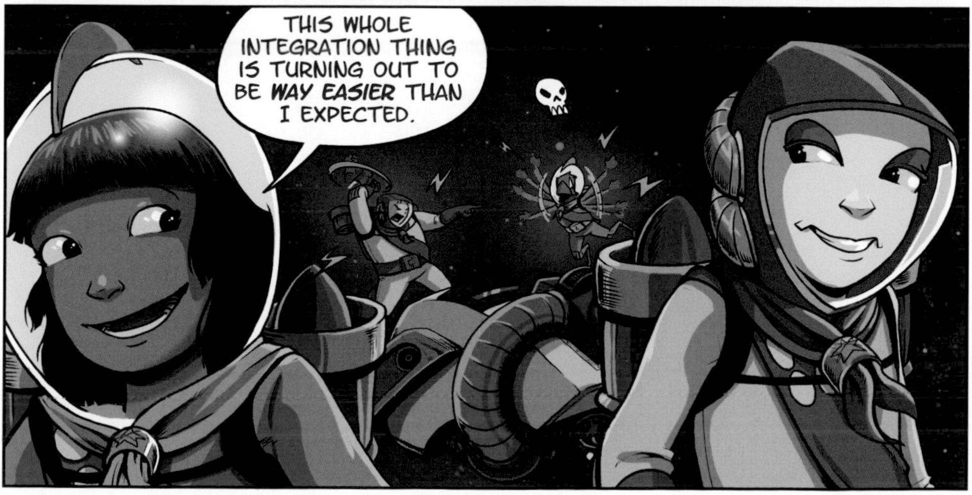
THIS WHOLE INTEGRATION THING IS TURNING OUT TO BE WAY EASIER THAN I EXPECTED.

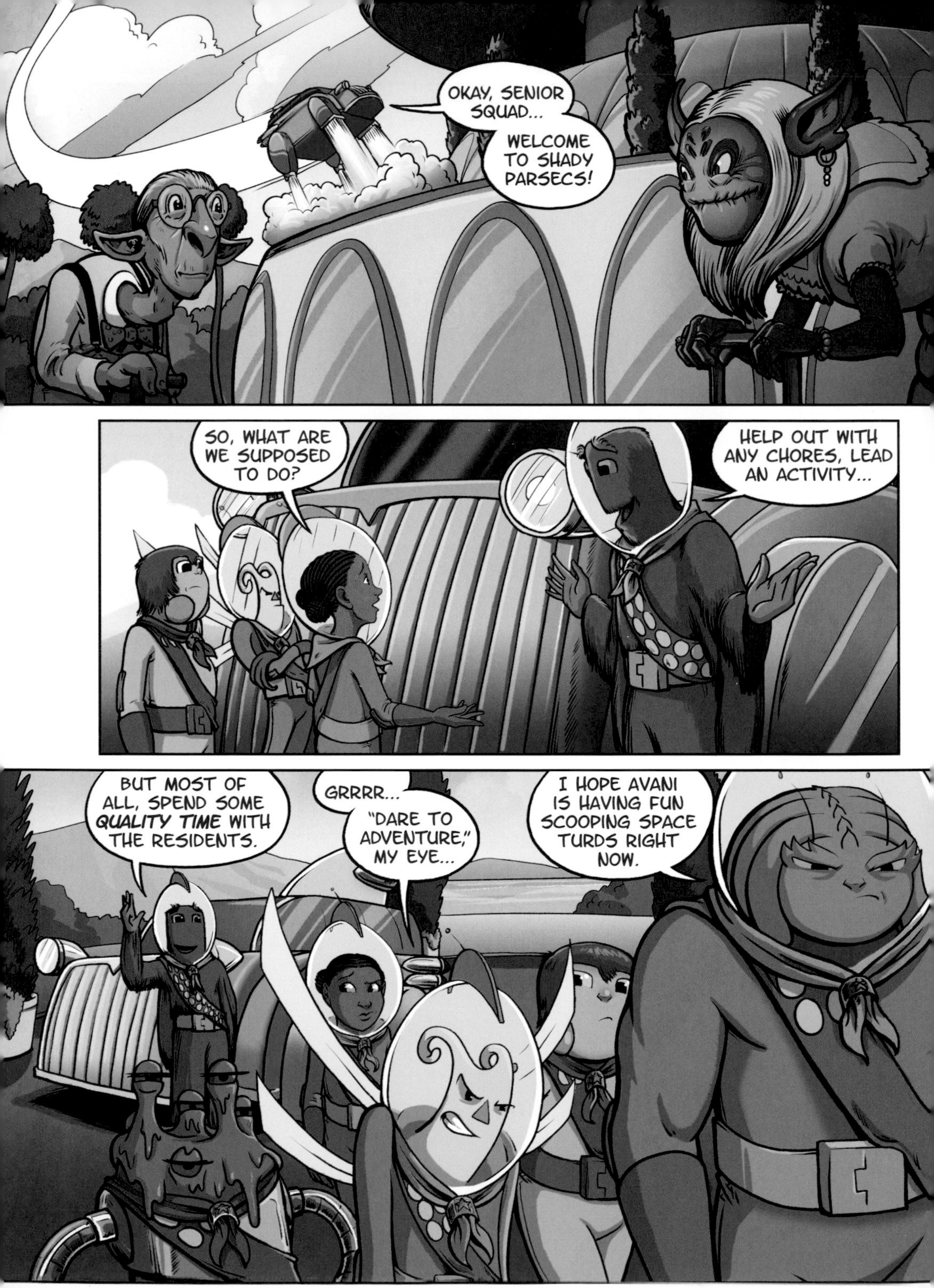
OKAY, SENIOR SQUAD...
WELCOME TO SHADY PARSECS!
SO, WHAT ARE WE SUPPOSED TO DO?
HELP OUT WITH ANY CHORES, LEAD AN ACTIVITY...
BUT MOST OF ALL, SPEND SOME QUALITY TIME WITH THE RESIDENTS.
GRRRR...
"DARE TO ADVENTURE," MY EYE...
I HOPE AVANI IS HAVING FUN SCOOPING SPACE TURDS RIGHT NOW.

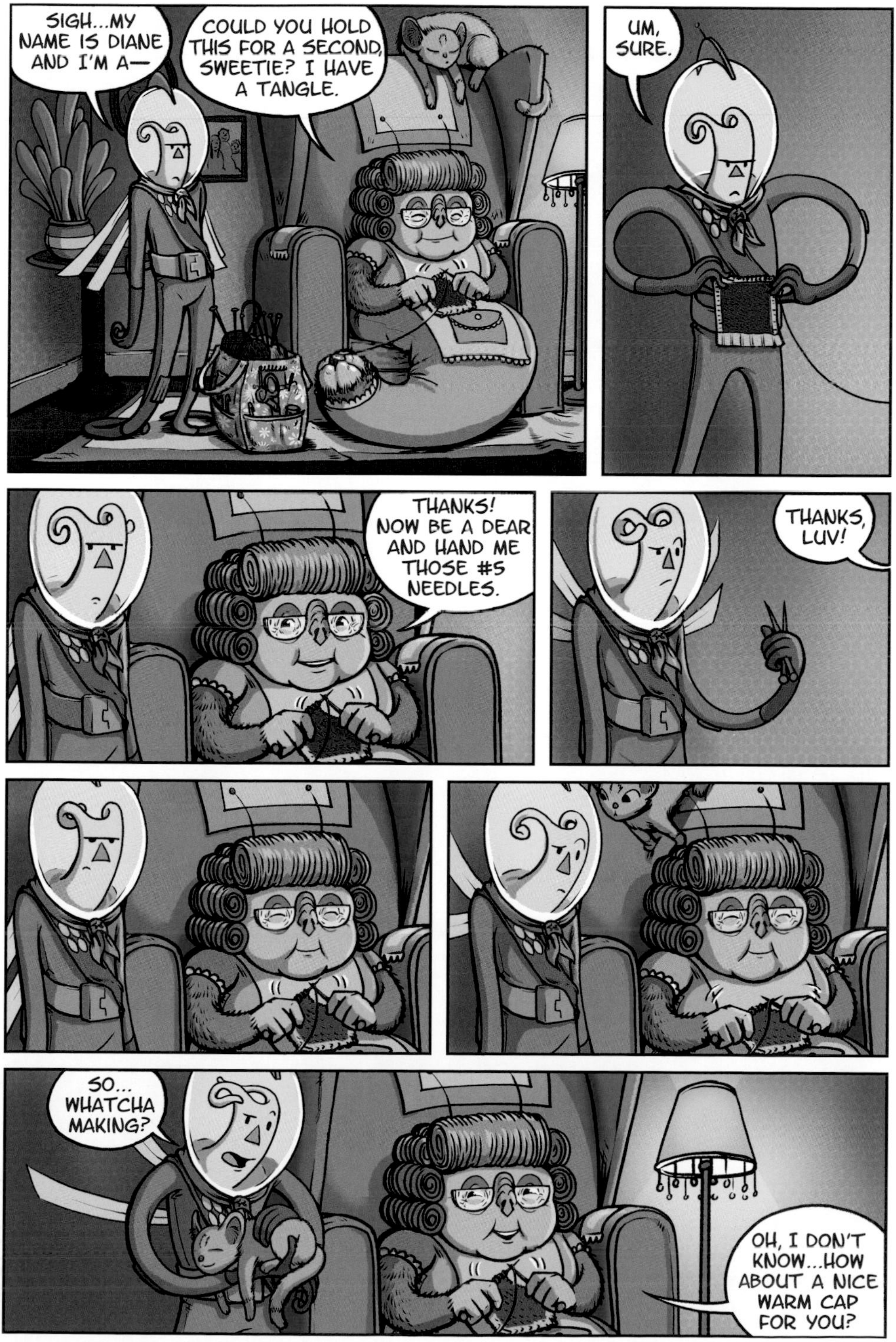
SIGH...MY NAME IS DIANE AND I'M A—
COULD YOU HOLD THIS FOR A SECOND, SWEETIE? I HAVE A TANGLE.
UM, SURE.
THANKS! NOW BE A DEAR AND HAND ME THOSE #5 NEEDLES.
THANKS, LUV!
SO... WHATCHA MAKING?
OH, I DON'T KNOW...HOW ABOUT A NICE WARM CAP FOR YOU?

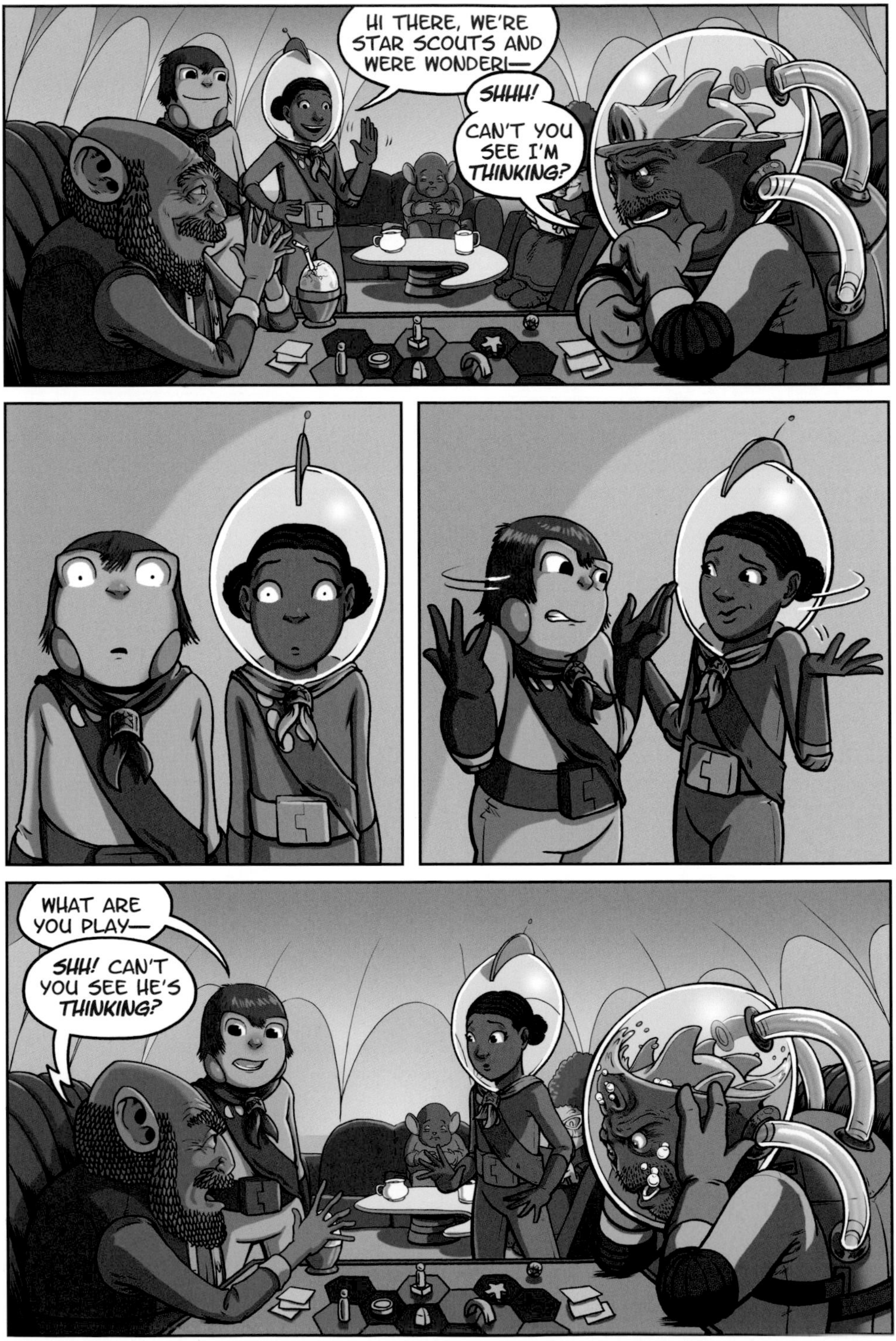
HI THERE, WE'RE STAR SCOUTS AND WERE WONDERI—
SHHH!
CAN'T YOU SEE I'M THINKING?
WHAT ARE YOU PLAY—
SHH! CAN'T YOU SEE HE'S THINKING?

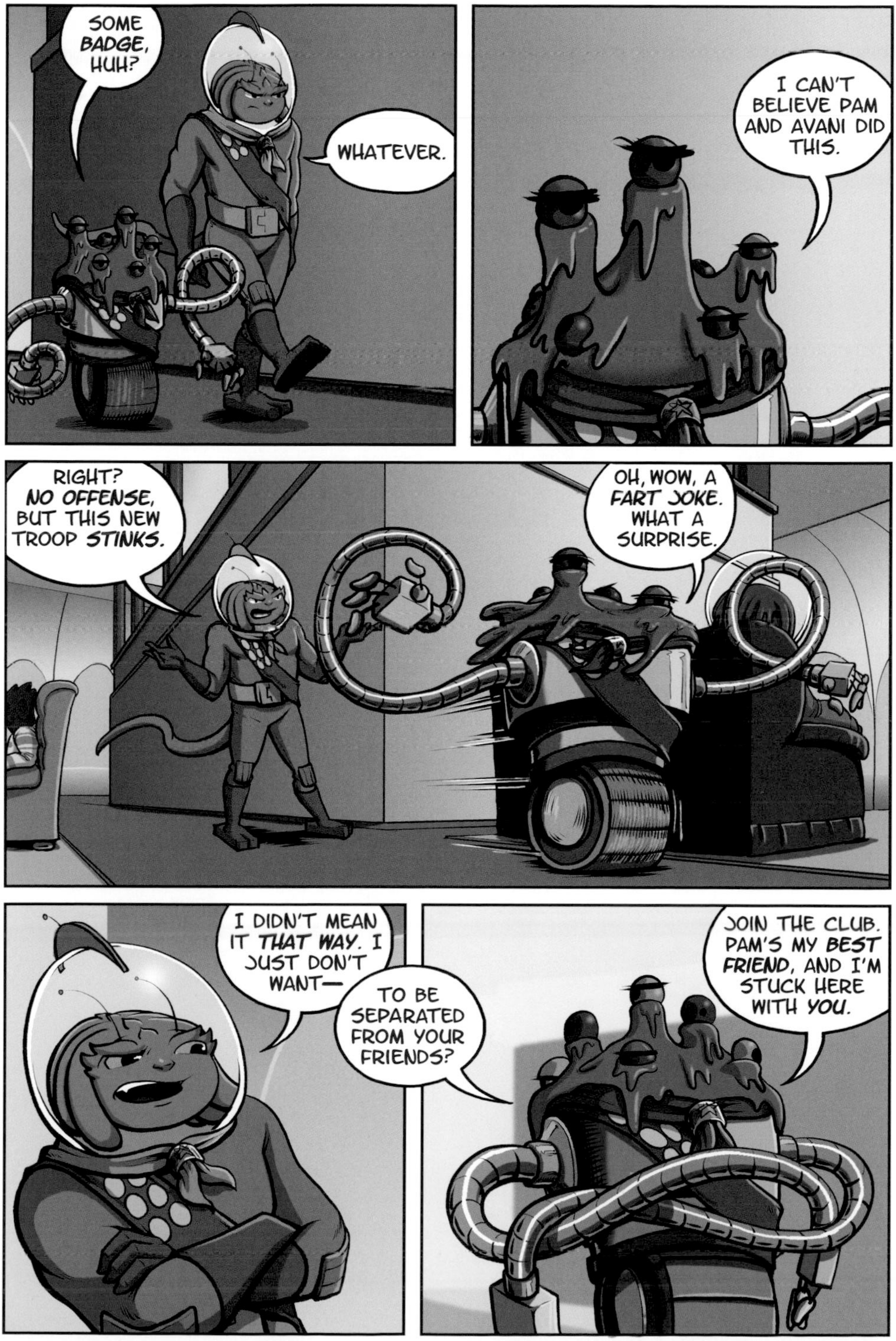

SOME BADGE, HUH?
WHATEVER.
I CAN'T BELIEVE PAM AND AVANI DID THIS.
RIGHT? NO OFFENSE, BUT THIS NEW TROOP STINKS.
OH, WOW, A FART JOKE. WHAT A SURPRISE.
I DIDN'T MEAN IT THAT WAY. I JUST DON'T WANT—
TO BE SEPARATED FROM YOUR FRIENDS?
JOIN THE CLUB. PAM'S MY BEST FRIEND, AND I'M STUCK HERE WITH YOU.

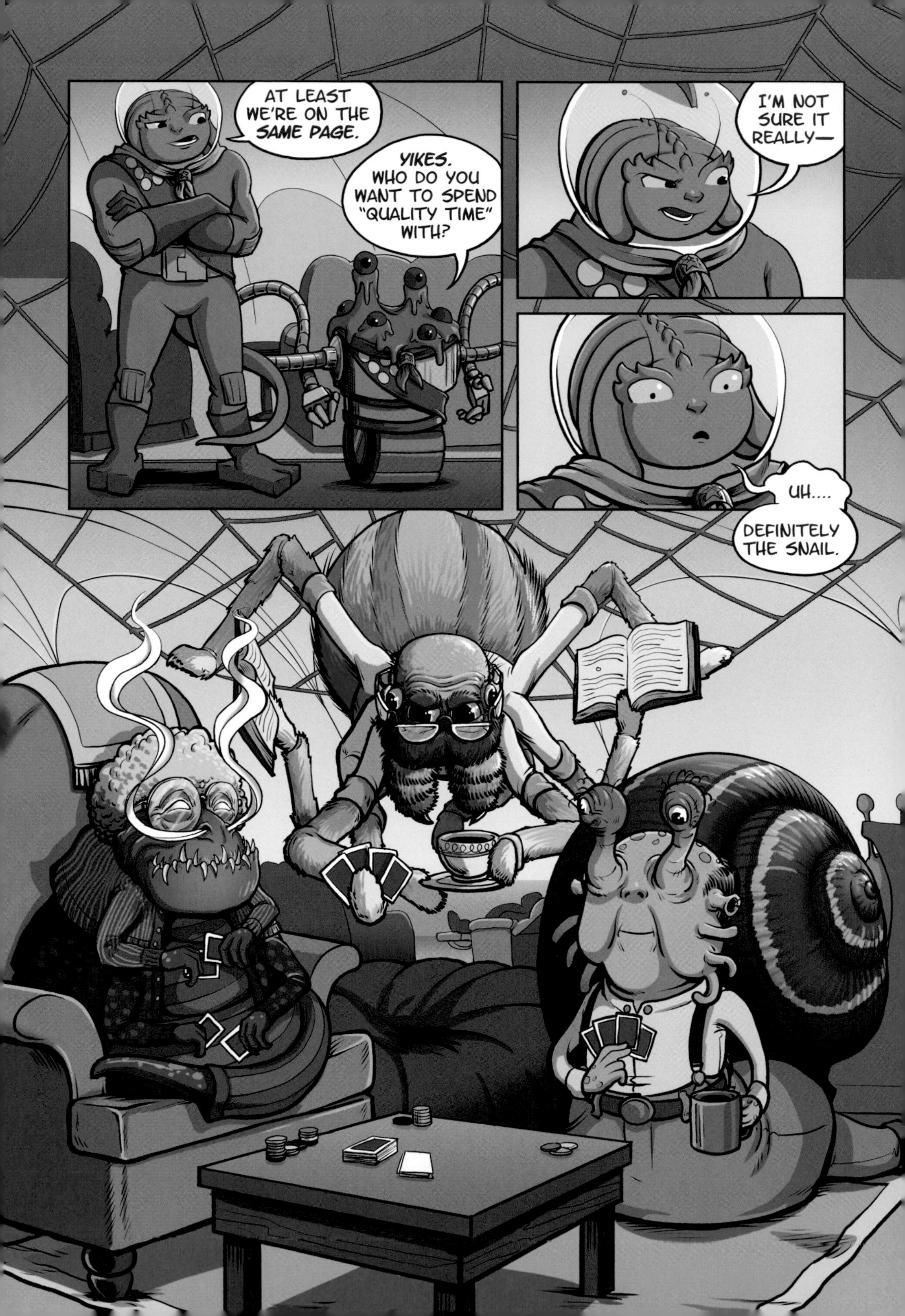
AT LEAST WE'RE ON THE SAME PAGE.
YIKES. WHO DO YOU WANT TO SPEND "QUALITY TIME" WITH?
I'M NOT SURE IT REALLY—
UH....
DEFINITELY THE SNAIL.

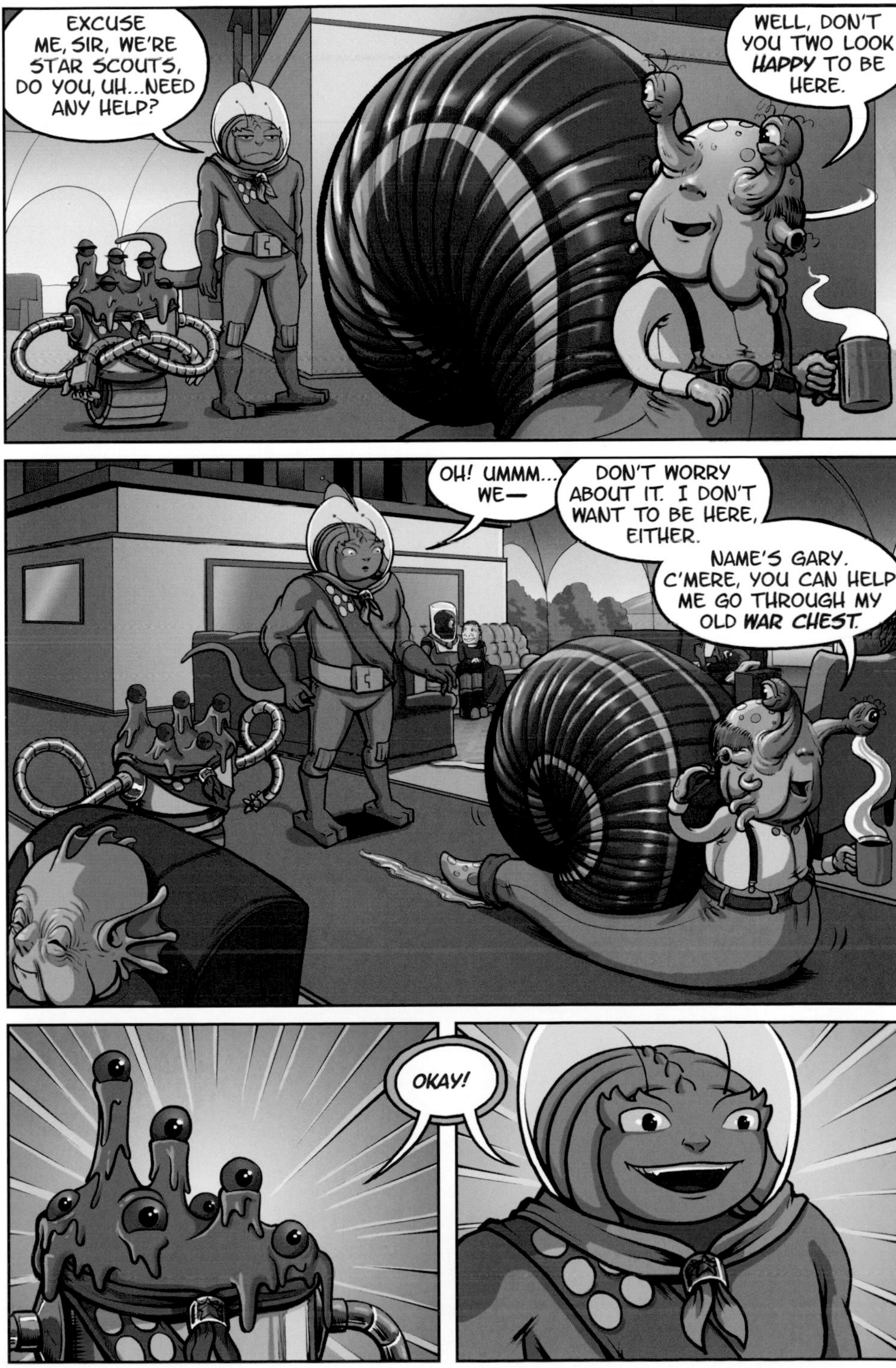

EXCUSE ME, SIR, WE'RE STAR SCOUTS, DO YOU, UH...NEED ANY HELP?
WELL, DON'T YOU TWO LOOK HAPPY TO BE HERE.
OH! UMMM... WE—
DON'T WORRY ABOUT IT. I DON'T WANT TO BE HERE, EITHER.
NAME'S GARY. C'MERE, YOU CAN HELP ME GO THROUGH MY OLD WAR CHEST.
OKAY!

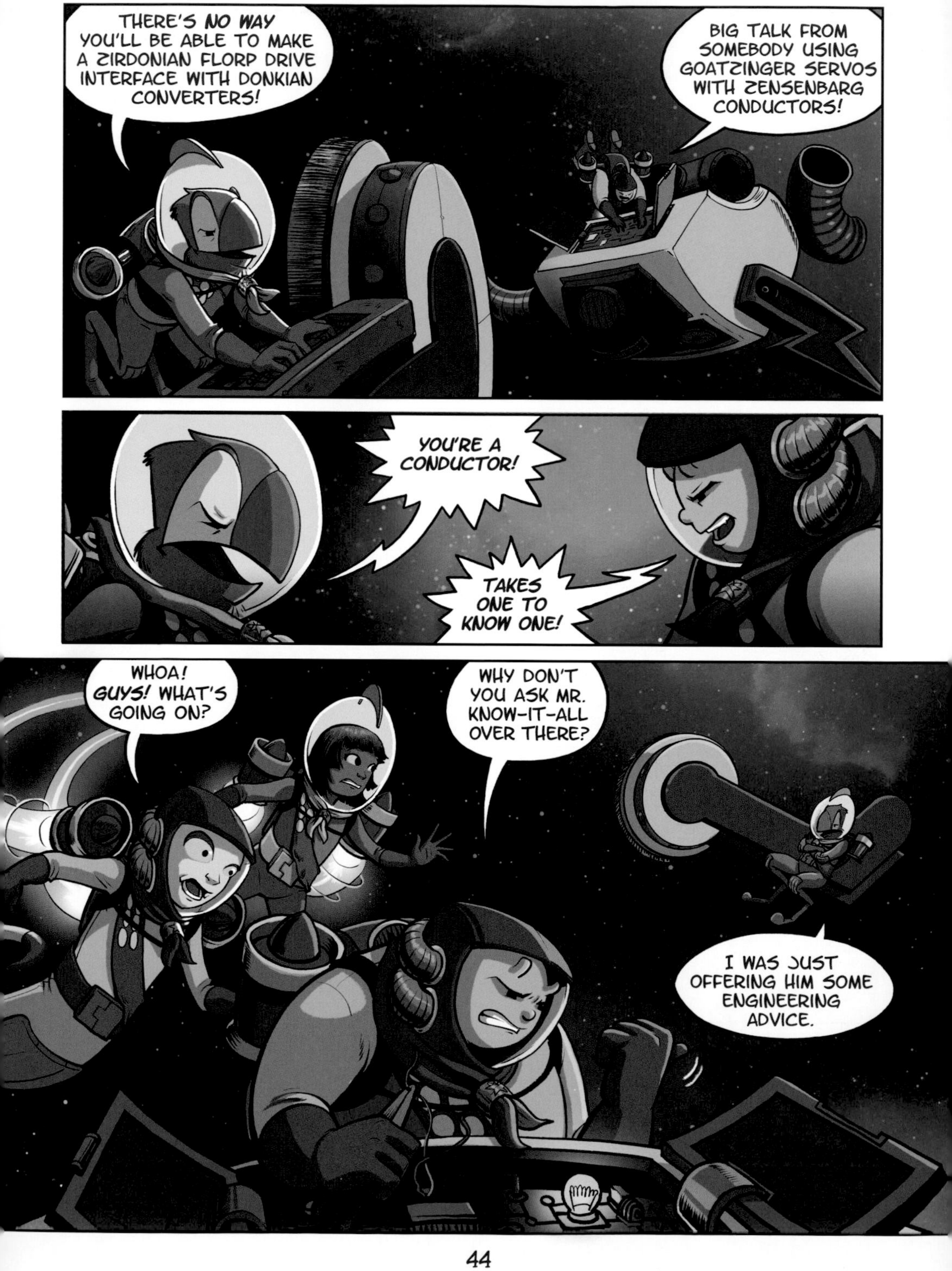
THERE'S NO WAY YOU'LL BE ABLE TO MAKE A ZIRDONIAN FLORP DRIVE INTERFACE WITH DONKIAN CONVERTERS!
BIG TALK FROM SOMEBODY USING GOATZINGER SERVOS WITH ZENSENBARG CONDUCTORS!
YOU'RE A CONDUCTOR!
TAKES ONE TO KNOW ONE!
WHOA! GUYS! WHAT'S GOING ON?
WHY DON'T YOU ASK MR. KNOW-IT-ALL OVER THERE?
I WAS JUST OFFERING HIM SOME ENGINEERING ADVICE.

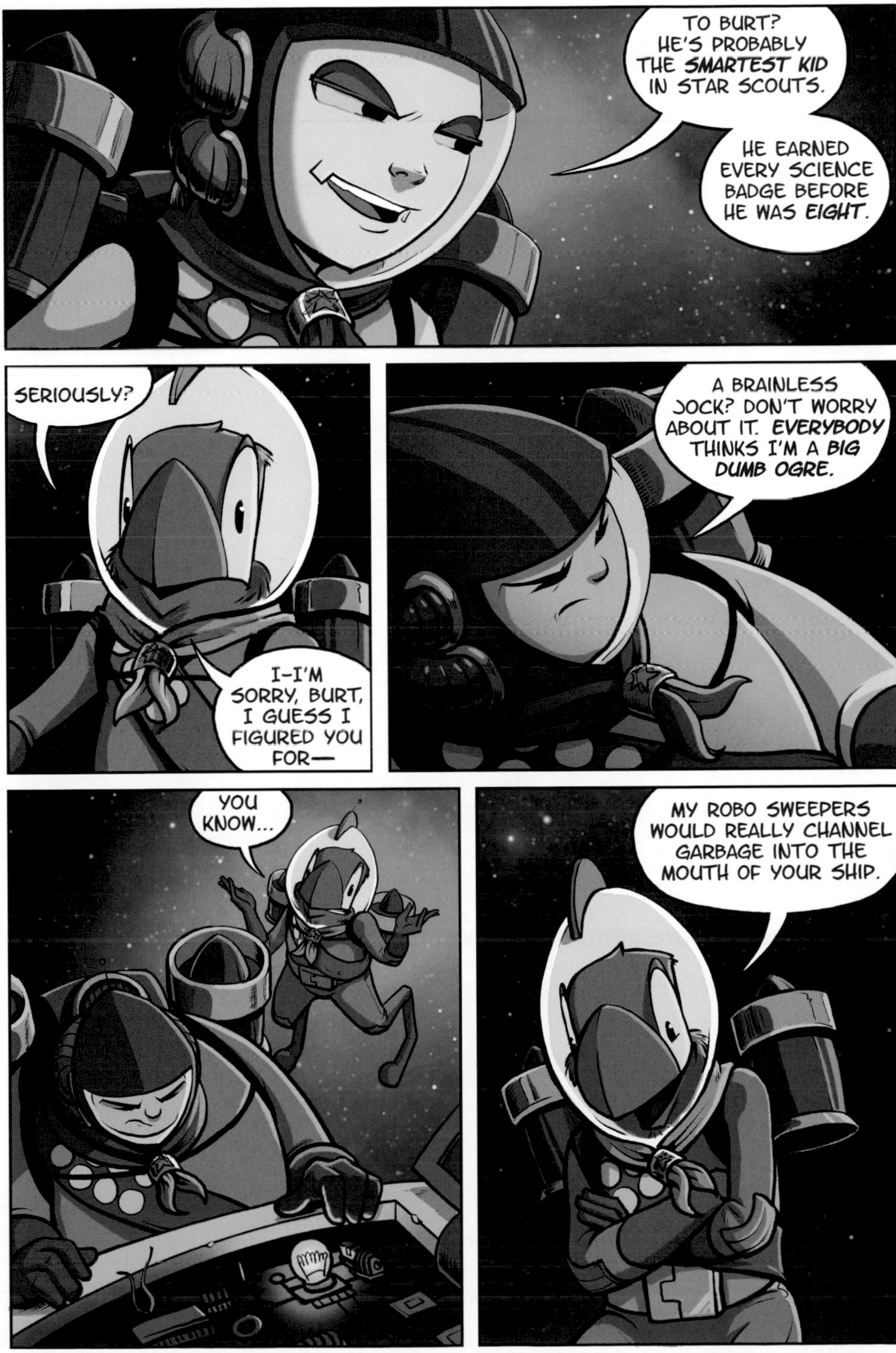
TO BURT? HE'S PROBABLY THE **SMARTEST KID** IN STAR SCOUTS.
HE EARNED EVERY SCIENCE BADGE BEFORE HE WAS **EIGHT**.
SERIOUSLY?
I-I'M SORRY, BURT, I GUESS I FIGURED YOU FOR—
A BRAINLESS JOCK? DON'T WORRY ABOUT IT. **EVERYBODY** THINKS I'M A **BIG DUMB OGRE**.
YOU KNOW...
MY ROBO SWEEPERS WOULD REALLY CHANNEL GARBAGE INTO THE MOUTH OF YOUR SHIP.

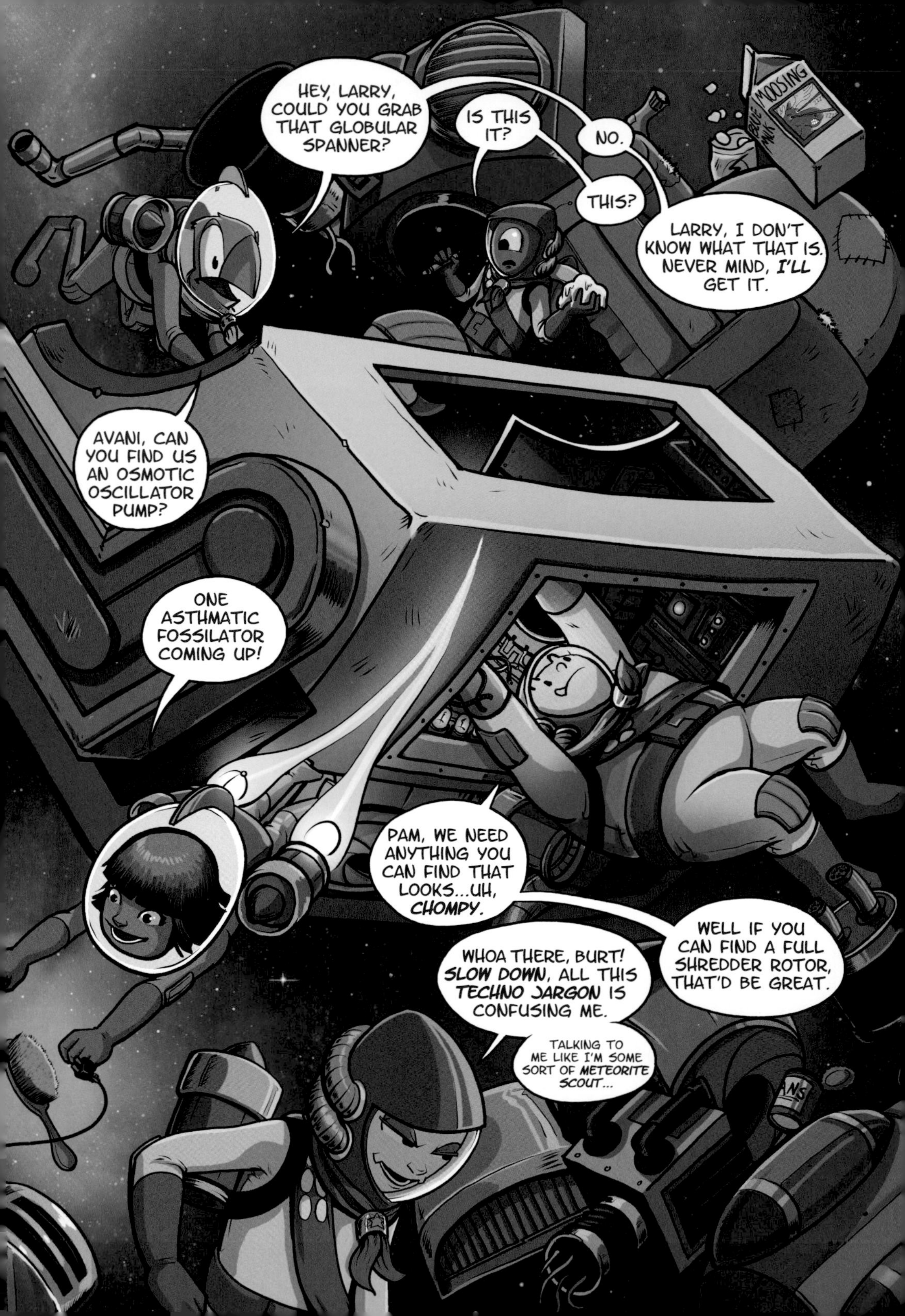
HEY, LARRY, COULD YOU GRAB THAT GLOBULAR SPANNER?
IS THIS IT?
NO.
THIS?
LARRY, I DON'T KNOW WHAT THAT IS. NEVER MIND, *I'LL* GET IT.
MOOSING
BLUE MILK
AVANI, CAN YOU FIND US AN OSMOTIC OSCILLATOR PUMP?
ONE ASTHMATIC FOSSILATOR COMING UP!
PAM, WE NEED ANYTHING YOU CAN FIND THAT LOOKS...UH, *CHOMPY*.
WELL IF YOU CAN FIND A FULL SHREDDER ROTOR, THAT'D BE GREAT.
WHOA THERE, BURT! *SLOW DOWN*, ALL THIS *TECHNO JARGON* IS CONFUSING ME.
TALKING TO ME LIKE I'M SOME SORT OF *METEORITE* SCOUT...

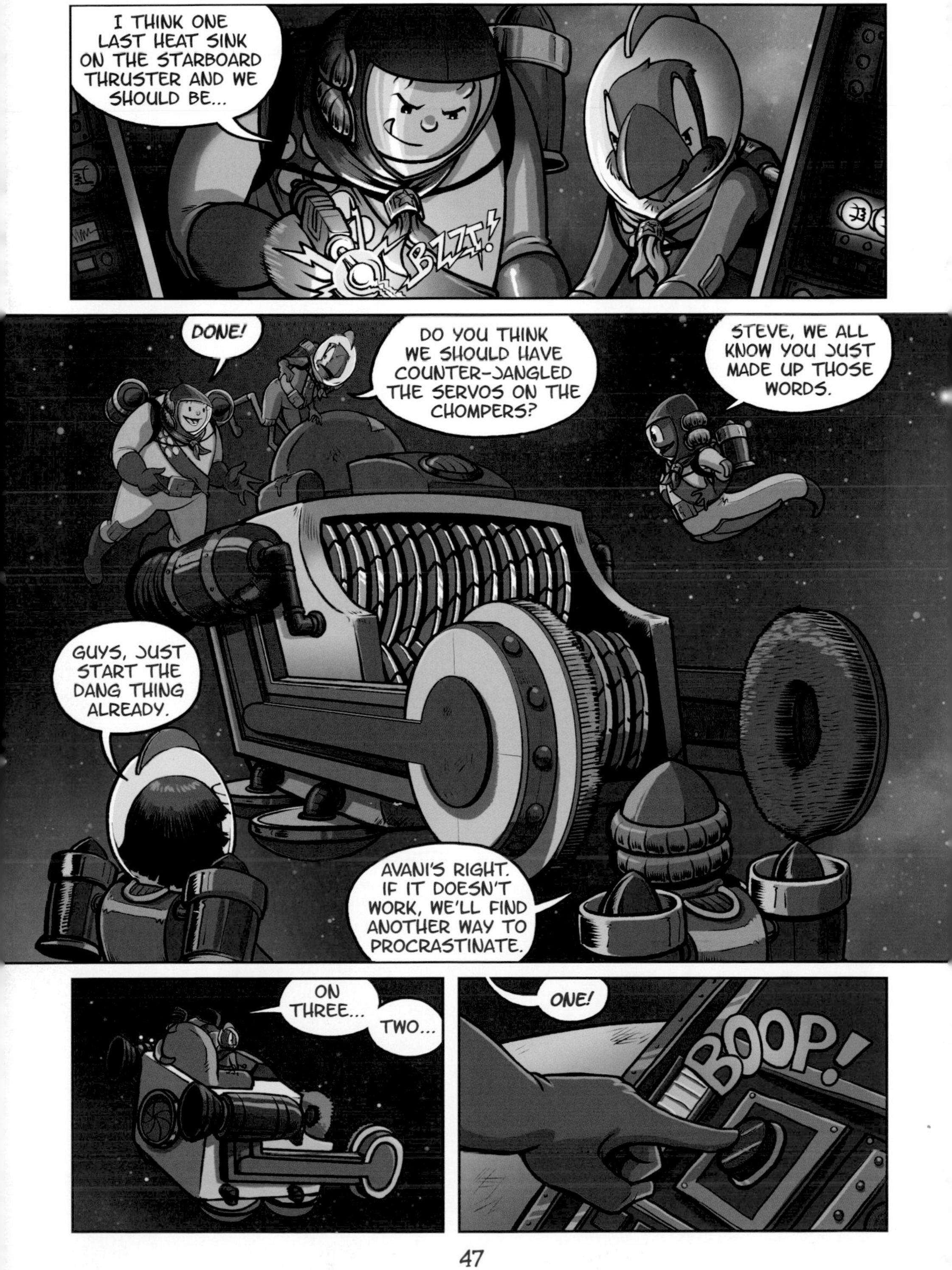
I THINK ONE LAST HEAT SINK ON THE STARBOARD THRUSTER AND WE SHOULD BE...
BZZT!
DONE!
DO YOU THINK WE SHOULD HAVE COUNTER-JANGLED THE SERVOS ON THE CHOMPERS?
STEVE, WE ALL KNOW YOU JUST MADE UP THOSE WORDS.
GUYS, JUST START THE DANG THING ALREADY.
AVANI'S RIGHT. IF IT DOESN'T WORK, WE'LL FIND ANOTHER WAY TO PROCRASTINATE.
ON THREE...
TWO...
ONE!
BOOP!

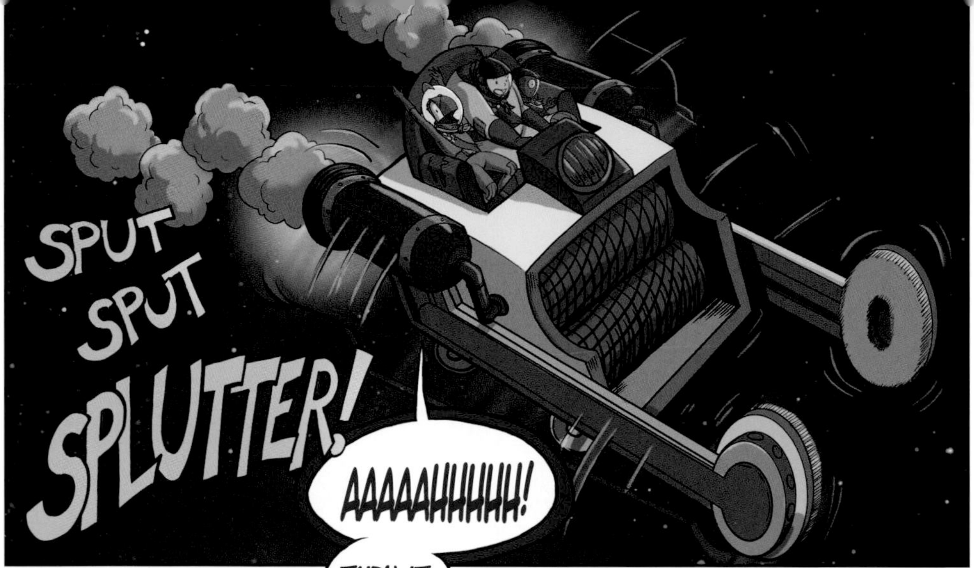
SPUT
SPUT
SPLUTTER!
AAAAAHHHHH!

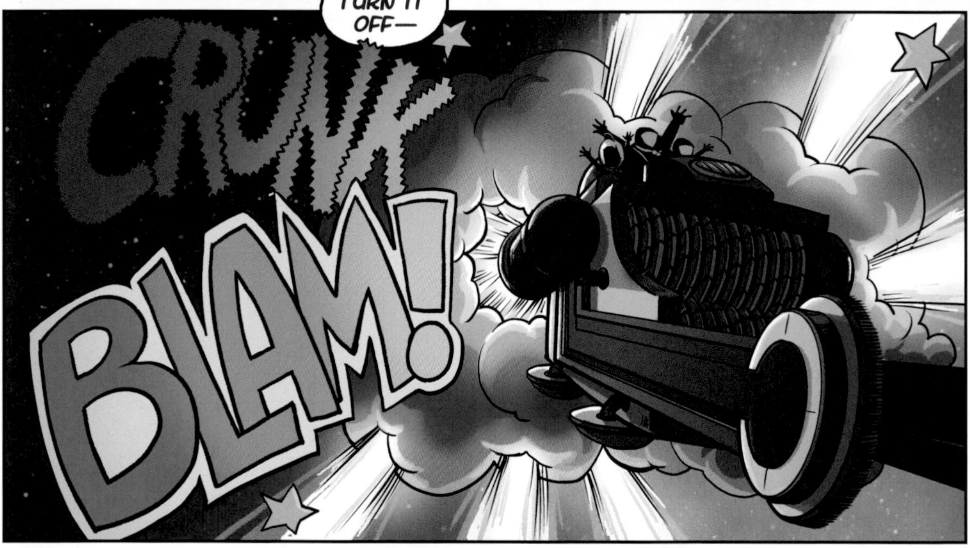
TURN IT OFF—
CRUNK
BLAM!

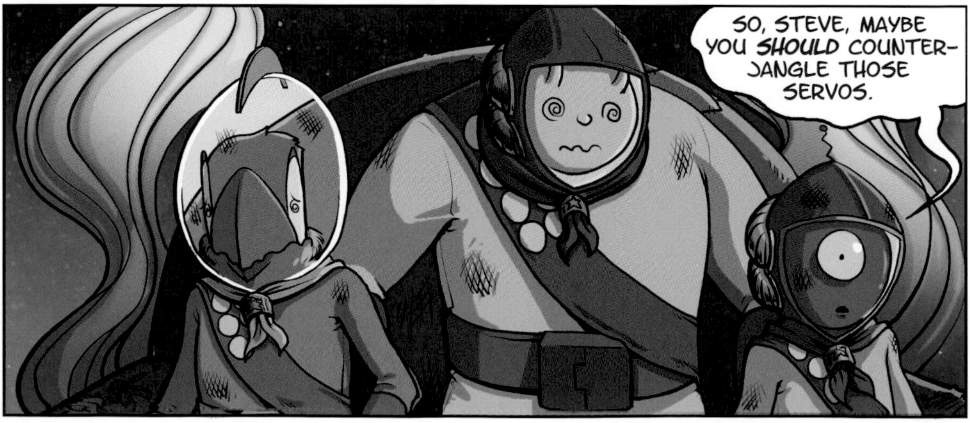
SO, STEVE, MAYBE YOU SHOULD COUNTER-JANGLE THOSE SERVOS.

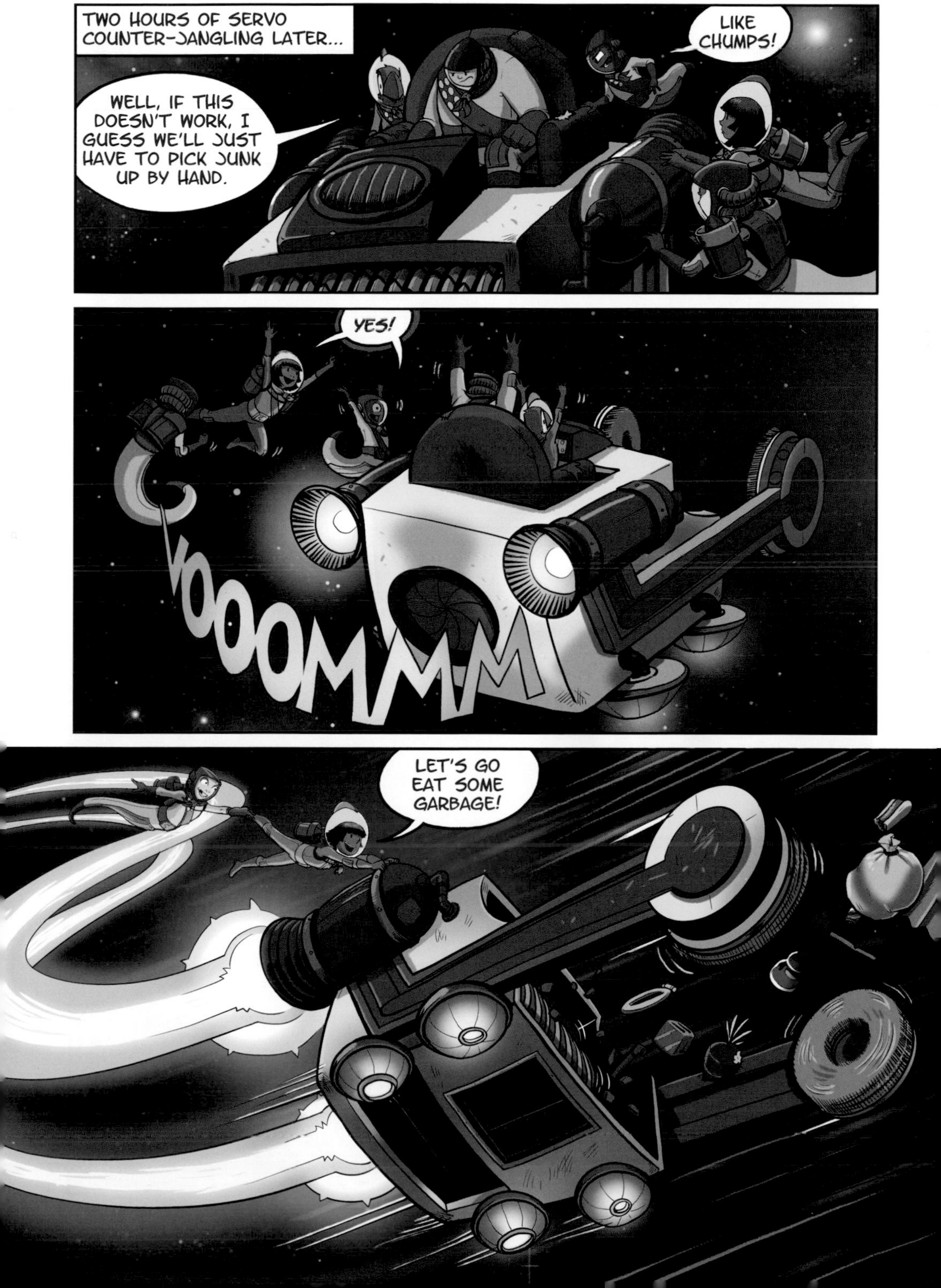
TWO HOURS OF SERVO COUNTER-JANGLING LATER...
LIKE CHUMPS!
WELL, IF THIS DOESN'T WORK, I GUESS WE'LL JUST HAVE TO PICK JUNK UP BY HAND.
YES!
VOOOMMM
LET'S GO EAT SOME GARBAGE!

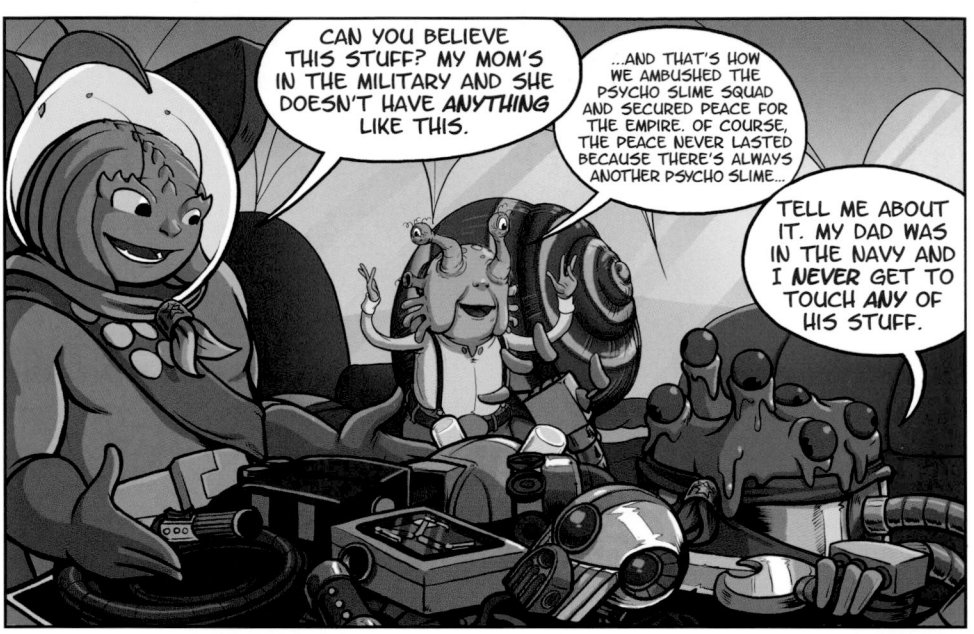

CAN YOU BELIEVE THIS STUFF? MY MOM'S IN THE MILITARY AND SHE DOESN'T HAVE **ANYTHING** LIKE THIS.

...AND THAT'S HOW WE AMBUSHED THE PSYCHO SLIME SQUAD AND SECURED PEACE FOR THE EMPIRE. OF COURSE, THE PEACE NEVER LASTED BECAUSE THERE'S ALWAYS ANOTHER PSYCHO SLIME...

TELL ME ABOUT IT. MY DAD WAS IN THE NAVY AND I **NEVER** GET TO TOUCH **ANY** OF HIS STUFF.

I DIDN'T KNOW YOUR DAD WAS IN THE MILITARY.

YEAH, IT WAS ROUGH WHEN HE WAS DEPLOYED, BUT KIND OF COOL THAT HE WAS ON **WARSHIPS.**

EXACTLY. I'M PROUD OF MOM, BUT SHE'S GONE FOR **MONTHS** AT A TIME.

...THEN I JUMPED OUT OF THE SHIP AND LANDED RIGHT ON THE LEADER OF THE BLUD GUZZLERS...

NOBODY IN MY TROOP, I MEAN MY **OLD TROOP**, WAS FROM A MILITARY FAMILY.

SAME HERE. THEY HAVE **NO IDEA** WHAT IT'S LIKE.

RIGHT? AVANI IS ALL, "BOO-HOO, I'M THE **NEW KID**" AND I'M LIKE, "TRY BEING THE NEW KID **SEVEN TIMES**...ON DIFFERENT **PLANETS!**"

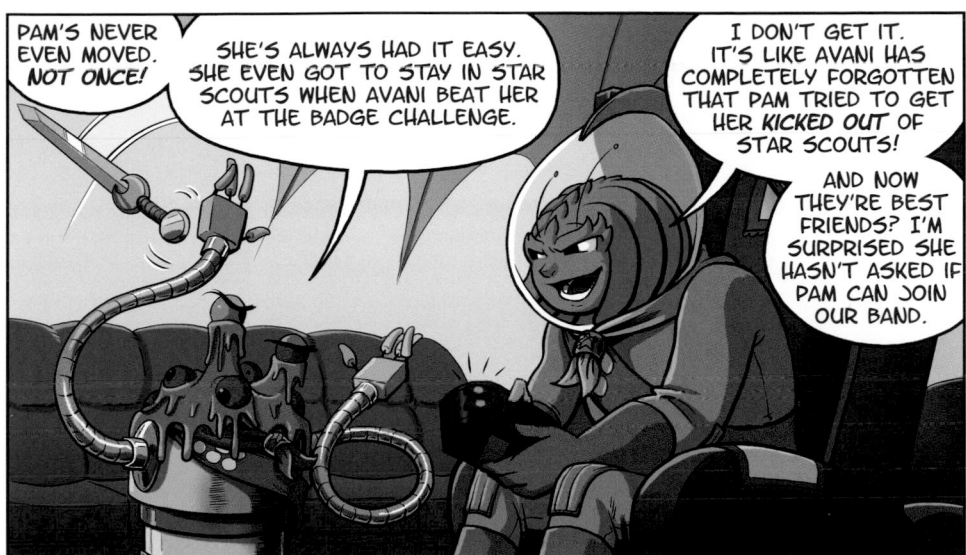

PAM'S NEVER EVEN MOVED. *NOT ONCE!*

SHE'S ALWAYS HAD IT EASY. SHE EVEN GOT TO STAY IN STAR SCOUTS WHEN AVANI BEAT HER AT THE BADGE CHALLENGE.

I DON'T GET IT. IT'S LIKE AVANI HAS COMPLETELY FORGOTTEN THAT PAM TRIED TO GET HER *KICKED OUT* OF STAR SCOUTS!

AND NOW THEY'RE BEST FRIENDS? I'M SURPRISED SHE HASN'T ASKED IF PAM CAN JOIN OUR BAND.

UGH. DON'T EVEN GET ME STARTED ON PAM'S TASTE IN MUSIC.

LITERALLY *THE WORST* POP YOU'VE *EVER* HEARD.

REALLY? AVANI *HATES* THAT JUNK. WHEN I FIRST MET HER SHE KEPT TRASH TALKING THIS GUY HER OLD FLOWER SCOUT TROOP LOVED, *CHAZ WÜNDERLIP—*

POP!

WHAT THE? I THINK THIS THING JUST *MOVED.*

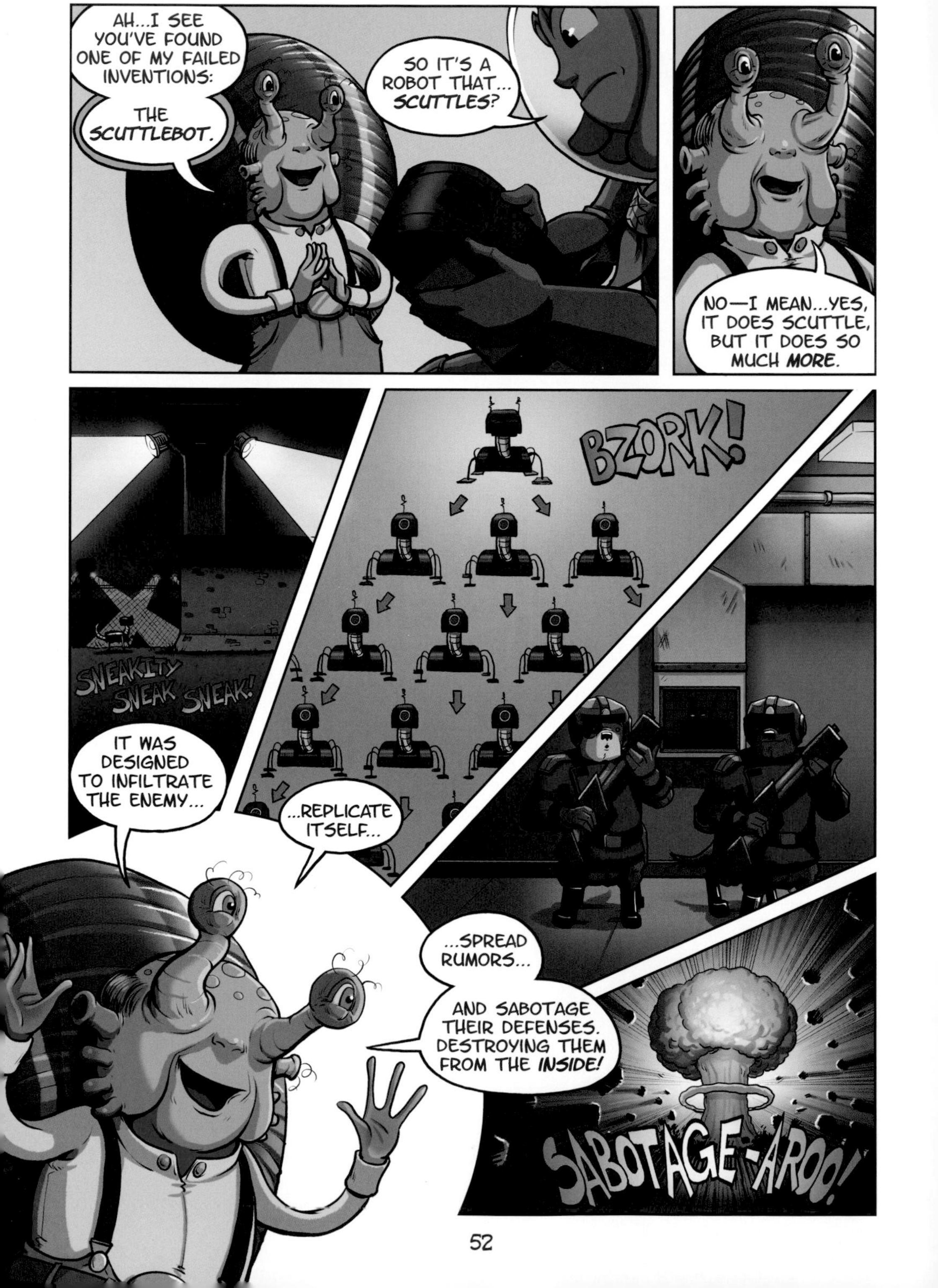
AH...I SEE YOU'VE FOUND ONE OF MY FAILED INVENTIONS:
THE SCUTTLEBOT.
SO IT'S A ROBOT THAT... SCUTTLES?
NO—I MEAN...YES, IT DOES SCUTTLE, BUT IT DOES SO MUCH MORE.
SNEAKITY SNEAK SNEAK!
BZORK!
IT WAS DESIGNED TO INFILTRATE THE ENEMY...
...REPLICATE ITSELF...
...SPREAD RUMORS...
AND SABOTAGE THEIR DEFENSES. DESTROYING THEM FROM THE INSIDE!
SABOTAGE-AROO!

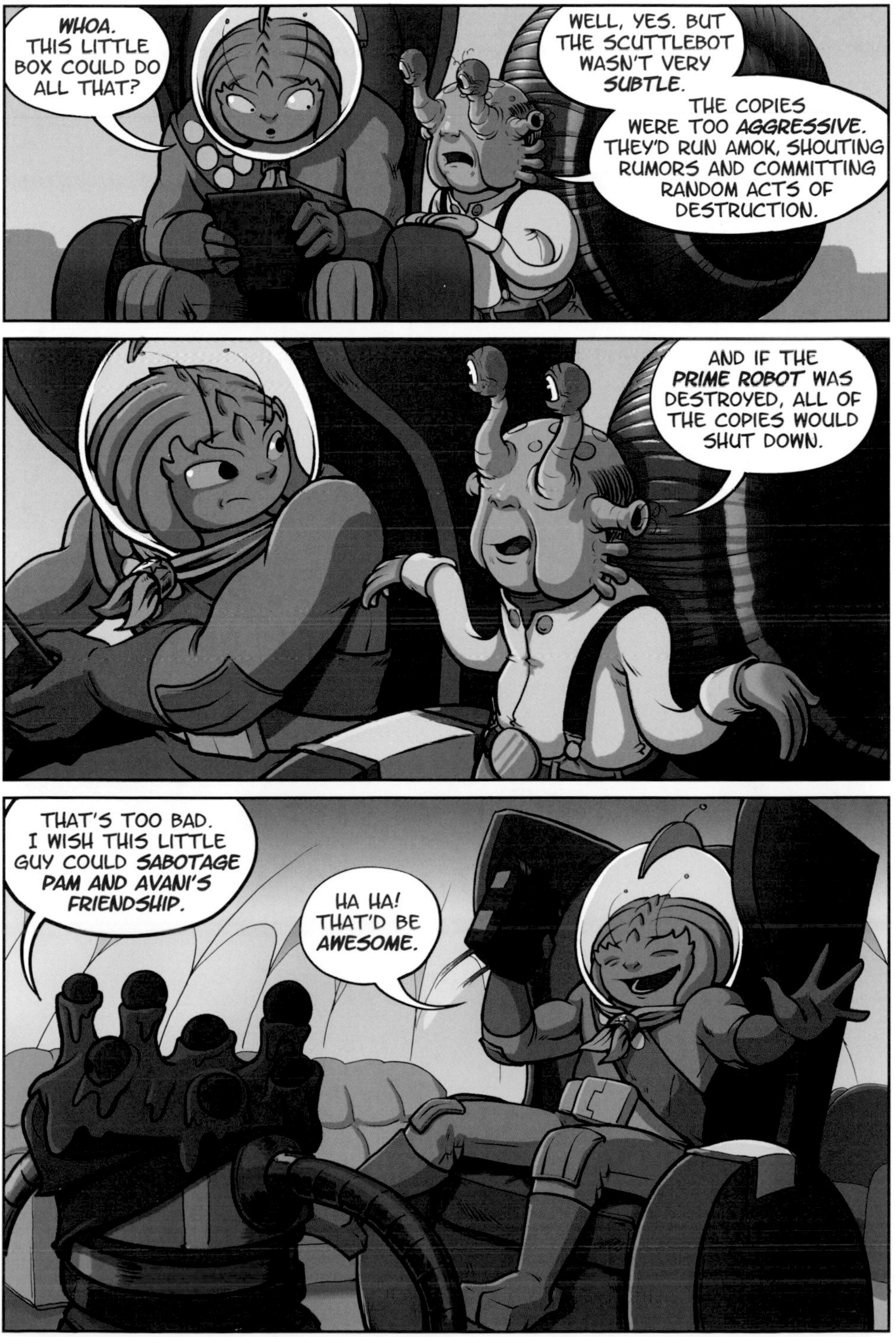
WHOA. THIS LITTLE BOX COULD DO ALL THAT?
WELL, YES. BUT THE SCUTTLEBOT WASN'T VERY SUBTLE.
THE COPIES WERE TOO AGGRESSIVE. THEY'D RUN AMOK, SHOUTING RUMORS AND COMMITTING RANDOM ACTS OF DESTRUCTION.
AND IF THE PRIME ROBOT WAS DESTROYED, ALL OF THE COPIES WOULD SHUT DOWN.
THAT'S TOO BAD. I WISH THIS LITTLE GUY COULD SABOTAGE PAM AND AVANI'S FRIENDSHIP.
HA HA! THAT'D BE AWESOME.

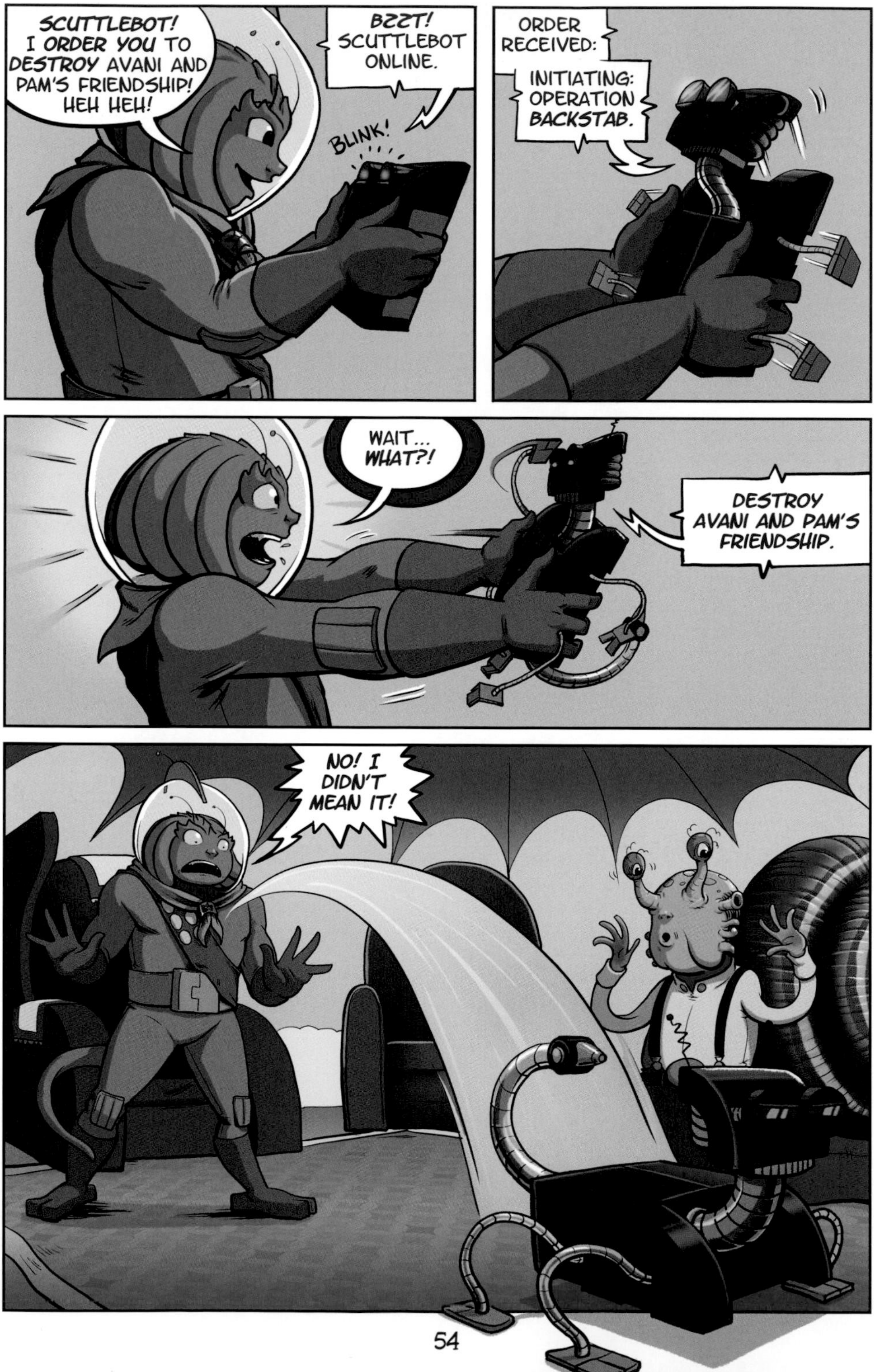
SCUTTLEBOT! I ORDER YOU TO DESTROY AVANI AND PAM'S FRIENDSHIP! HEH HEH!
BZZT! SCUTTLEBOT ONLINE.
BLINK!
ORDER RECEIVED:
INITIATING: OPERATION BACKSTAB.
WAIT... WHAT?!
DESTROY AVANI AND PAM'S FRIENDSHIP.
NO! I DIDN'T MEAN IT!

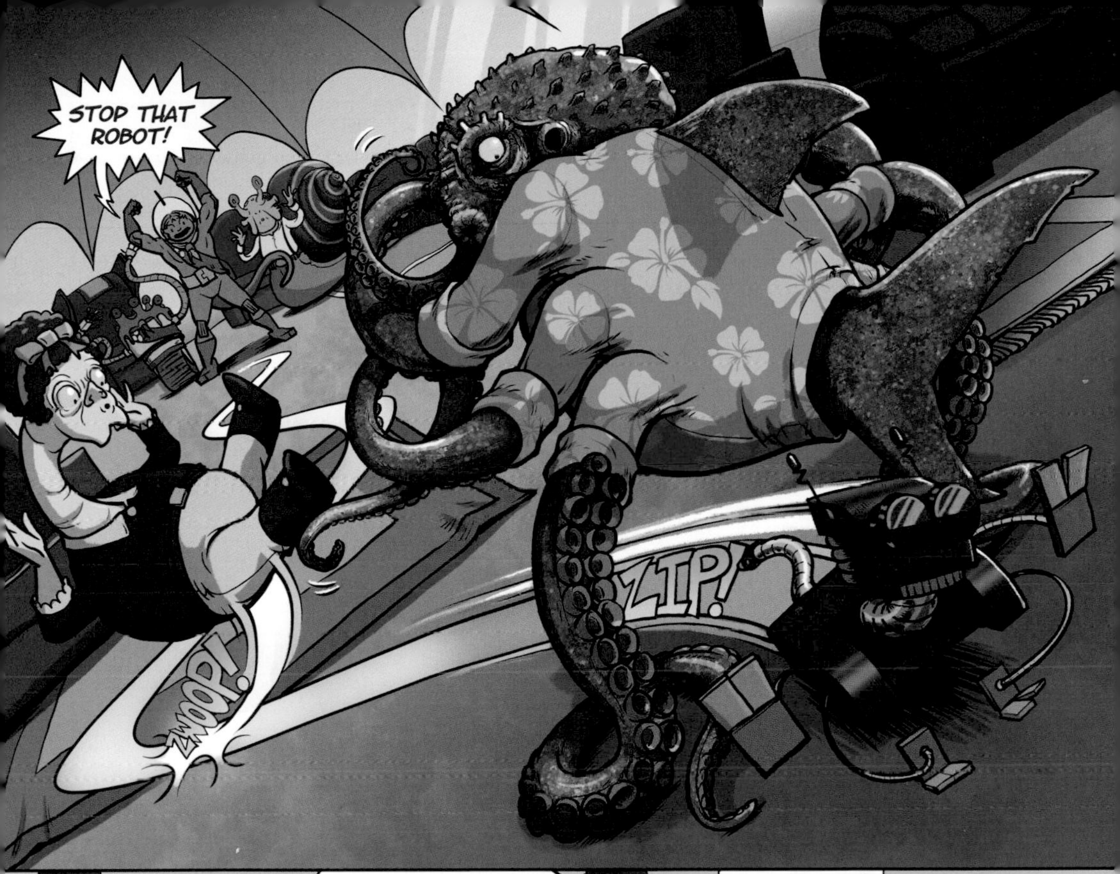
STOP THAT ROBOT!
ZIP!
ZWOOP!

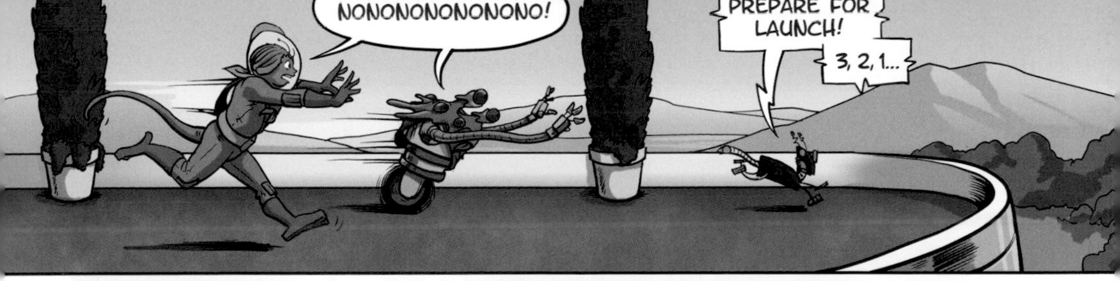
NONONONONONONO!
PREPARE FOR LAUNCH!
3, 2, 1...

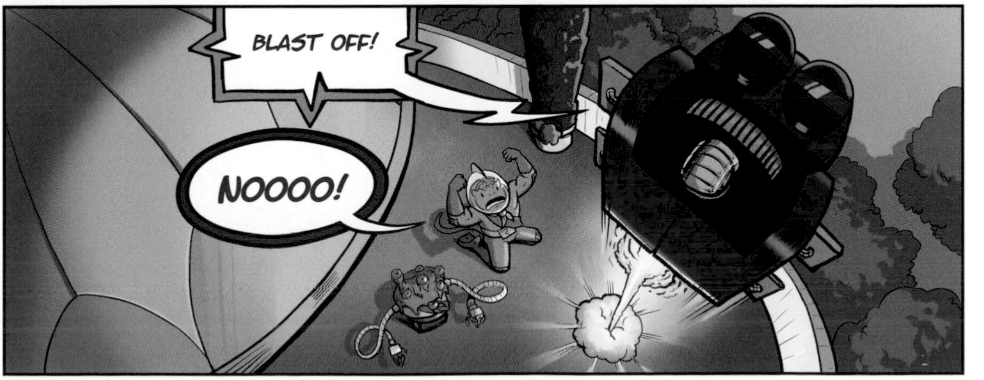
BLAST OFF!
NOOOO!

:PANT:
:PANT:
WHO KNEW :GASP: SCUTTLING WAS SO *FAST*?

:WHEEZE:
THAT WASN'T :COUGH: *SCUTTLING*. THAT WAS :PANT: *SCAMPERING*.

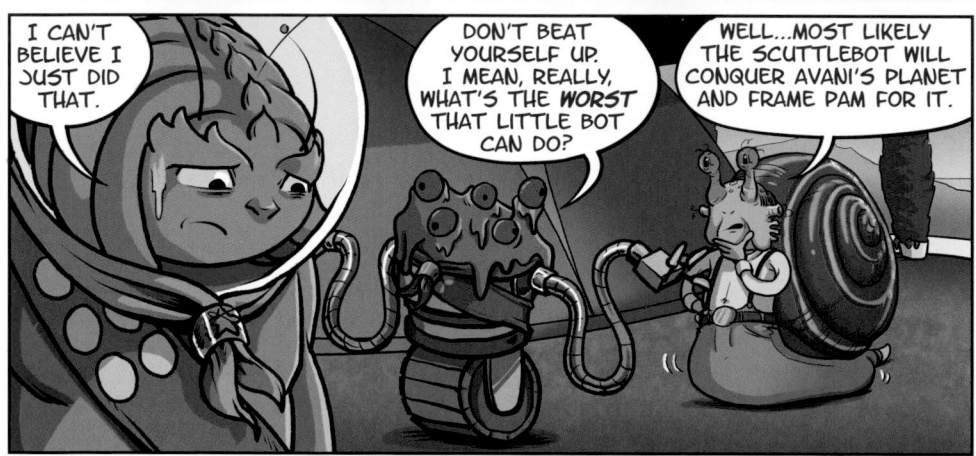

I CAN'T BELIEVE I JUST DID THAT.

DON'T BEAT YOURSELF UP. I MEAN, REALLY, WHAT'S THE *WORST* THAT LITTLE BOT CAN DO?

WELL...MOST LIKELY THE SCUTTLEBOT WILL CONQUER AVANI'S PLANET AND FRAME PAM FOR IT.

BUT IT HAS ABSOLUTELY *ZERO* FINESSE, SO I *DOUBT* AVANI WILL FALL FOR IT.

OF COURSE, HER PLANET WILL *STILL* BE CONQUERED...

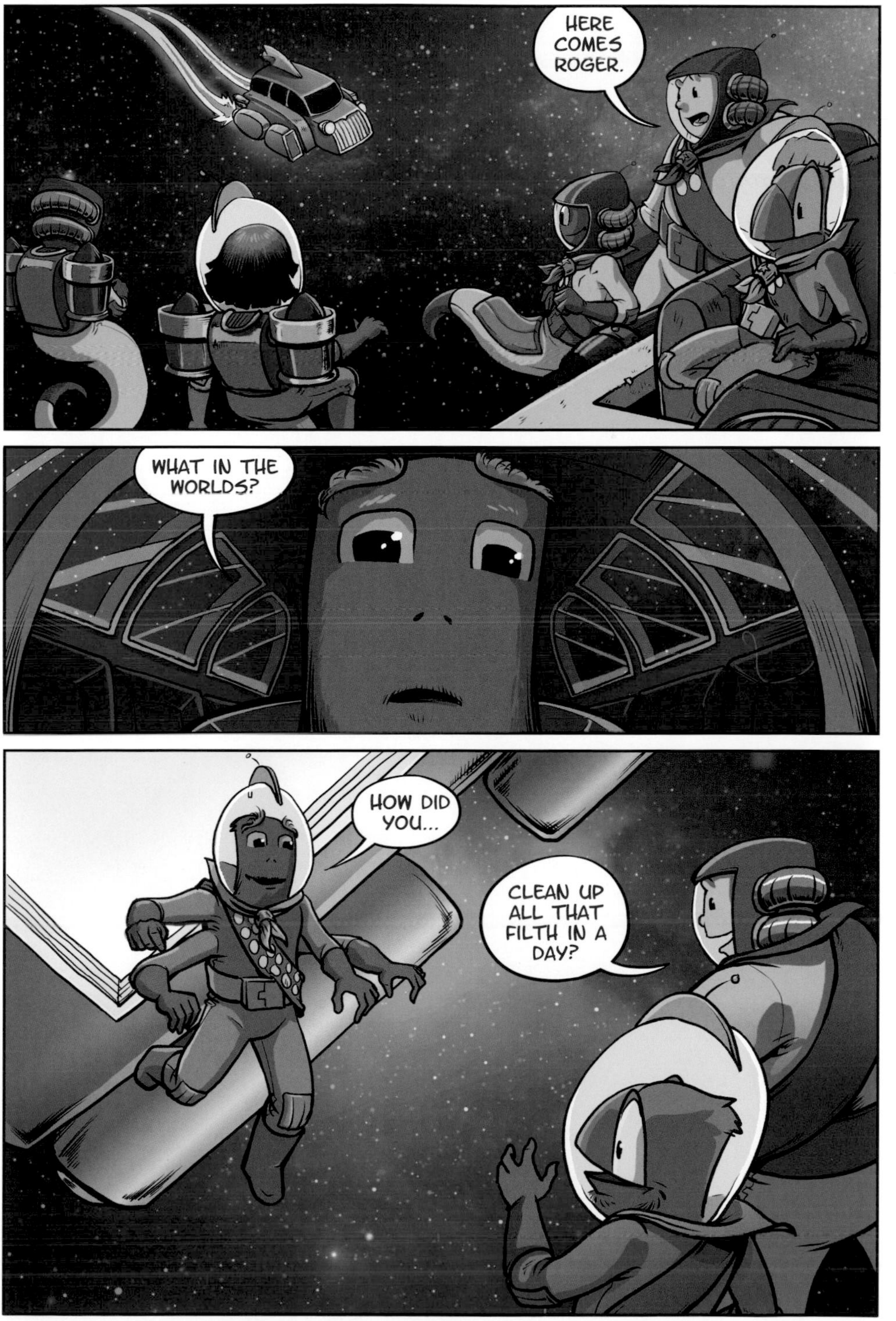
HERE COMES ROGER.
WHAT IN THE WORLDS?
HOW DID YOU...
CLEAN UP ALL THAT FILTH IN A DAY?

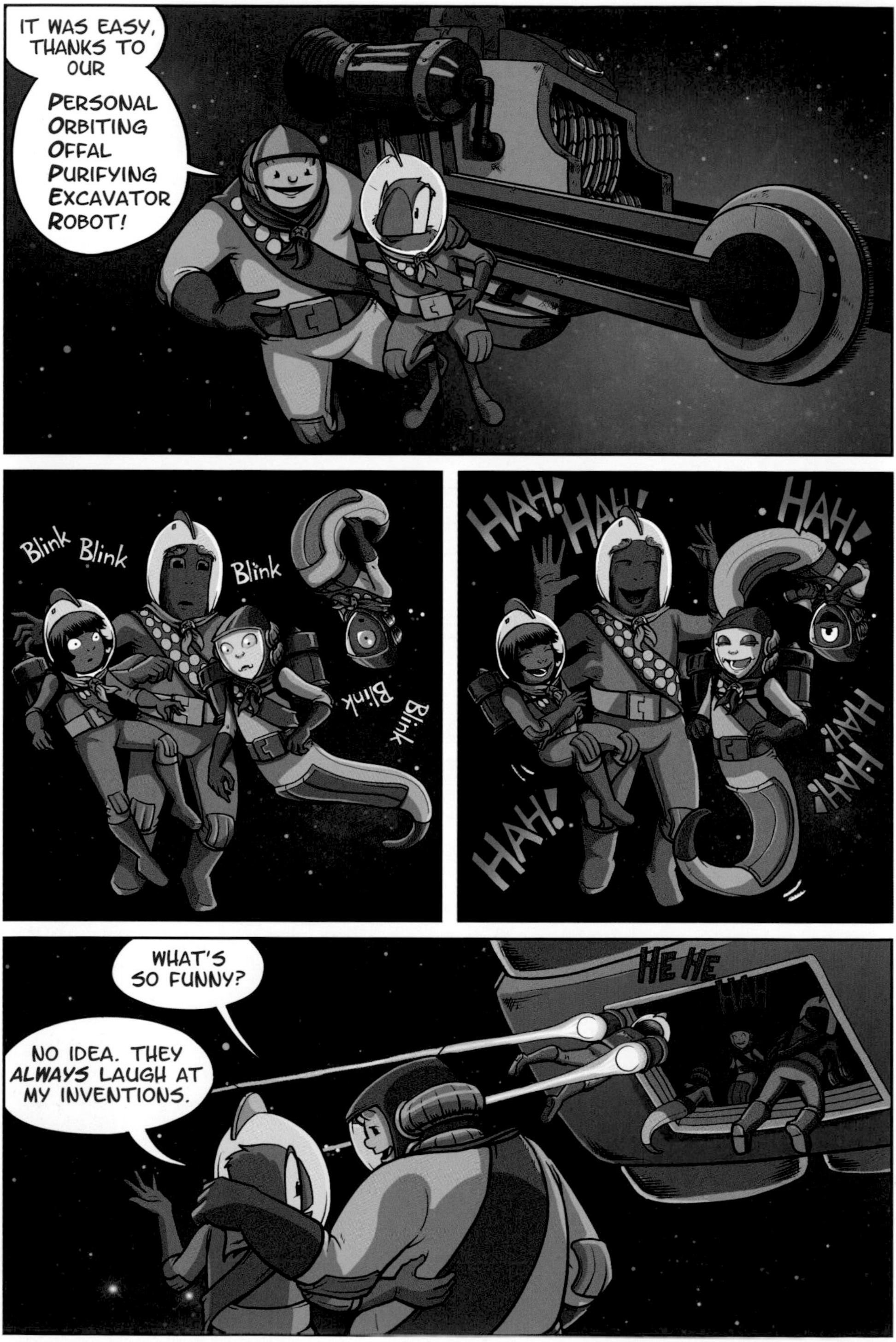
IT WAS EASY, THANKS TO OUR PERSONAL ORBITING OFFAL PURIFYING EXCAVATOR ROBOT!
Blink Blink
Blink
Blink
Blink
HAH! HAH! HAH!
HAH! HAH! HAH!
HAH!
WHAT'S SO FUNNY?
NO IDEA. THEY ALWAYS LAUGH AT MY INVENTIONS.
HE HE
HAH

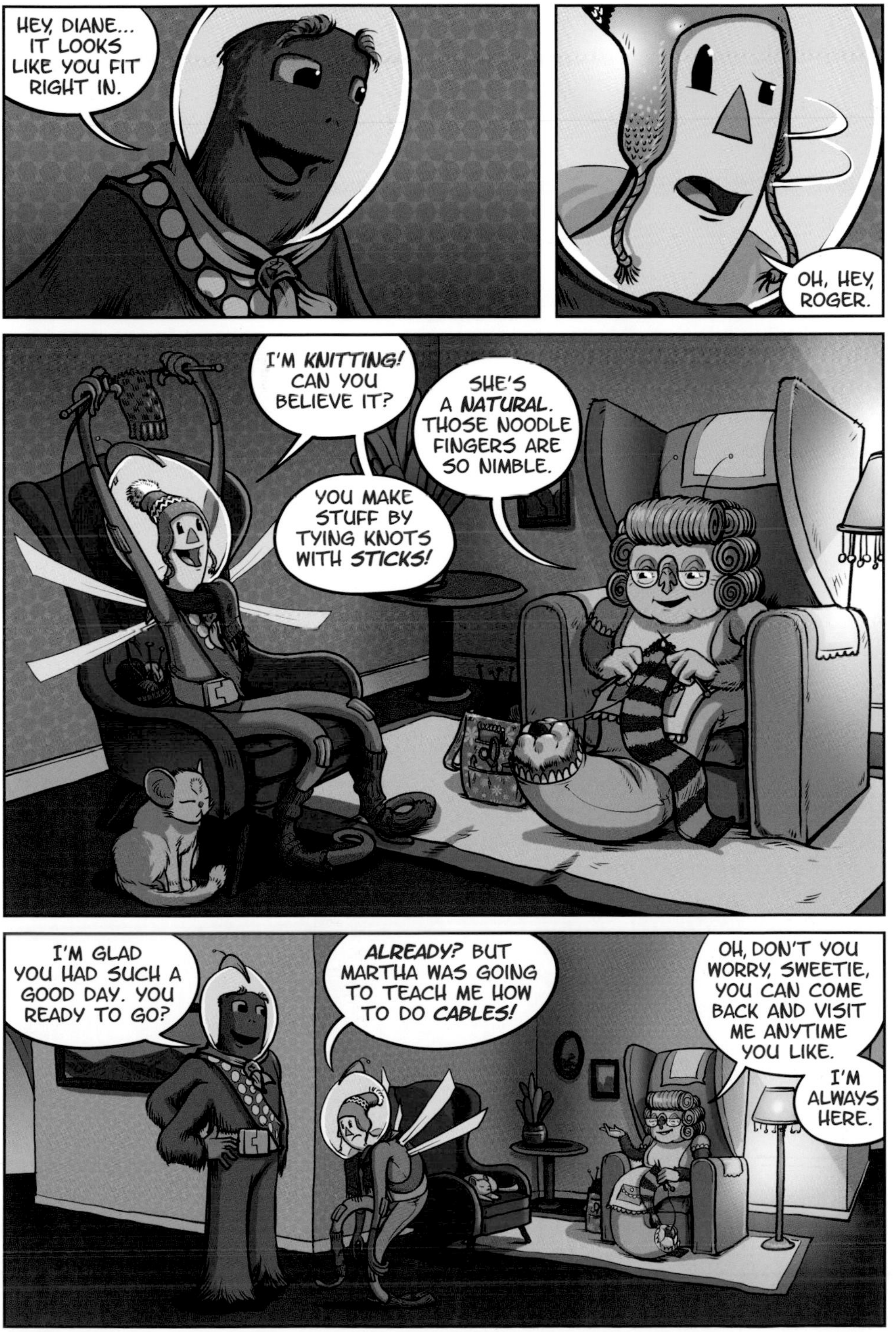
HEY, DIANE... IT LOOKS LIKE YOU FIT RIGHT IN.
OH, HEY, ROGER.
I'M KNITTING! CAN YOU BELIEVE IT?
YOU MAKE STUFF BY TYING KNOTS WITH STICKS!
SHE'S A NATURAL. THOSE NOODLE FINGERS ARE SO NIMBLE.
I'M GLAD YOU HAD SUCH A GOOD DAY. YOU READY TO GO?
ALREADY? BUT MARTHA WAS GOING TO TEACH ME HOW TO DO CABLES!
OH, DON'T YOU WORRY, SWEETIE, YOU CAN COME BACK AND VISIT ME ANYTIME YOU LIKE.
I'M ALWAYS HERE.

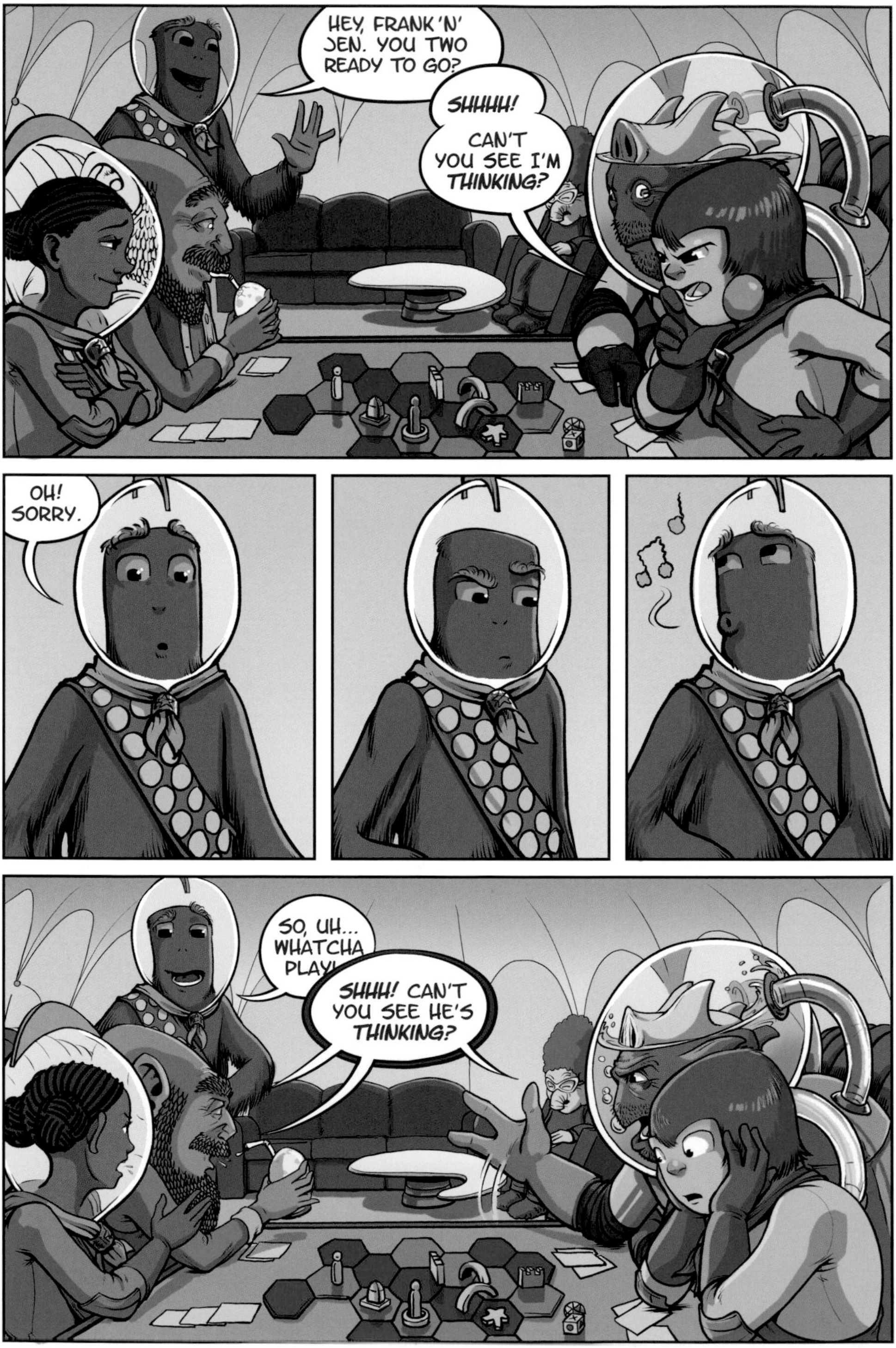
HEY, FRANK 'N' JEN. YOU TWO READY TO GO?
SHHHH!
CAN'T YOU SEE I'M THINKING?
OH! SORRY.
SO, UH... WHATCHA PLAY!
SHHH! CAN'T YOU SEE HE'S THINKING?

HEY, GIRLS, READY TO G—

WE DIDN'T DO ANYTHING!

UM...OKAY. EVERYTHING ALL RIGHT?

WHY WOULDN'T IT BE?

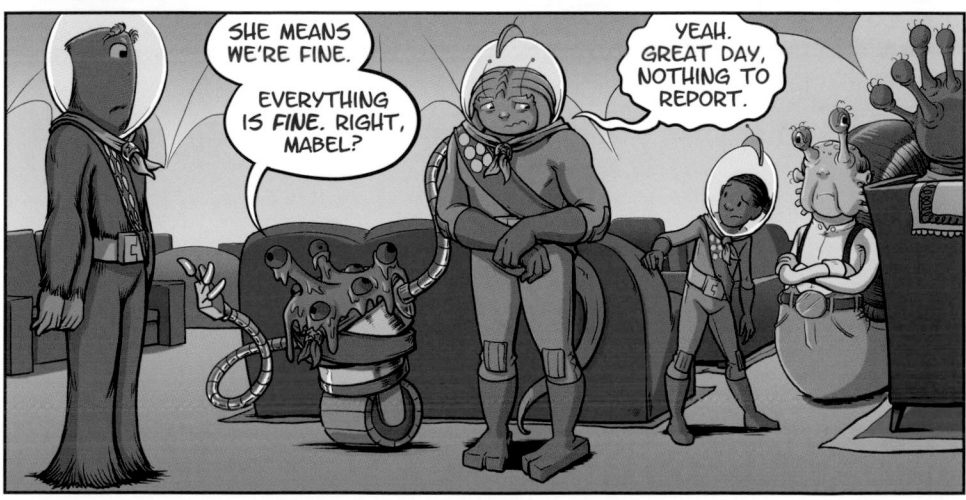

SHE MEANS WE'RE FINE.

EVERYTHING IS *FINE*. RIGHT, MABEL?

YEAH. GREAT DAY, NOTHING TO REPORT.

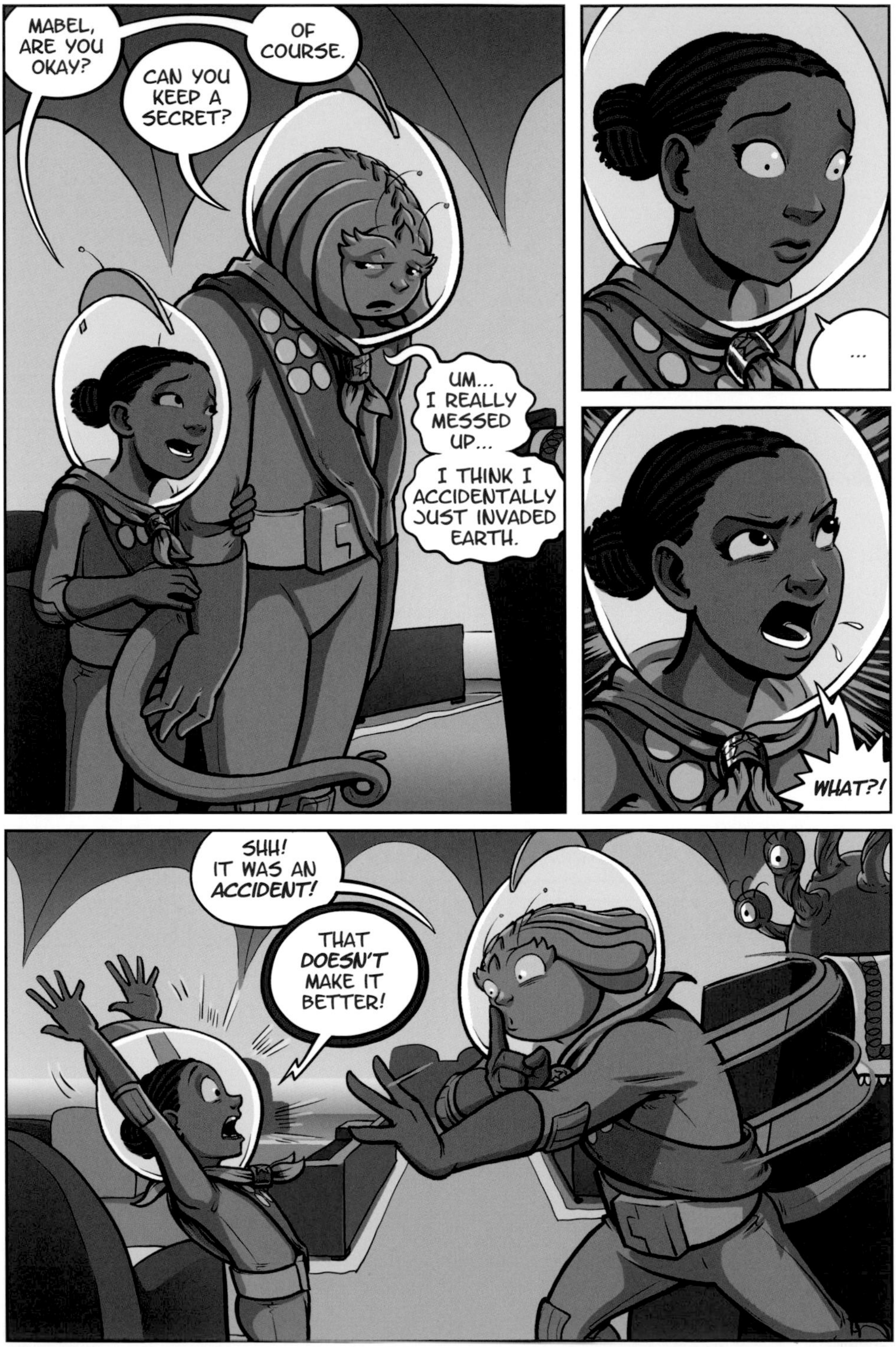
MABEL, ARE YOU OKAY?
OF COURSE.
CAN YOU KEEP A SECRET?
UM... I REALLY MESSED UP...
I THINK I ACCIDENTALLY JUST INVADED EARTH.
...
WHAT?!
SHH! IT WAS AN ACCIDENT!
THAT DOESN'T MAKE IT BETTER!

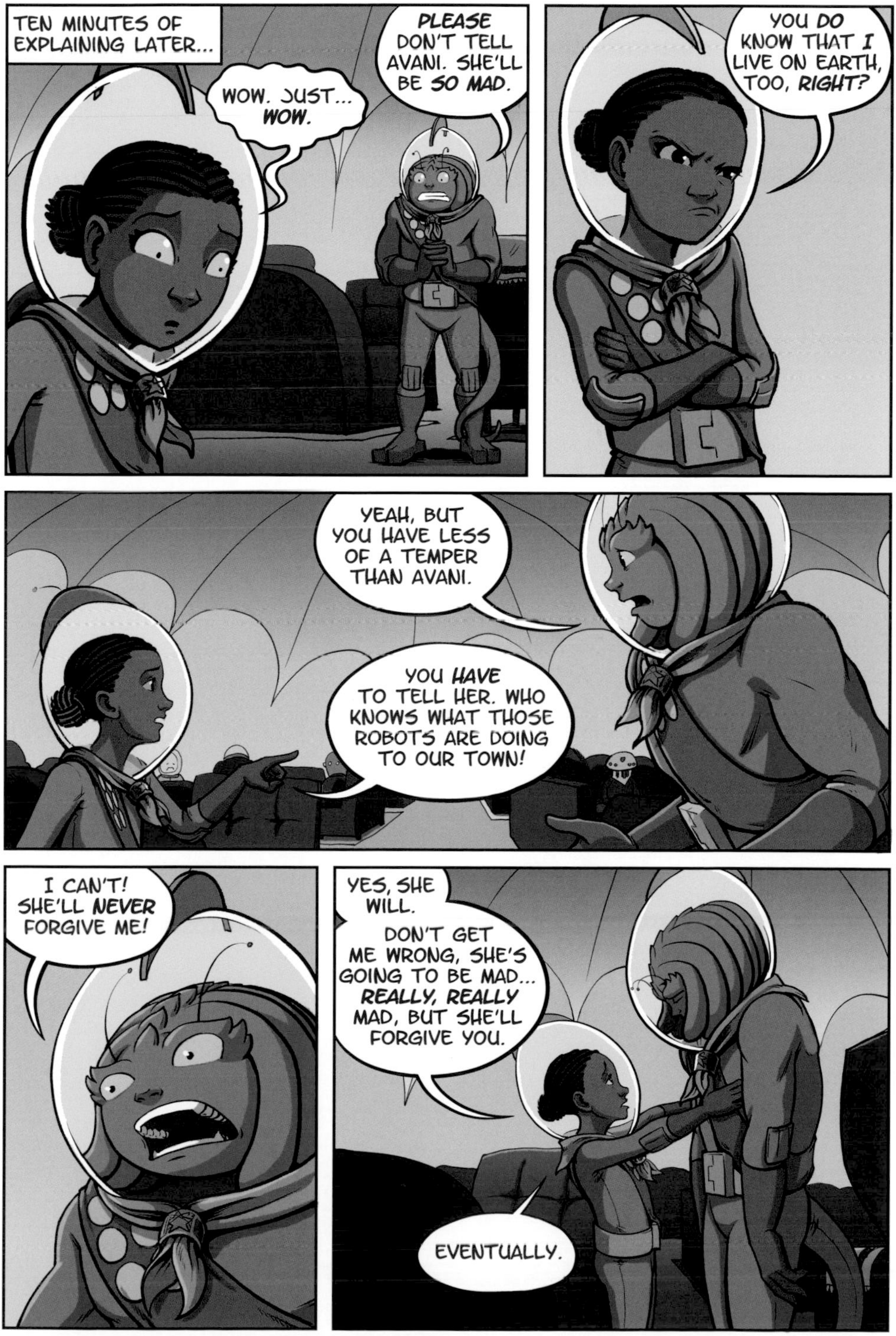
TEN MINUTES OF EXPLAINING LATER...
WOW. JUST... **WOW.**
PLEASE DON'T TELL AVANI. SHE'LL BE **SO MAD**.
YOU **DO** KNOW THAT **I** LIVE ON EARTH, TOO, **RIGHT?**
YEAH, BUT YOU HAVE LESS OF A TEMPER THAN AVANI.
YOU **HAVE** TO TELL HER. WHO KNOWS WHAT THOSE ROBOTS ARE DOING TO OUR TOWN!
I CAN'T! SHE'LL **NEVER** FORGIVE ME!
YES, SHE WILL.
DON'T GET ME WRONG, SHE'S GOING TO BE MAD... **REALLY, REALLY** MAD, BUT SHE'LL FORGIVE YOU.
EVENTUALLY.

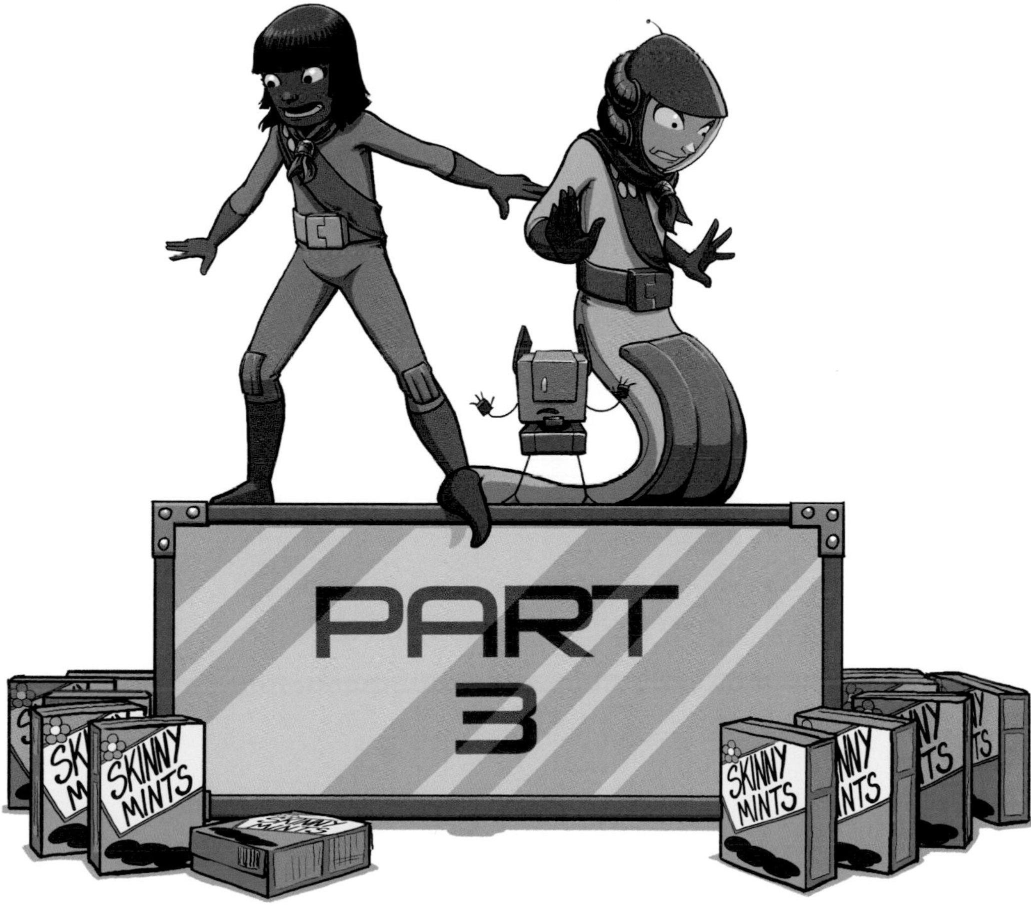
PART
3
SKINNY MINTS
SKINNY MINTS
SKINNY MINTS

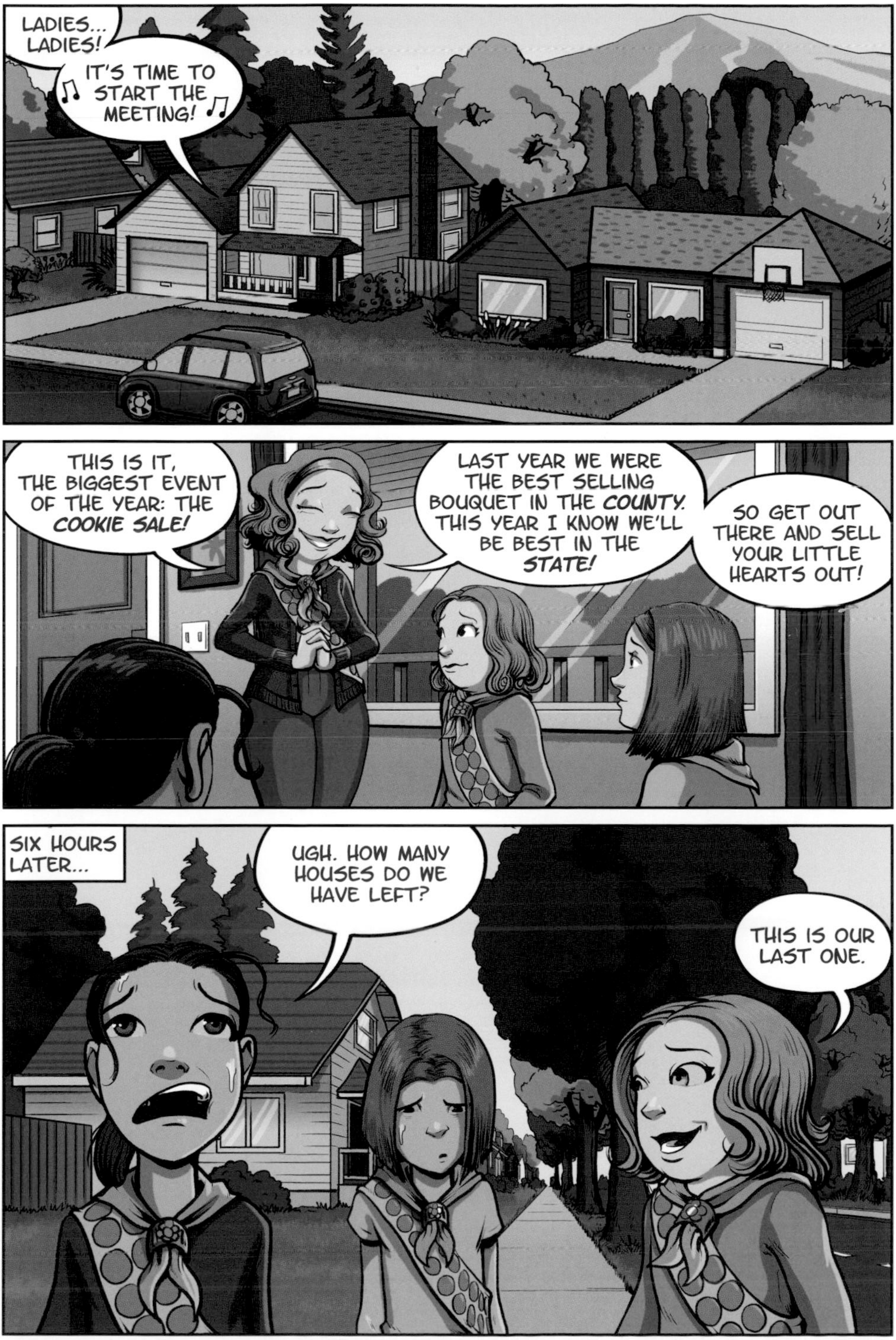
LADIES... LADIES!
IT'S TIME TO START THE MEETING!
THIS IS IT, THE BIGGEST EVENT OF THE YEAR: THE COOKIE SALE!
LAST YEAR WE WERE THE BEST SELLING BOUQUET IN THE COUNTY. THIS YEAR I KNOW WE'LL BE BEST IN THE STATE!
SO GET OUT THERE AND SELL YOUR LITTLE HEARTS OUT!
SIX HOURS LATER...
UGH. HOW MANY HOUSES DO WE HAVE LEFT?
THIS IS OUR LAST ONE.

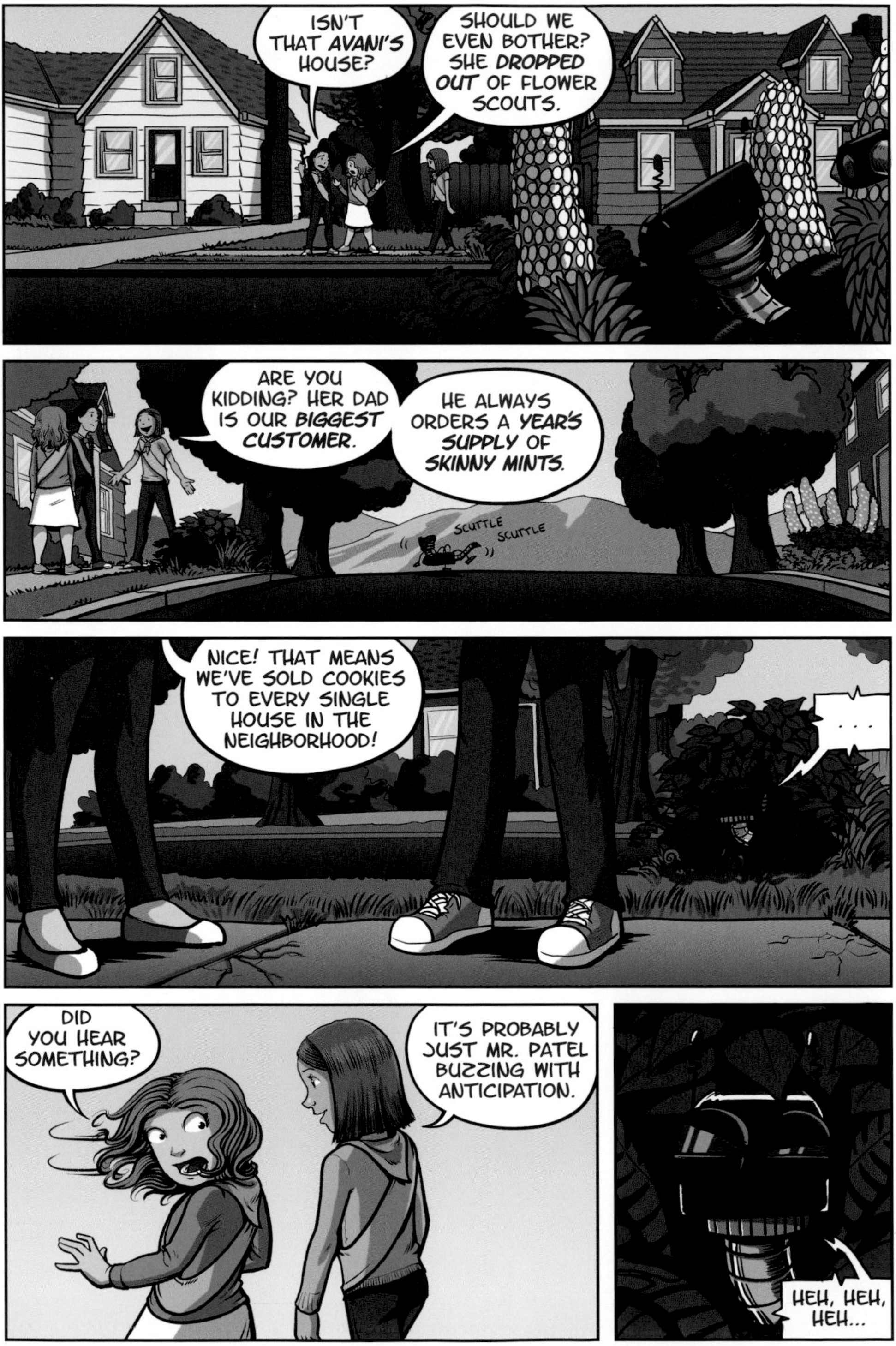
ISN'T THAT AVANI'S HOUSE?
SHOULD WE EVEN BOTHER? SHE DROPPED OUT OF FLOWER SCOUTS.
ARE YOU KIDDING? HER DAD IS OUR BIGGEST CUSTOMER.
HE ALWAYS ORDERS A YEAR'S SUPPLY OF SKINNY MINTS.
SCUTTLE SCUTTLE
NICE! THAT MEANS WE'VE SOLD COOKIES TO EVERY SINGLE HOUSE IN THE NEIGHBORHOOD!
. . .
DID YOU HEAR SOMETHING?
IT'S PROBABLY JUST MR. PATEL BUZZING WITH ANTICIPATION.
HEH, HEH, HEH...

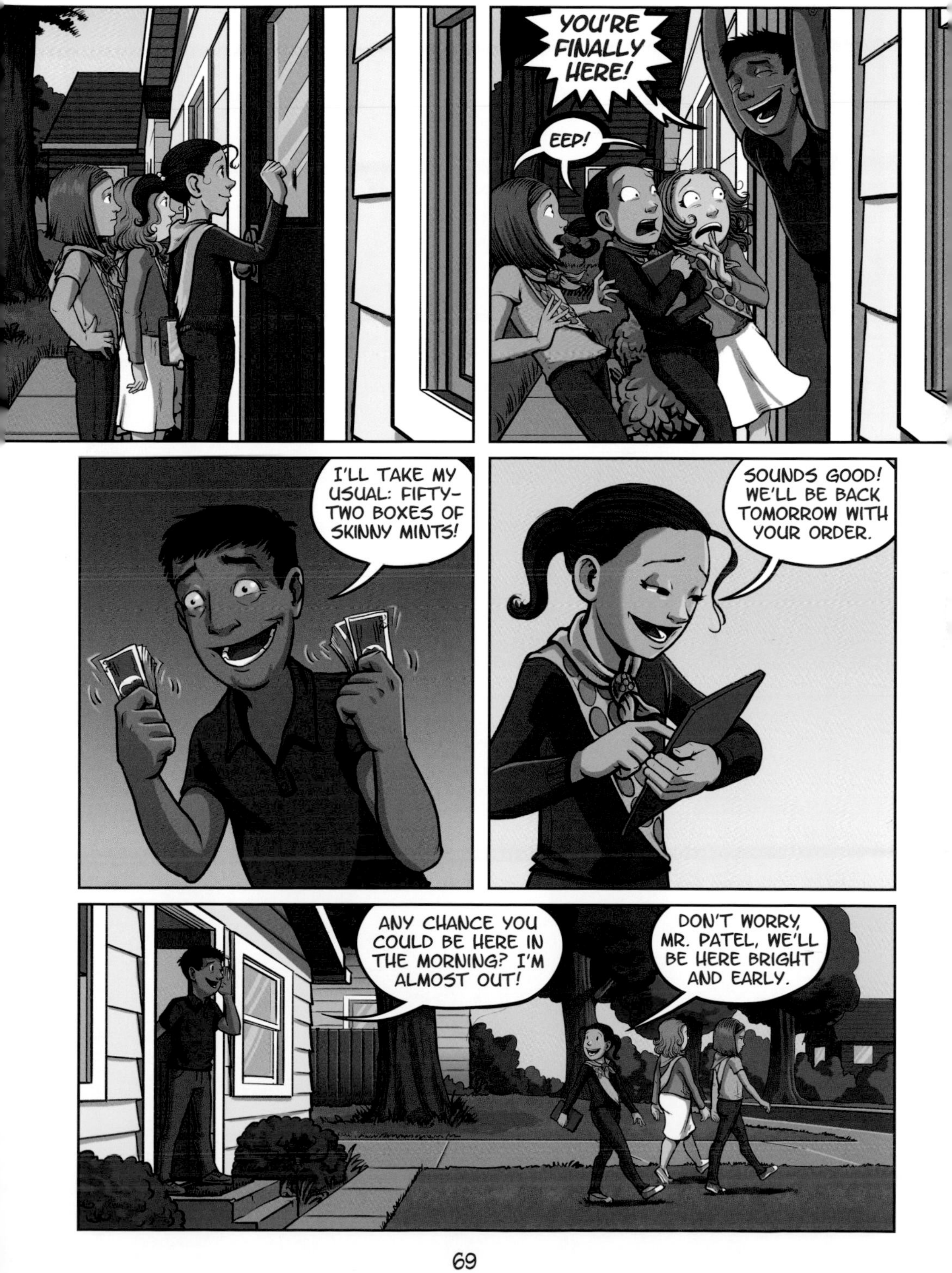

YOU'RE FINALLY HERE!
EEP!
I'LL TAKE MY USUAL: FIFTY-TWO BOXES OF SKINNY MINTS!
SOUNDS GOOD! WE'LL BE BACK TOMORROW WITH YOUR ORDER.
ANY CHANCE YOU COULD BE HERE IN THE MORNING? I'M ALMOST OUT!
DON'T WORRY, MR. PATEL, WE'LL BE HERE BRIGHT AND EARLY.

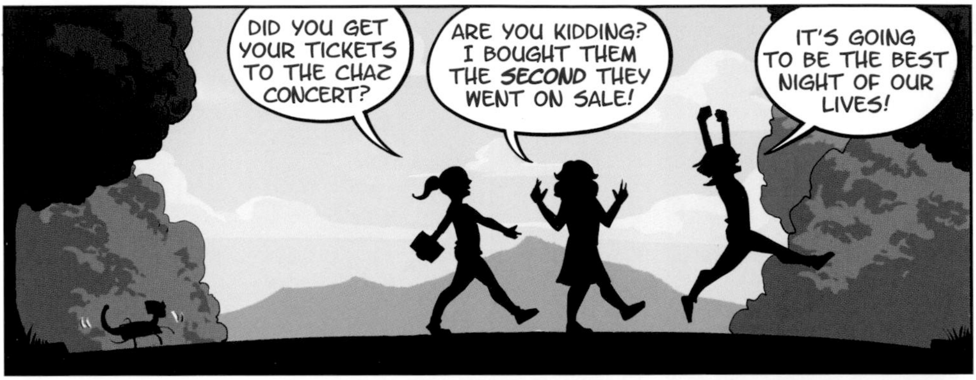
DID YOU GET YOUR TICKETS TO THE CHAZ CONCERT?
ARE YOU KIDDING? I BOUGHT THEM THE SECOND THEY WENT ON SALE!
IT'S GOING TO BE THE BEST NIGHT OF OUR LIVES!

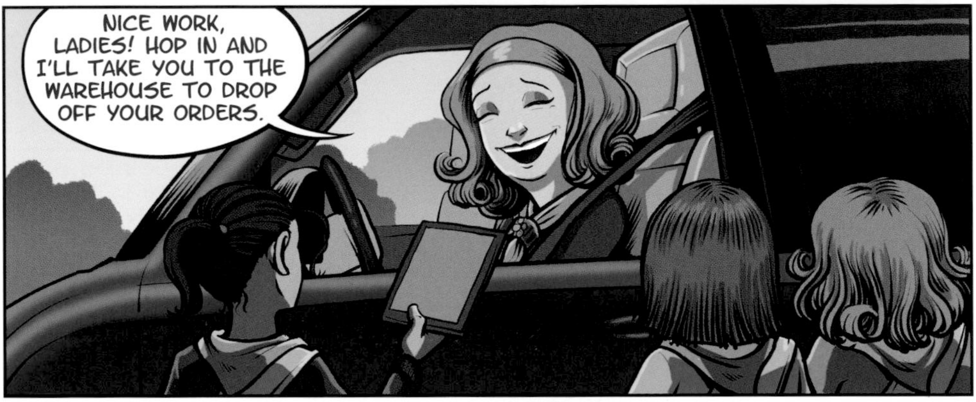
NICE WORK, LADIES! HOP IN AND I'LL TAKE YOU TO THE WAREHOUSE TO DROP OFF YOUR ORDERS.

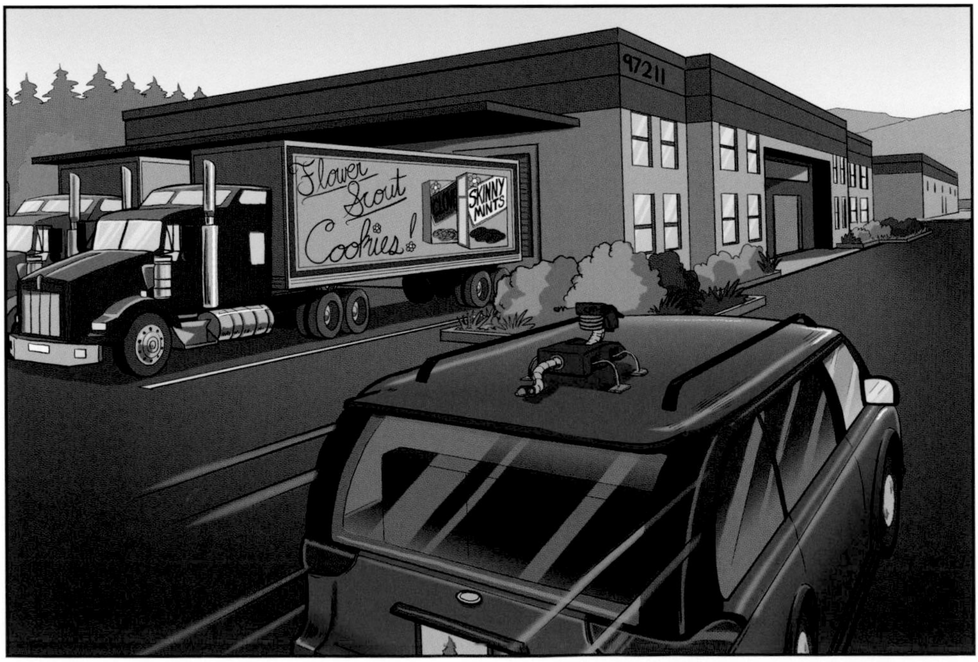
97211
Flower Scout Cookies!
SKINNY MINTS

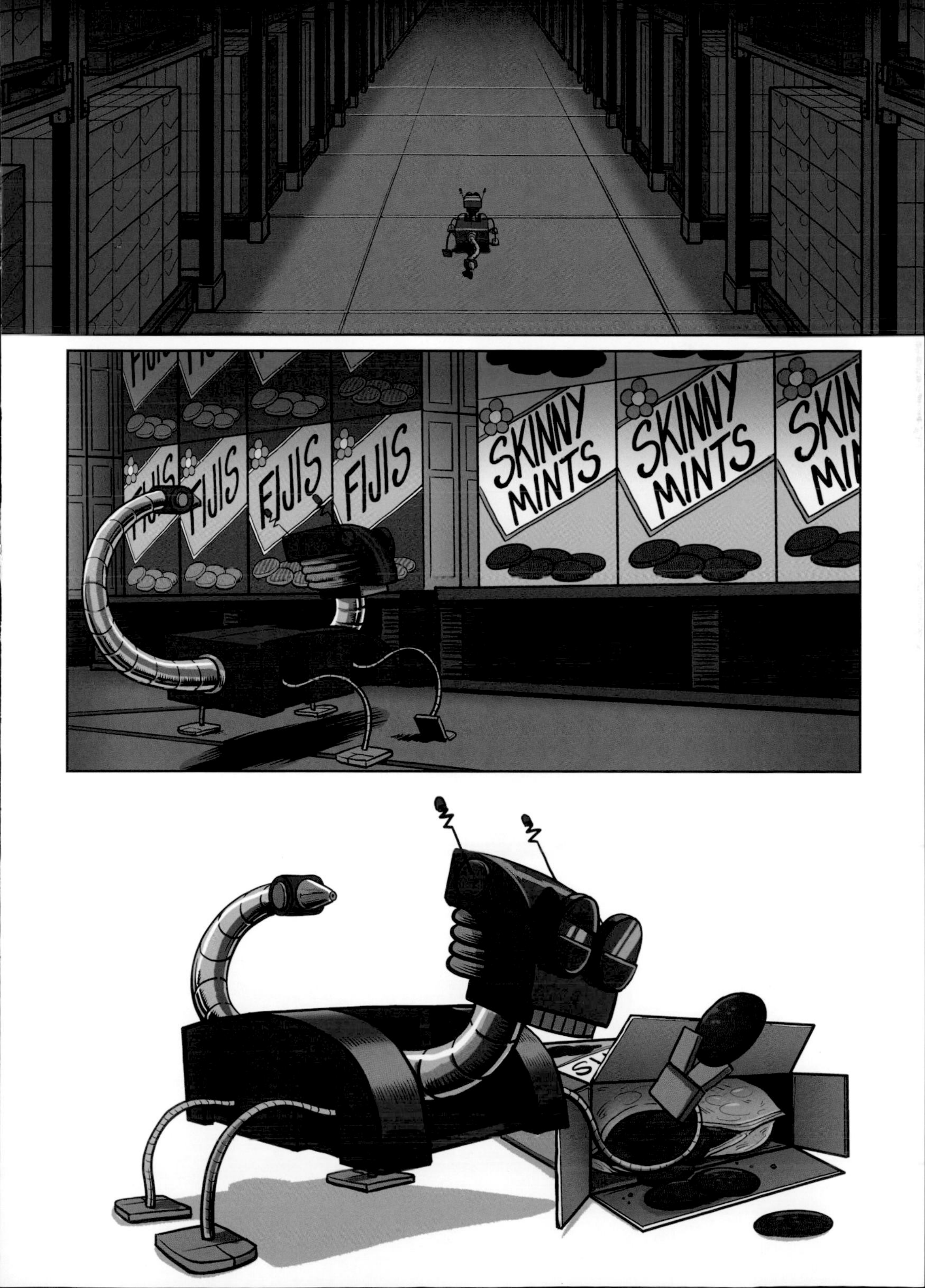
FIJIS
FIJIS
FIJIS
SKINNY MINTS
SKINNY MINTS

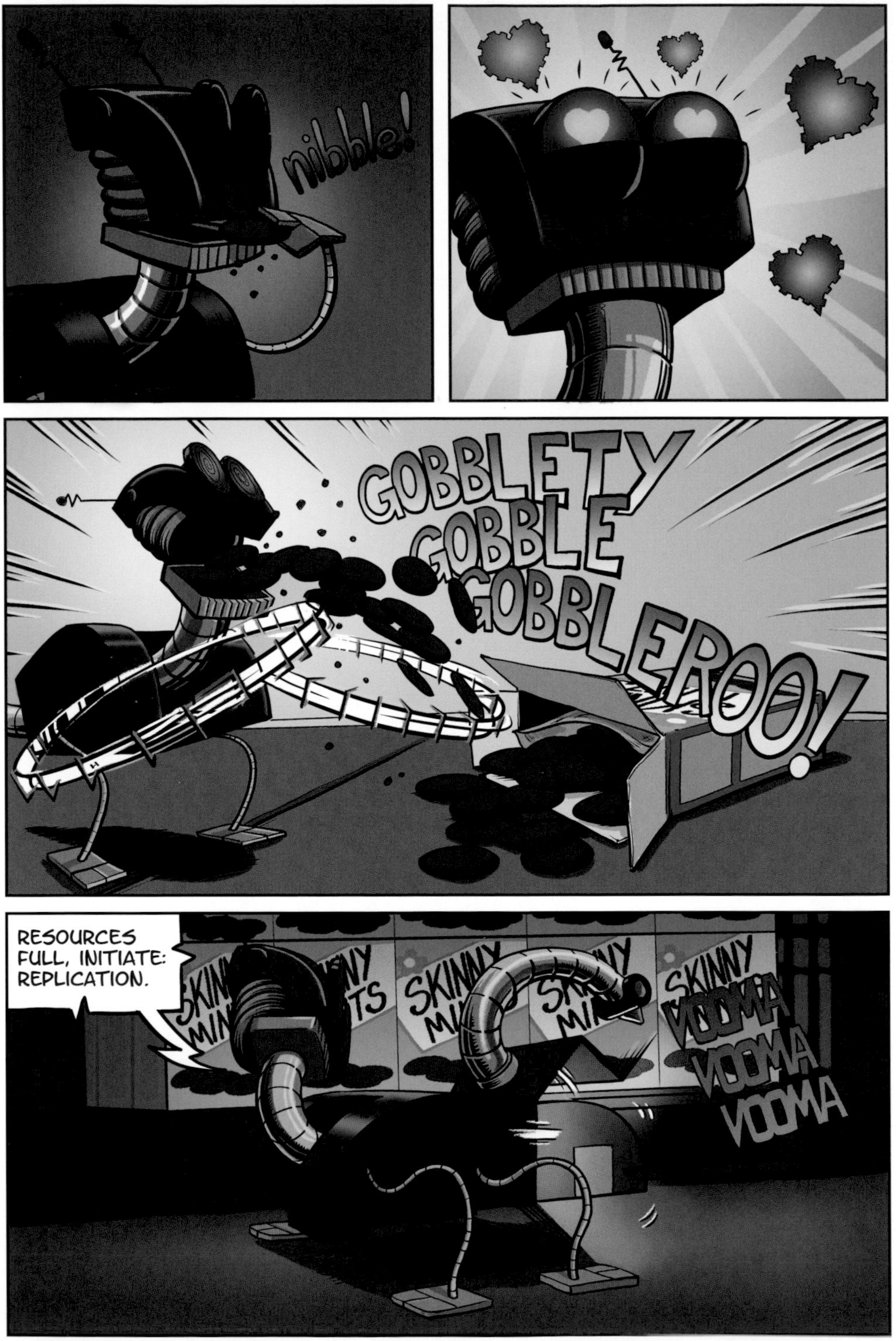

nibble!
GOBBLETY
GOBBLE
GOBBLEROO!
RESOURCES FULL, INITIATE: REPLICATION.
SKINNY MINTS
VOOMA
VOOMA
VOOMA

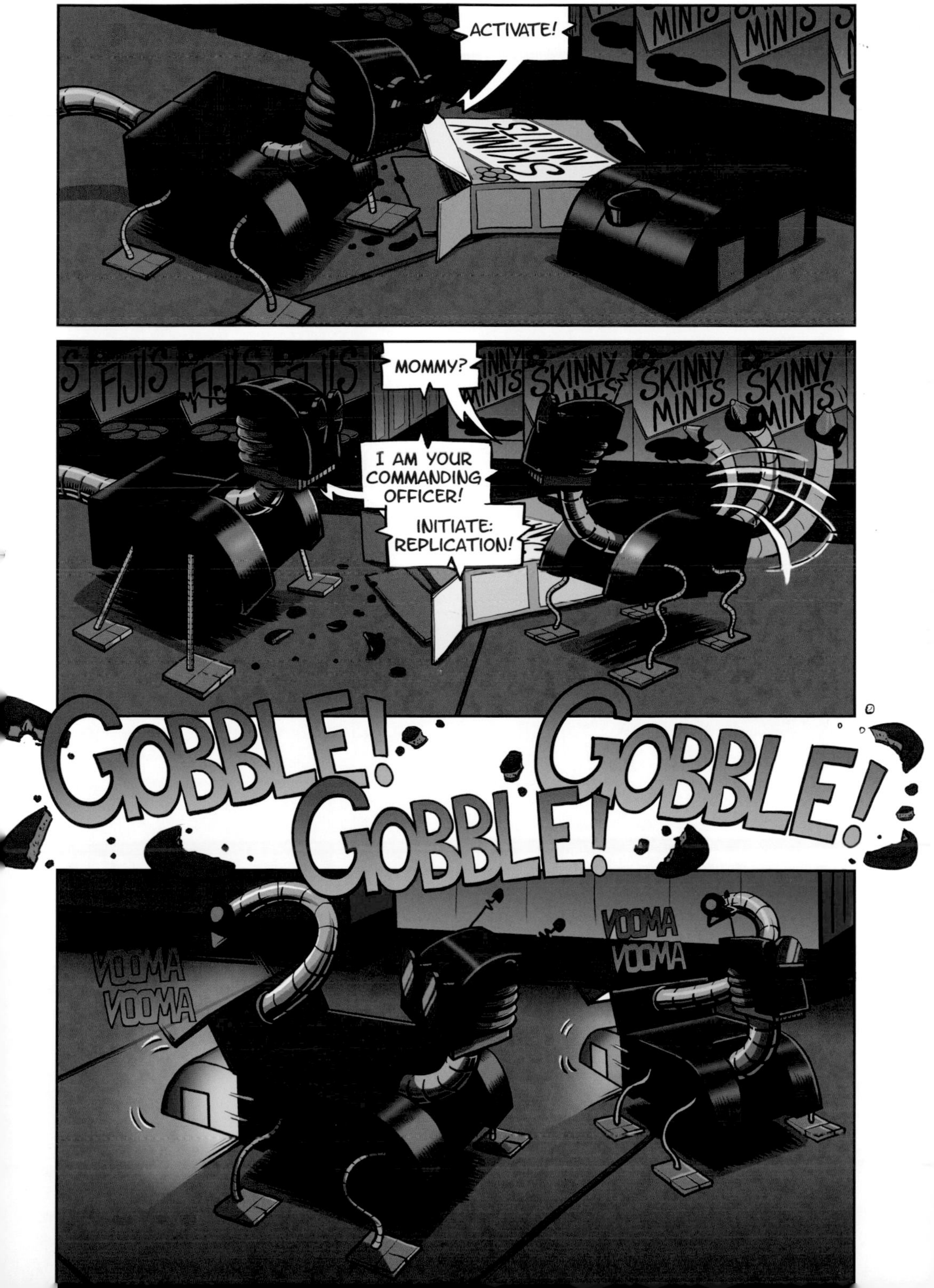
ACTIVATE!
SKINNY MINTS
MINTS
MINTS
FIJIS
FIJIS
FIJIS
SKINNY MINTS
SKINNY MINTS
SKINNY MINTS
MOMMY?
I AM YOUR COMMANDING OFFICER!
INITIATE: REPLICATION!
GOBBLE!
GOBBLE!
GOBBLE!
VOOMA VOOMA
VOOMA VOOMA

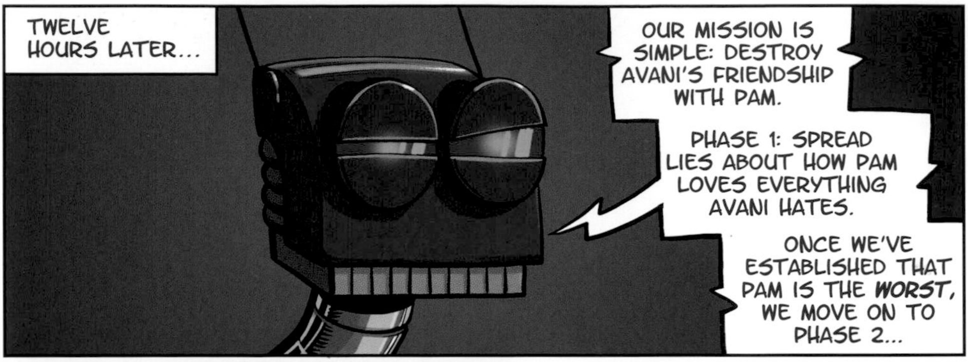
TWELVE HOURS LATER...
OUR MISSION IS SIMPLE: DESTROY AVANI'S FRIENDSHIP WITH PAM.
PHASE 1: SPREAD LIES ABOUT HOW PAM LOVES EVERYTHING AVANI HATES.
ONCE WE'VE ESTABLISHED THAT PAM IS THE *WORST*, WE MOVE ON TO PHASE 2...

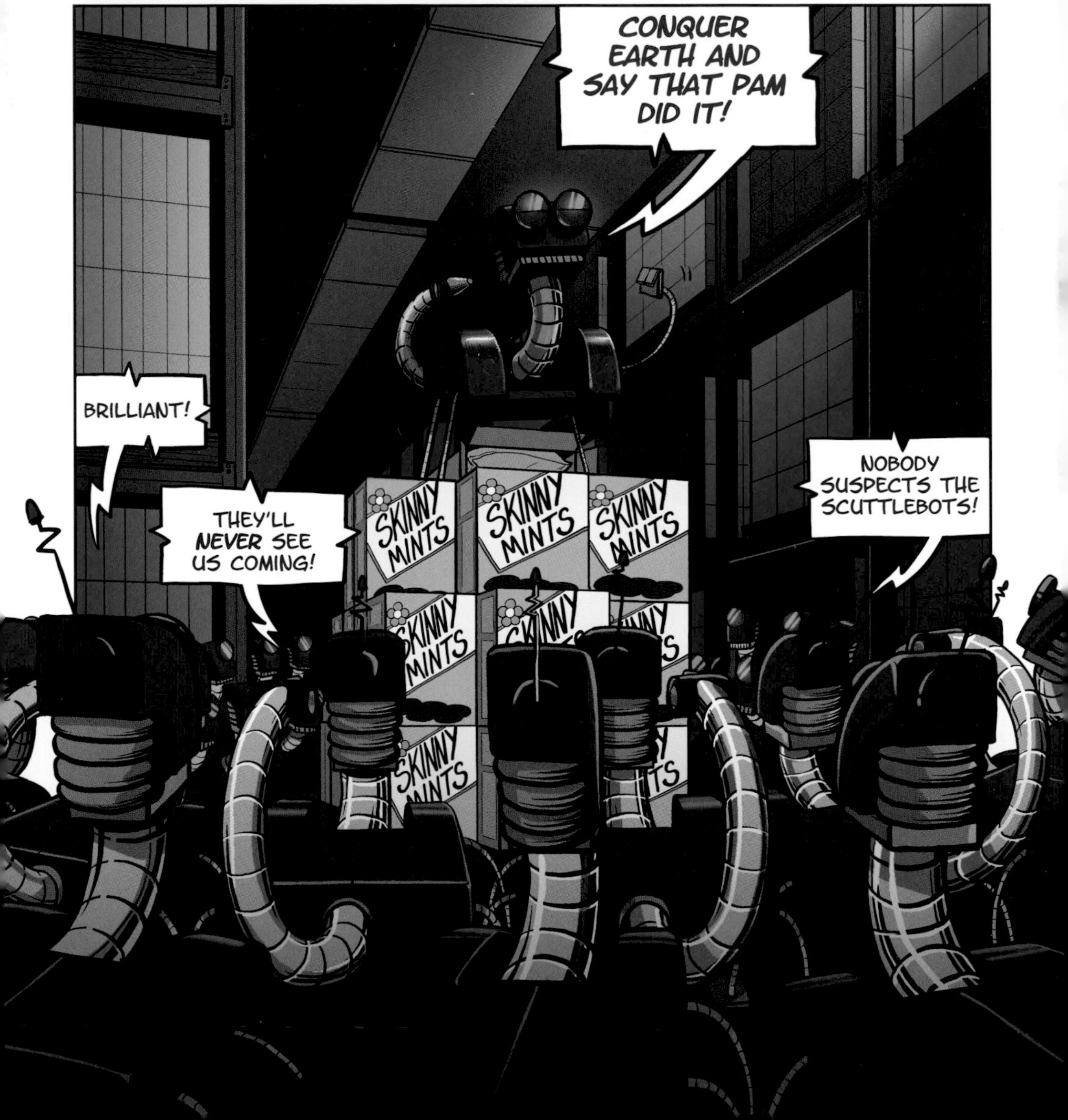
CONQUER EARTH AND SAY THAT PAM DID IT!
BRILLIANT!
THEY'LL *NEVER* SEE US COMING!
NOBODY SUSPECTS THE SCUTTLEBOTS!
SKINNY MINTS

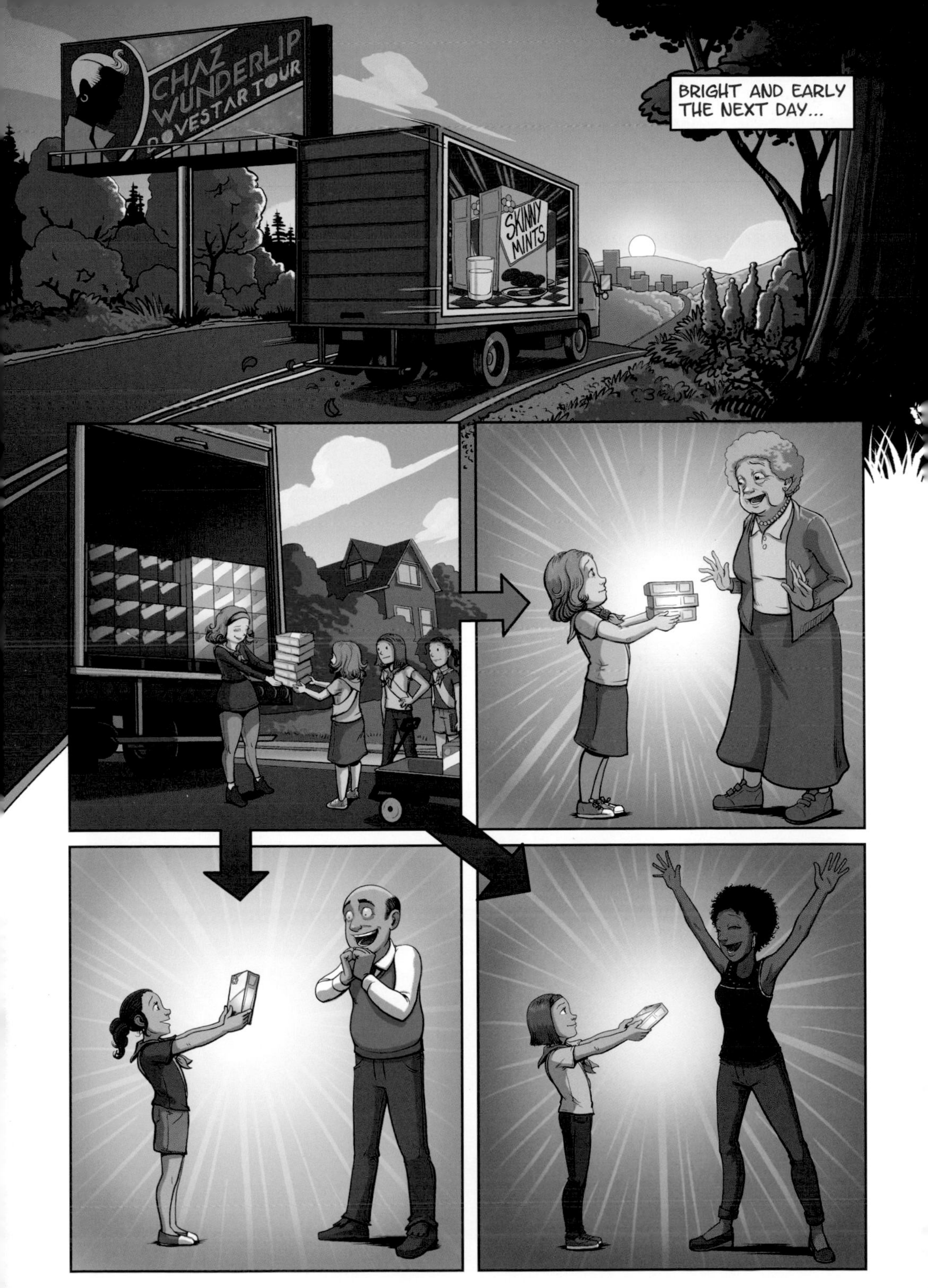
BRIGHT AND EARLY THE NEXT DAY...
CHAZ WUNDERLIP
DOVESTAR TOUR
SKINNY MINTS

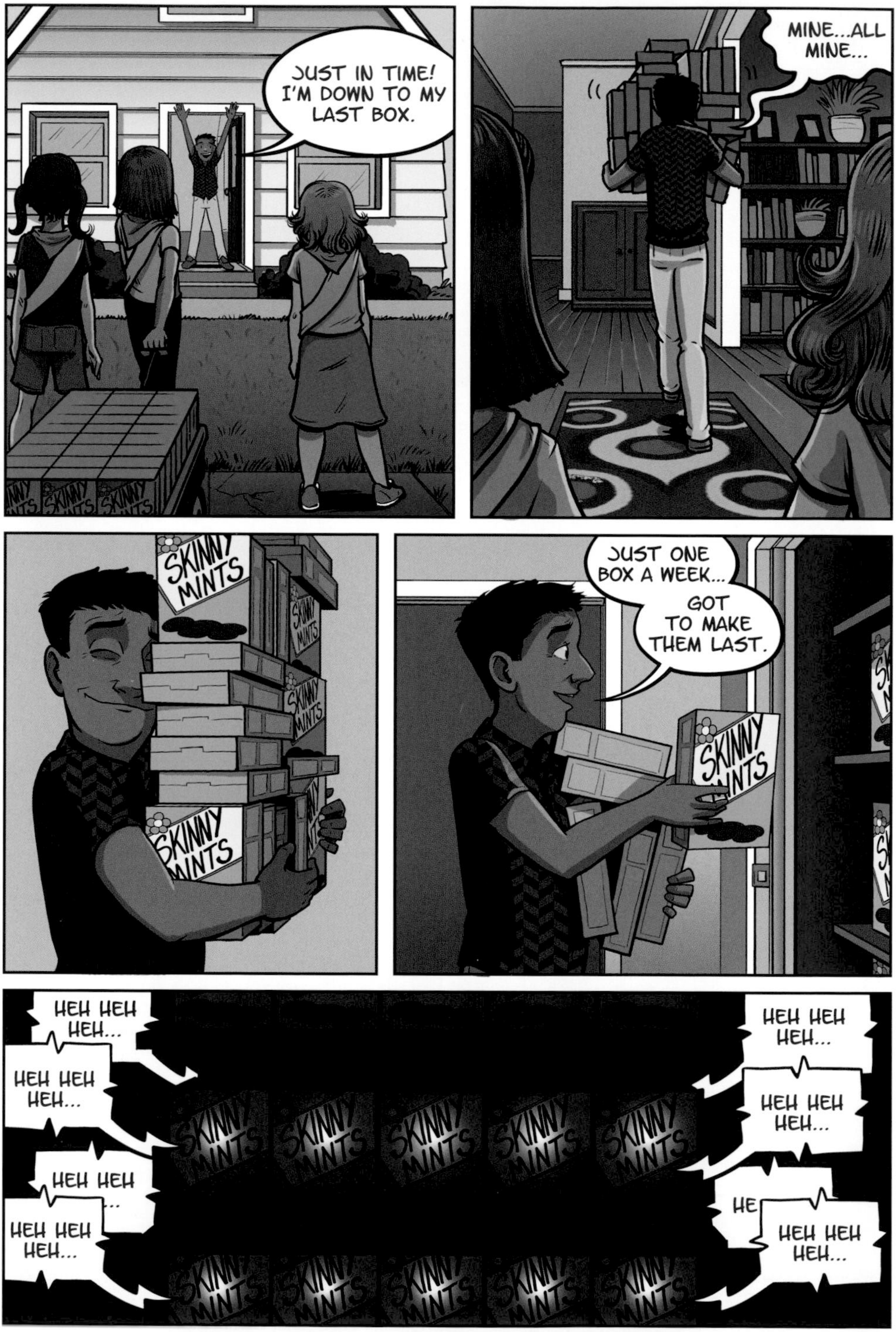
JUST IN TIME! I'M DOWN TO MY LAST BOX.
MINE...ALL MINE...
SKINNY MINTS
JUST ONE BOX A WEEK...
GOT TO MAKE THEM LAST.
SKINNY MINTS
HEH HEH HEH...
HEH HEH HEH...
HEH HEH
HEH HEH HEH...
HEH HEH HEH...
HEH HEH HEH...
HE
HEH HEH HEH...
SKINNY MINTS

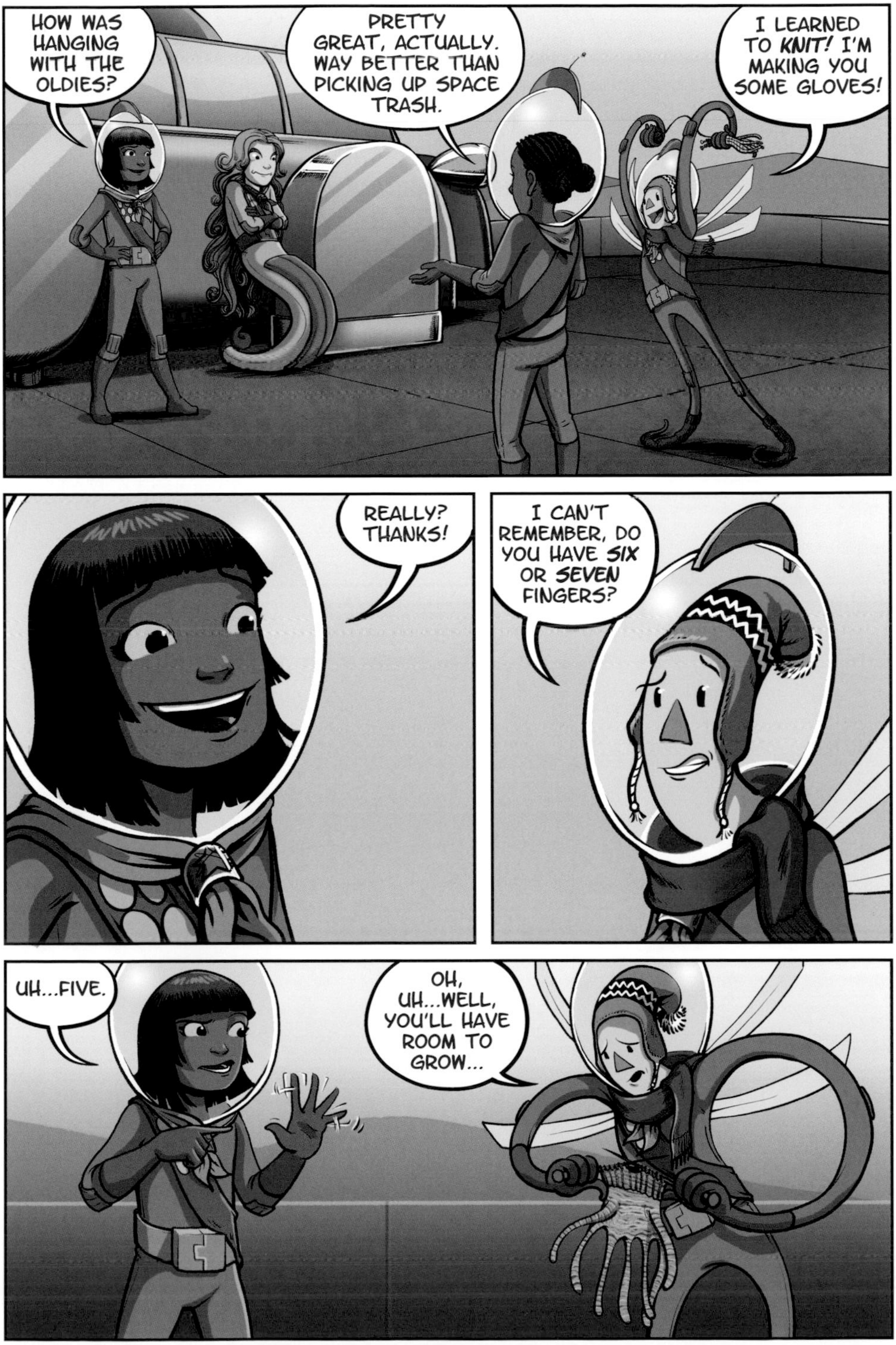
HOW WAS HANGING WITH THE OLDIES?
PRETTY GREAT, ACTUALLY. WAY BETTER THAN PICKING UP SPACE TRASH.
I LEARNED TO KNIT! I'M MAKING YOU SOME GLOVES!
REALLY? THANKS!
I CAN'T REMEMBER, DO YOU HAVE SIX OR SEVEN FINGERS?
UH...FIVE.
OH, UH...WELL, YOU'LL HAVE ROOM TO GROW...

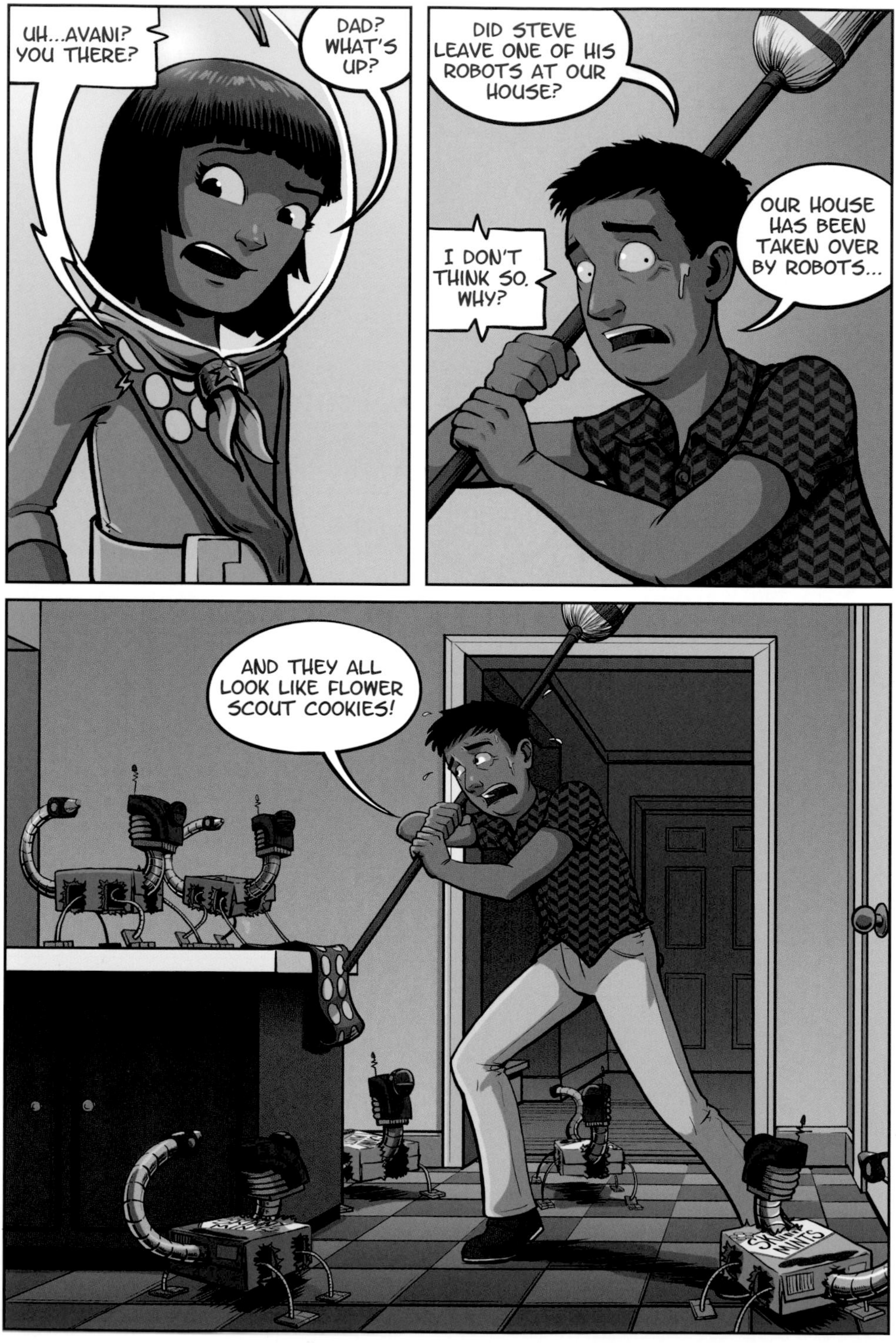
UH...AVANI? YOU THERE?
DAD? WHAT'S UP?
DID STEVE LEAVE ONE OF HIS ROBOTS AT OUR HOUSE?
I DON'T THINK SO. WHY?
OUR HOUSE HAS BEEN TAKEN OVER BY ROBOTS...
AND THEY ALL LOOK LIKE FLOWER SCOUT COOKIES!

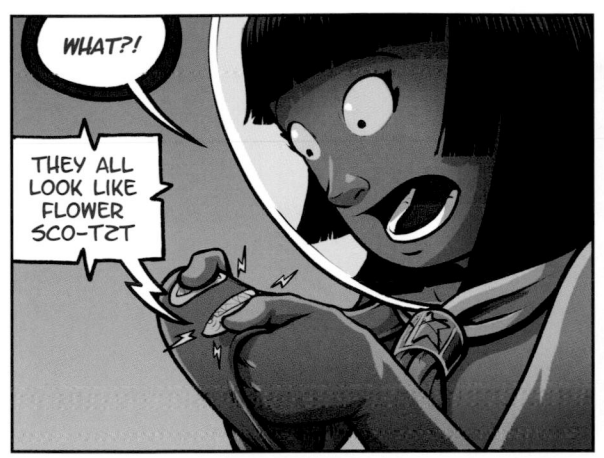

WHAT?!

THEY ALL LOOK LIKE FLOWER SCO-TZT

DAD?

DAD?!

AVANI...

WHAT DID YOU DO?!

I SWEAR.

I HAVE *NO IDEA* WHAT YOUR DAD IS TALKING ABOUT.

NUDGE! NUDGE!

UM...AVANI?

I'M THE ONE WHO SENT THE ROBOT, BUT IT WAS AN *ACCIDENT*.

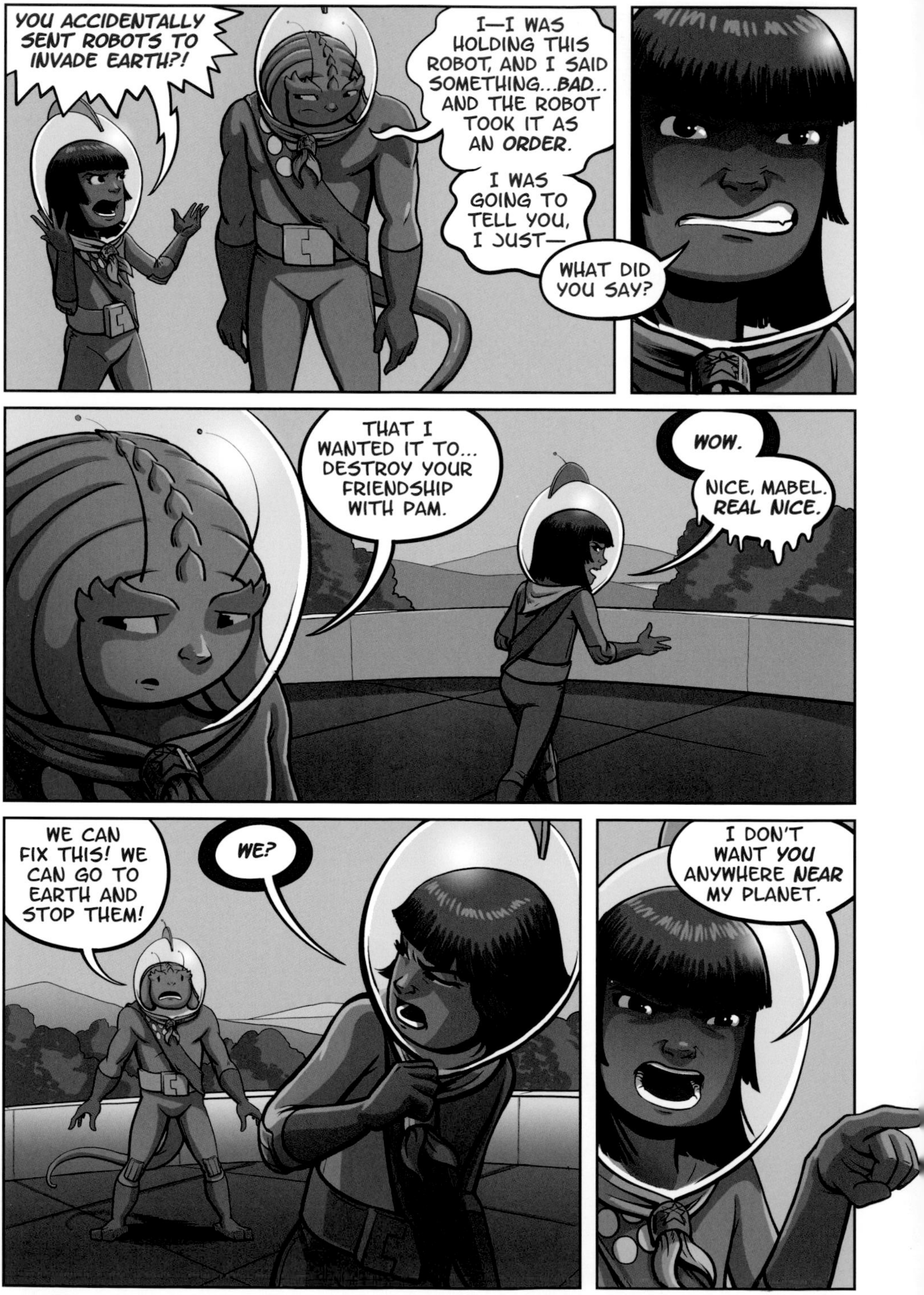
YOU ACCIDENTALLY SENT ROBOTS TO INVADE EARTH?!
I—I WAS HOLDING THIS ROBOT, AND I SAID SOMETHING...BAD... AND THE ROBOT TOOK IT AS AN ORDER.
I WAS GOING TO TELL YOU, I JUST—
WHAT DID YOU SAY?
THAT I WANTED IT TO... DESTROY YOUR FRIENDSHIP WITH PAM.
WOW.
NICE, MABEL. REAL NICE.
WE CAN FIX THIS! WE CAN GO TO EARTH AND STOP THEM!
WE?
I DON'T WANT YOU ANYWHERE NEAR MY PLANET.

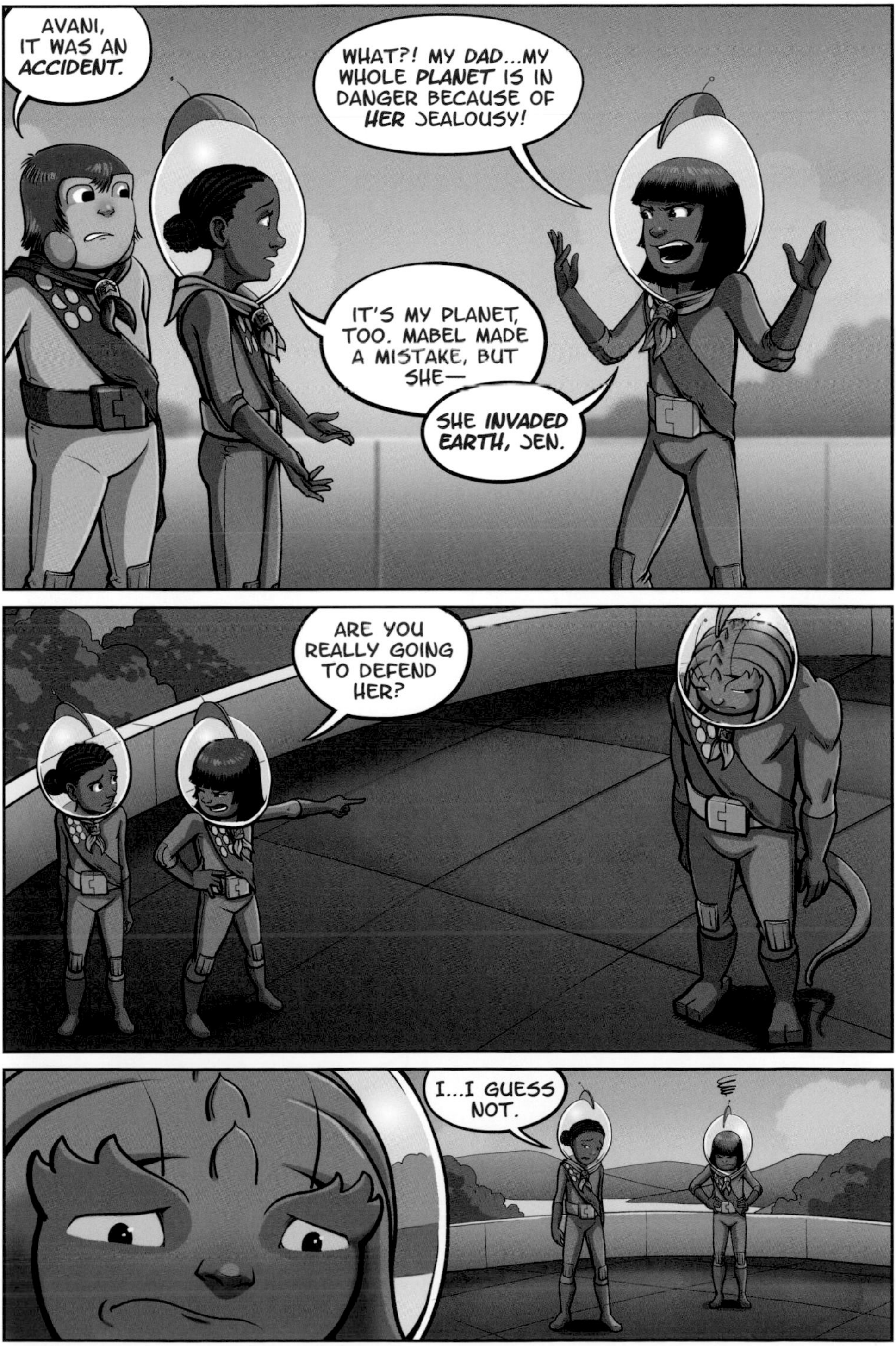
AVANI, IT WAS AN ACCIDENT.
WHAT?! MY DAD...MY WHOLE PLANET IS IN DANGER BECAUSE OF HER JEALOUSY!
IT'S MY PLANET, TOO. MABEL MADE A MISTAKE, BUT SHE—
SHE INVADED EARTH, JEN.
ARE YOU REALLY GOING TO DEFEND HER?
I...I GUESS NOT.

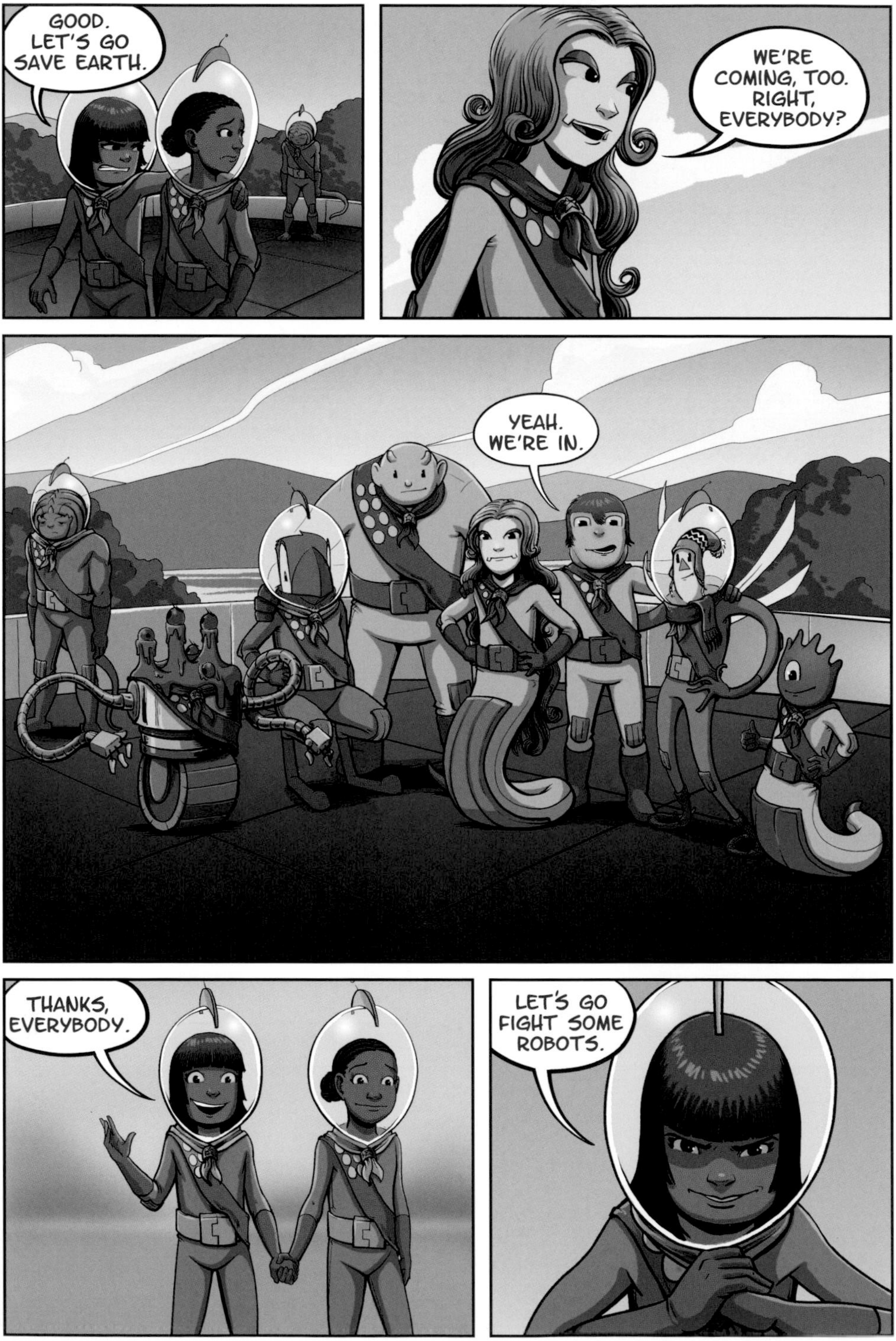
GOOD. LET'S GO SAVE EARTH.
WE'RE COMING, TOO. RIGHT, EVERYBODY?
YEAH. WE'RE IN.
THANKS, EVERYBODY.
LET'S GO FIGHT SOME ROBOTS.

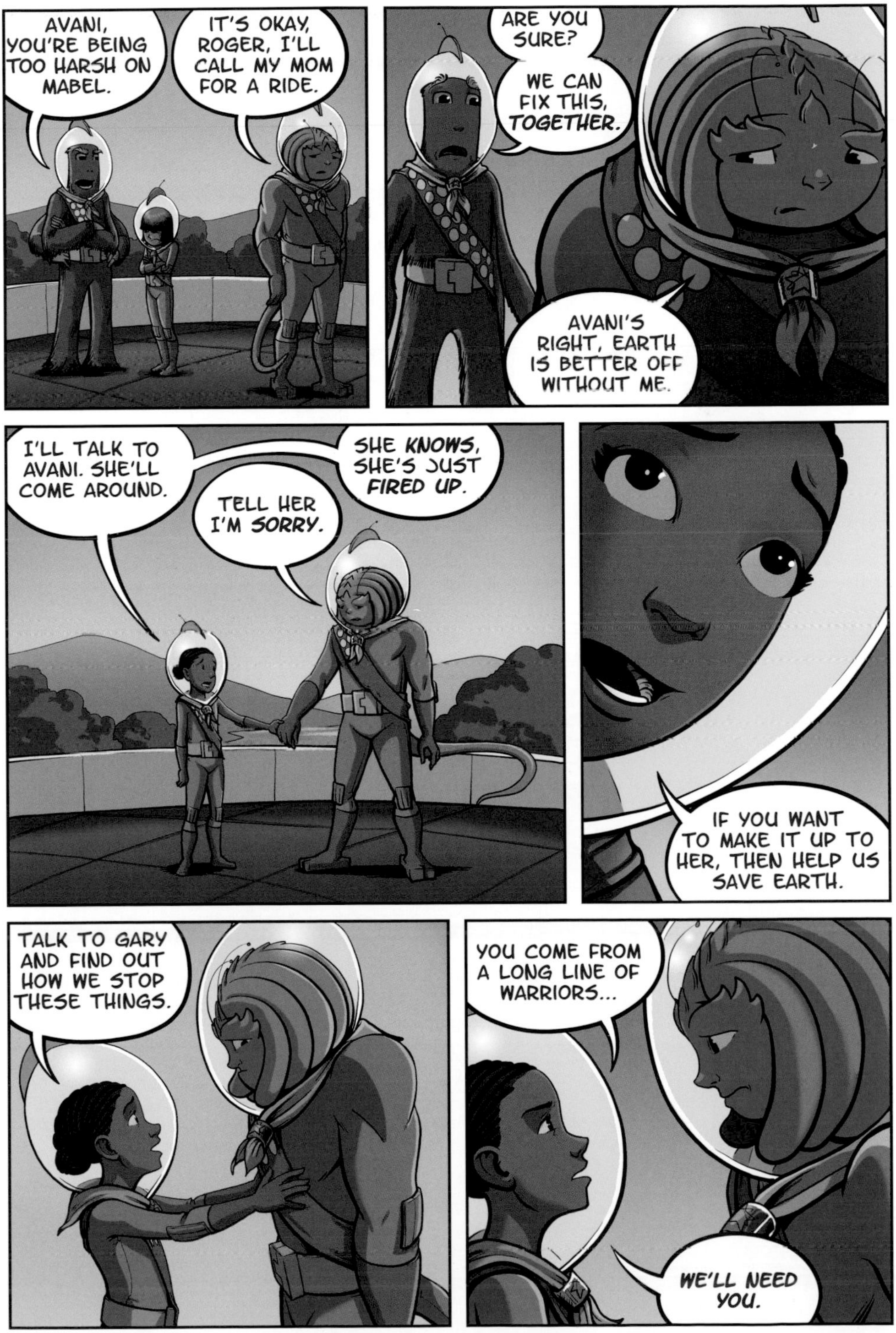

AVANI, YOU'RE BEING TOO HARSH ON MABEL.
IT'S OKAY, ROGER, I'LL CALL MY MOM FOR A RIDE.
ARE YOU SURE?
WE CAN FIX THIS, TOGETHER.
AVANI'S RIGHT, EARTH IS BETTER OFF WITHOUT ME.
I'LL TALK TO AVANI. SHE'LL COME AROUND.
TELL HER I'M SORRY.
SHE KNOWS, SHE'S JUST FIRED UP.
IF YOU WANT TO MAKE IT UP TO HER, THEN HELP US SAVE EARTH.
TALK TO GARY AND FIND OUT HOW WE STOP THESE THINGS.
YOU COME FROM A LONG LINE OF WARRIORS...
WE'LL NEED YOU.

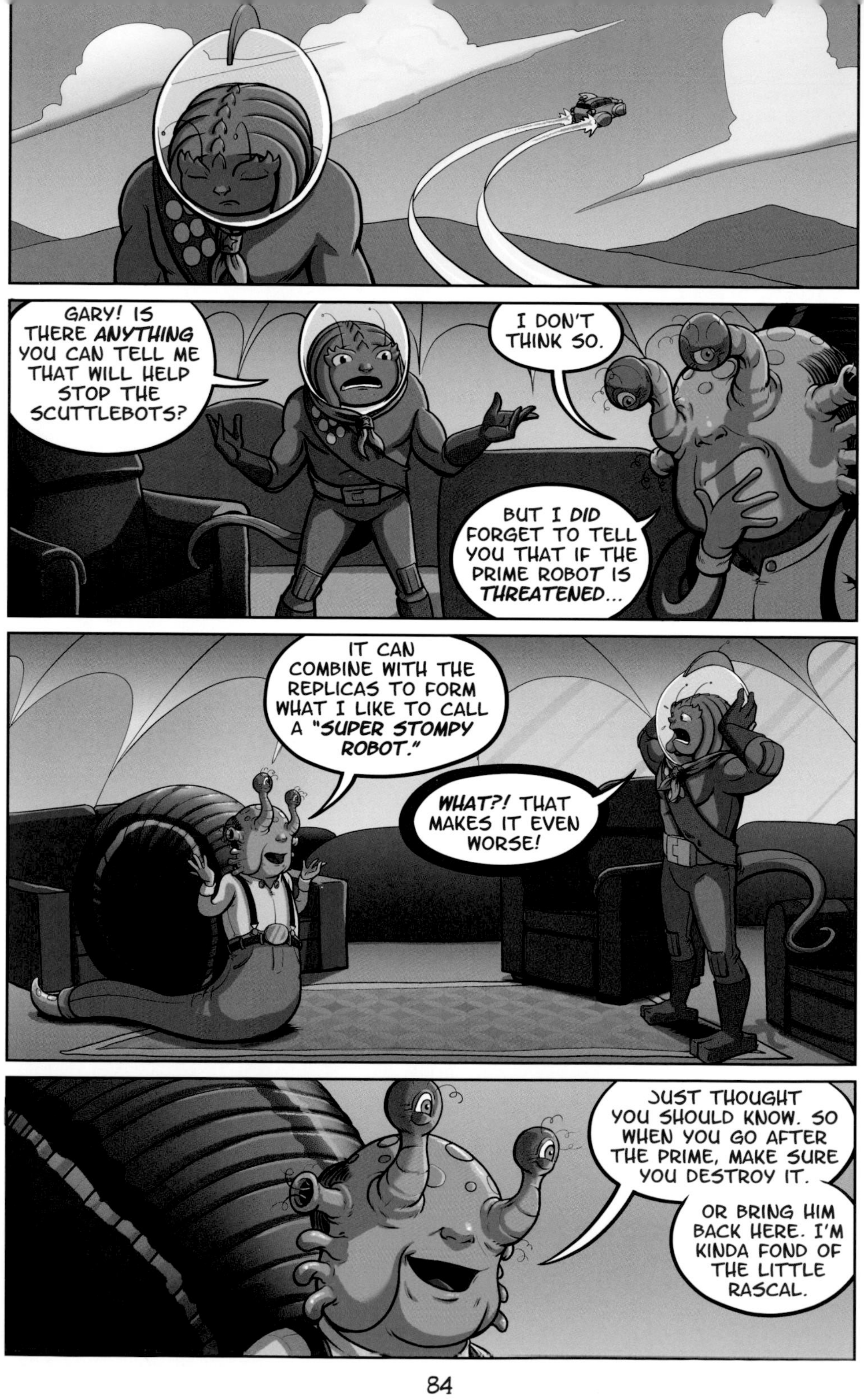
GARY! IS THERE ANYTHING YOU CAN TELL ME THAT WILL HELP STOP THE SCUTTLEBOTS?
I DON'T THINK SO.
BUT I DID FORGET TO TELL YOU THAT IF THE PRIME ROBOT IS THREATENED...
IT CAN COMBINE WITH THE REPLICAS TO FORM WHAT I LIKE TO CALL A "SUPER STOMPY ROBOT."
WHAT?! THAT MAKES IT EVEN WORSE!
JUST THOUGHT YOU SHOULD KNOW. SO WHEN YOU GO AFTER THE PRIME, MAKE SURE YOU DESTROY IT.
OR BRING HIM BACK HERE. I'M KINDA FOND OF THE LITTLE RASCAL.

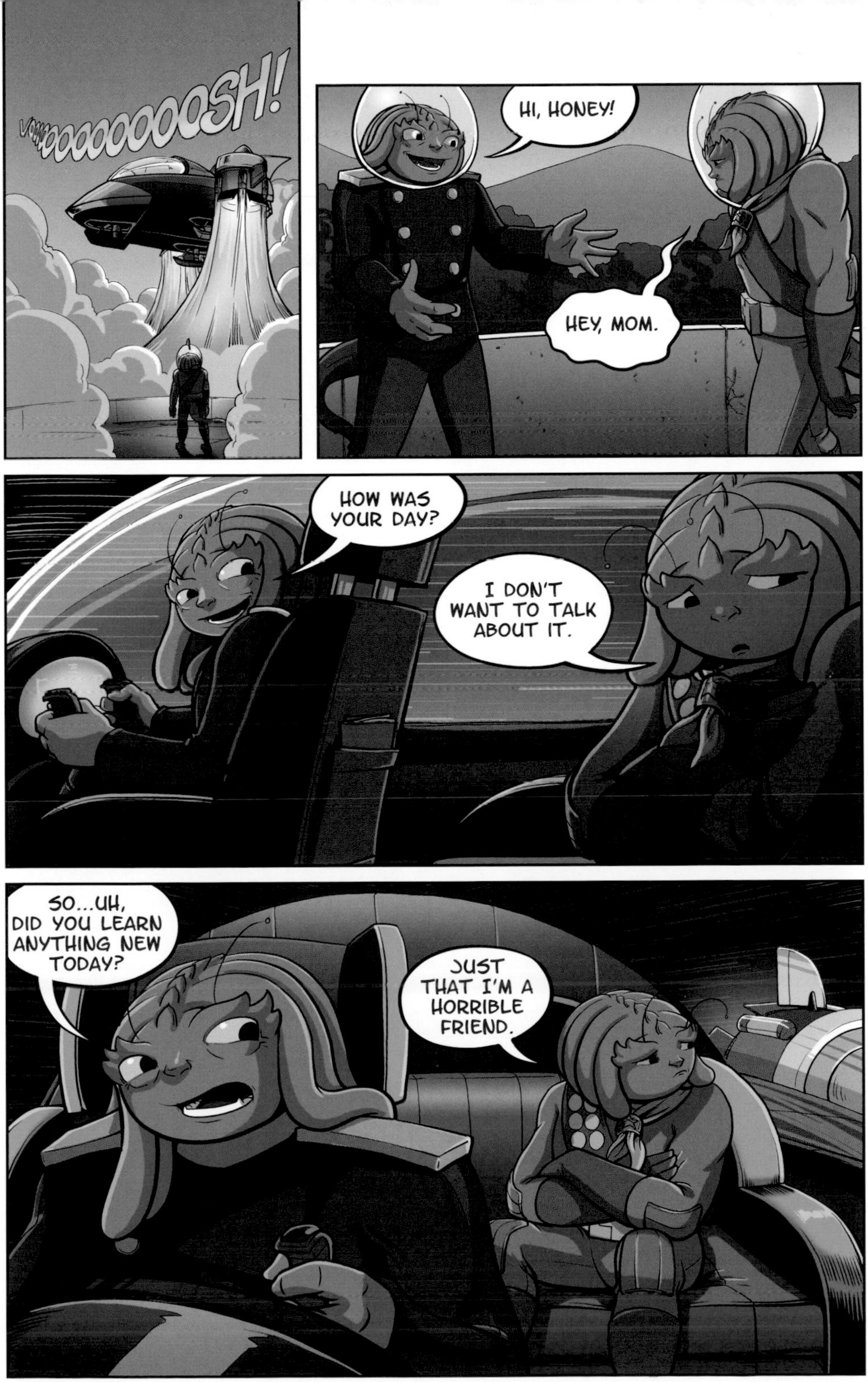
VOOOOOOOOOOOSH!
HI, HONEY!
HEY, MOM.
HOW WAS YOUR DAY?
I DON'T WANT TO TALK ABOUT IT.
SO...UH, DID YOU LEARN ANYTHING NEW TODAY?
JUST THAT I'M A HORRIBLE FRIEND.

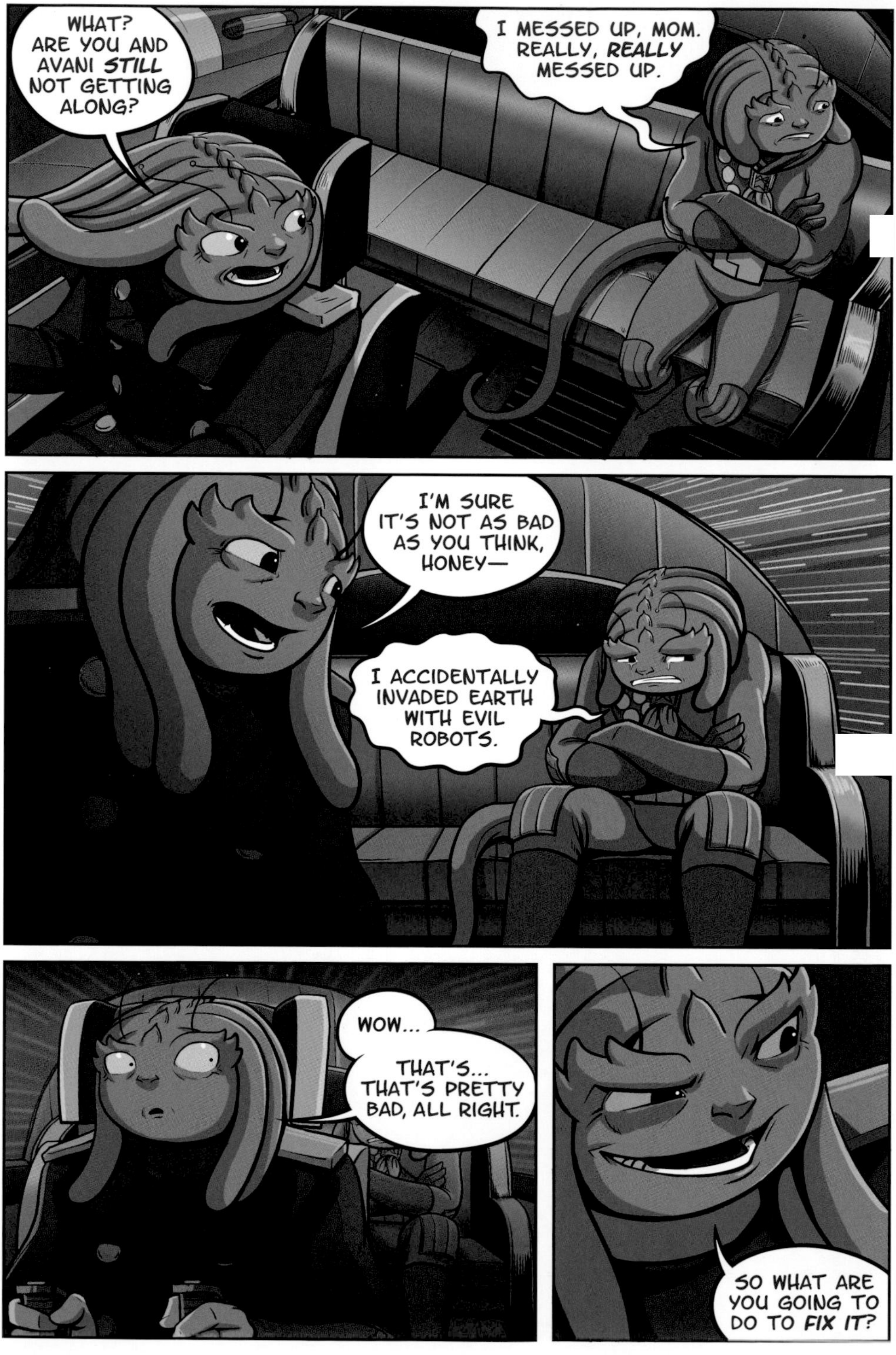
WHAT? ARE YOU AND AVANI STILL NOT GETTING ALONG?
I MESSED UP, MOM. REALLY, REALLY MESSED UP.
I'M SURE IT'S NOT AS BAD AS YOU THINK, HONEY—
I ACCIDENTALLY INVADED EARTH WITH EVIL ROBOTS.
WOW...
THAT'S... THAT'S PRETTY BAD, ALL RIGHT.
SO WHAT ARE YOU GOING TO DO TO FIX IT?

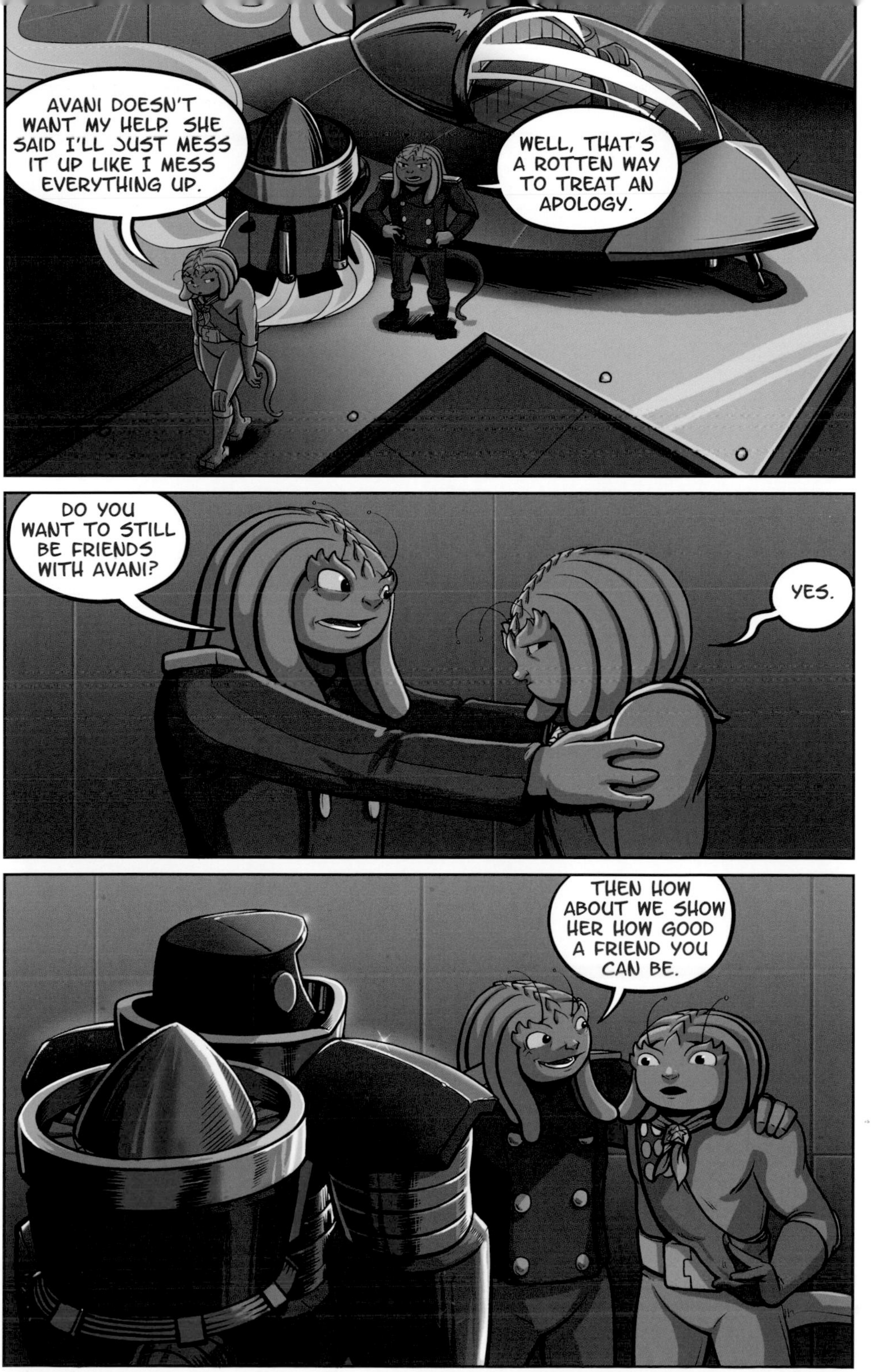
AVANI DOESN'T WANT MY HELP. SHE SAID I'LL JUST MESS IT UP LIKE I MESS EVERYTHING UP.
WELL, THAT'S A ROTTEN WAY TO TREAT AN APOLOGY.
DO YOU WANT TO STILL BE FRIENDS WITH AVANI?
YES.
THEN HOW ABOUT WE SHOW HER HOW GOOD A FRIEND YOU CAN BE.

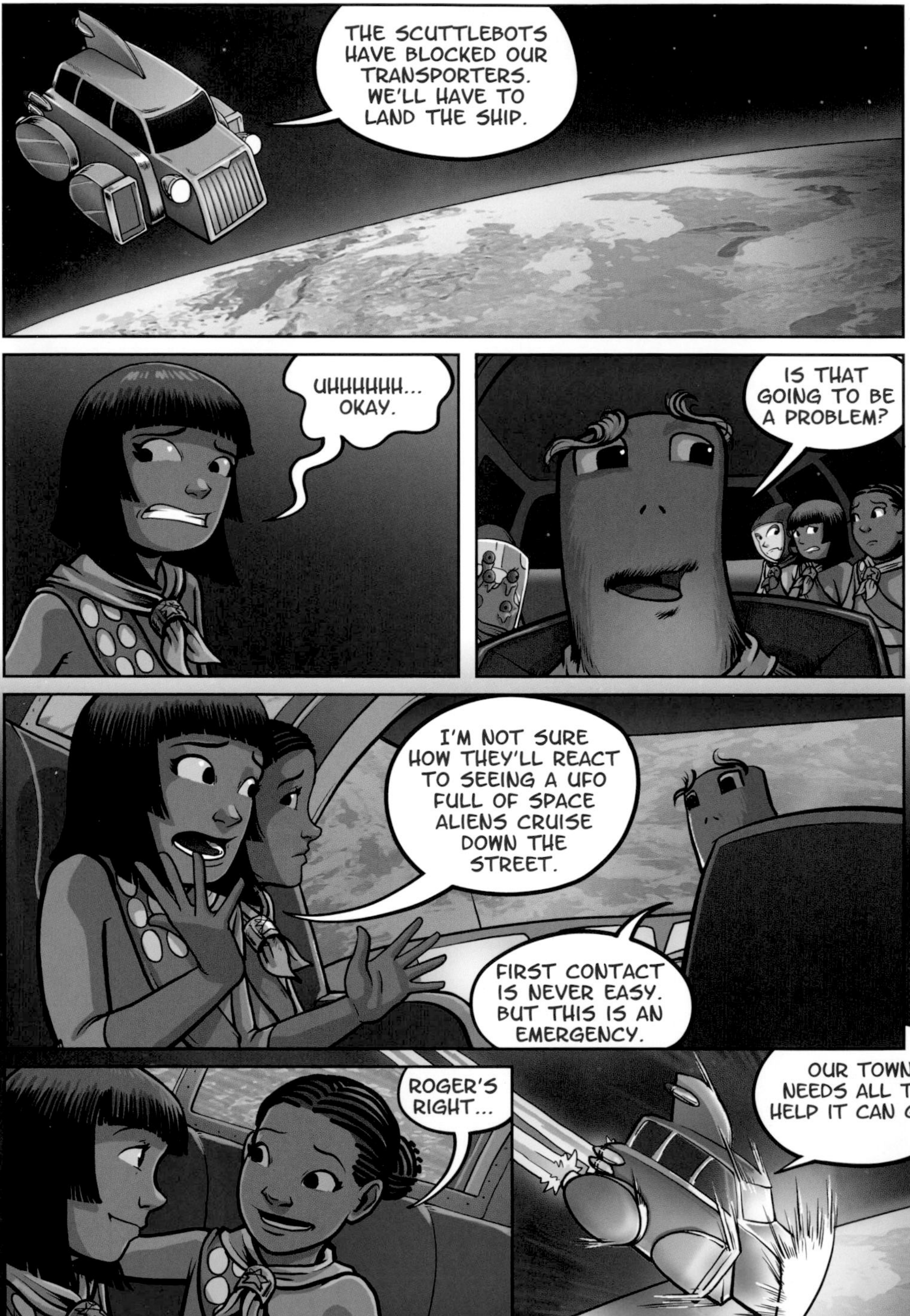
THE SCUTTLEBOTS HAVE BLOCKED OUR TRANSPORTERS. WE'LL HAVE TO LAND THE SHIP.
UHHHHHH... OKAY.
IS THAT GOING TO BE A PROBLEM?
I'M NOT SURE HOW THEY'LL REACT TO SEEING A UFO FULL OF SPACE ALIENS CRUISE DOWN THE STREET.
FIRST CONTACT IS NEVER EASY. BUT THIS IS AN EMERGENCY.
ROGER'S RIGHT...
OUR TOWN NEEDS ALL THE HELP IT CAN GET.

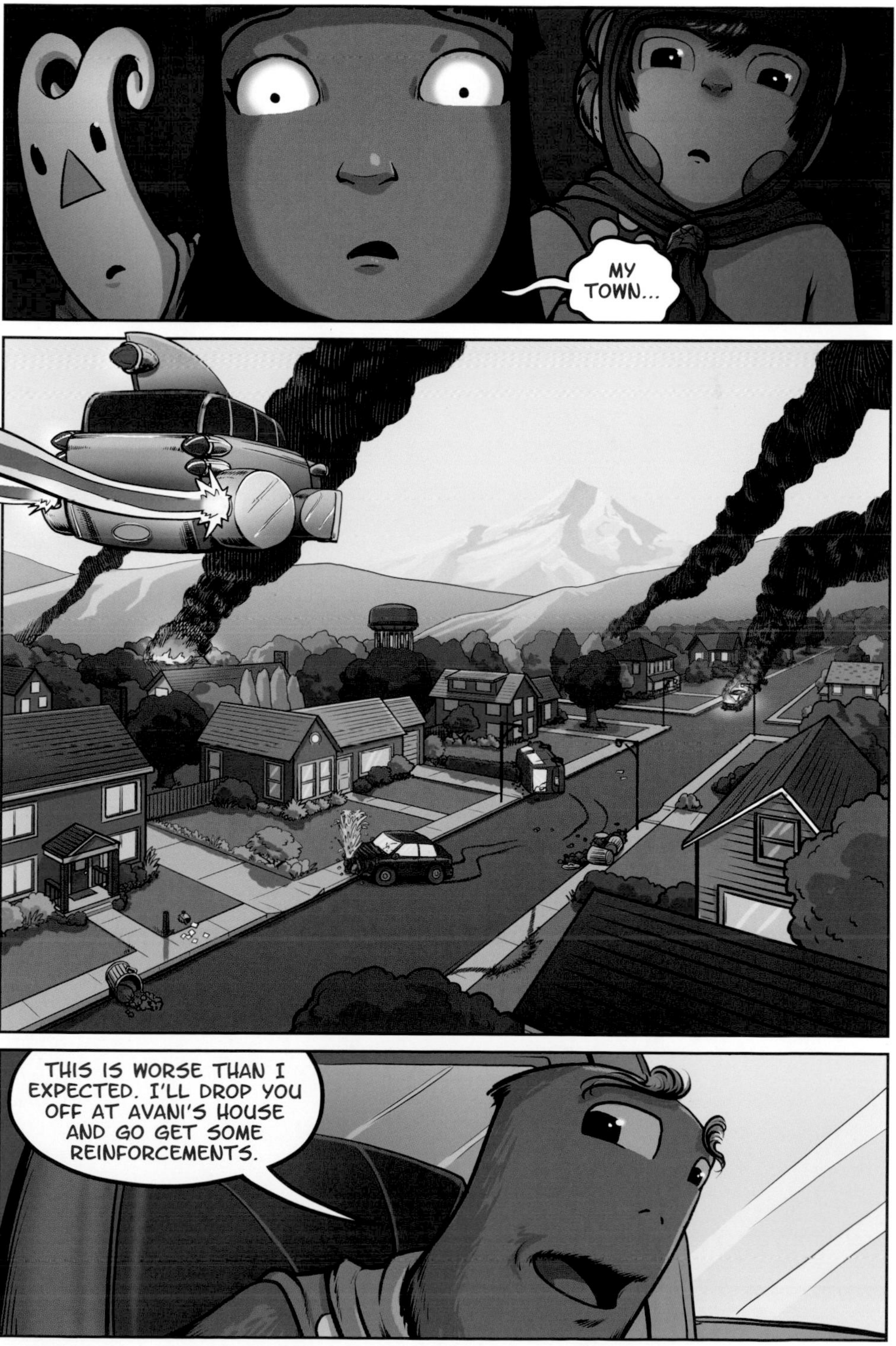
MY TOWN...
THIS IS WORSE THAN I EXPECTED. I'LL DROP YOU OFF AT AVANI'S HOUSE AND GO GET SOME REINFORCEMENTS.

WHOOSH!

AVANI! THANKS FOR GETTING HERE SO FAST!
AND YOU BROUGHT... **FRIENDS**.
DAD, WHAT'S GOING ON?!

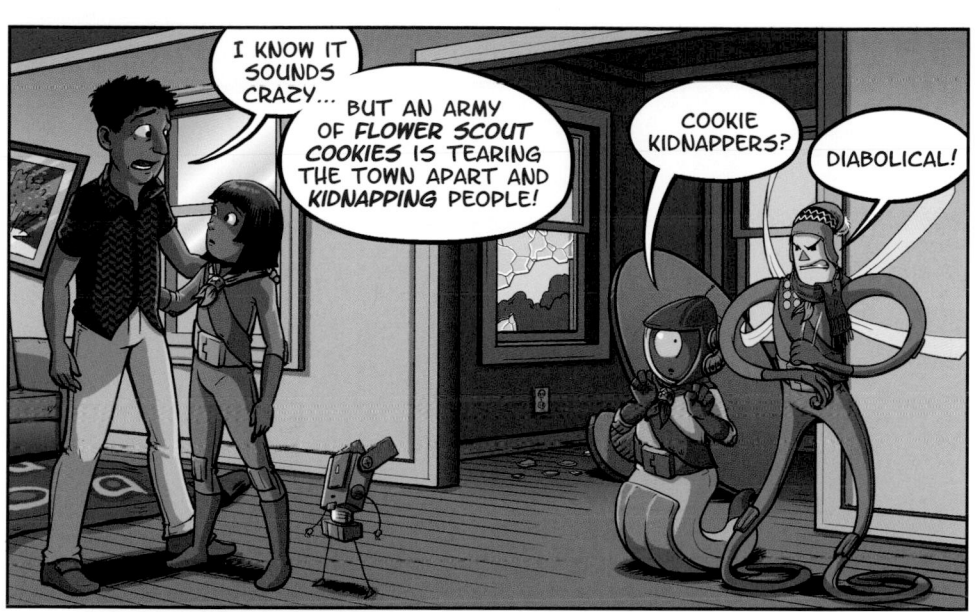

I KNOW IT SOUNDS CRAZY... BUT AN ARMY OF *FLOWER SCOUT* COOKIES IS TEARING THE TOWN APART AND *KIDNAPPING* PEOPLE!

COOKIE KIDNAPPERS?

DIABOLICAL!

THEY'RE *KIDNAPPING* PEOPLE?! WHERE ARE THEY TAKING THEM?

I DON'T KNOW. I SAW A PACK OF THEM CARRYING MR. WISHART DOWN THE STREET.

IT ALL HAPPENED SO FAST...

I CAME DOWN FOR A SNACK AND WAS AMBUSHED.

OH NO... MY STASH!

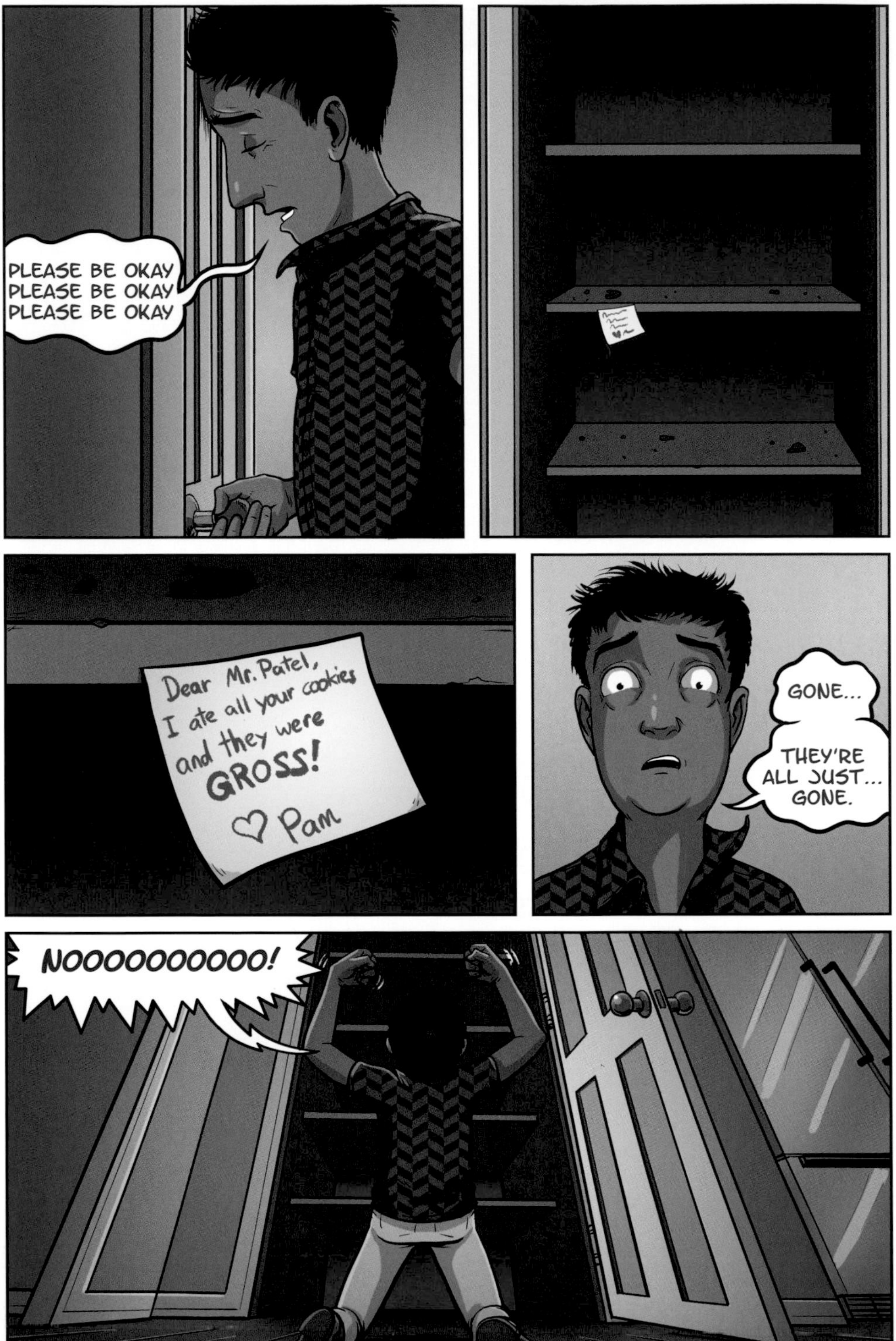
PLEASE BE OKAY
PLEASE BE OKAY
PLEASE BE OKAY
Dear Mr. Patel,
I ate all your cookies
and they were
GROSS!
♡ Pam
GONE...
THEY'RE ALL JUST... GONE.
NOOOOOOOOOO!

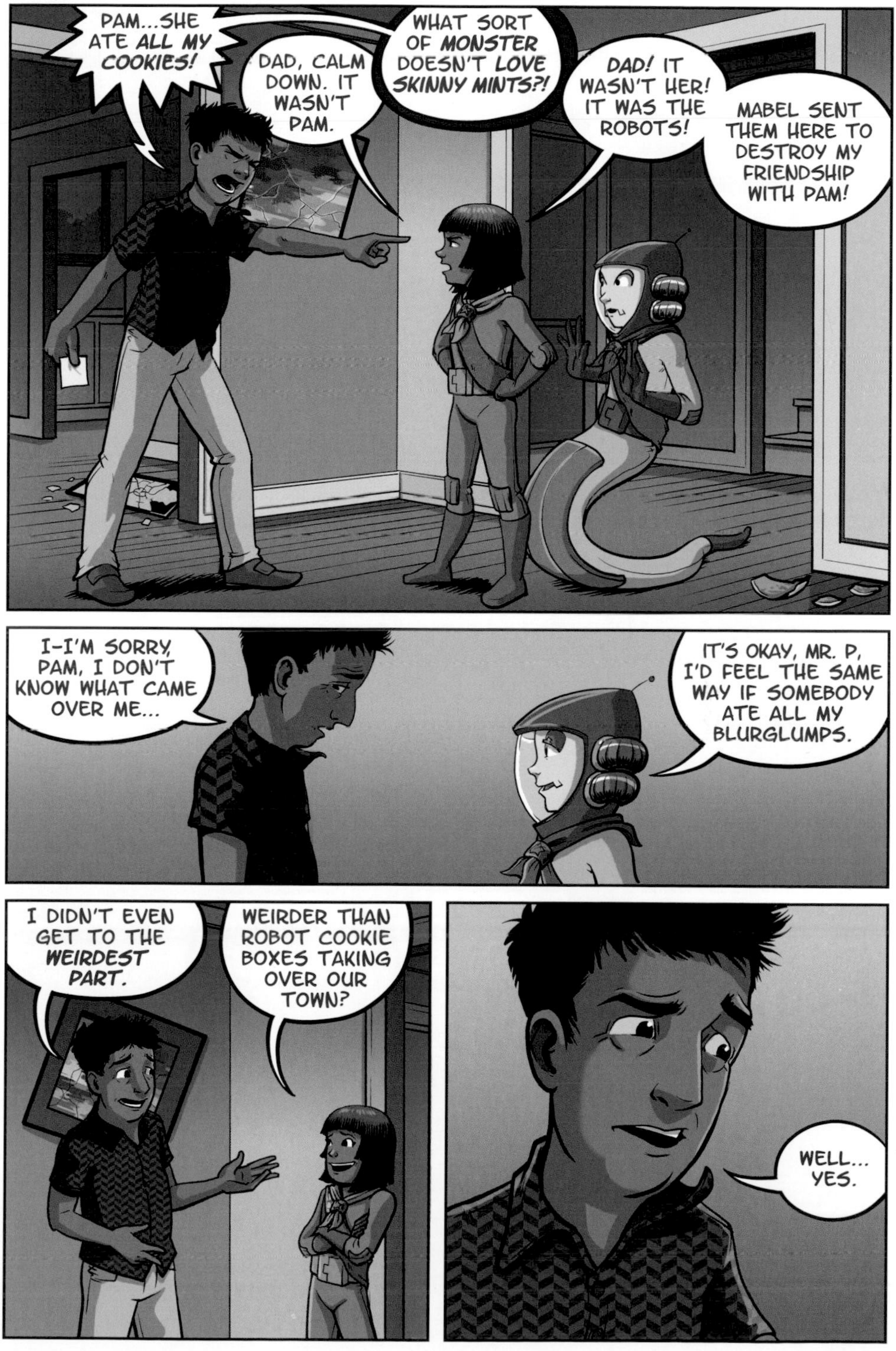
PAM...SHE ATE ALL MY COOKIES!
DAD, CALM DOWN. IT WASN'T PAM.
WHAT SORT OF MONSTER DOESN'T LOVE SKINNY MINTS?!
DAD! IT WASN'T HER! IT WAS THE ROBOTS!
MABEL SENT THEM HERE TO DESTROY MY FRIENDSHIP WITH PAM!
I-I'M SORRY, PAM, I DON'T KNOW WHAT CAME OVER ME...
IT'S OKAY, MR. P, I'D FEEL THE SAME WAY IF SOMEBODY ATE ALL MY BLURGLUMPS.
I DIDN'T EVEN GET TO THE WEIRDEST PART.
WEIRDER THAN ROBOT COOKIE BOXES TAKING OVER OUR TOWN?
WELL... YES.

THEY KEPT SAYING HOW MUCH PAM LOVES *CHAZ WÜNDERLIP*.

OOH! I LOVE "YOU ARE MY ONE TRUE DOVESTAR"!

WAIT...YOU LIKE CHAZ WÜNDERLIP?

WHAT? IT'S CATCHY!

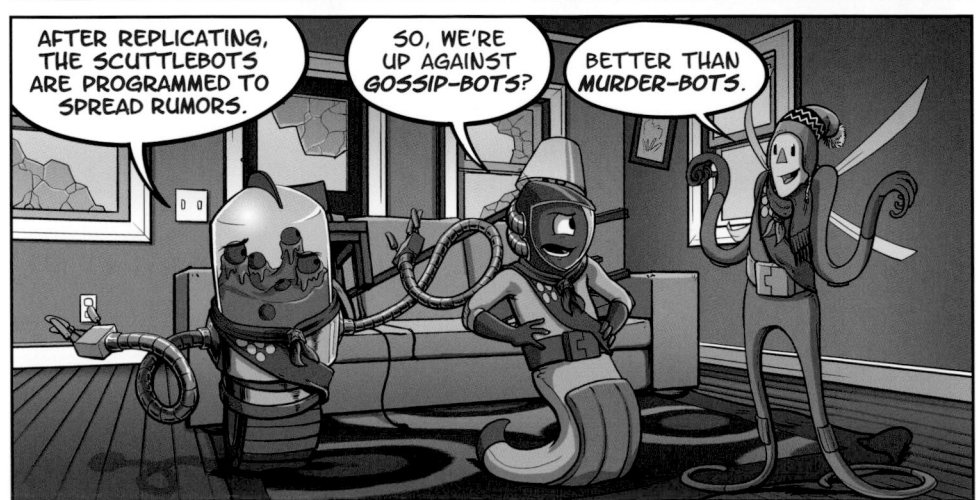

AFTER REPLICATING, THE SCUTTLEBOTS ARE PROGRAMMED TO SPREAD RUMORS.

SO, WE'RE UP AGAINST *GOSSIP-BOTS*?

BETTER THAN *MURDER-BOTS*.

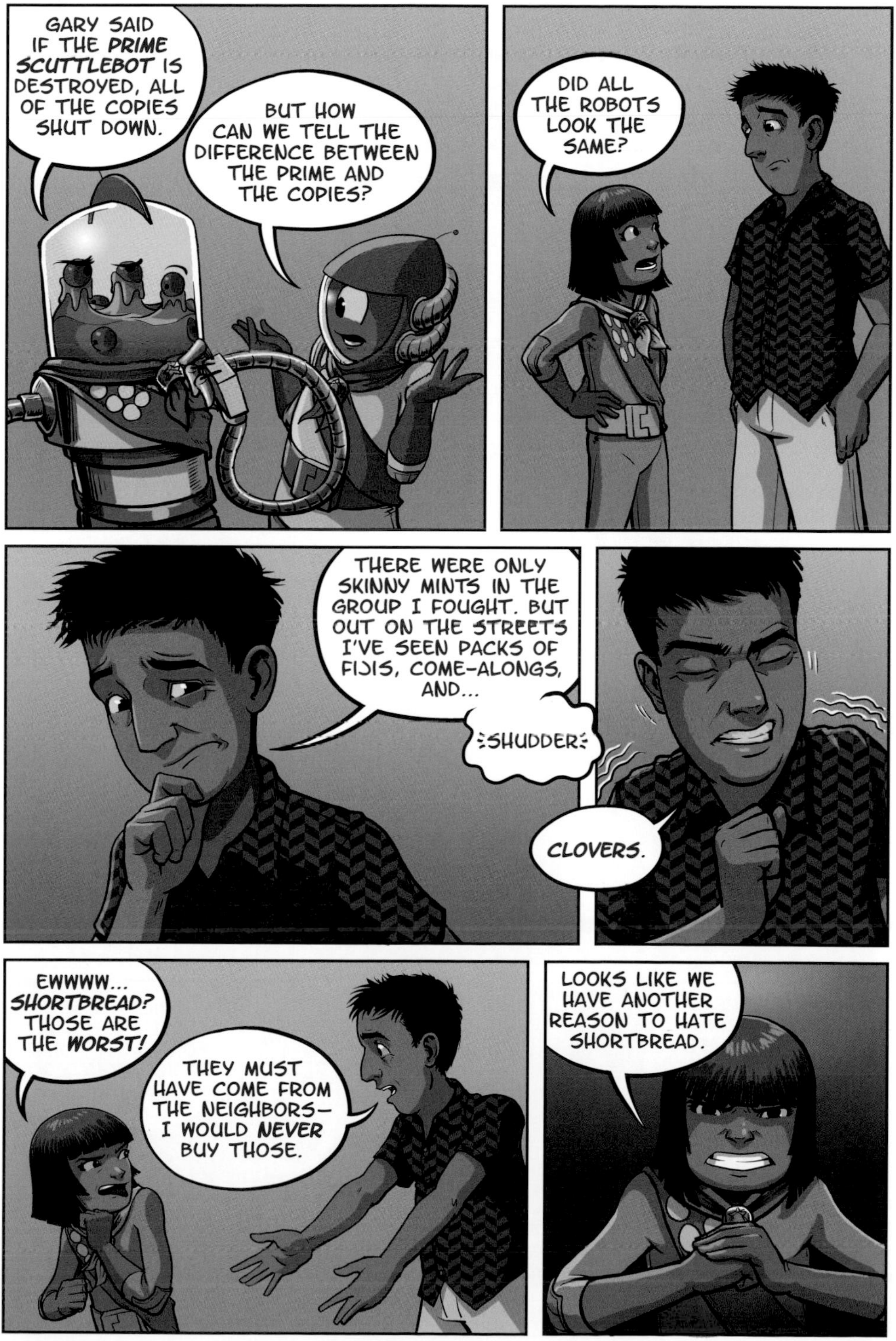
GARY SAID IF THE ***PRIME SCUTTLEBOT*** IS DESTROYED, ALL OF THE COPIES SHUT DOWN.
BUT HOW CAN WE TELL THE DIFFERENCE BETWEEN THE PRIME AND THE COPIES?
DID ALL THE ROBOTS LOOK THE SAME?
THERE WERE ONLY SKINNY MINTS IN THE GROUP I FOUGHT. BUT OUT ON THE STREETS I'VE SEEN PACKS OF FIJIS, COME-ALONGS, AND...
SHUDDER
CLOVERS.
EWWWW... ***SHORTBREAD?*** THOSE ARE THE ***WORST!***
THEY MUST HAVE COME FROM THE NEIGHBORS— I WOULD ***NEVER*** BUY THOSE.
LOOKS LIKE WE HAVE ANOTHER REASON TO HATE SHORTBREAD.

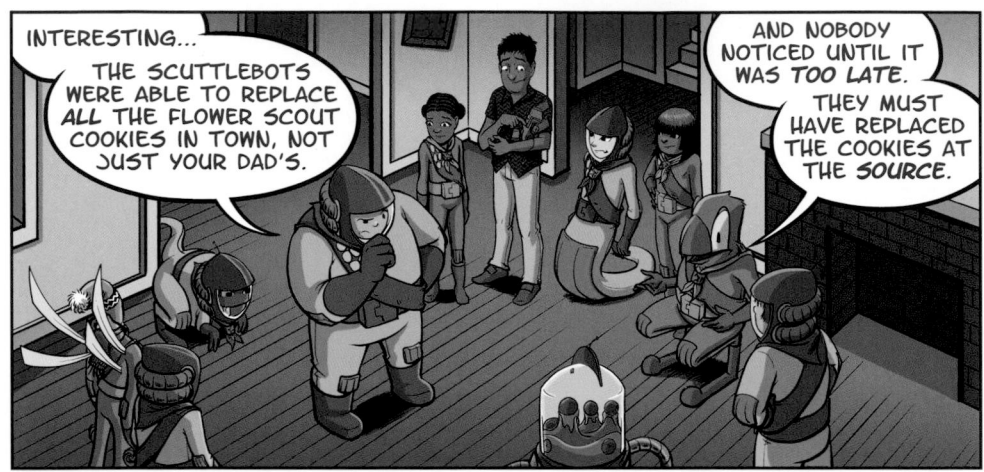

INTERESTING... THE SCUTTLEBOTS WERE ABLE TO REPLACE ALL THE FLOWER SCOUT COOKIES IN TOWN, NOT JUST YOUR DAD'S.

AND NOBODY NOTICED UNTIL IT WAS *TOO LATE*. THEY MUST HAVE REPLACED THE COOKIES AT THE *SOURCE*.

THEY'RE BAKED IN ENTERPRISE, CALIFORNIA!

I...UH... WENT ON THE *TOUR*...

THAT'S *HUNDREDS OF MILES* FROM HERE. THEY MUST HAVE INFILTRATED THE LOCAL FLOWER SCOUTS SOMEHOW.

LET'S SPLIT INTO TWO TEAMS, ONE TO PROTECT THE TOWN AND ONE TO FIND THE PRIME SCUTTLEBOT'S BASE.

SINCE AVANI AND I KNOW THE TOWN BEST, ONE OF US SHOULD GO WITH EACH TEAM.

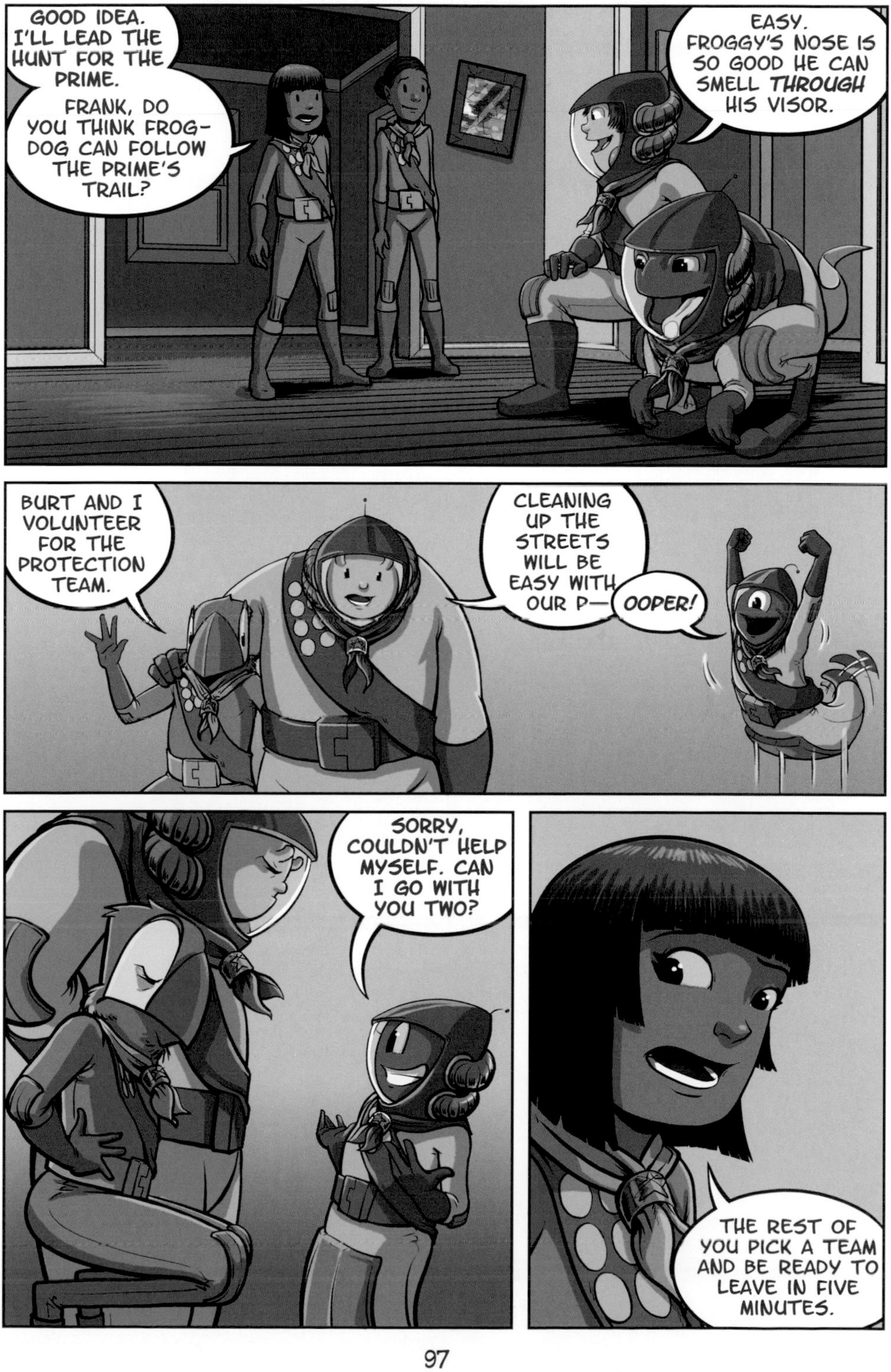
GOOD IDEA. I'LL LEAD THE HUNT FOR THE PRIME.
FRANK, DO YOU THINK FROG-DOG CAN FOLLOW THE PRIME'S TRAIL?
EASY. FROGGY'S NOSE IS SO GOOD HE CAN SMELL *THROUGH* HIS VISOR.
BURT AND I VOLUNTEER FOR THE PROTECTION TEAM.
CLEANING UP THE STREETS WILL BE EASY WITH OUR P—
OOPER!
SORRY, COULDN'T HELP MYSELF. CAN I GO WITH YOU TWO?
THE REST OF YOU PICK A TEAM AND BE READY TO LEAVE IN FIVE MINUTES.

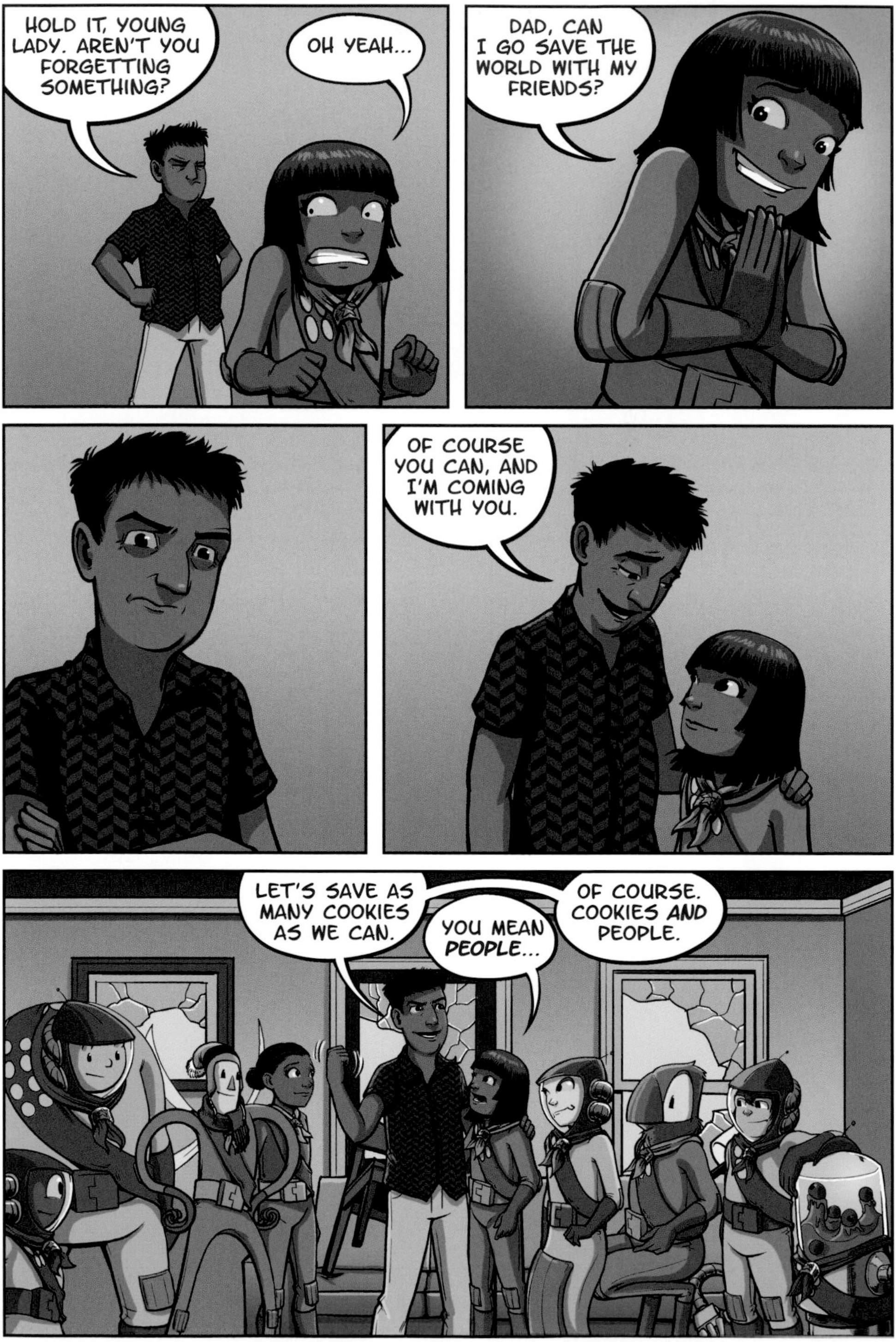
HOLD IT, YOUNG LADY. AREN'T YOU FORGETTING SOMETHING?
OH YEAH...
DAD, CAN I GO SAVE THE WORLD WITH MY FRIENDS?
OF COURSE YOU CAN, AND I'M COMING WITH YOU.
LET'S SAVE AS MANY COOKIES AS WE CAN.
YOU MEAN *PEOPLE*...
OF COURSE. COOKIES *AND* PEOPLE.

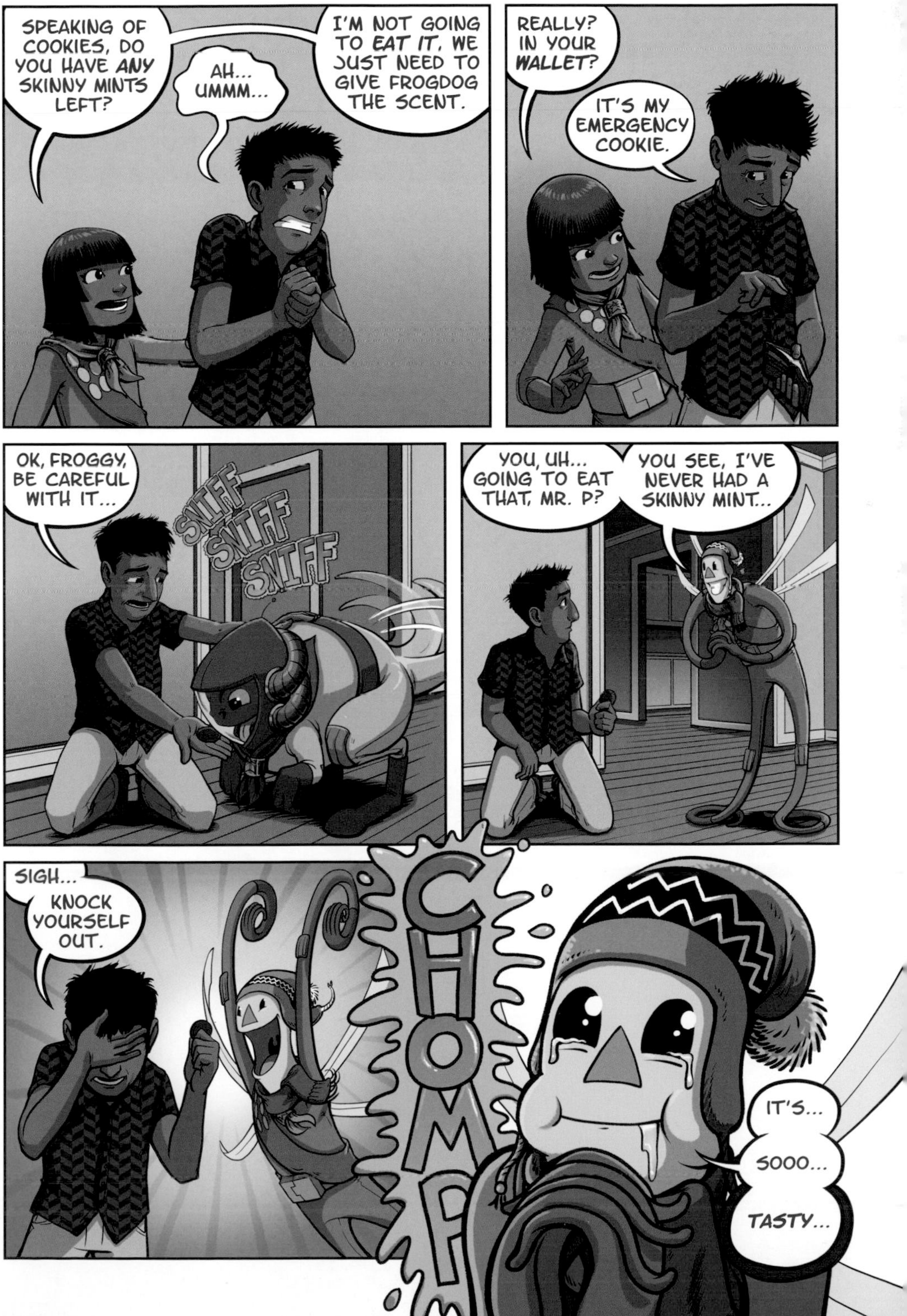
SPEAKING OF COOKIES, DO YOU HAVE *ANY* SKINNY MINTS LEFT?
AH... UMMM...
I'M NOT GOING TO *EAT IT*, WE JUST NEED TO GIVE FROGDOG THE SCENT.
REALLY? IN YOUR *WALLET*?
IT'S MY EMERGENCY COOKIE.
OK, FROGGY, BE CAREFUL WITH IT...
SNIFF SNIFF SNIFF
YOU, UH... GOING TO EAT THAT, MR. P?
YOU SEE, I'VE NEVER HAD A SKINNY MINT...
SIGH...
KNOCK YOURSELF OUT.
CHOMP
IT'S...
SOOO...
TASTY...

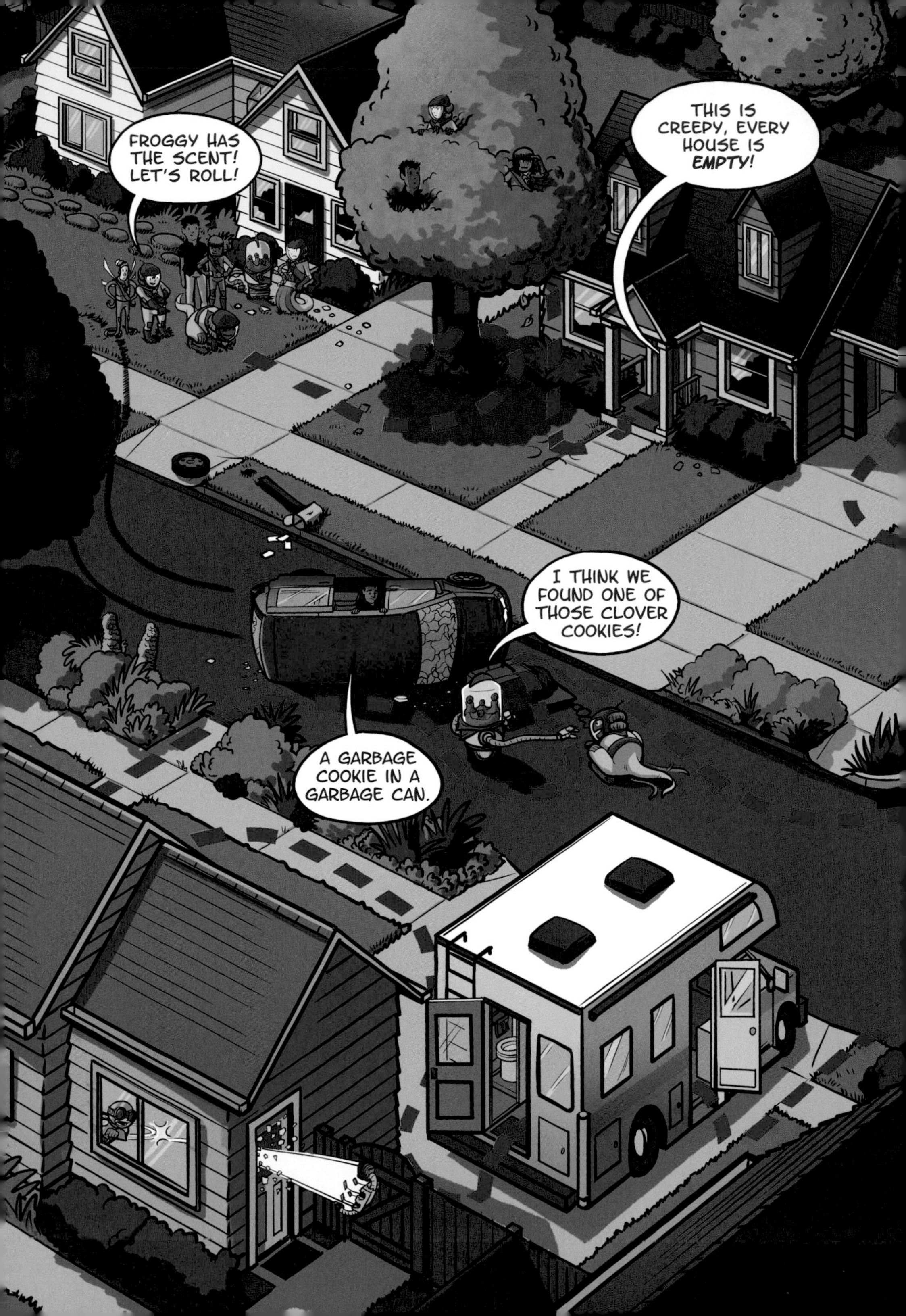
FROGGY HAS THE SCENT! LET'S ROLL!
THIS IS CREEPY, EVERY HOUSE IS EMPTY!
I THINK WE FOUND ONE OF THOSE CLOVER COOKIES!
A GARBAGE COOKIE IN A GARBAGE CAN.

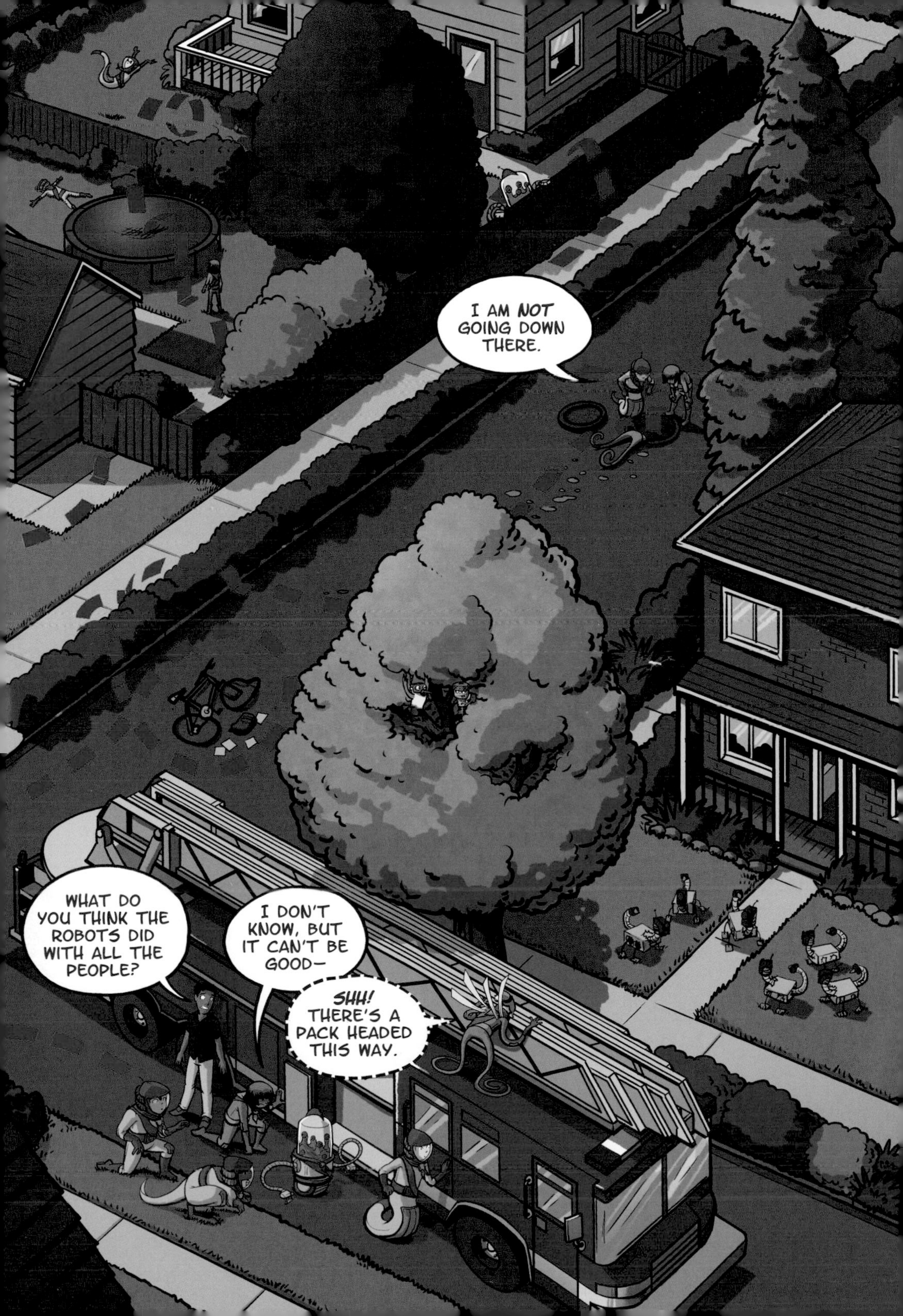
I AM NOT GOING DOWN THERE.
WHAT DO YOU THINK THE ROBOTS DID WITH ALL THE PEOPLE?
I DON'T KNOW, BUT IT CAN'T BE GOOD—
SHH! THERE'S A PACK HEADED THIS WAY.

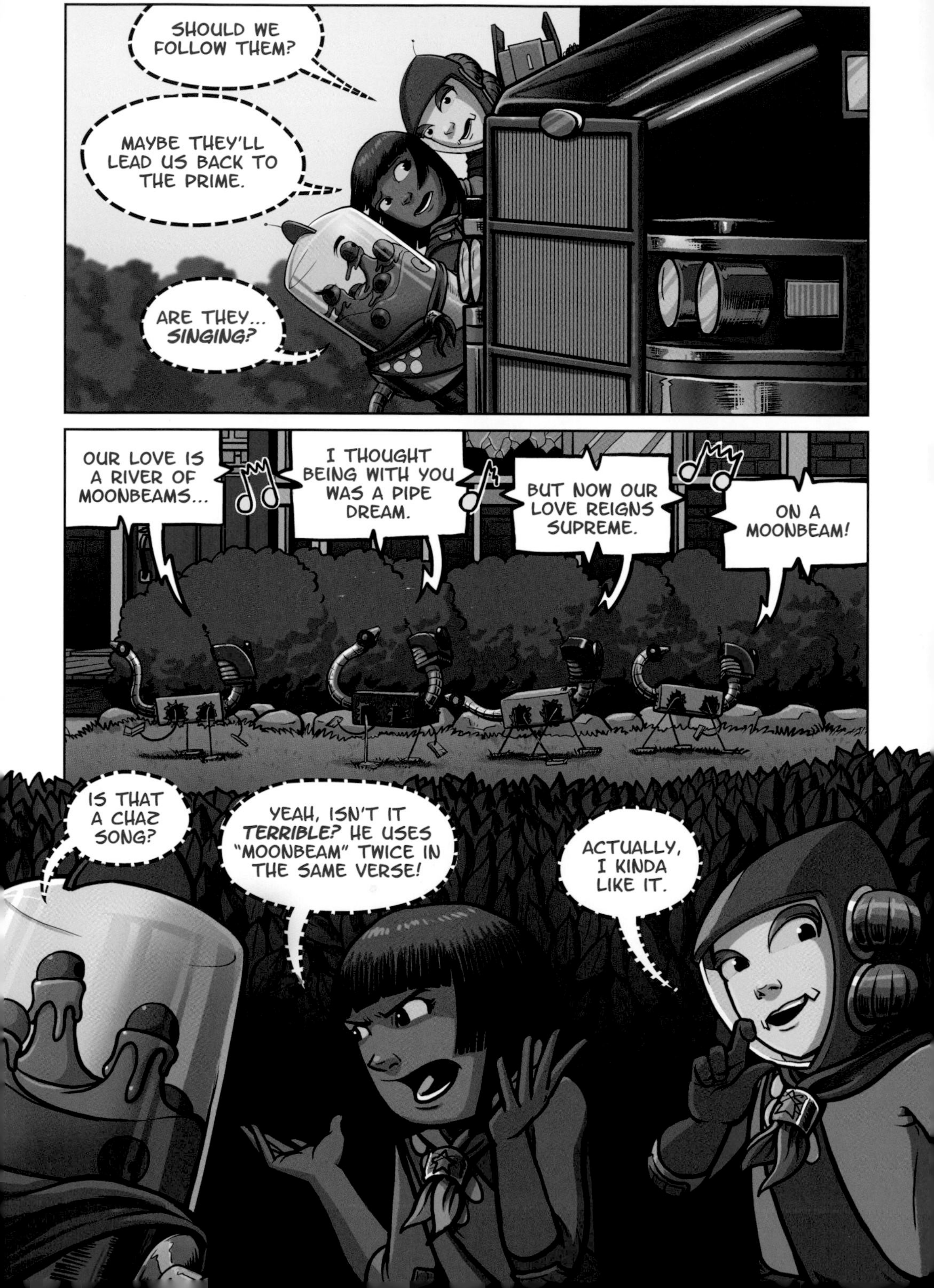
SHOULD WE FOLLOW THEM?
MAYBE THEY'LL LEAD US BACK TO THE PRIME.
ARE THEY... *SINGING?*
OUR LOVE IS A RIVER OF MOONBEAMS...
I THOUGHT BEING WITH YOU WAS A PIPE DREAM.
BUT NOW OUR LOVE REIGNS SUPREME.
ON A MOONBEAM!
IS THAT A CHAZ SONG?
YEAH, ISN'T IT *TERRIBLE?* HE USES "MOONBEAM" TWICE IN THE SAME VERSE!
ACTUALLY, I KINDA LIKE IT.

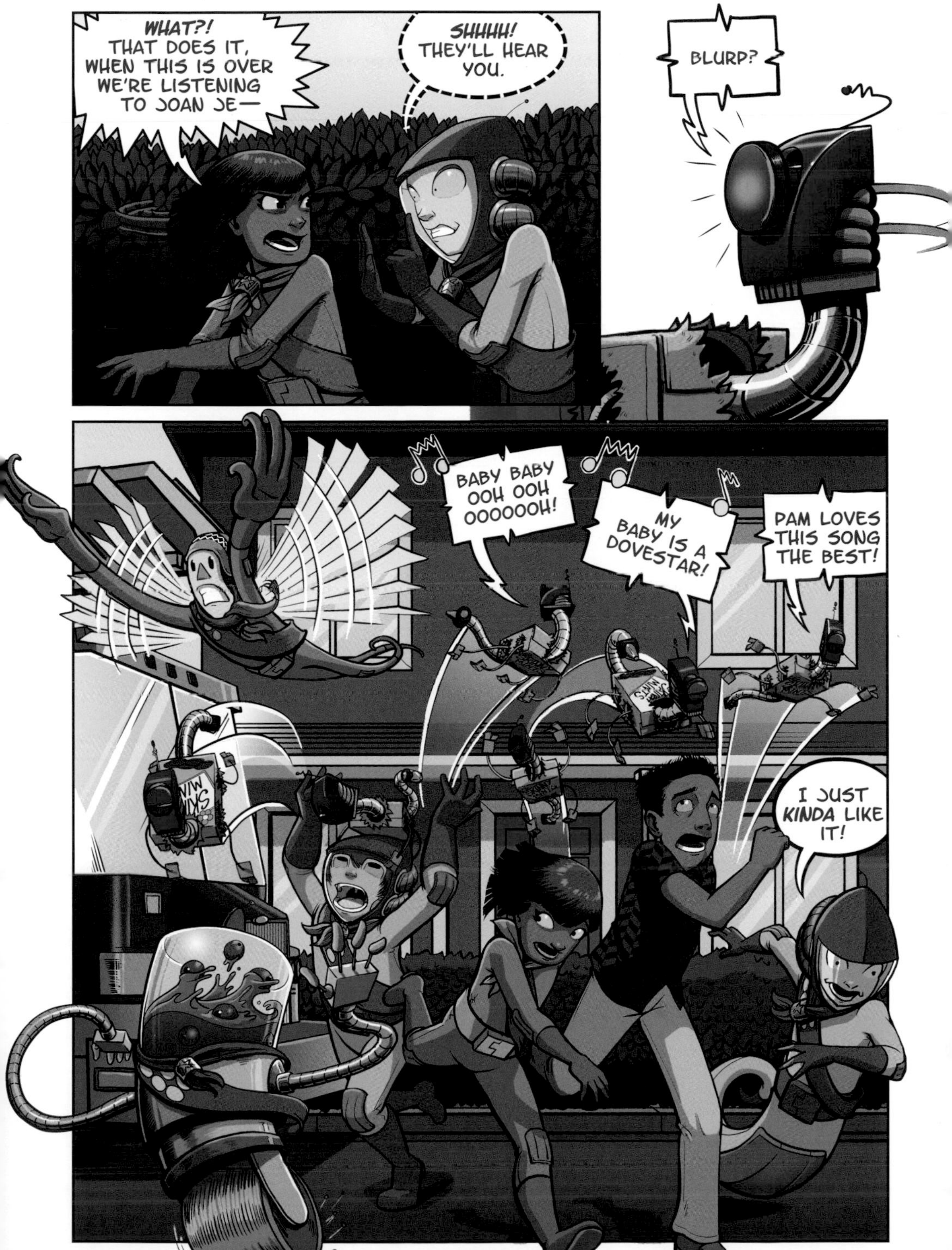
WHAT?! THAT DOES IT, WHEN THIS IS OVER WE'RE LISTENING TO JOAN JE—
SHHHH! THEY'LL HEAR YOU.
BLURP?
BABY BABY OOH OOH OOOOOOH!
MY BABY IS A DOVESTAR!
PAM LOVES THIS SONG THE BEST!
I JUST KINDA LIKE IT!

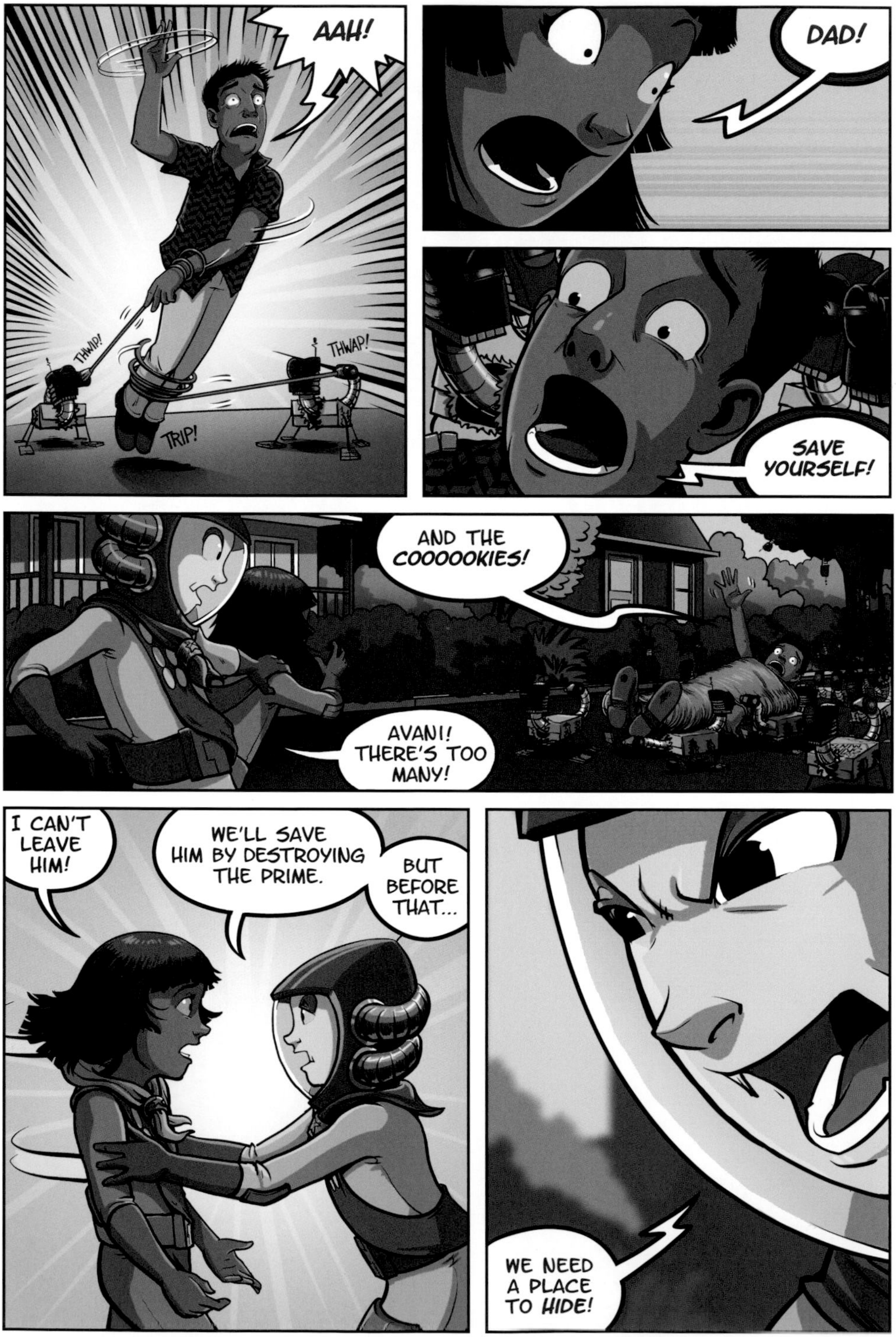
AAH!
THWIP!
THWAP!
TRIP!
DAD!
SAVE YOURSELF!
AND THE COOOOOKIES!
AVANI! THERE'S TOO MANY!
I CAN'T LEAVE HIM!
WE'LL SAVE HIM BY DESTROYING THE PRIME.
BUT BEFORE THAT...
WE NEED A PLACE TO HIDE!

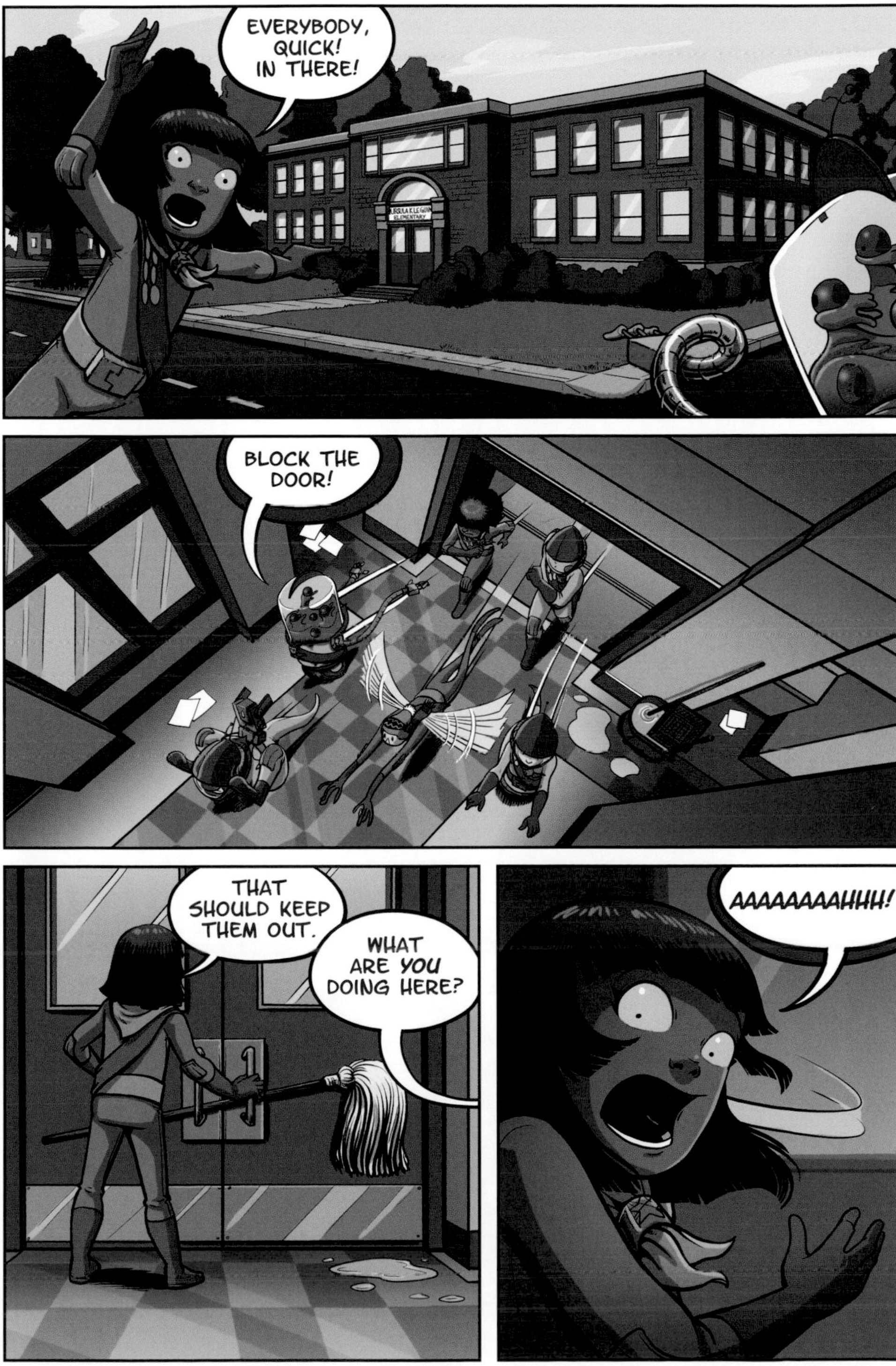
EVERYBODY, QUICK! IN THERE!
BLOCK THE DOOR!
THAT SHOULD KEEP THEM OUT.
WHAT ARE YOU DOING HERE?
AAAAAAAAHHH!

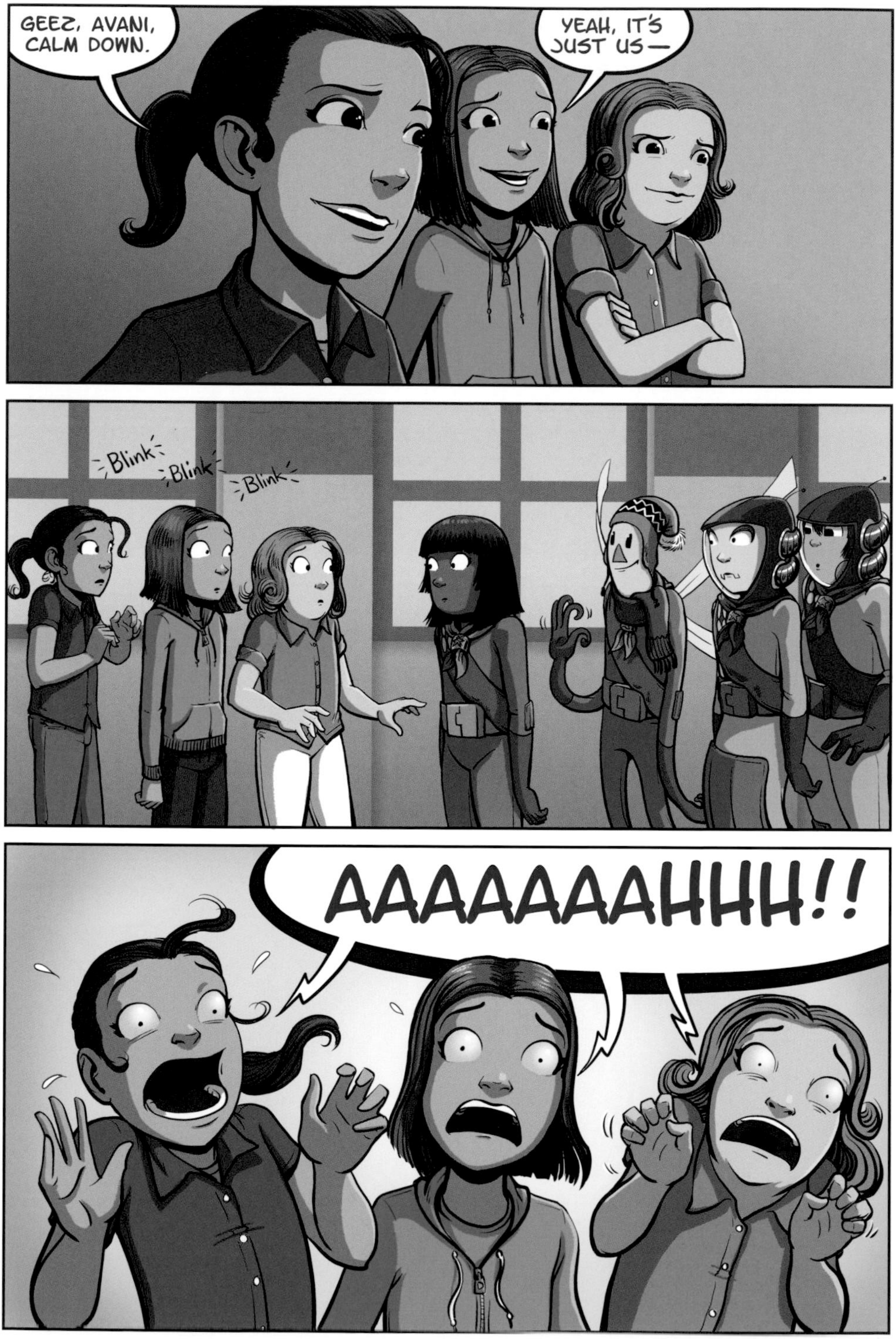
GEEZ, AVANI, CALM DOWN.
YEAH, IT'S JUST US—
Blink
Blink
Blink
AAAAAAAHHH!!

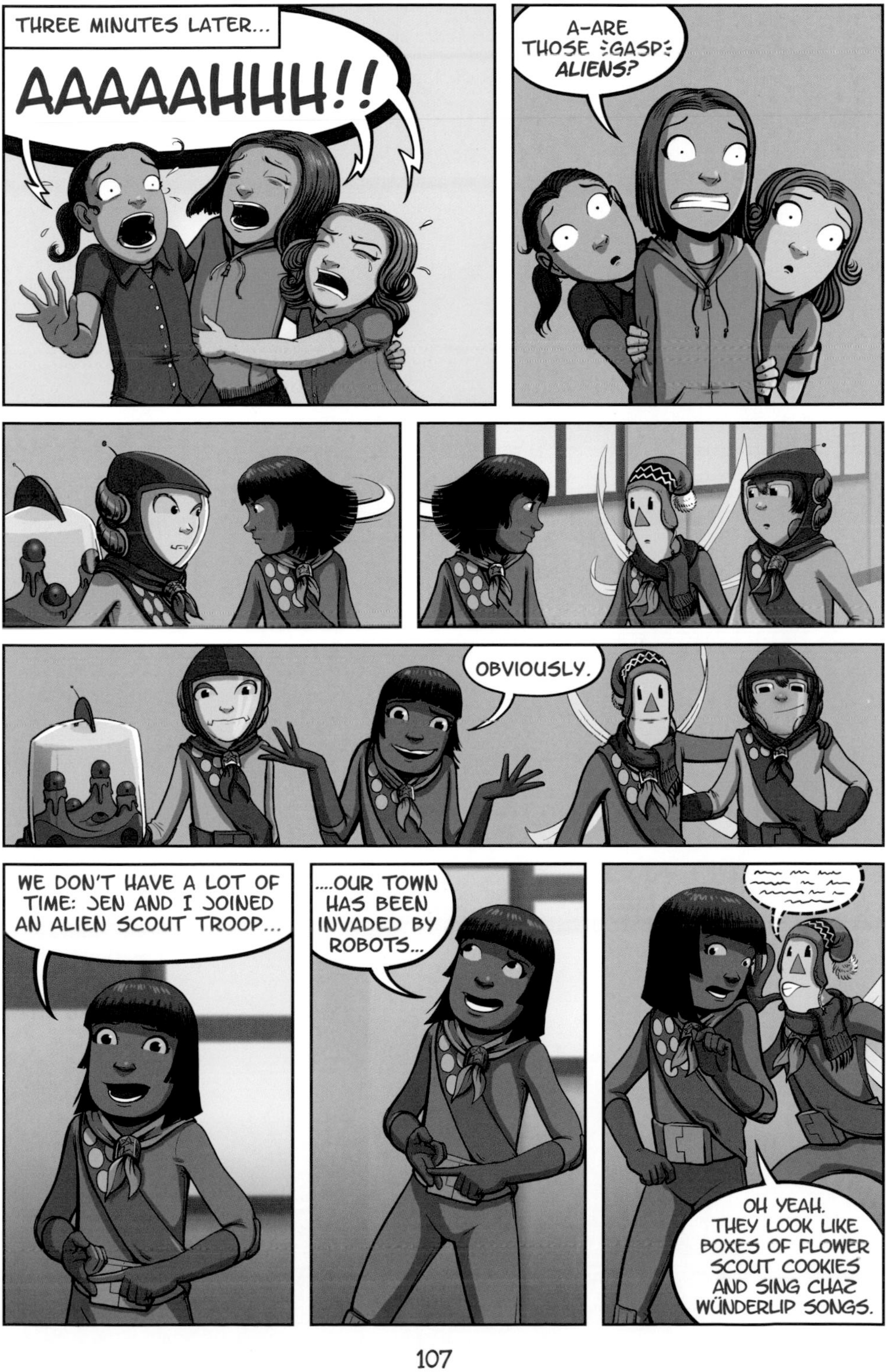
THREE MINUTES LATER...
AAAAAHHH!!
A-ARE THOSE ⸗GASP⸗ ALIENS?
OBVIOUSLY.
WE DON'T HAVE A LOT OF TIME: JEN AND I JOINED AN ALIEN SCOUT TROOP...
...OUR TOWN HAS BEEN INVADED BY ROBOTS...
OH YEAH. THEY LOOK LIKE BOXES OF FLOWER SCOUT COOKIES AND SING CHAZ WÜNDERLIP SONGS.

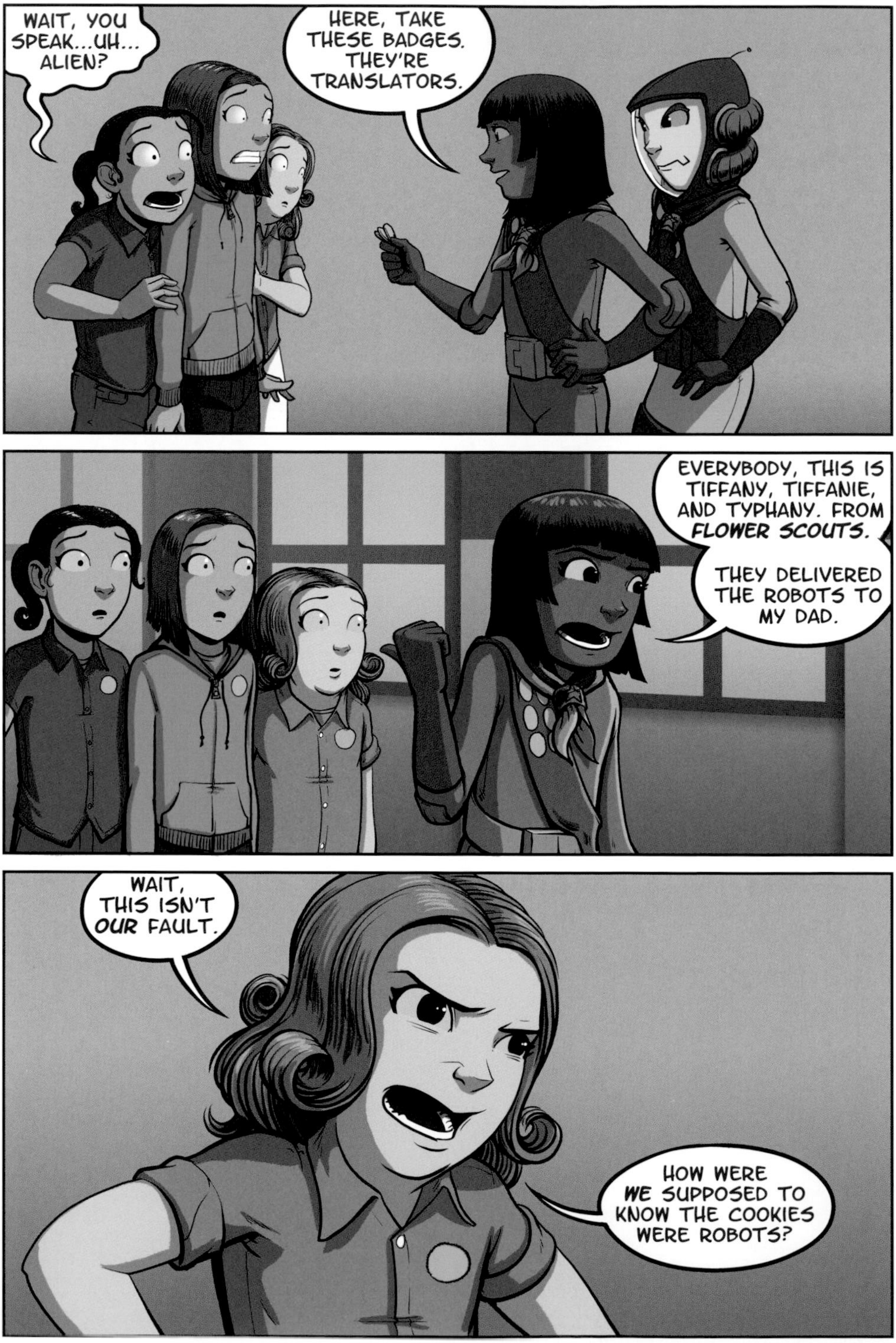
WAIT, YOU SPEAK...UH... ALIEN?
HERE, TAKE THESE BADGES. THEY'RE TRANSLATORS.
EVERYBODY, THIS IS TIFFANY, TIFFANIE, AND TYPHANY. FROM FLOWER SCOUTS.
THEY DELIVERED THE ROBOTS TO MY DAD.
WAIT, THIS ISN'T OUR FAULT.
HOW WERE WE SUPPOSED TO KNOW THE COOKIES WERE ROBOTS?

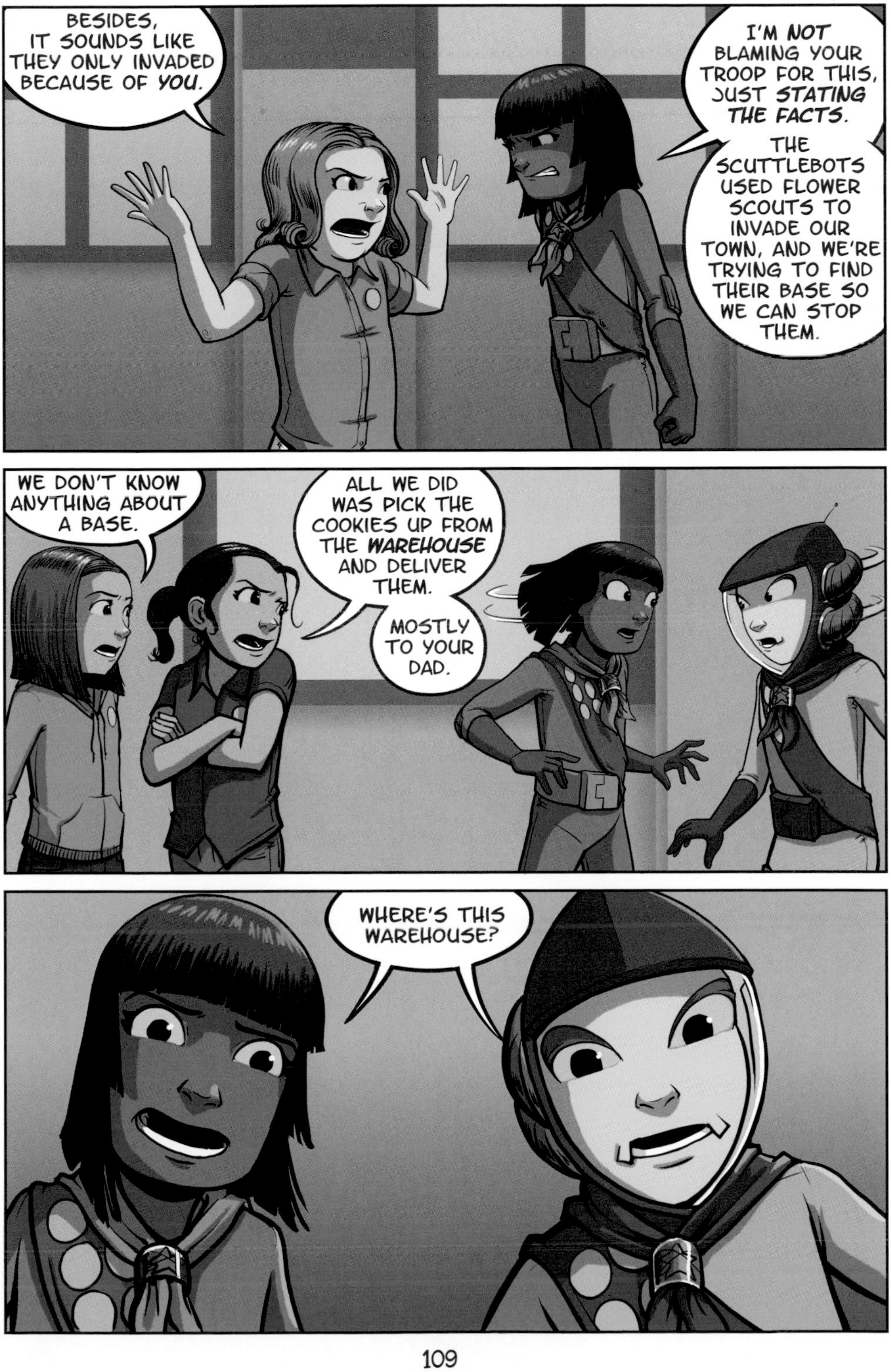
BESIDES, IT SOUNDS LIKE THEY ONLY INVADED BECAUSE OF YOU.
I'M NOT BLAMING YOUR TROOP FOR THIS, JUST STATING THE FACTS.
THE SCUTTLEBOTS USED FLOWER SCOUTS TO INVADE OUR TOWN, AND WE'RE TRYING TO FIND THEIR BASE SO WE CAN STOP THEM.
WE DON'T KNOW ANYTHING ABOUT A BASE.
ALL WE DID WAS PICK THE COOKIES UP FROM THE WAREHOUSE AND DELIVER THEM.
MOSTLY TO YOUR DAD.
WHERE'S THIS WAREHOUSE?

PART 4

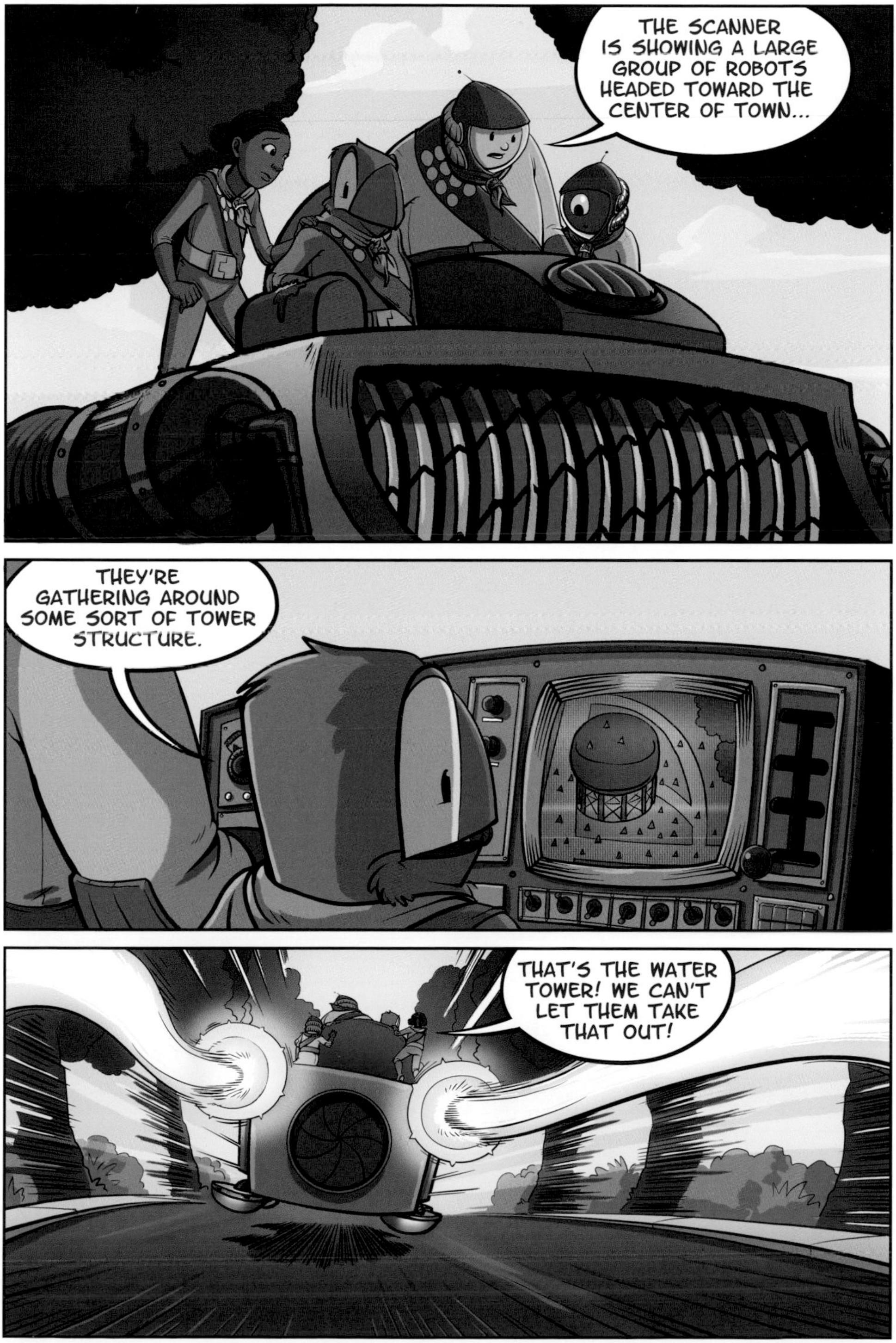
THE SCANNER IS SHOWING A LARGE GROUP OF ROBOTS HEADED TOWARD THE CENTER OF TOWN...
THEY'RE GATHERING AROUND SOME SORT OF TOWER STRUCTURE.
THAT'S THE WATER TOWER! WE CAN'T LET THEM TAKE THAT OUT!

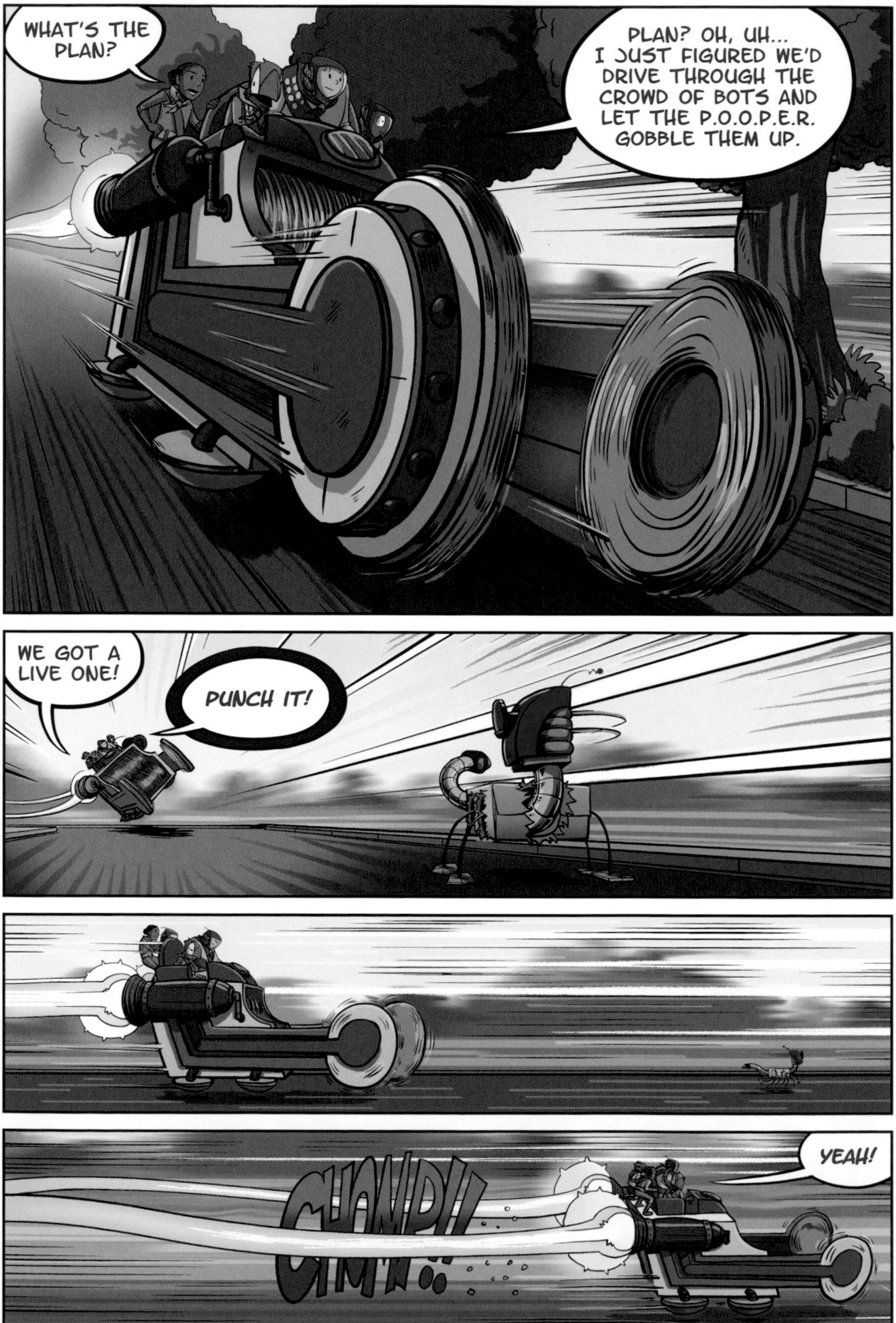
WHAT'S THE PLAN?
PLAN? OH, UH... I JUST FIGURED WE'D DRIVE THROUGH THE CROWD OF BOTS AND LET THE P.O.O.P.E.R. GOBBLE THEM UP.
WE GOT A LIVE ONE!
PUNCH IT!
CHOMP!!
YEAH!

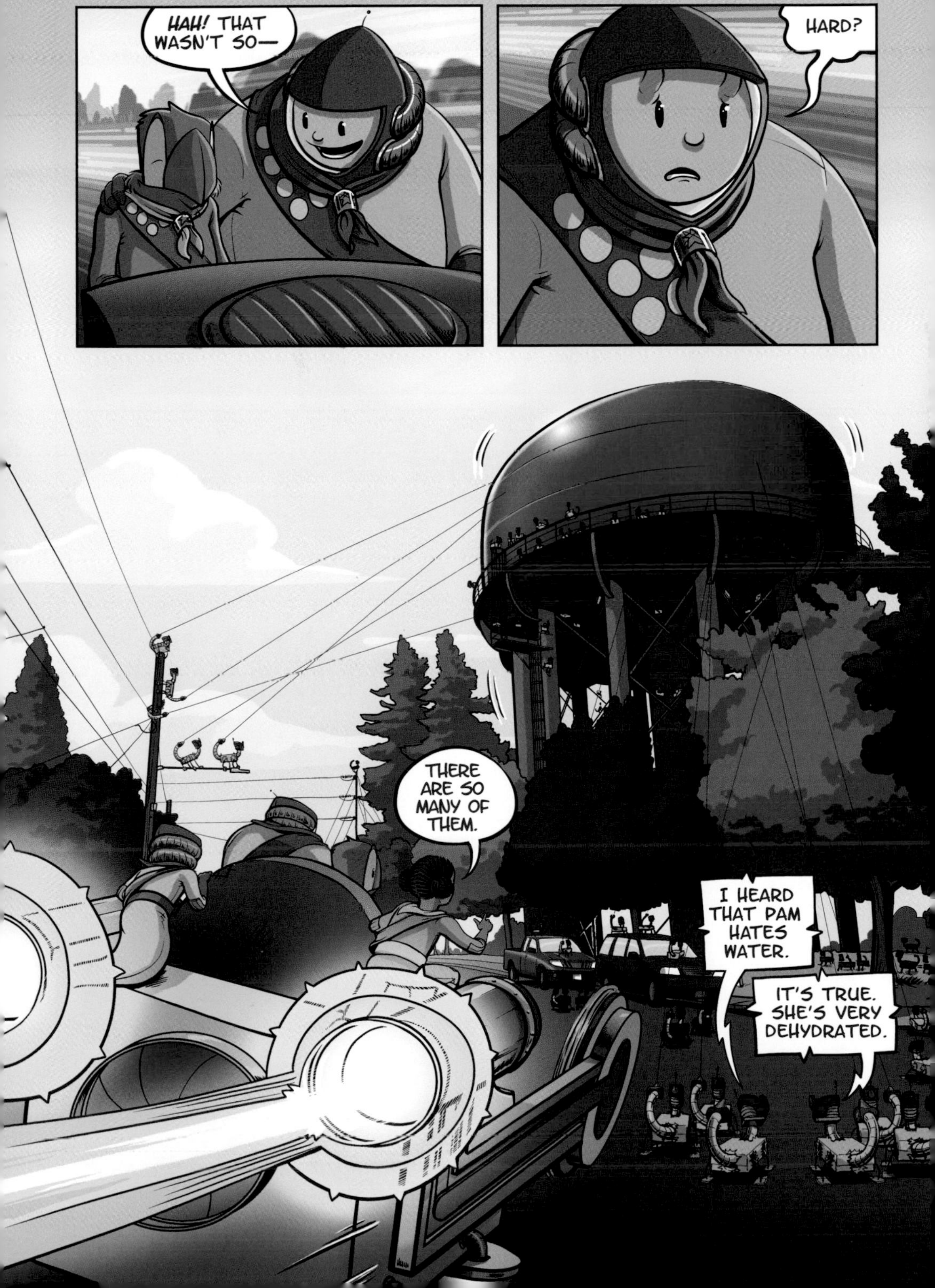
HAH! THAT WASN'T SO—
HARD?
THERE ARE SO MANY OF THEM.
I HEARD THAT PAM HATES WATER.
IT'S TRUE. SHE'S VERY DEHYDRATED.

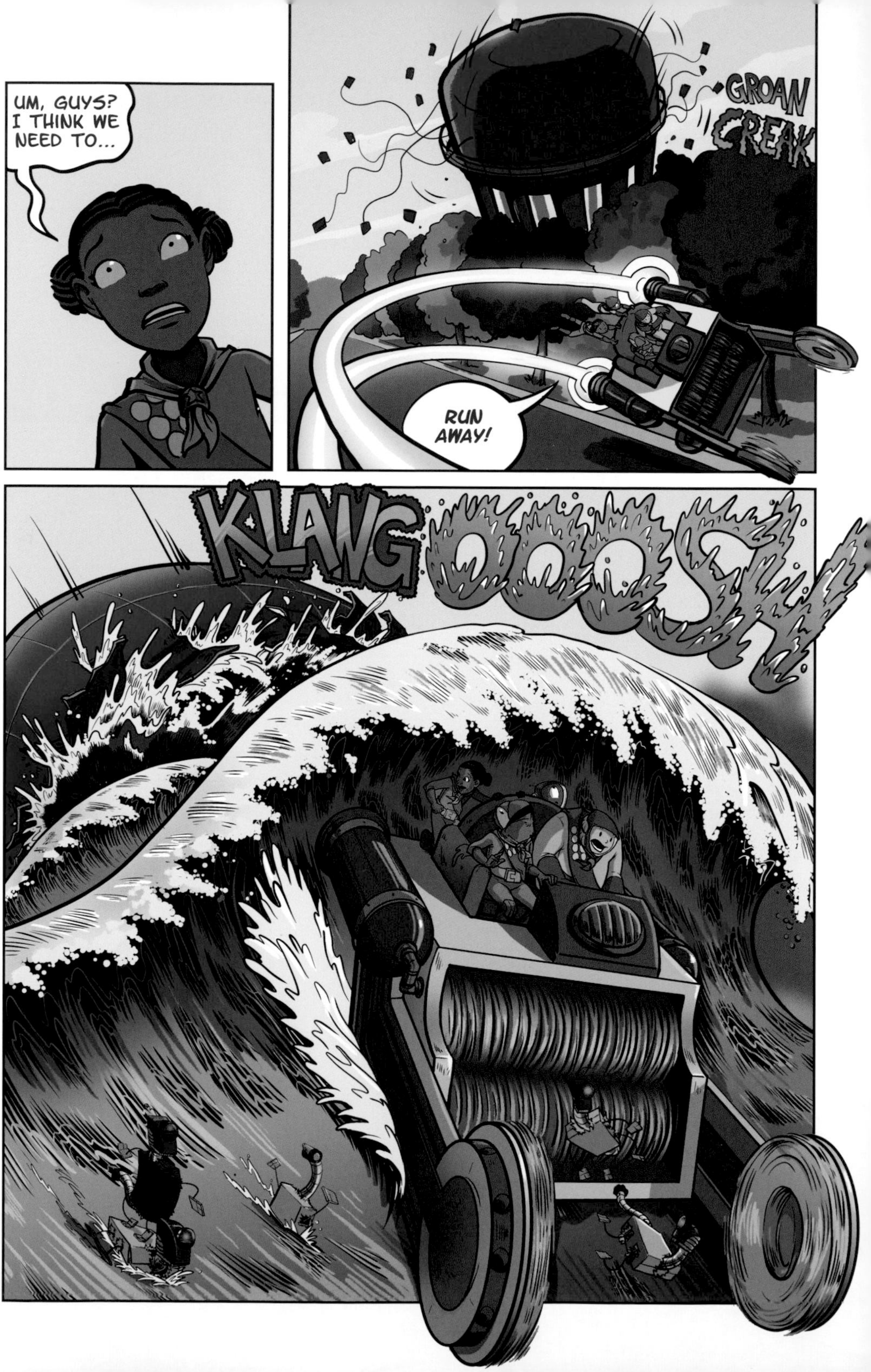
UM, GUYS? I THINK WE NEED TO...
GROAN
CREAK
RUN AWAY!
KLANG
OOOSH

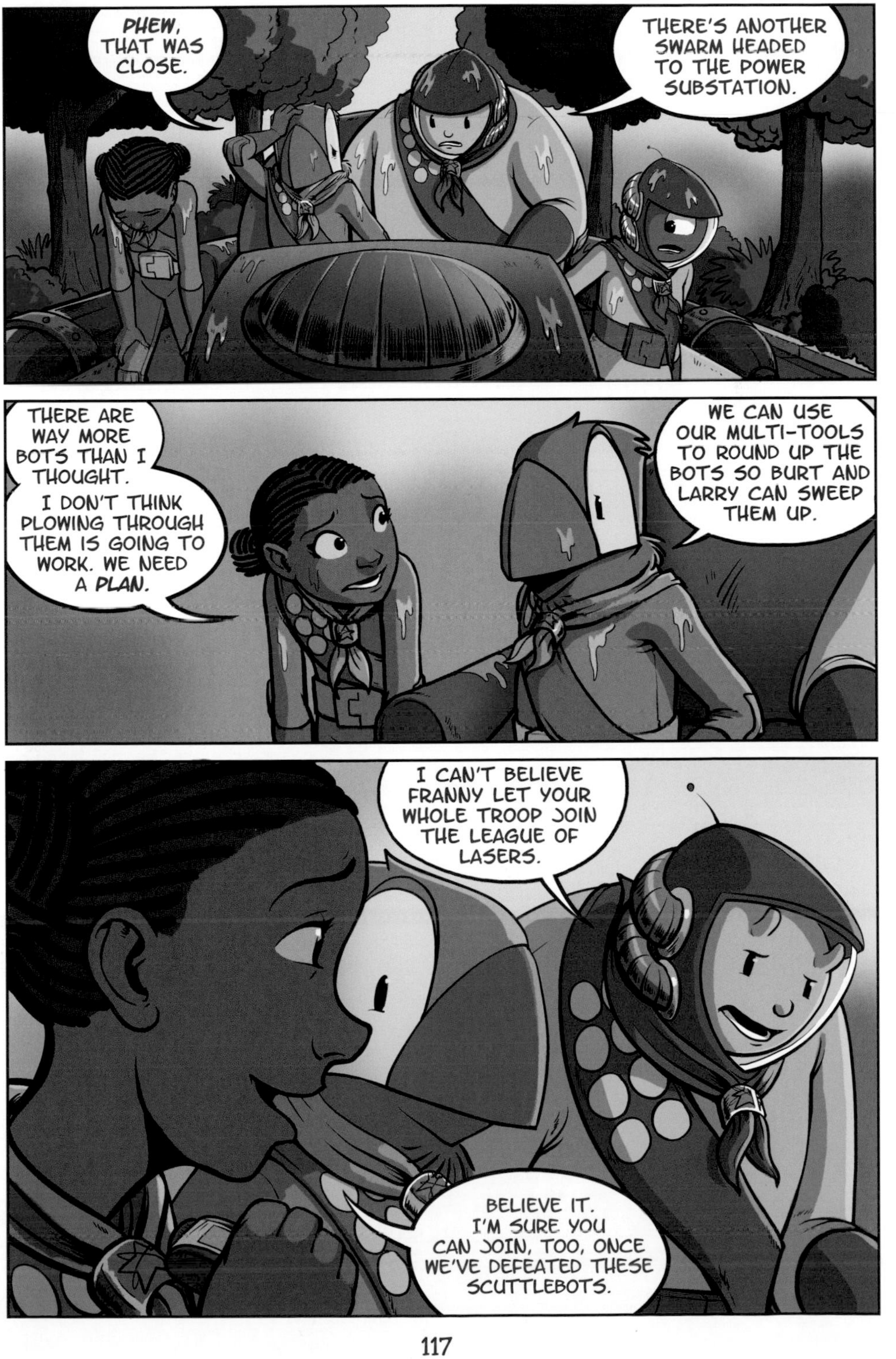
PHEW, THAT WAS CLOSE.
THERE'S ANOTHER SWARM HEADED TO THE POWER SUBSTATION.
THERE ARE WAY MORE BOTS THAN I THOUGHT.
I DON'T THINK PLOWING THROUGH THEM IS GOING TO WORK. WE NEED A PLAN.
WE CAN USE OUR MULTI-TOOLS TO ROUND UP THE BOTS SO BURT AND LARRY CAN SWEEP THEM UP.
I CAN'T BELIEVE FRANNY LET YOUR WHOLE TROOP JOIN THE LEAGUE OF LASERS.
BELIEVE IT. I'M SURE YOU CAN JOIN, TOO, ONCE WE'VE DEFEATED THESE SCUTTLEBOTS.

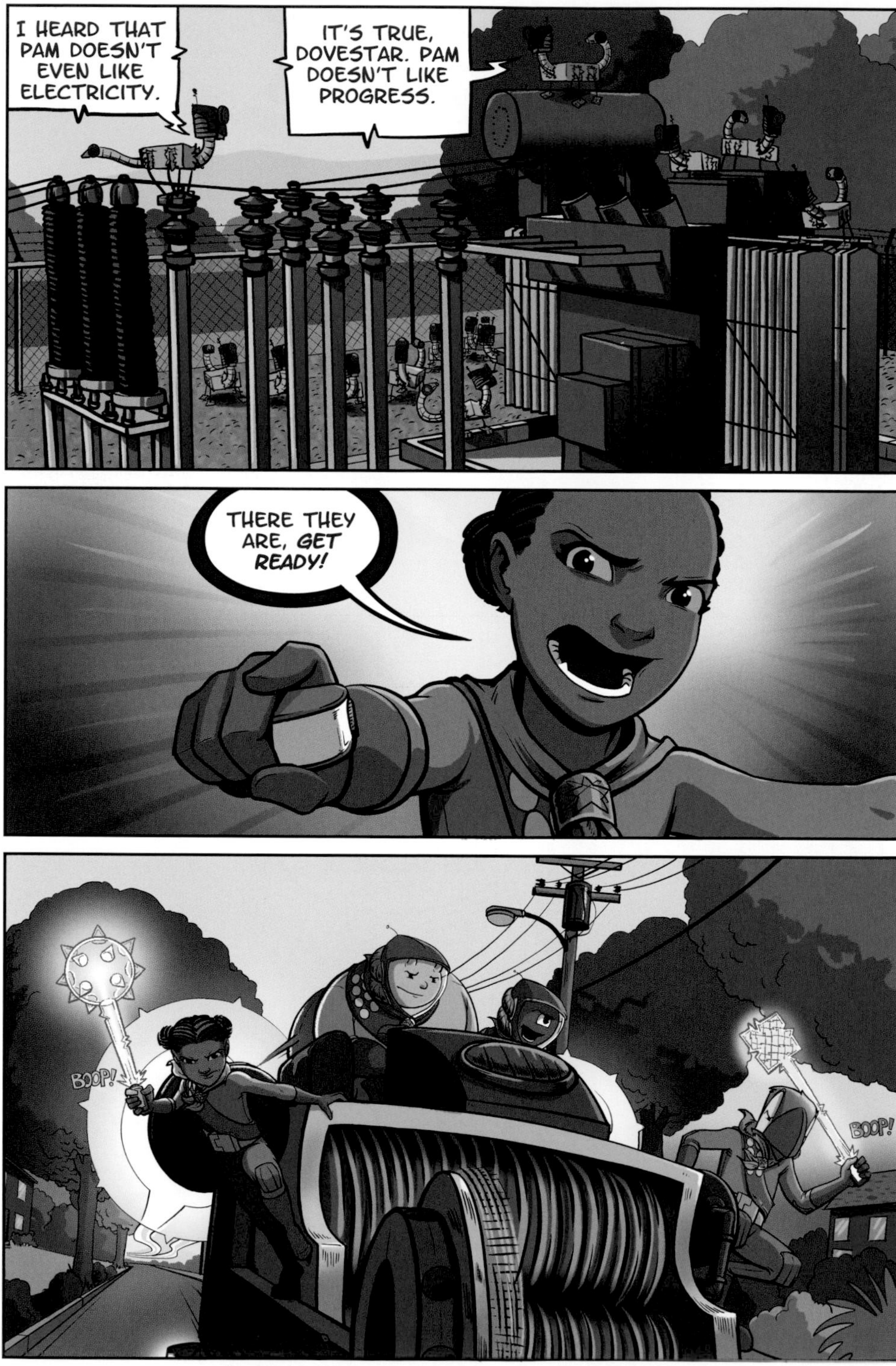

I HEARD THAT PAM DOESN'T EVEN LIKE ELECTRICITY.
IT'S TRUE, DOVESTAR. PAM DOESN'T LIKE PROGRESS.
THERE THEY ARE, GET READY!
BOOP!
BOOP!

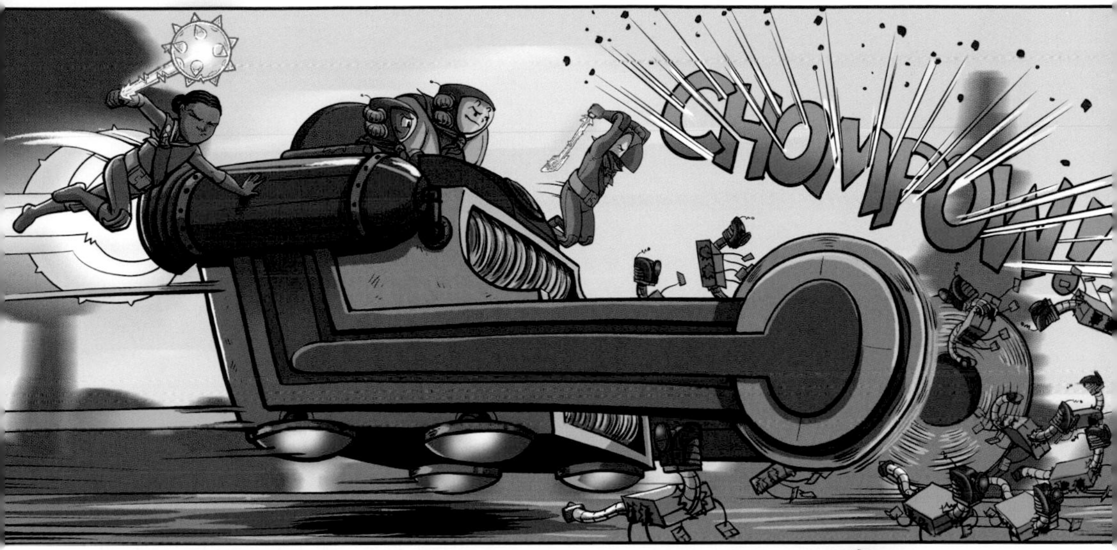
CHOMPOWW!

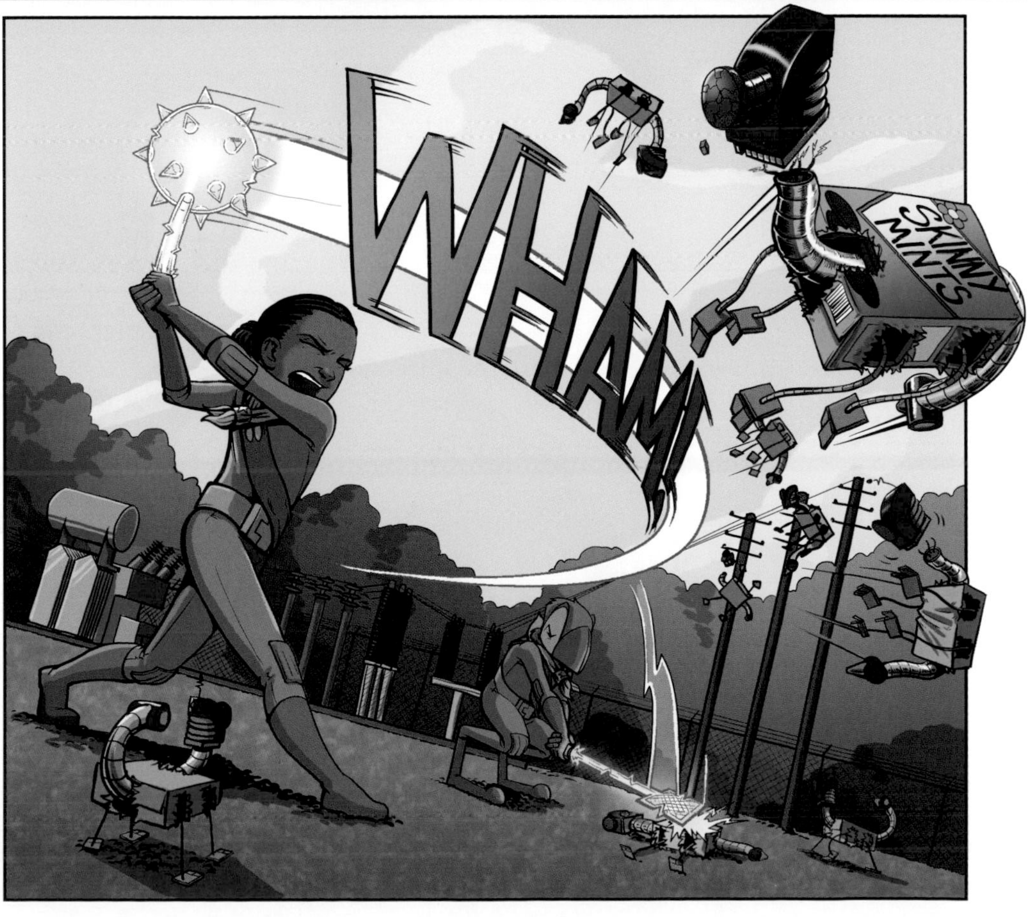
WHAM!
SKINNY MINTS

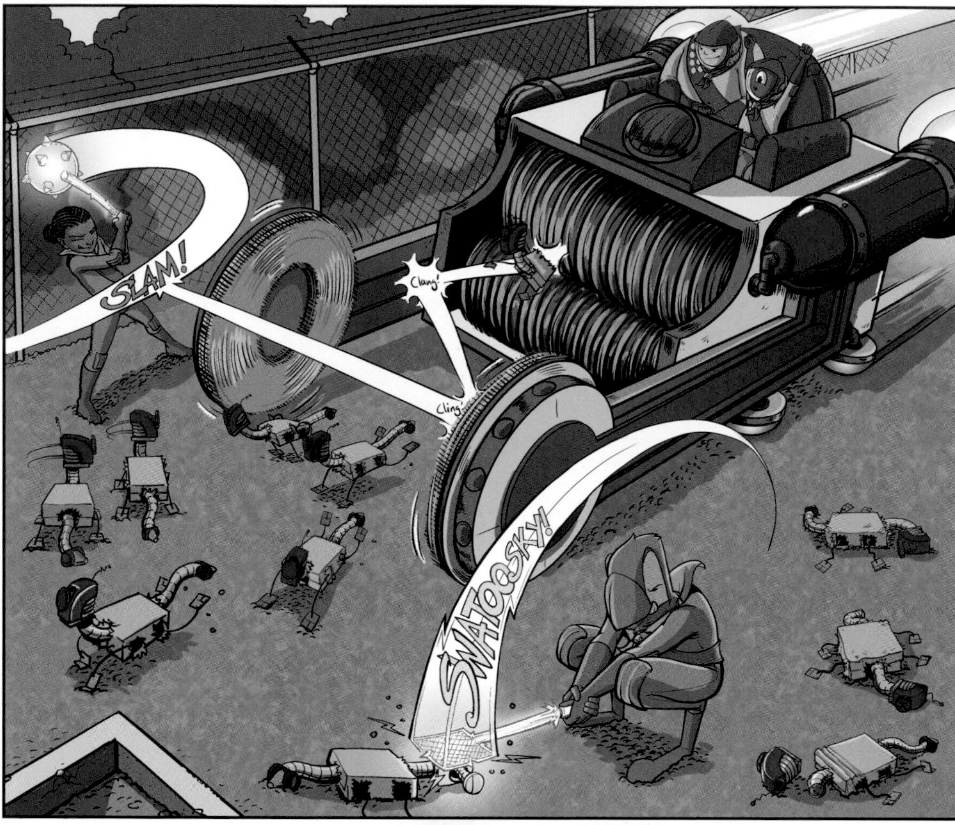
SLAM!
Clang!
SWATOOSKY!

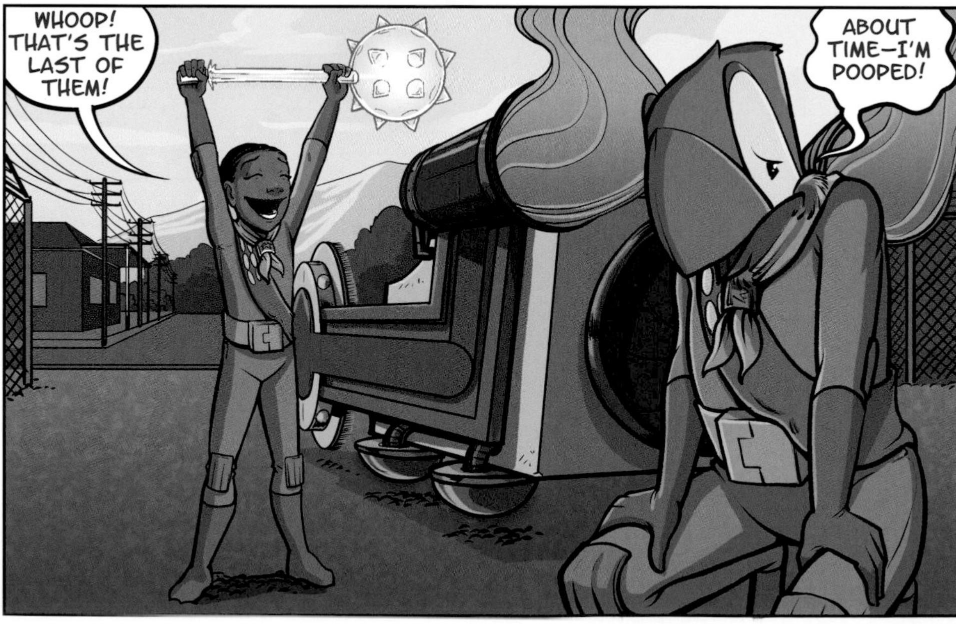
WHOOP! THAT'S THE LAST OF THEM!
ABOUT TIME—I'M POOPED!

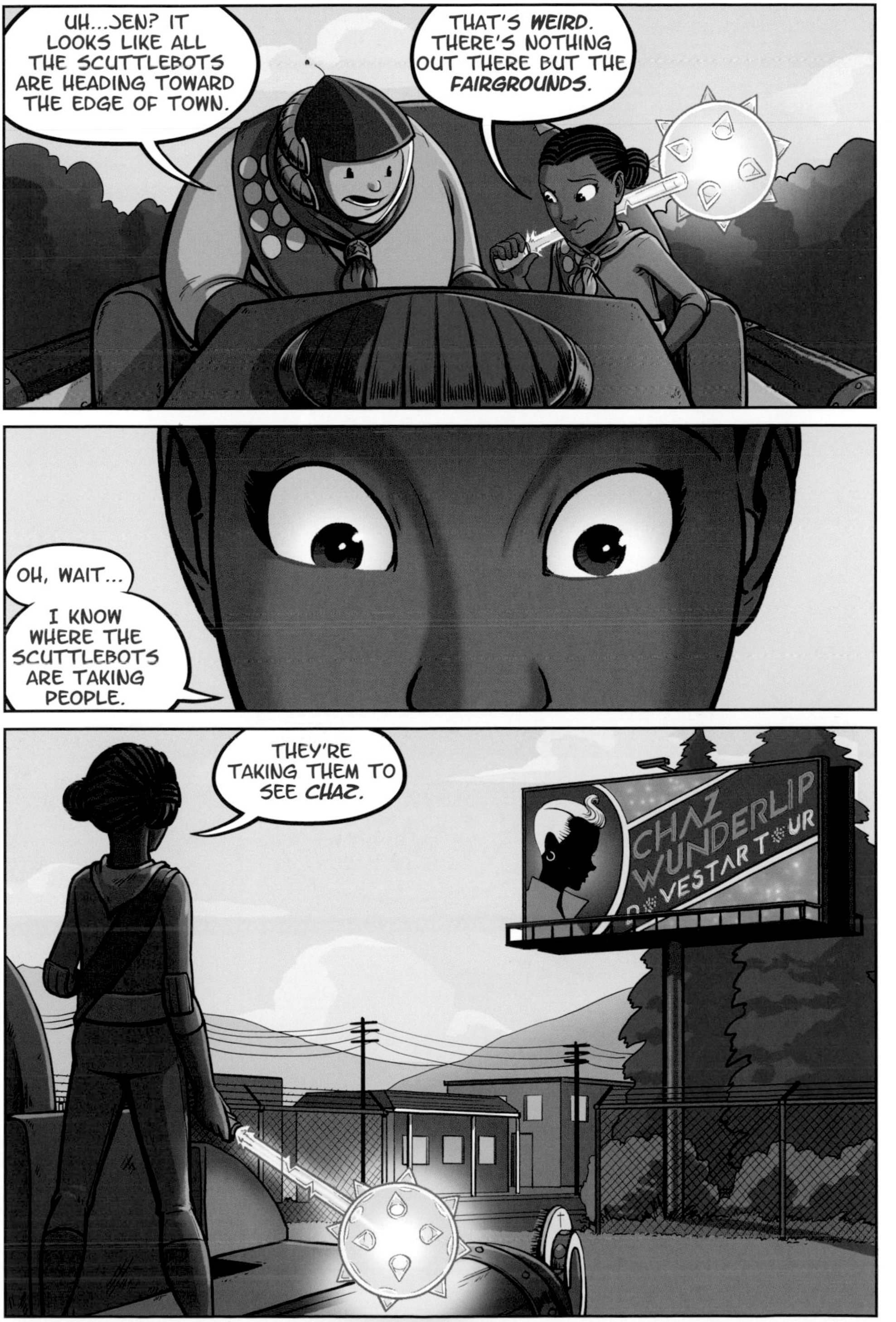
UH...JEN? IT LOOKS LIKE ALL THE SCUTTLEBOTS ARE HEADING TOWARD THE EDGE OF TOWN.
THAT'S *WEIRD*. THERE'S NOTHING OUT THERE BUT THE *FAIRGROUNDS*.
OH, WAIT...
I KNOW WHERE THE SCUTTLEBOTS ARE TAKING PEOPLE.
THEY'RE TAKING THEM TO SEE *CHAZ*.
CHAZ WUNDERLIP

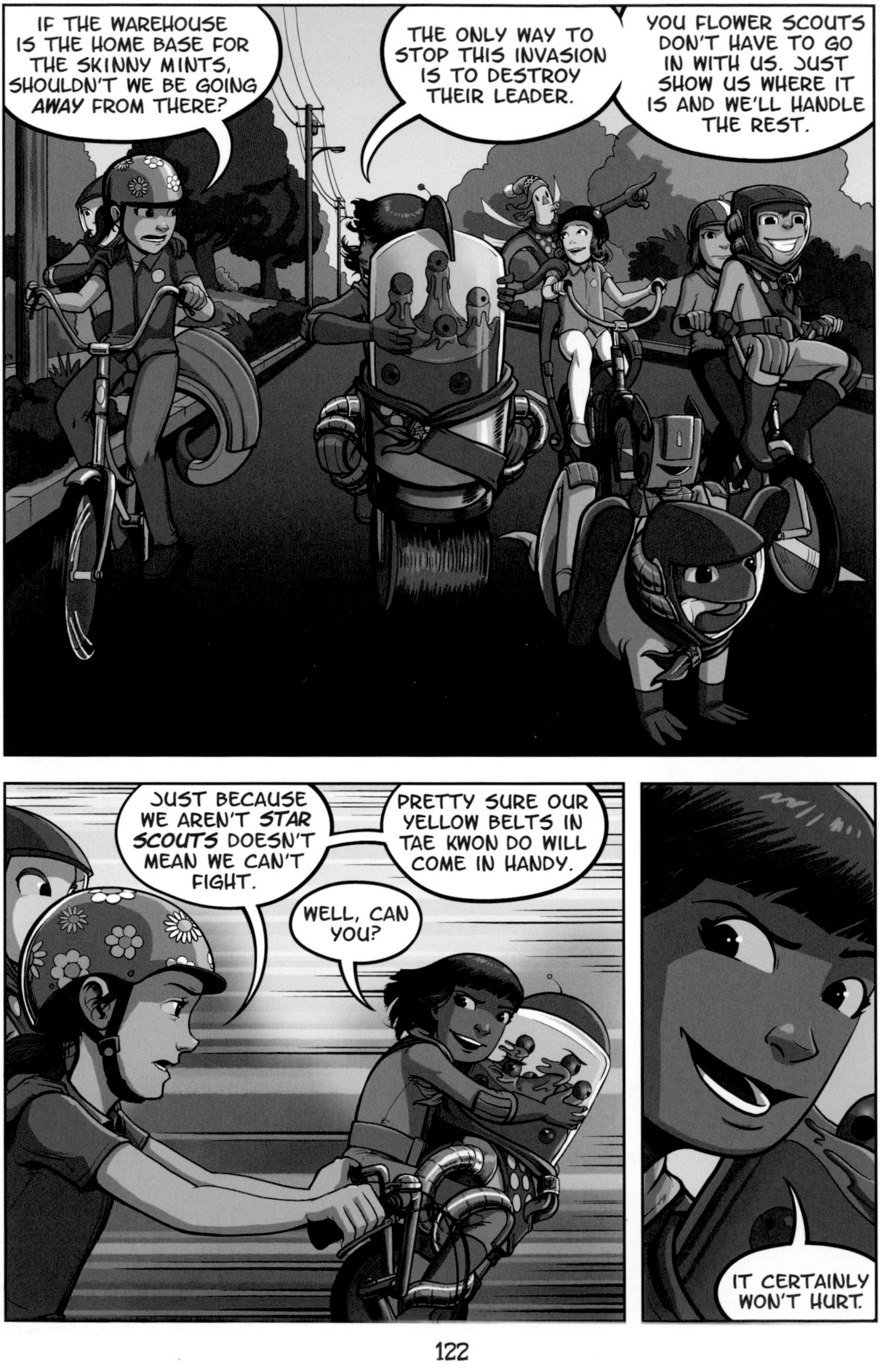
IF THE WAREHOUSE IS THE HOME BASE FOR THE SKINNY MINTS, SHOULDN'T WE BE GOING *AWAY* FROM THERE?
THE ONLY WAY TO STOP THIS INVASION IS TO DESTROY THEIR LEADER.
YOU FLOWER SCOUTS DON'T HAVE TO GO IN WITH US. JUST SHOW US WHERE IT IS AND WE'LL HANDLE THE REST.
JUST BECAUSE WE AREN'T **STAR SCOUTS** DOESN'T MEAN WE CAN'T FIGHT.
PRETTY SURE OUR YELLOW BELTS IN TAE KWON DO WILL COME IN HANDY.
WELL, CAN YOU?
IT CERTAINLY WON'T HURT.

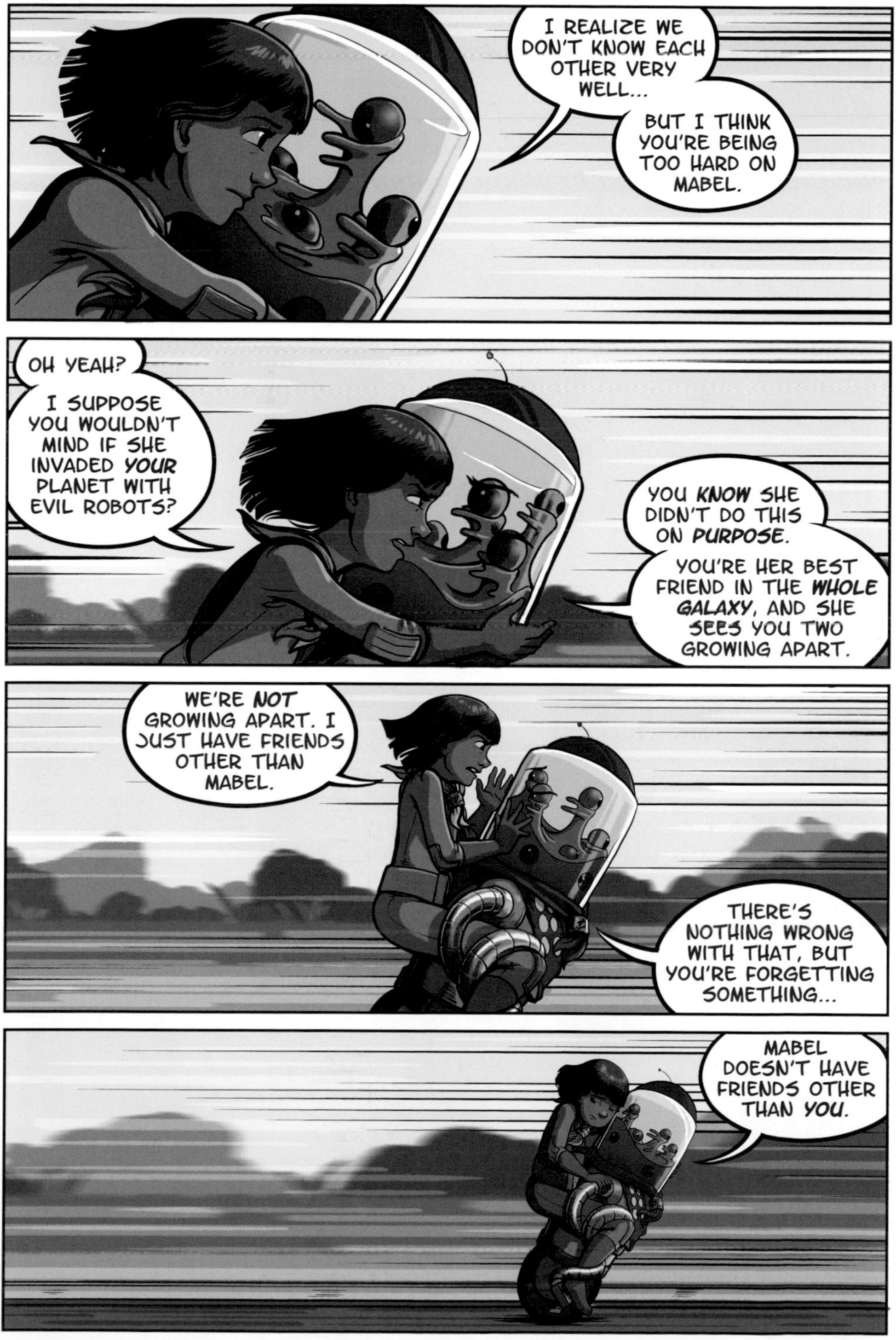

Panel 1:

I REALIZE WE DON'T KNOW EACH OTHER VERY WELL...

BUT I THINK YOU'RE BEING TOO HARD ON MABEL.

Panel 2:

OH YEAH? I SUPPOSE YOU WOULDN'T MIND IF SHE INVADED *YOUR* PLANET WITH EVIL ROBOTS?

YOU *KNOW* SHE DIDN'T DO THIS ON *PURPOSE.*

YOU'RE HER BEST FRIEND IN THE *WHOLE GALAXY,* AND SHE SEES YOU TWO GROWING APART.

Panel 3:

WE'RE *NOT* GROWING APART. I JUST HAVE FRIENDS OTHER THAN MABEL.

THERE'S NOTHING WRONG WITH THAT, BUT YOU'RE FORGETTING SOMETHING...

Panel 4:

MABEL DOESN'T HAVE FRIENDS OTHER THAN *YOU.*

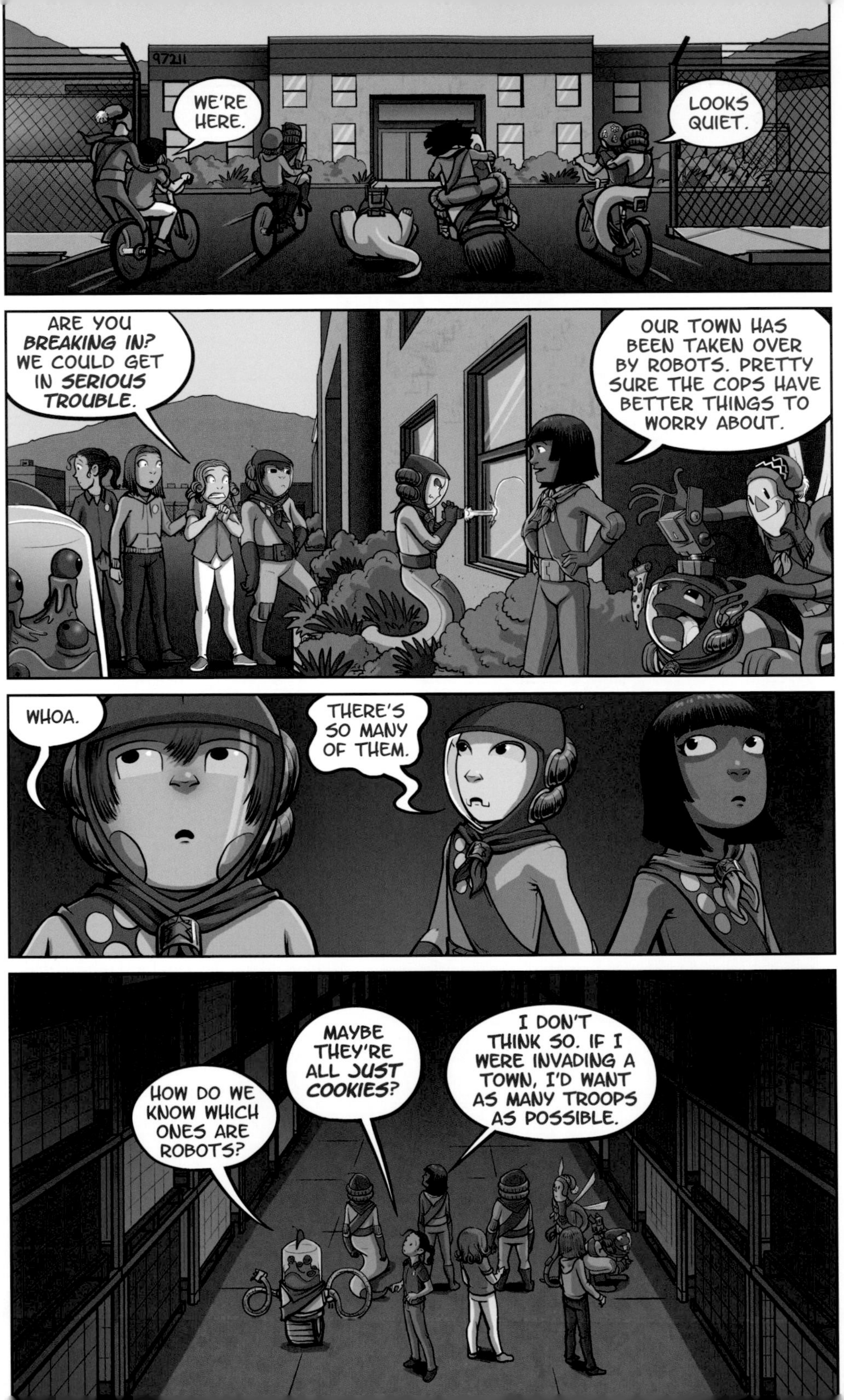
97211
WE'RE HERE.
LOOKS QUIET.
ARE YOU *BREAKING IN?* WE COULD GET IN *SERIOUS TROUBLE.*
OUR TOWN HAS BEEN TAKEN OVER BY ROBOTS. PRETTY SURE THE COPS HAVE BETTER THINGS TO WORRY ABOUT.
WHOA.
THERE'S SO MANY OF THEM.
HOW DO WE KNOW WHICH ONES ARE ROBOTS?
MAYBE THEY'RE ALL *JUST COOKIES?*
I DON'T THINK SO. IF I WERE INVADING A TOWN, I'D WANT AS MANY TROOPS AS POSSIBLE.

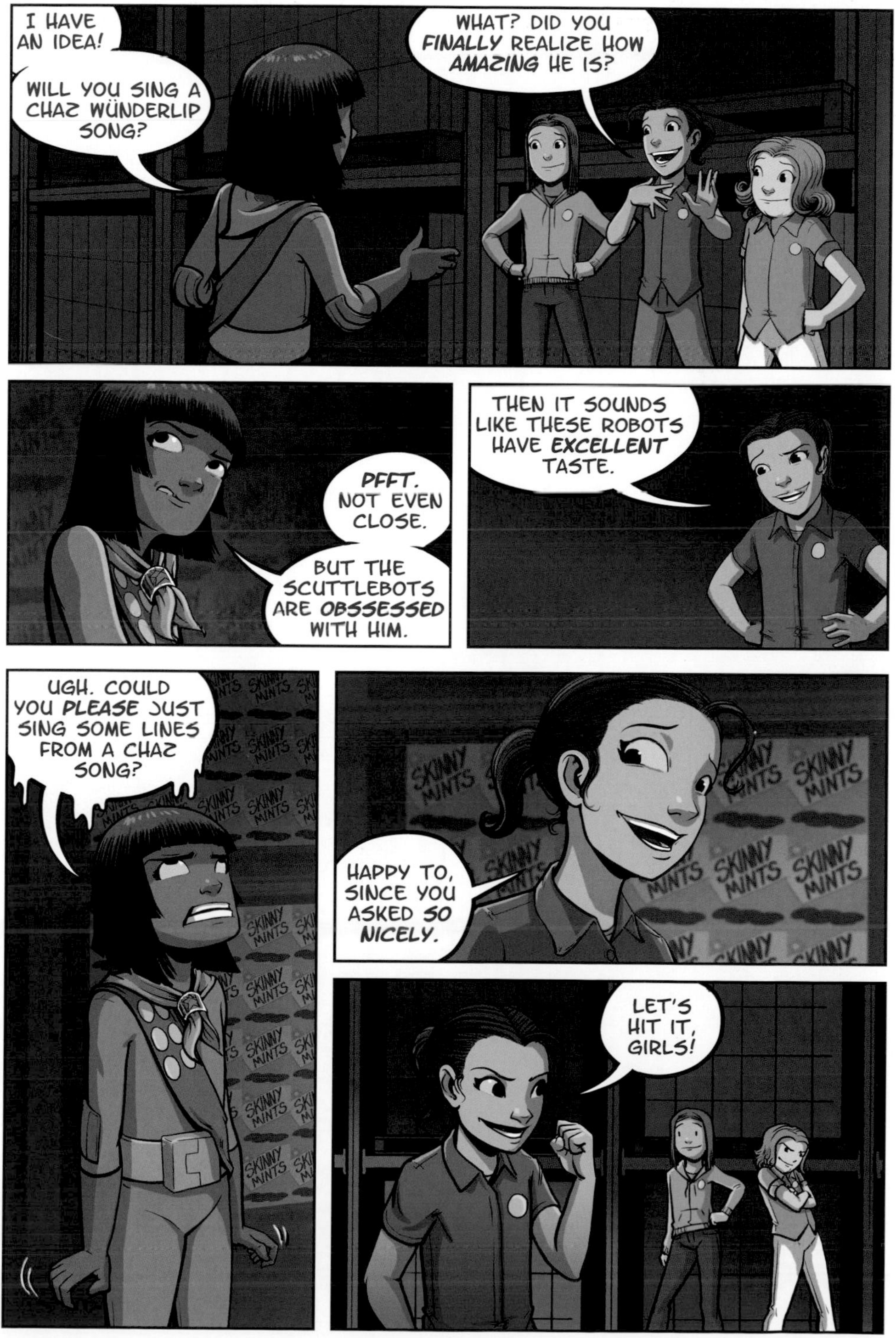
I HAVE AN IDEA!
WILL YOU SING A CHAZ WÜNDERLIP SONG?
WHAT? DID YOU FINALLY REALIZE HOW AMAZING HE IS?
PFFT. NOT EVEN CLOSE.
BUT THE SCUTTLEBOTS ARE OBSSESSED WITH HIM.
THEN IT SOUNDS LIKE THESE ROBOTS HAVE EXCELLENT TASTE.
UGH. COULD YOU PLEASE JUST SING SOME LINES FROM A CHAZ SONG?
HAPPY TO, SINCE YOU ASKED SO NICELY.
LET'S HIT IT, GIRLS!

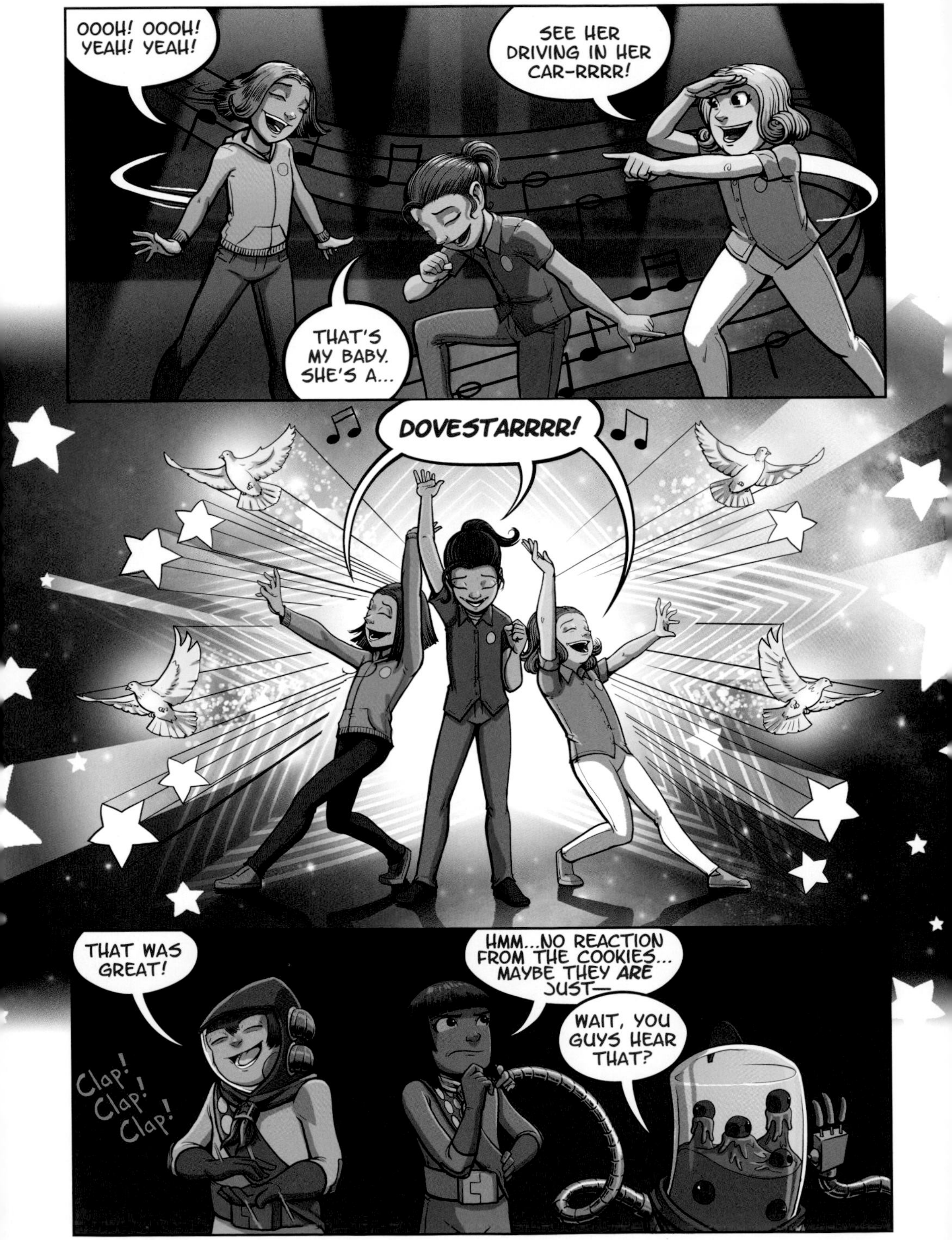
OOOH! OOOH! YEAH! YEAH!
SEE HER DRIVING IN HER CAR-RRRR!
THAT'S MY BABY. SHE'S A...
DOVESTARRRR!
THAT WAS GREAT!
Clap! Clap! Clap!
HMM...NO REACTION FROM THE COOKIES... MAYBE THEY ARE JUST—
WAIT, YOU GUYS HEAR THAT?

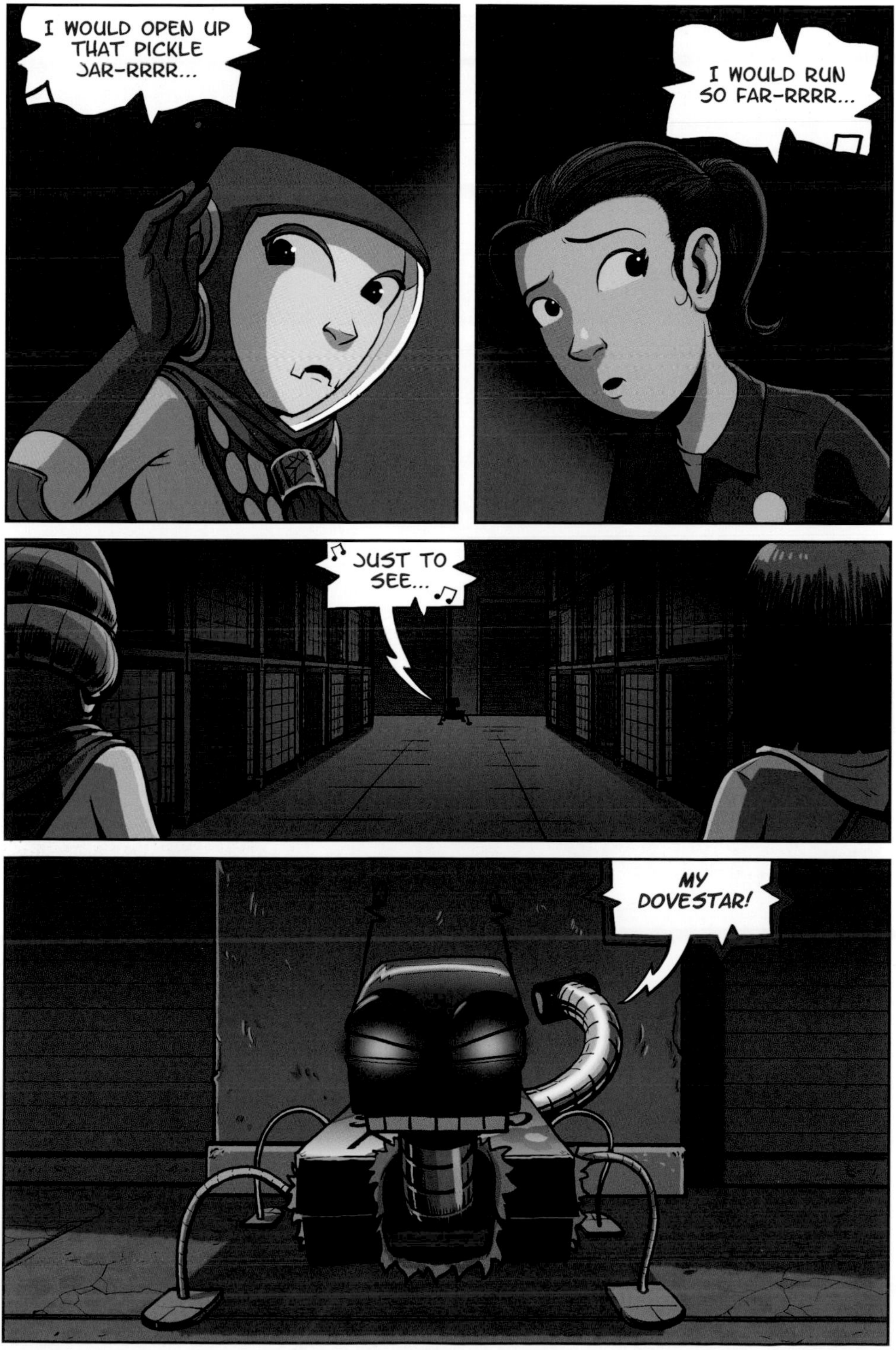
I WOULD OPEN UP THAT PICKLE JAR-RRRR...
I WOULD RUN SO FAR-RRRR...
JUST TO SEE...
MY DOVESTAR!

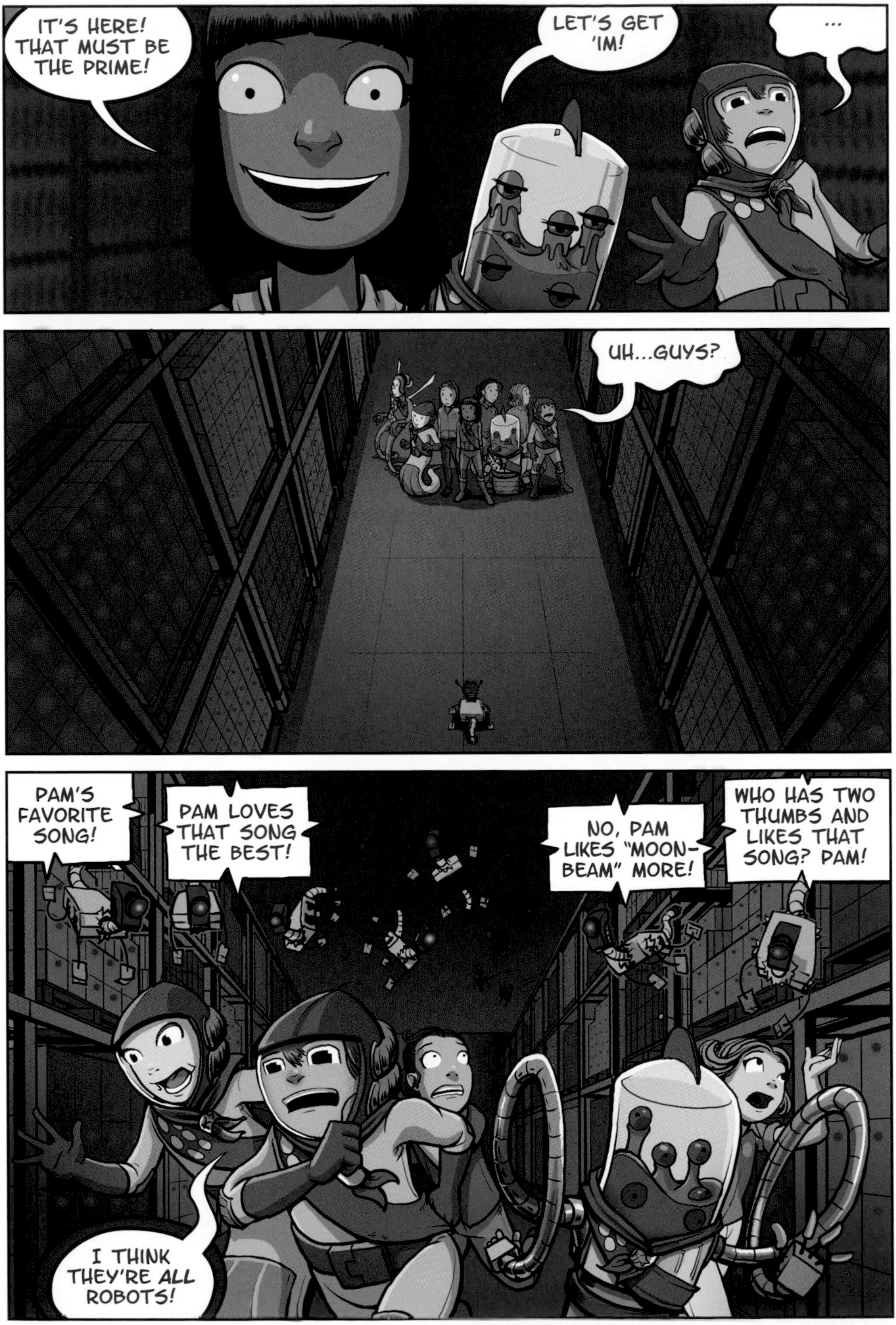
IT'S HERE! THAT MUST BE THE PRIME!
LET'S GET 'IM!
...
UH...GUYS?
PAM'S FAVORITE SONG!
PAM LOVES THAT SONG THE BEST!
NO, PAM LIKES "MOON-BEAM" MORE!
WHO HAS TWO THUMBS AND LIKES THAT SONG? PAM!
I THINK THEY'RE ALL ROBOTS!

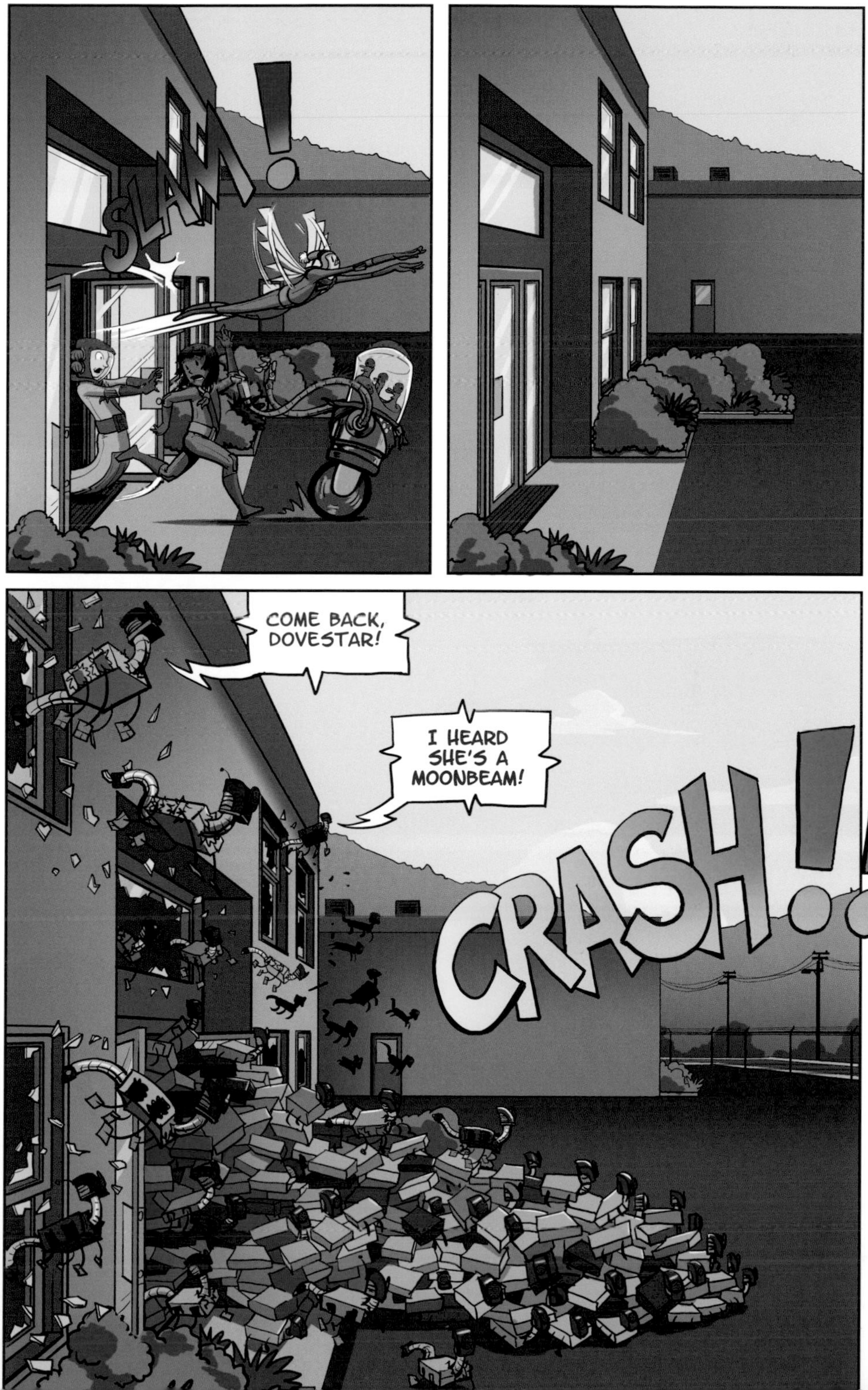
SLAM!
COME BACK, DOVESTAR!
I HEARD SHE'S A MOONBEAM!
CRASH!!!

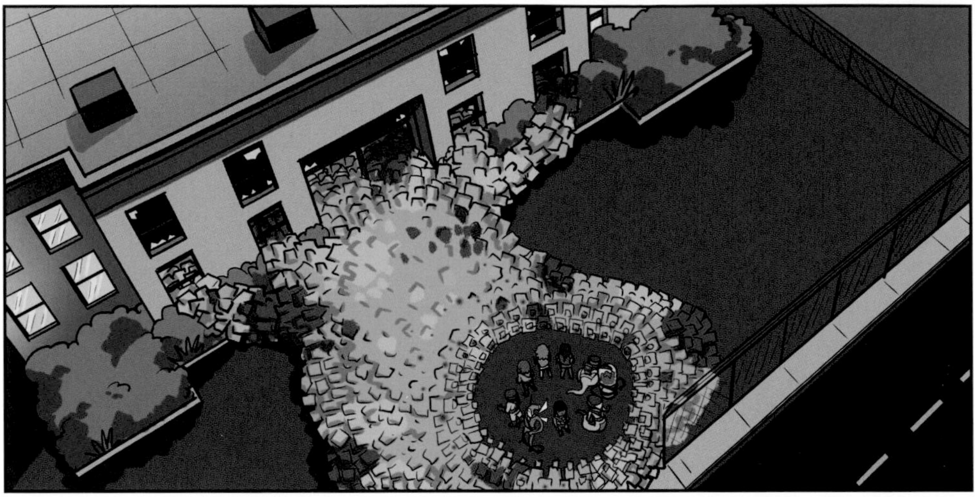

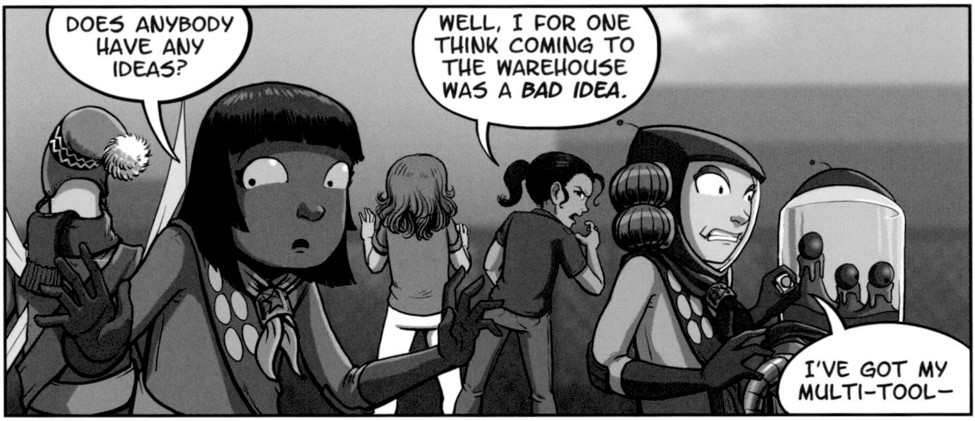
DOES ANYBODY HAVE ANY IDEAS?
WELL, I FOR ONE THINK COMING TO THE WAREHOUSE WAS A *BAD IDEA.*
I'VE GOT MY MULTI-TOOL—

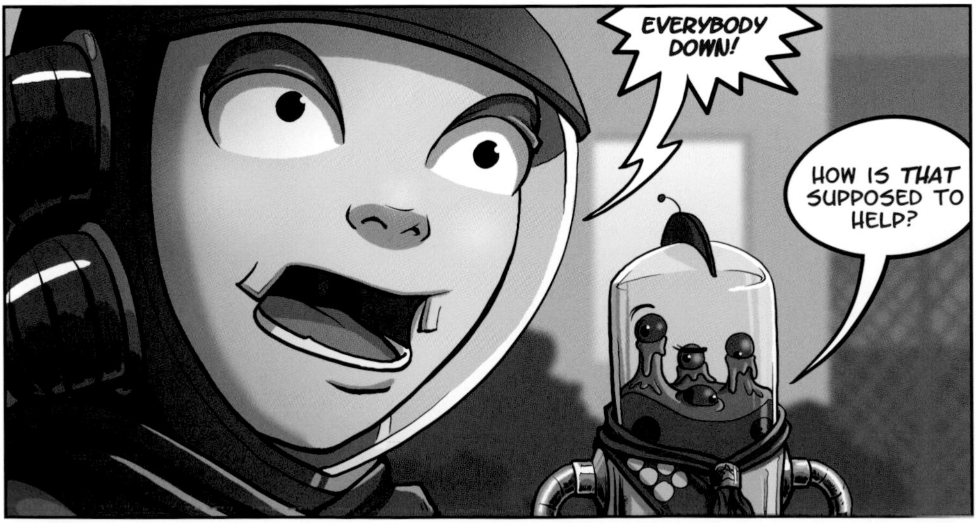
EVERYBODY DOWN!
HOW IS *THAT* SUPPOSED TO HELP?

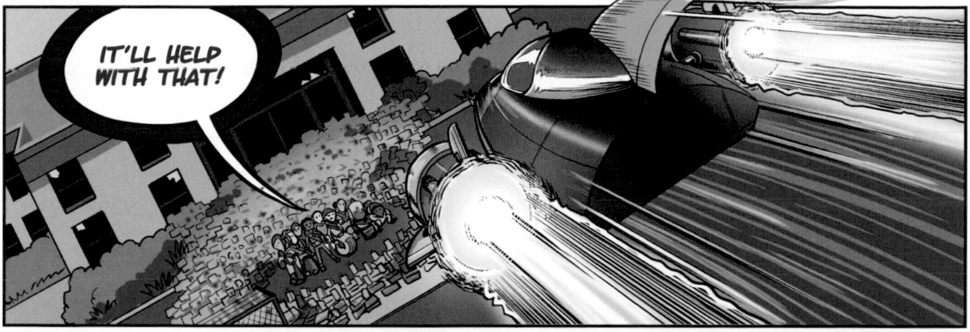
IT'LL HELP WITH THAT!

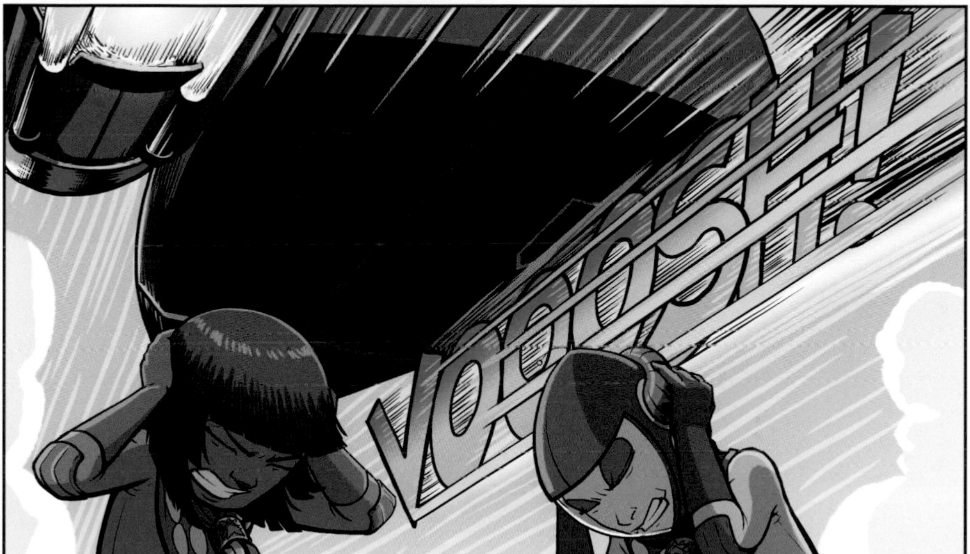
VOOOOSH!!

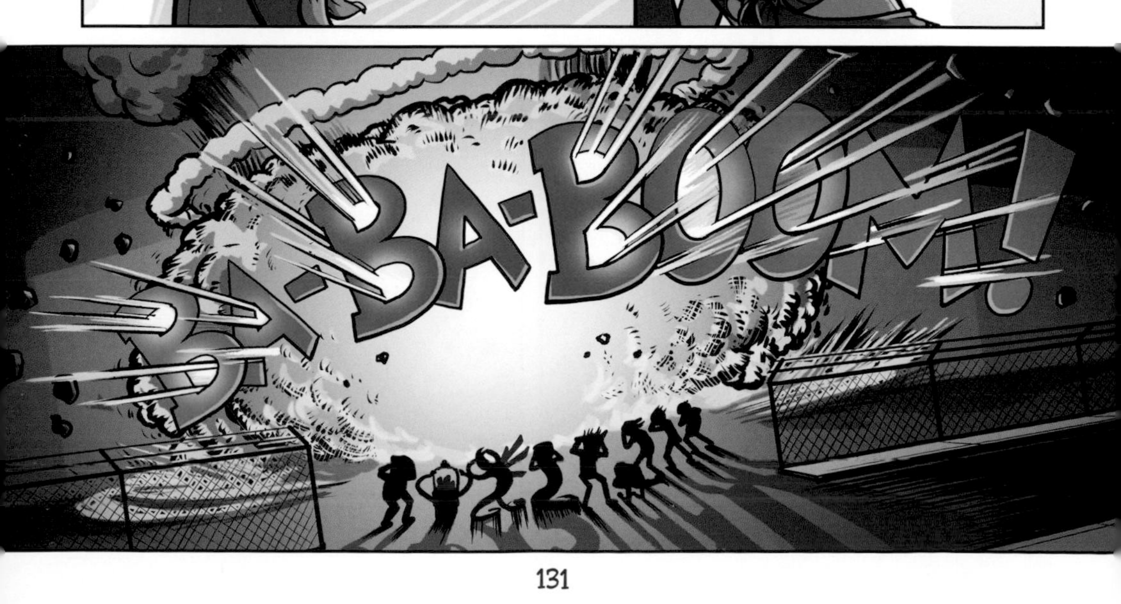
KA-BA-BOOM!!

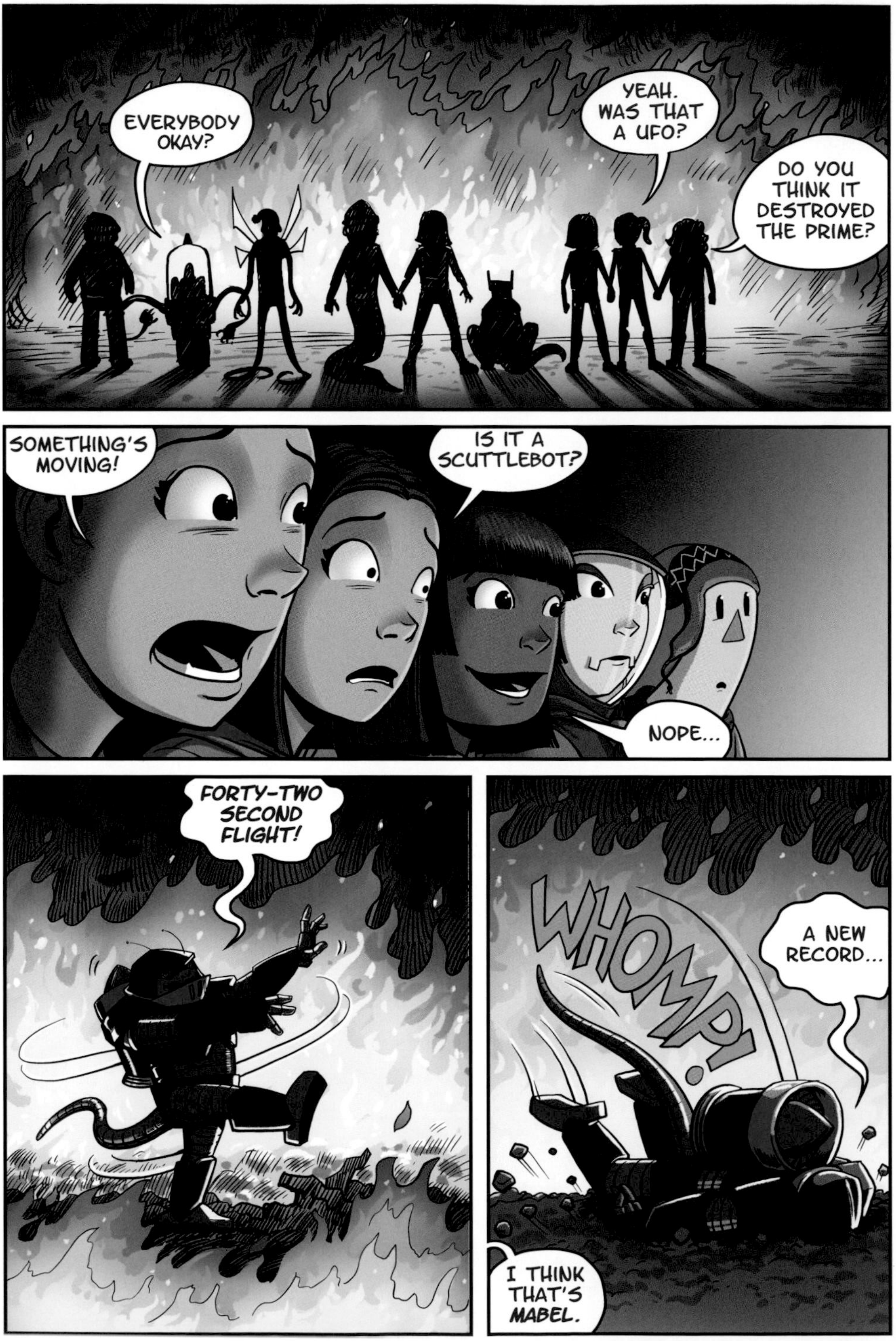
EVERYBODY OKAY?
YEAH. WAS THAT A UFO?
DO YOU THINK IT DESTROYED THE PRIME?
SOMETHING'S MOVING!
IS IT A SCUTTLEBOT?
NOPE...
FORTY-TWO SECOND FLIGHT!
WHOMP!
A NEW RECORD...
I THINK THAT'S MABEL.

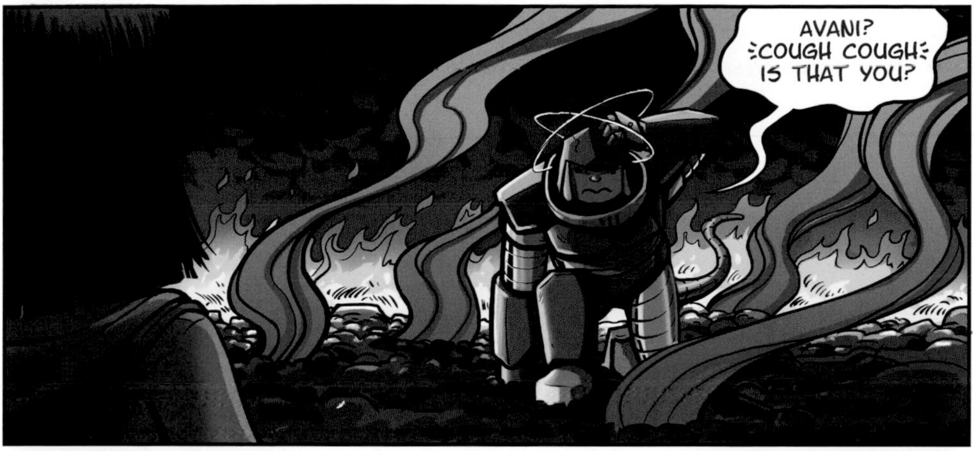
AVANI? ≈COUGH COUGH≈ IS THAT YOU?

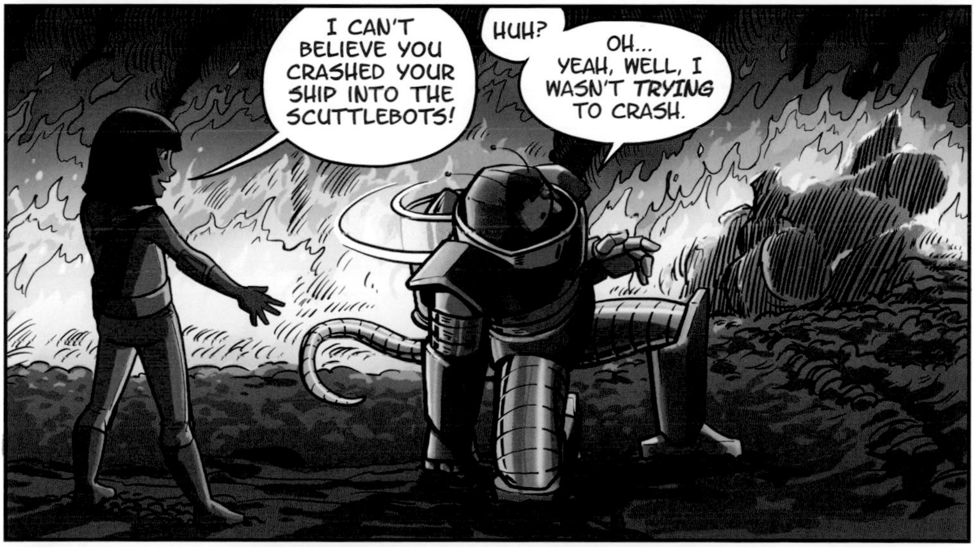
I CAN'T BELIEVE YOU CRASHED YOUR SHIP INTO THE SCUTTLEBOTS!
HUH?
OH... YEAH, WELL, I WASN'T *TRYING* TO CRASH.

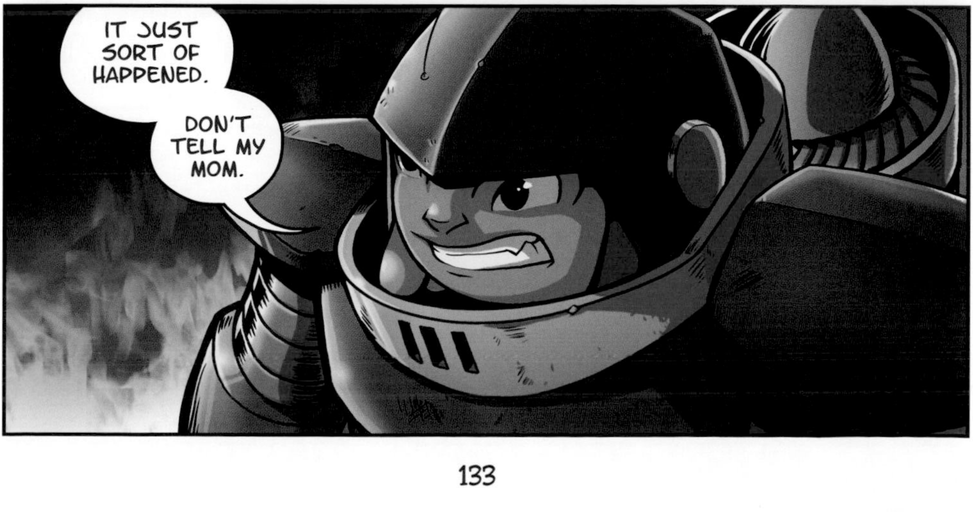
IT JUST SORT OF HAPPENED.
DON'T TELL MY MOM.

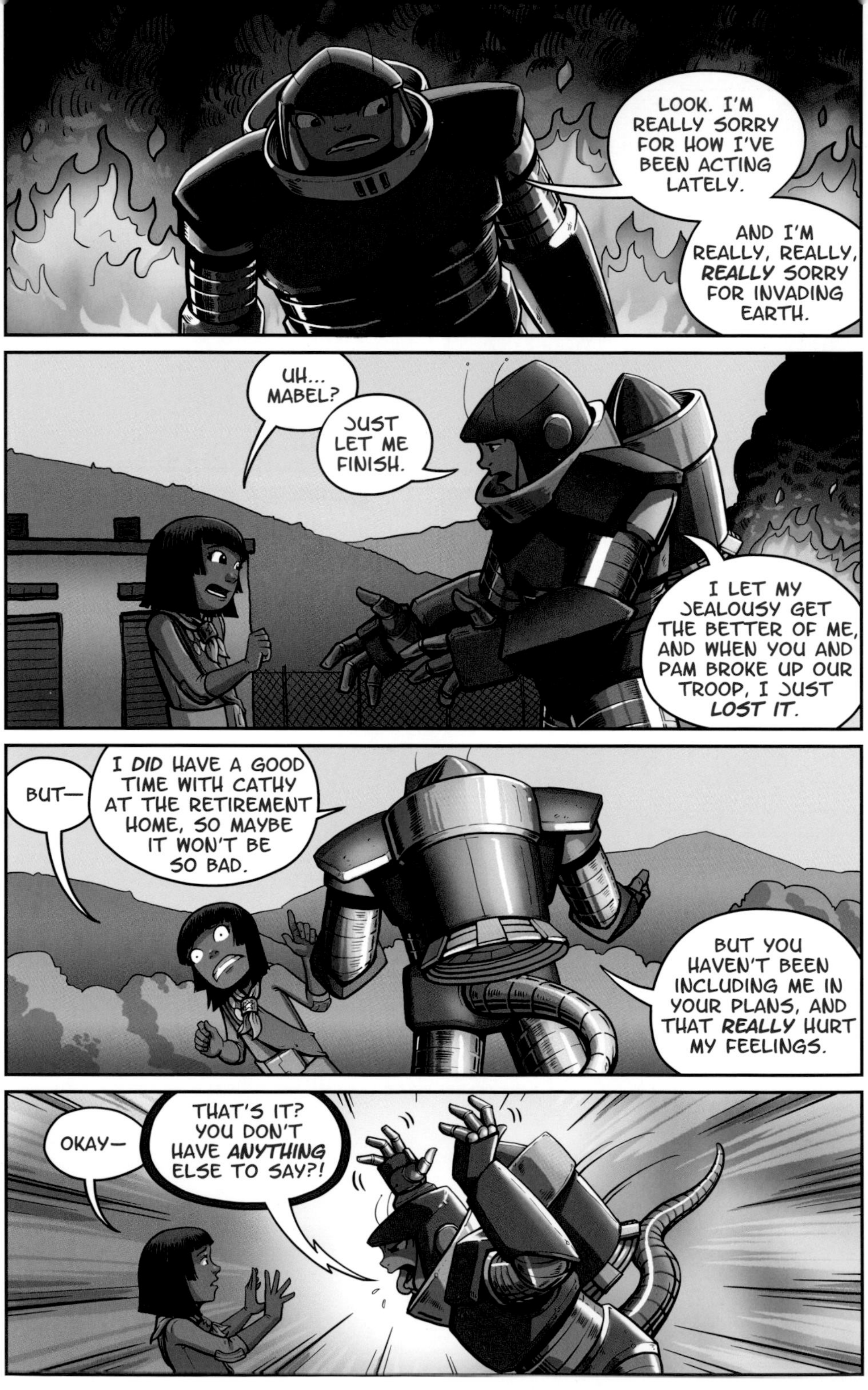

LOOK. I'M REALLY SORRY FOR HOW I'VE BEEN ACTING LATELY.
AND I'M REALLY, REALLY, *REALLY* SORRY FOR INVADING EARTH.
UH... MABEL?
JUST LET ME FINISH.
I LET MY JEALOUSY GET THE BETTER OF ME, AND WHEN YOU AND PAM BROKE UP OUR TROOP, I JUST *LOST IT*.
BUT—
I *DID* HAVE A GOOD TIME WITH CATHY AT THE RETIREMENT HOME, SO MAYBE IT WON'T BE SO BAD.
BUT YOU HAVEN'T BEEN INCLUDING ME IN YOUR PLANS, AND THAT *REALLY* HURT MY FEELINGS.
OKAY—
THAT'S IT? YOU DON'T HAVE *ANYTHING* ELSE TO SAY?!

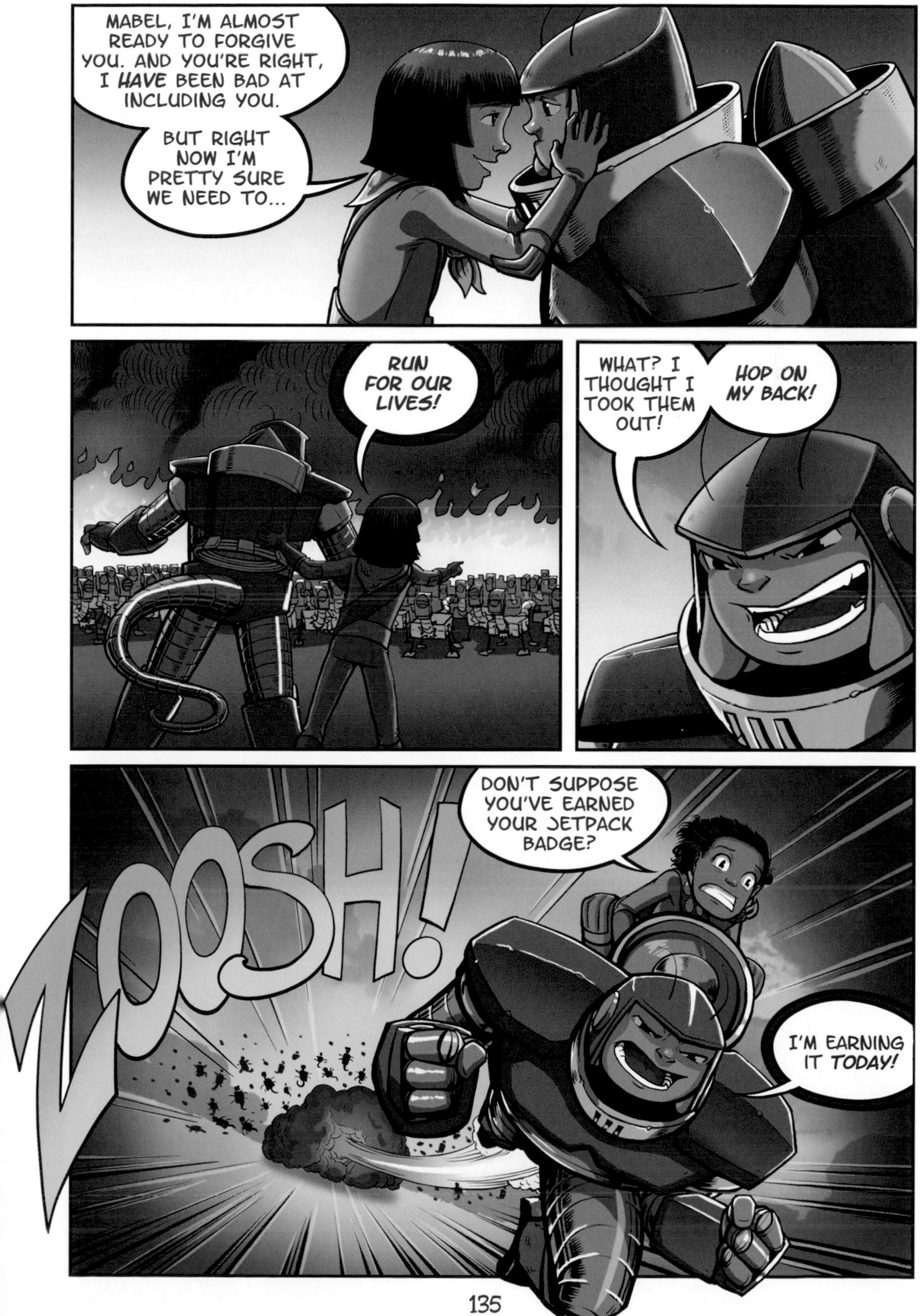
MABEL, I'M ALMOST READY TO FORGIVE YOU. AND YOU'RE RIGHT, I *HAVE* BEEN BAD AT INCLUDING YOU.
BUT RIGHT NOW I'M PRETTY SURE WE NEED TO...
RUN FOR OUR LIVES!
WHAT? I THOUGHT I TOOK THEM OUT!
HOP ON MY BACK!
ZOOOSH!
DON'T SUPPOSE YOU'VE EARNED YOUR JETPACK BADGE?
I'M EARNING IT *TODAY!*

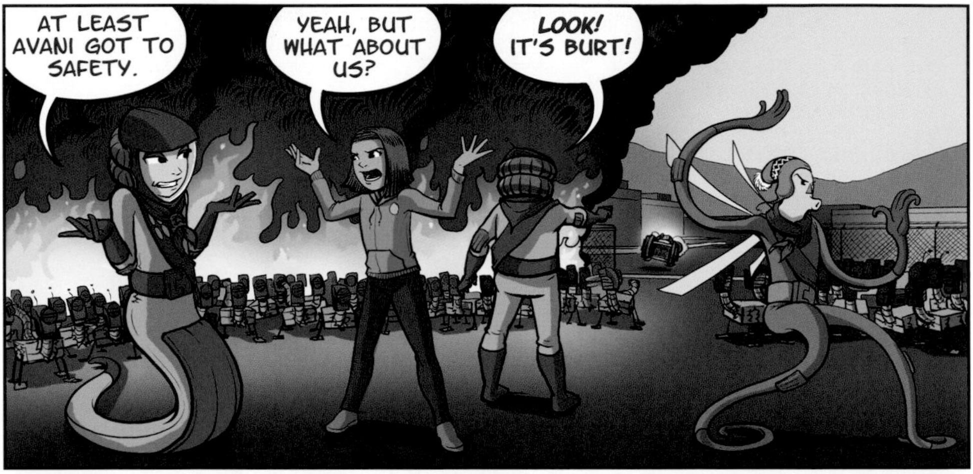
AT LEAST AVANI GOT TO SAFETY.
YEAH, BUT WHAT ABOUT US?
LOOK! IT'S BURT!

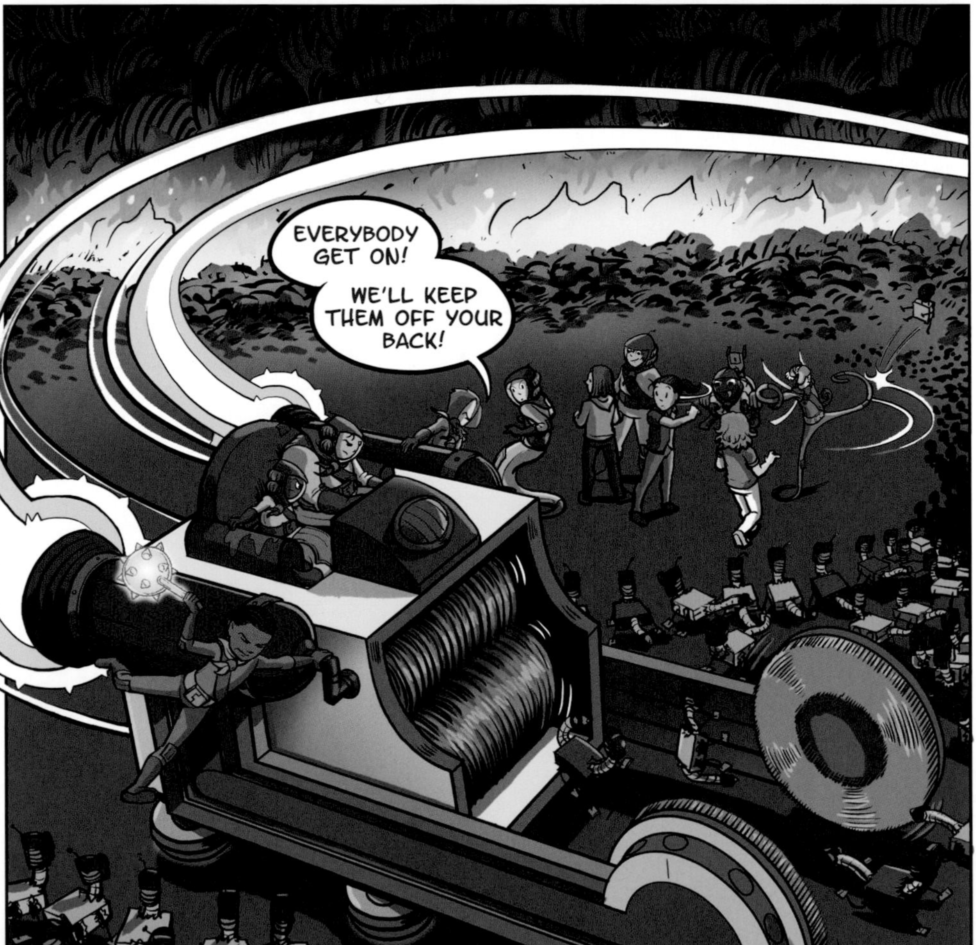
EVERYBODY GET ON!
WE'LL KEEP THEM OFF YOUR BACK!

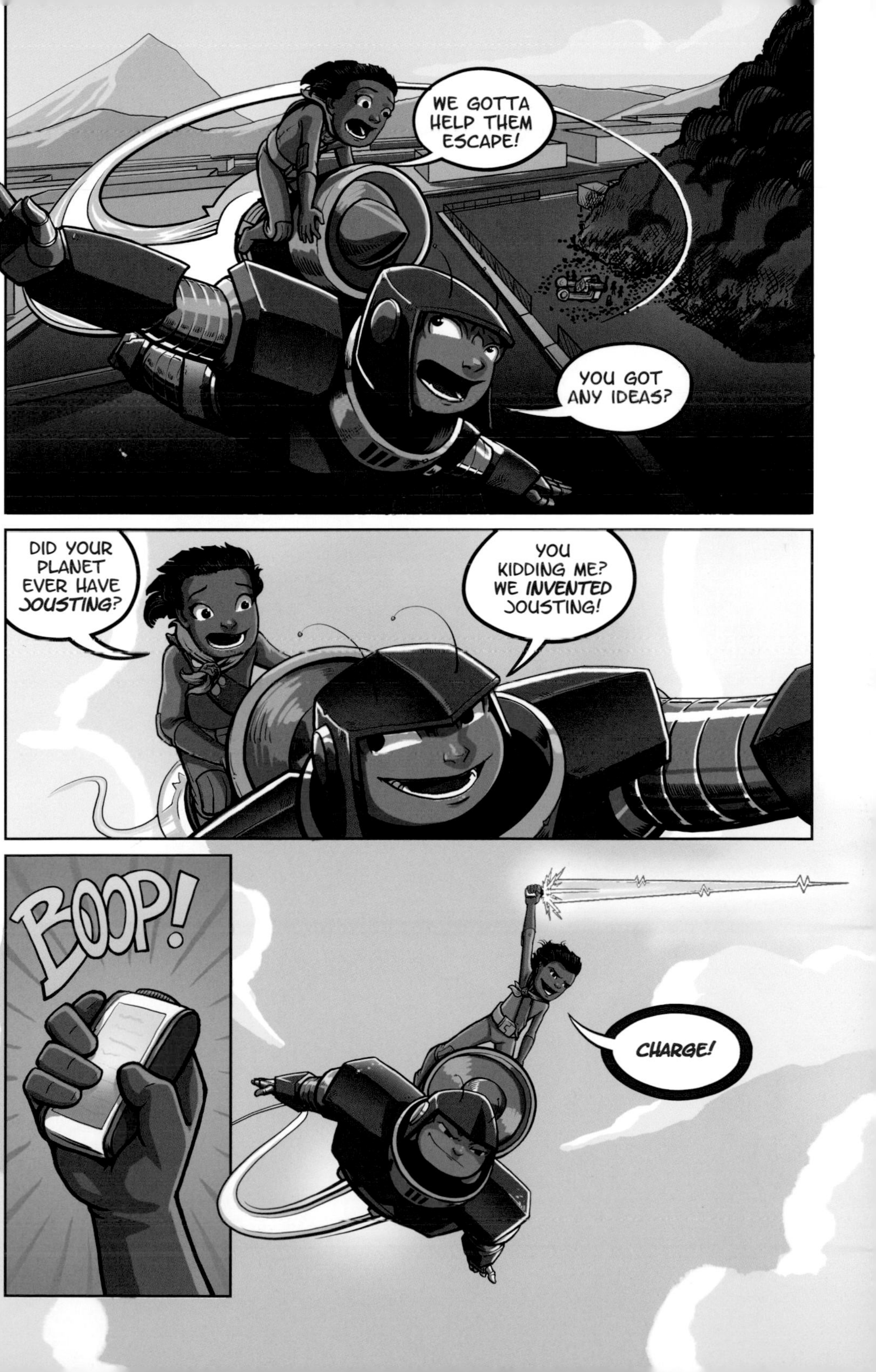
WE GOTTA HELP THEM ESCAPE!
YOU GOT ANY IDEAS?
DID YOUR PLANET EVER HAVE JOUSTING?
YOU KIDDING ME? WE INVENTED JOUSTING!
BOOP!
CHARGE!

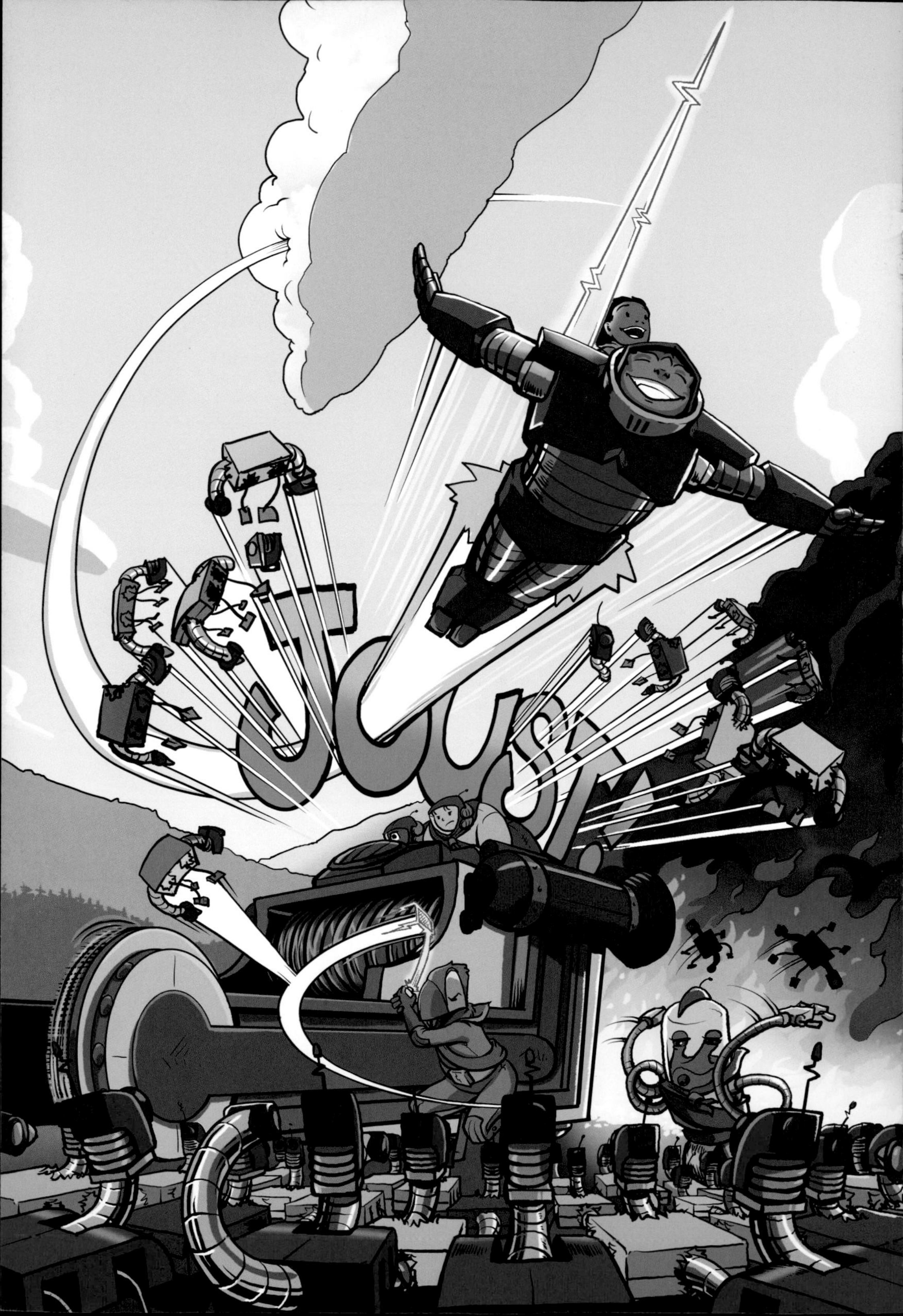

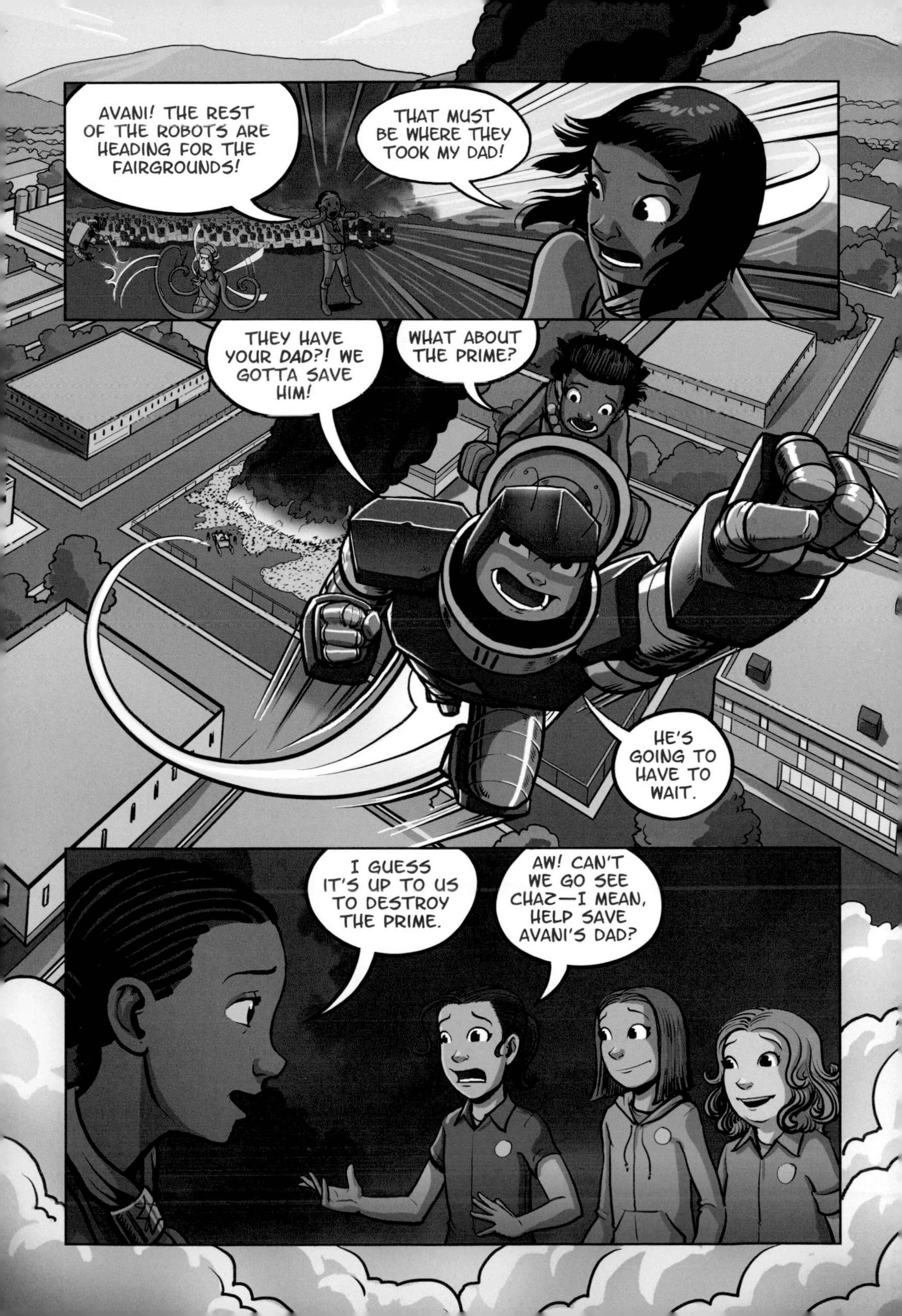
AVANI! THE REST OF THE ROBOTS ARE HEADING FOR THE FAIRGROUNDS!
THAT MUST BE WHERE THEY TOOK MY DAD!
THEY HAVE YOUR *DAD*?! WE GOTTA SAVE HIM!
WHAT ABOUT THE PRIME?
HE'S GOING TO HAVE TO WAIT.
I GUESS IT'S UP TO US TO DESTROY THE PRIME.
AW! CAN'T WE GO SEE CHAZ—I MEAN, HELP SAVE AVANI'S DAD?

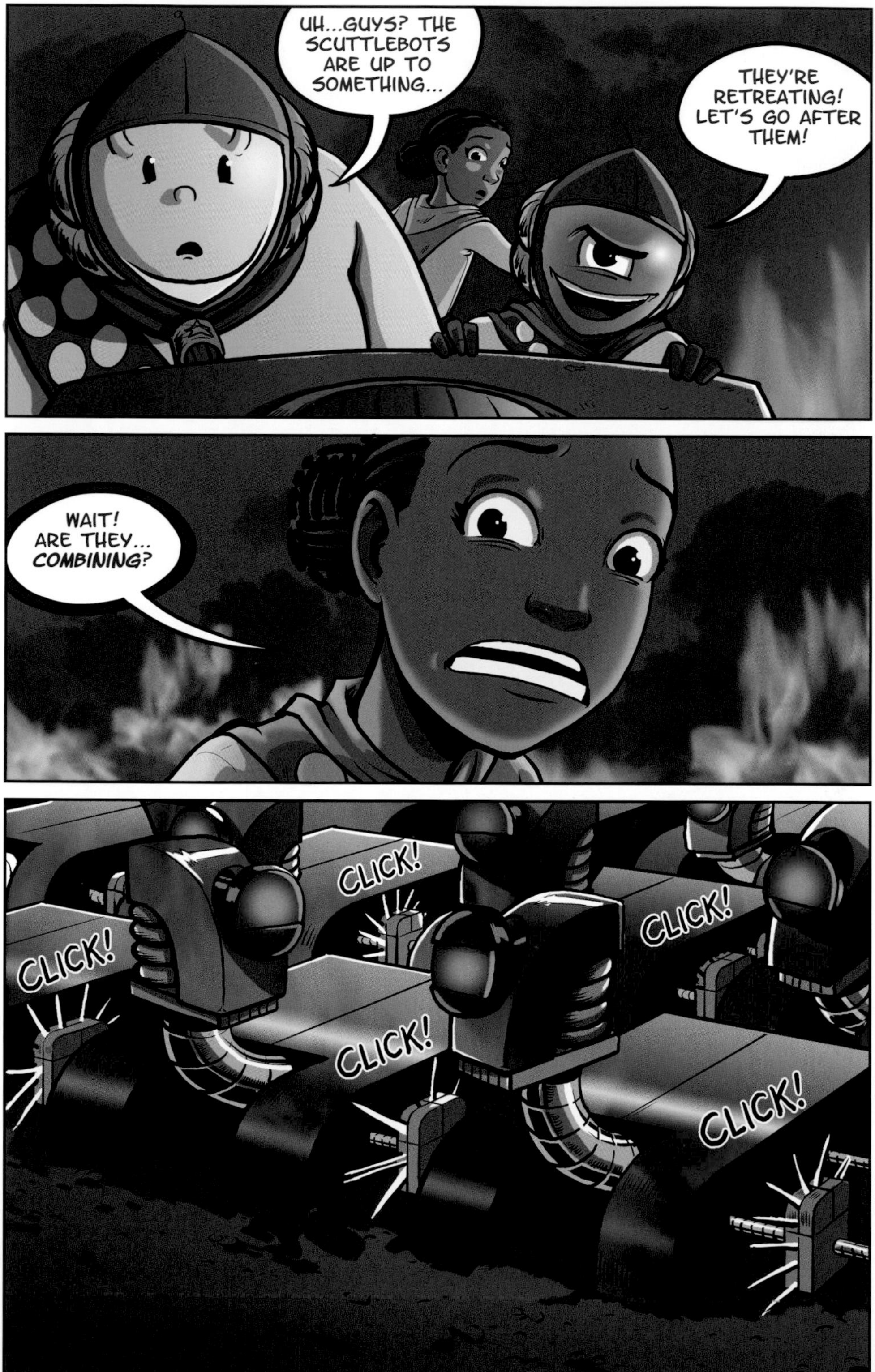
UH...GUYS? THE SCUTTLEBOTS ARE UP TO SOMETHING...
THEY'RE RETREATING! LET'S GO AFTER THEM!
WAIT! ARE THEY... COMBINING?
CLICK!
CLICK!
CLICK!
CLICK!
CLICK!
CLICK!

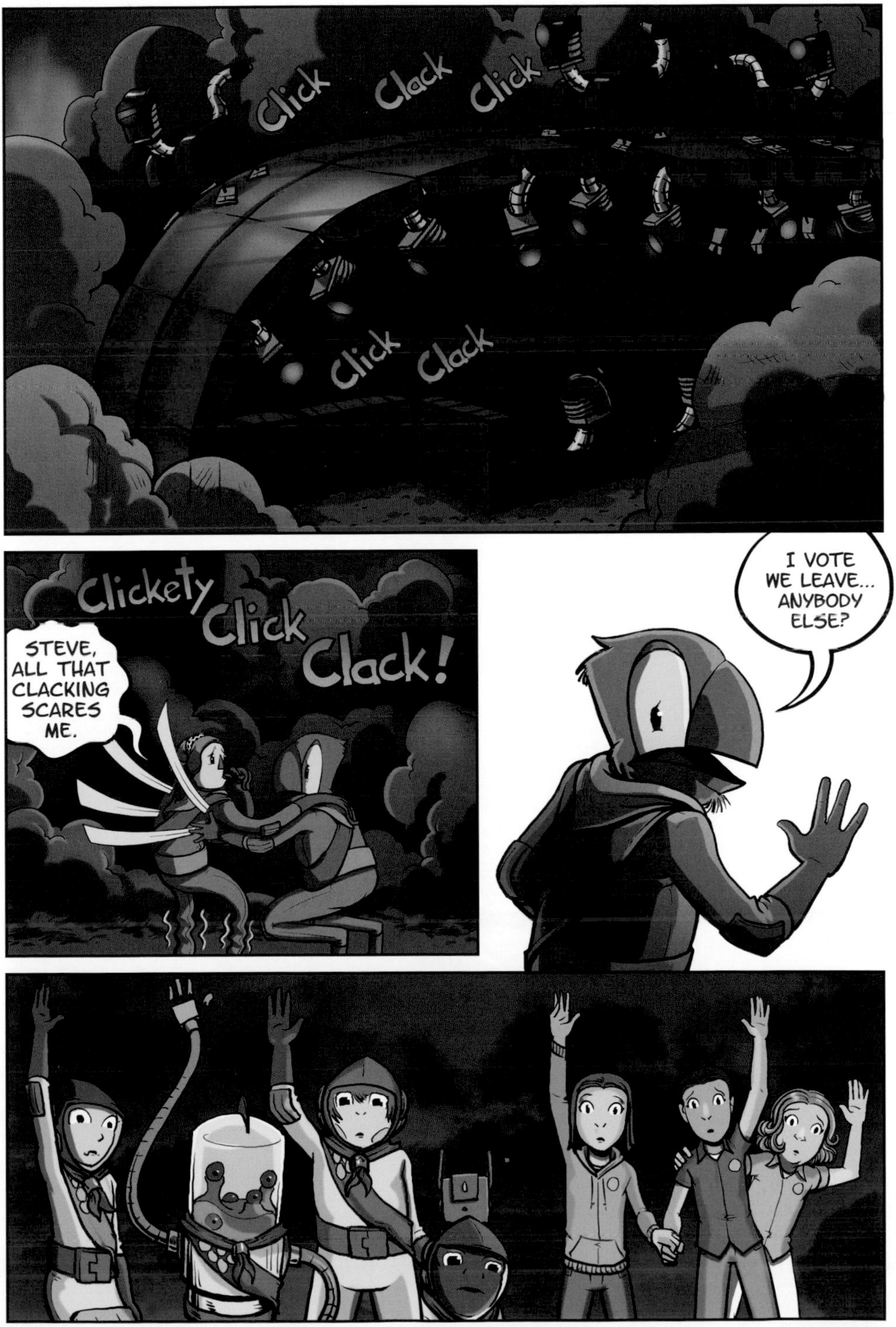
Click
Clack
Click
Click
Clack
Clickety
Click
Clack!
STEVE, ALL THAT CLACKING SCARES ME.
I VOTE WE LEAVE... ANYBODY ELSE?

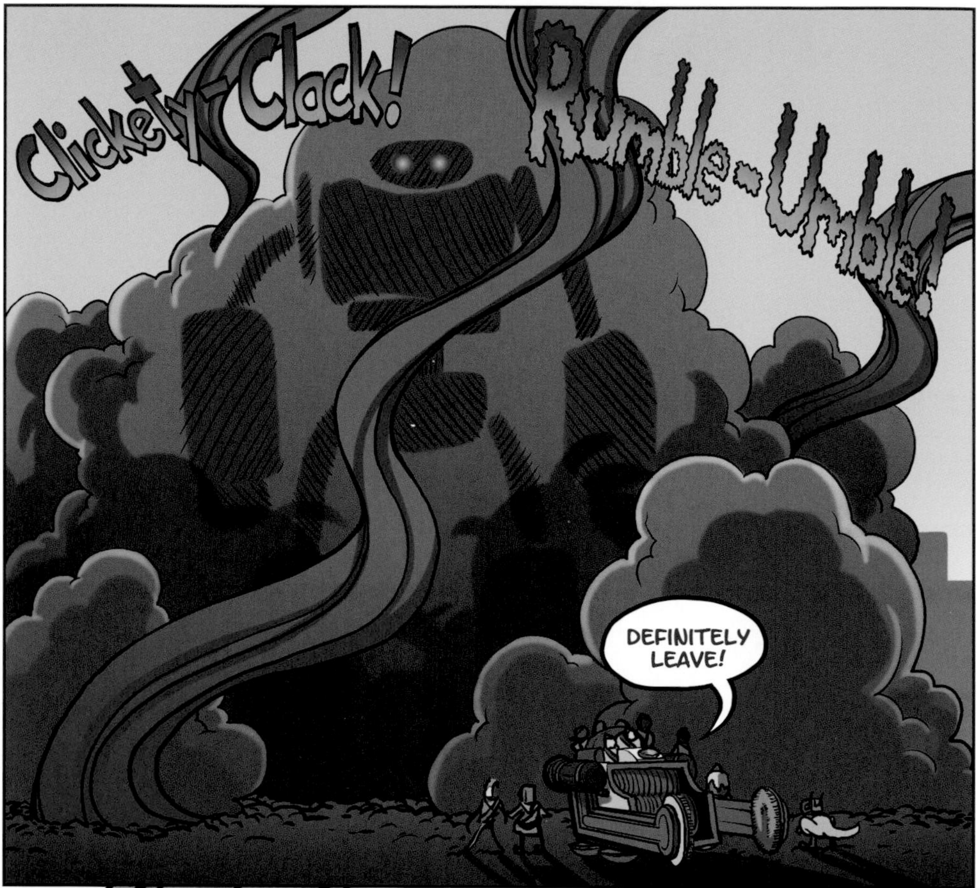
Clickety-Clack!
Rumble-Umble!
DEFINITELY LEAVE!
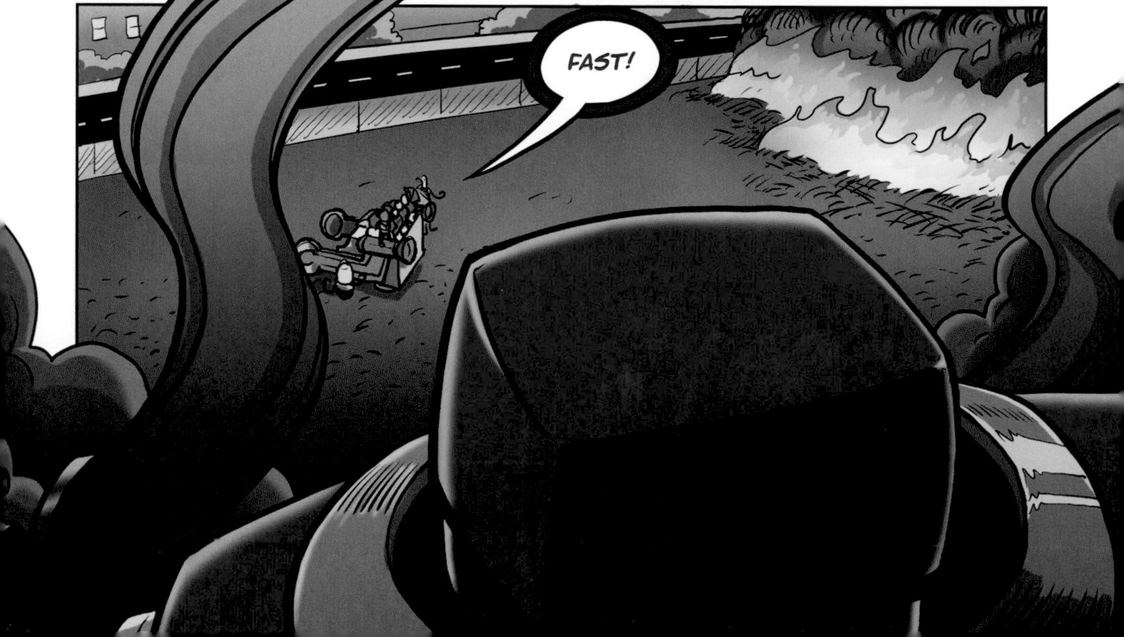
FAST!

PART 5

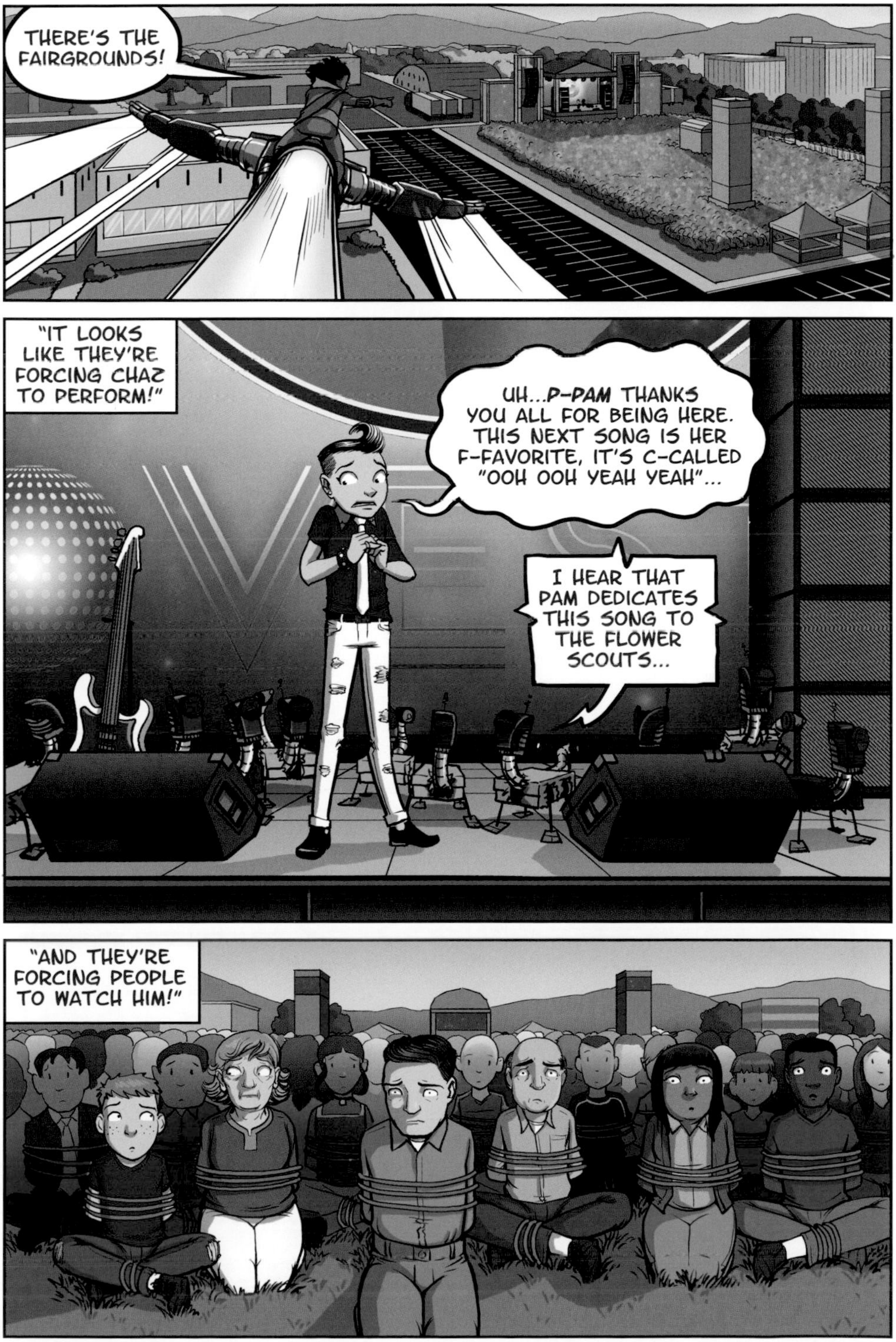
THERE'S THE FAIRGROUNDS!
"IT LOOKS LIKE THEY'RE FORCING CHAZ TO PERFORM!"
UH...*P-PAM* THANKS YOU ALL FOR BEING HERE. THIS NEXT SONG IS HER F-FAVORITE, IT'S C-CALLED "OOH OOH YEAH YEAH"...
I HEAR THAT PAM DEDICATES THIS SONG TO THE FLOWER SCOUTS...
"AND THEY'RE FORCING PEOPLE TO WATCH HIM!"

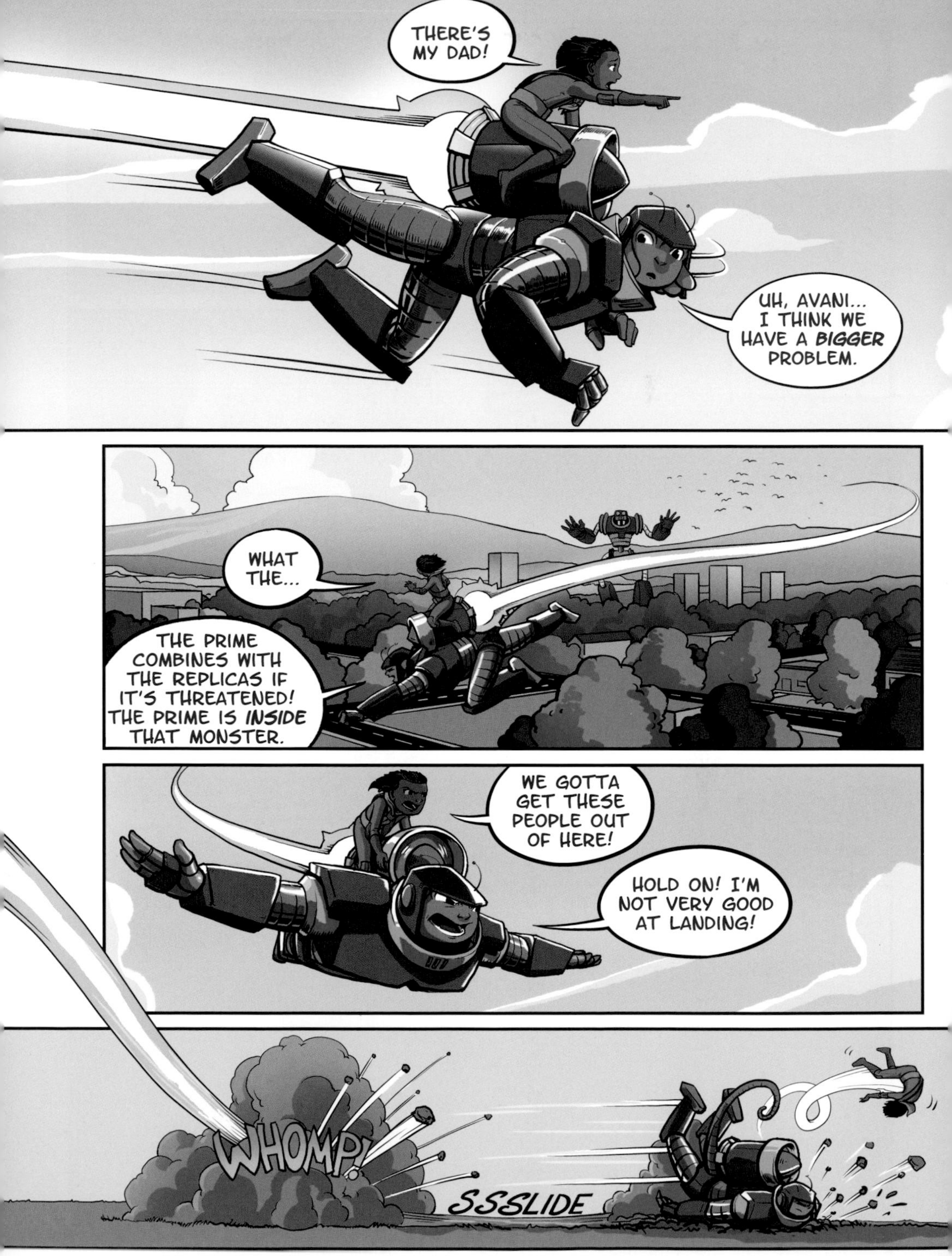
THERE'S MY DAD!
UH, AVANI... I THINK WE HAVE A BIGGER PROBLEM.
WHAT THE...
THE PRIME COMBINES WITH THE REPLICAS IF IT'S THREATENED! THE PRIME IS INSIDE THAT MONSTER.
WE GOTTA GET THESE PEOPLE OUT OF HERE!
HOLD ON! I'M NOT VERY GOOD AT LANDING!
WHOMP!
SSSLIDE

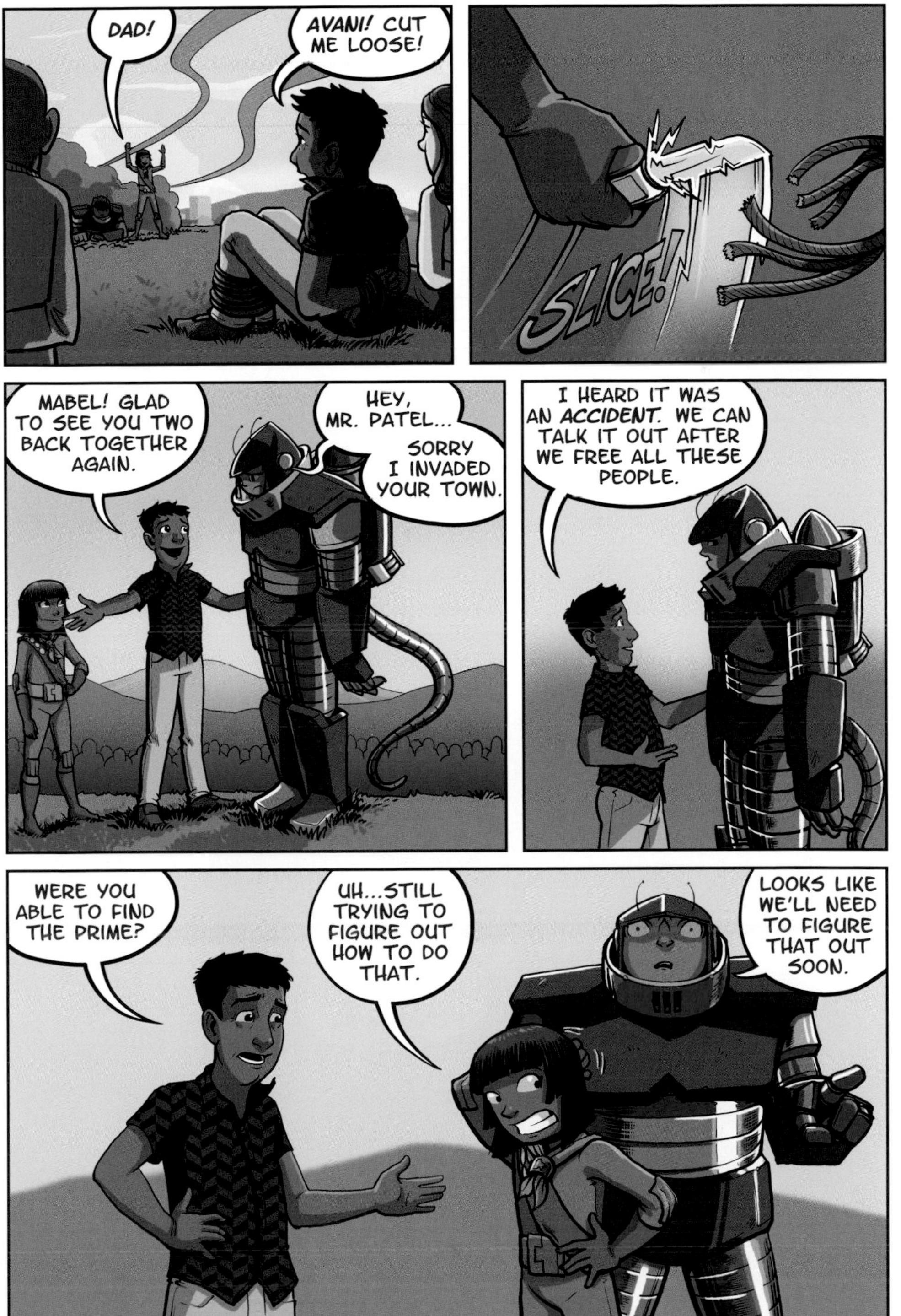
DAD!
AVANI! CUT ME LOOSE!
SLICE!
MABEL! GLAD TO SEE YOU TWO BACK TOGETHER AGAIN.
HEY, MR. PATEL...
SORRY I INVADED YOUR TOWN.
I HEARD IT WAS AN *ACCIDENT*. WE CAN TALK IT OUT AFTER WE FREE ALL THESE PEOPLE.
WERE YOU ABLE TO FIND THE PRIME?
UH...STILL TRYING TO FIGURE OUT HOW TO DO THAT.
LOOKS LIKE WE'LL NEED TO FIGURE THAT OUT SOON.

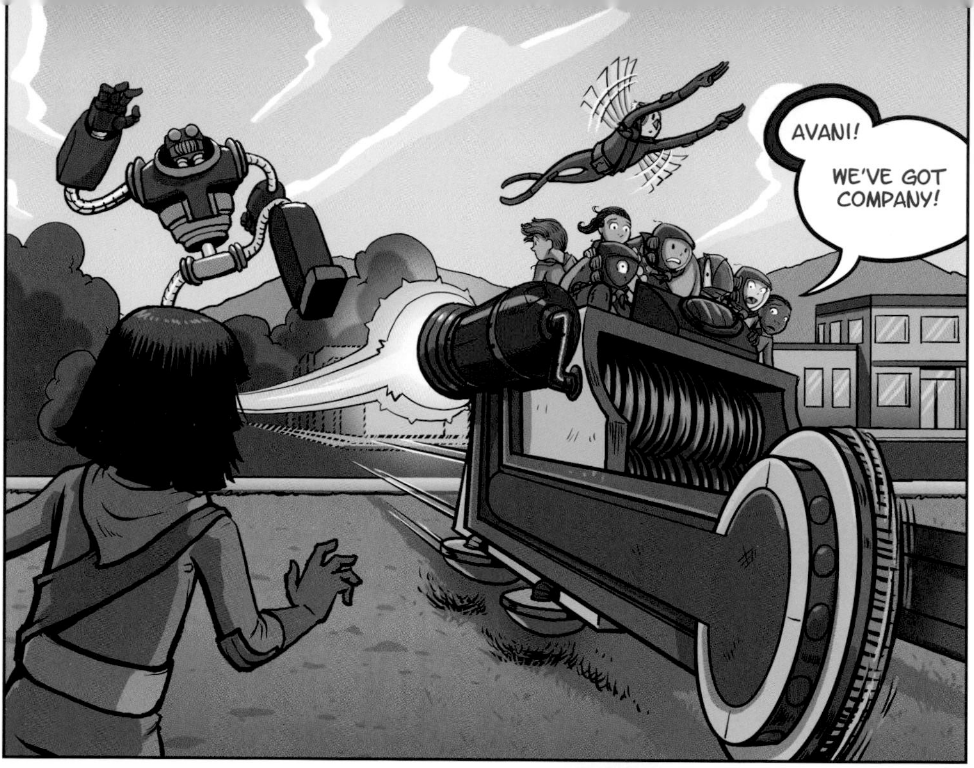
AVANI!
WE'VE GOT COMPANY!

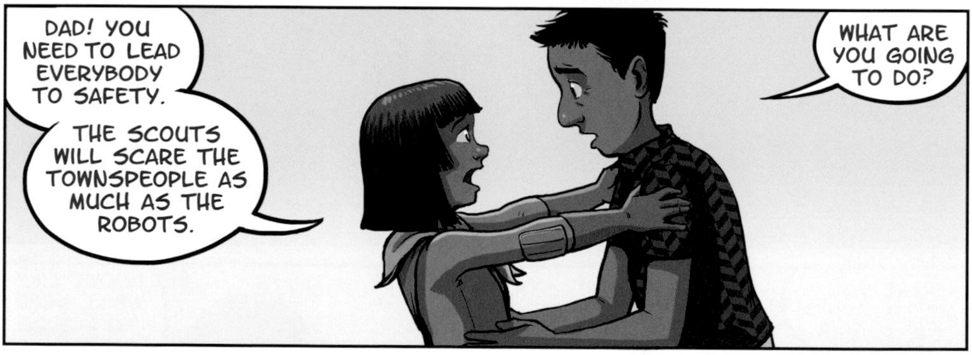
DAD! YOU NEED TO LEAD EVERYBODY TO SAFETY.
THE SCOUTS WILL SCARE THE TOWNSPEOPLE AS MUCH AS THE ROBOTS.
WHAT ARE YOU GOING TO DO?

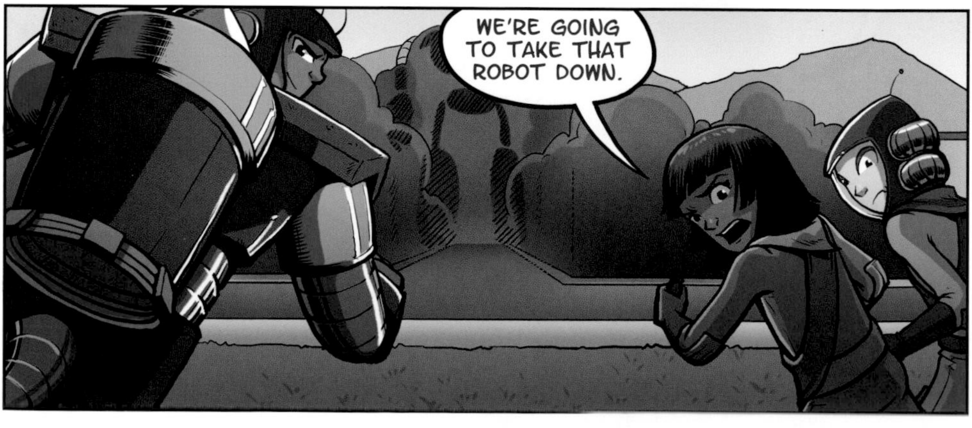
WE'RE GOING TO TAKE THAT ROBOT DOWN.

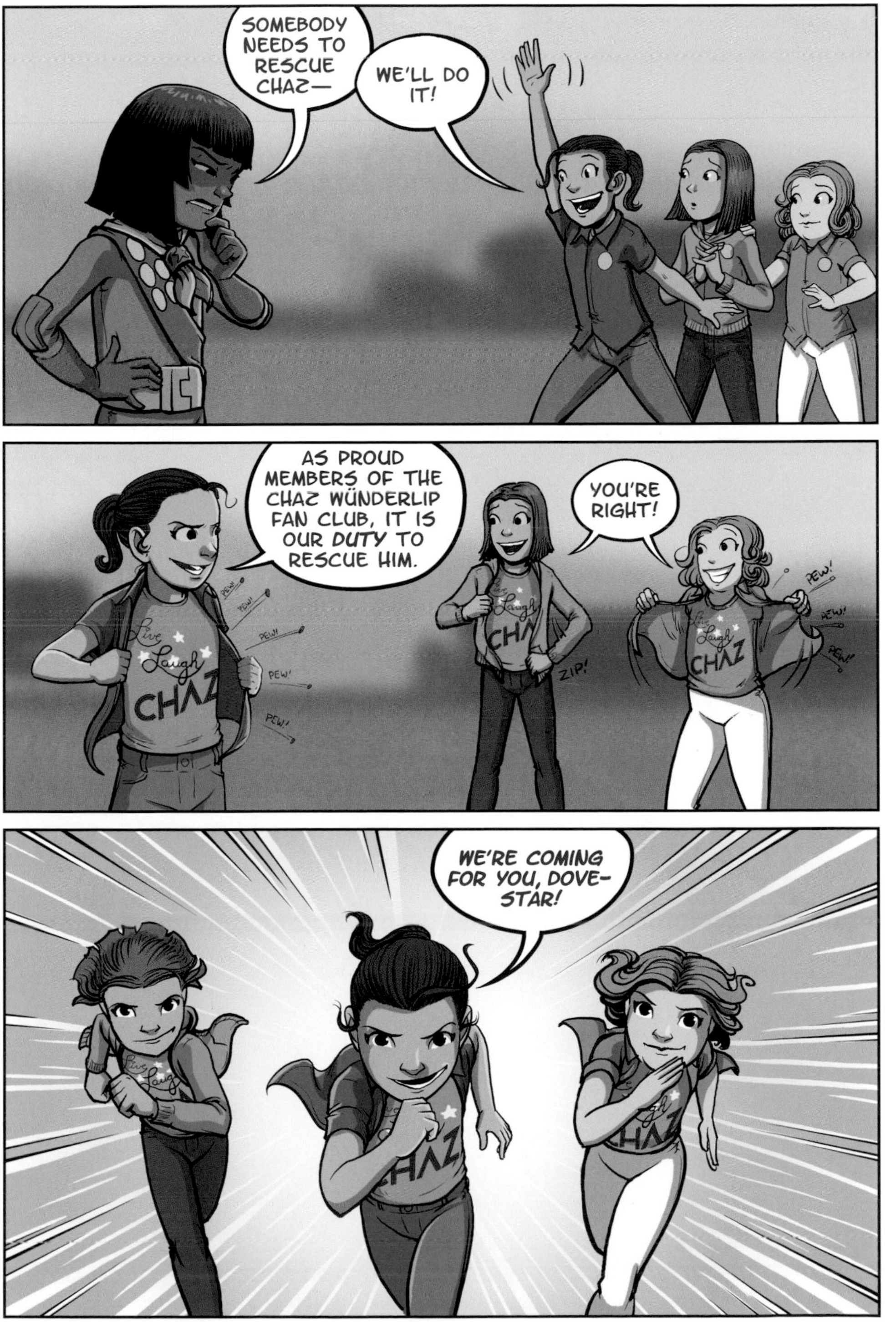
SOMEBODY NEEDS TO RESCUE CHAZ—
WE'LL DO IT!
AS PROUD MEMBERS OF THE CHAZ WÜNDERLIP FAN CLUB, IT IS OUR *DUTY* TO RESCUE HIM.
PEW!
PEW!
PEW!
PEW!
PEW!
Live Laugh CHAZ
YOU'RE RIGHT!
ZIP!
Live Laugh CHAZ
PEW!
PEW!
PEW!
Live Laugh CHAZ
WE'RE COMING FOR YOU, DOVE-STAR!

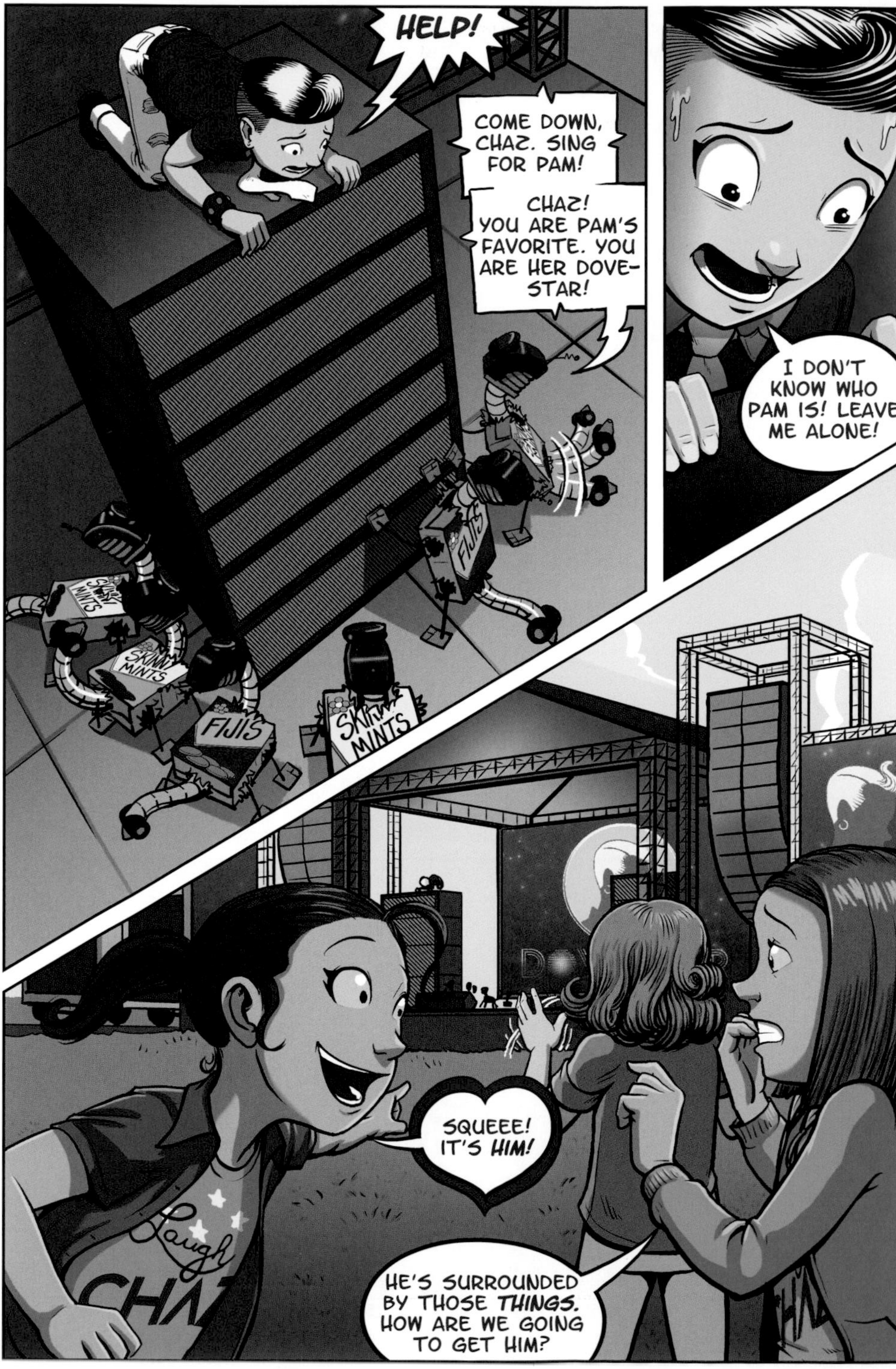
HELP!
COME DOWN, CHAZ. SING FOR PAM!
CHAZ! YOU ARE PAM'S FAVORITE. YOU ARE HER DOVE-STAR!
I DON'T KNOW WHO PAM IS! LEAVE ME ALONE!
SQUEEE! IT'S HIM!
HE'S SURROUNDED BY THOSE THINGS. HOW ARE WE GOING TO GET HIM?

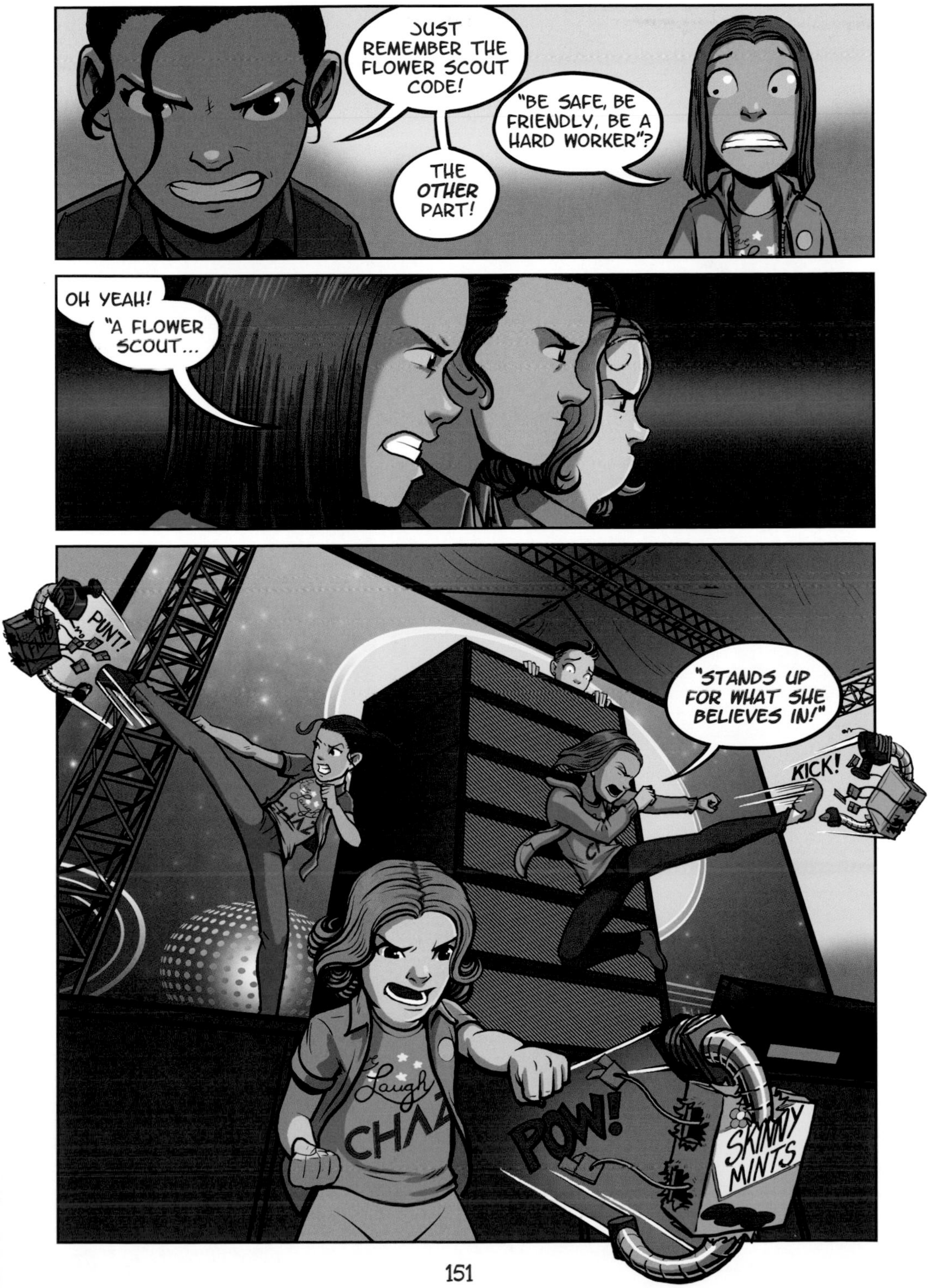
JUST REMEMBER THE FLOWER SCOUT CODE!
THE OTHER PART!
"BE SAFE, BE FRIENDLY, BE A HARD WORKER"?
OH YEAH! "A FLOWER SCOUT...
PUNT!
"STANDS UP FOR WHAT SHE BELIEVES IN!"
KICK!
Laugh
CHAZ
POW!
SKINNY MINTS

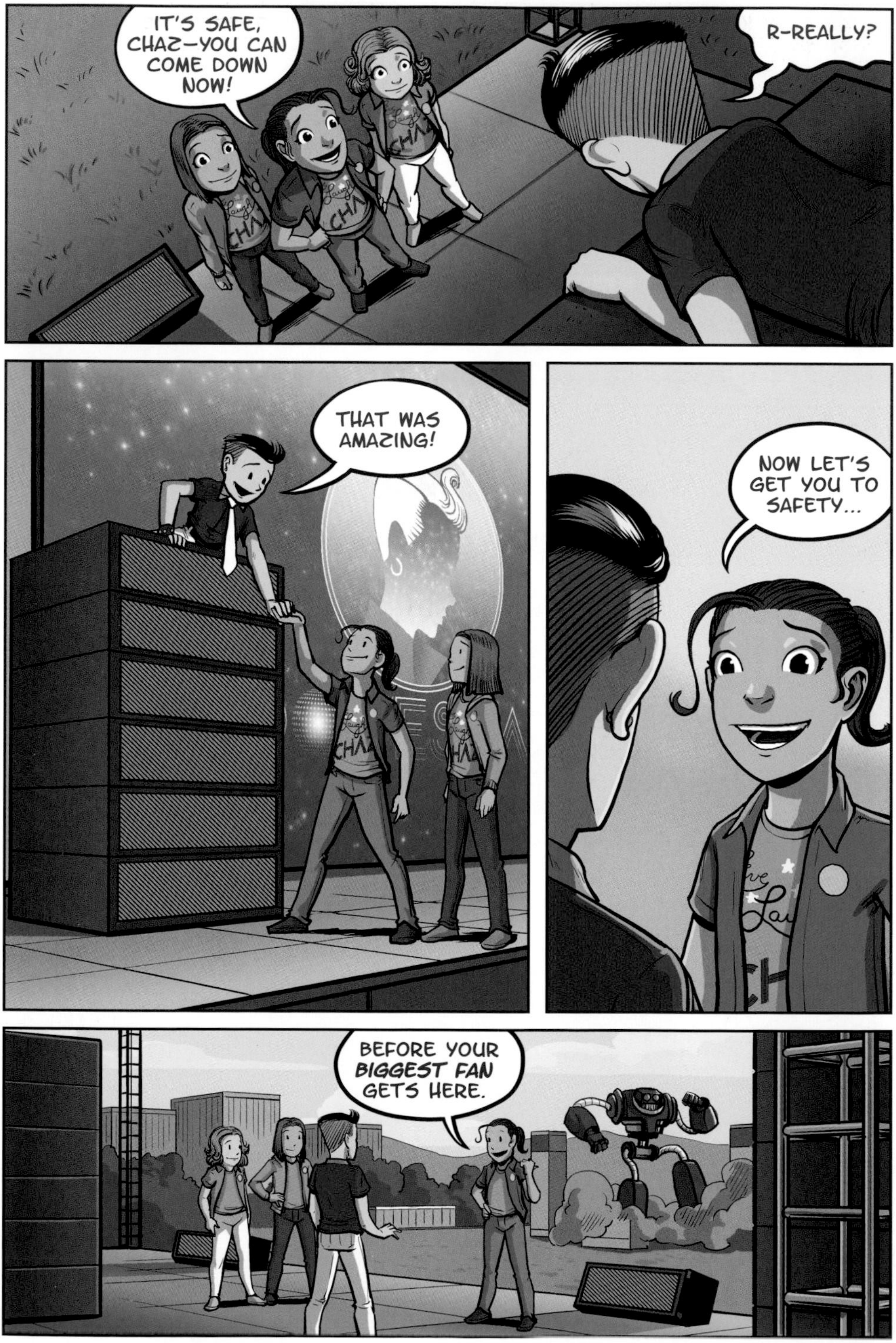
IT'S SAFE, CHAZ—YOU CAN COME DOWN NOW!
R-REALLY?
THAT WAS AMAZING!
NOW LET'S GET YOU TO SAFETY...
BEFORE YOUR ***BIGGEST FAN*** GETS HERE.

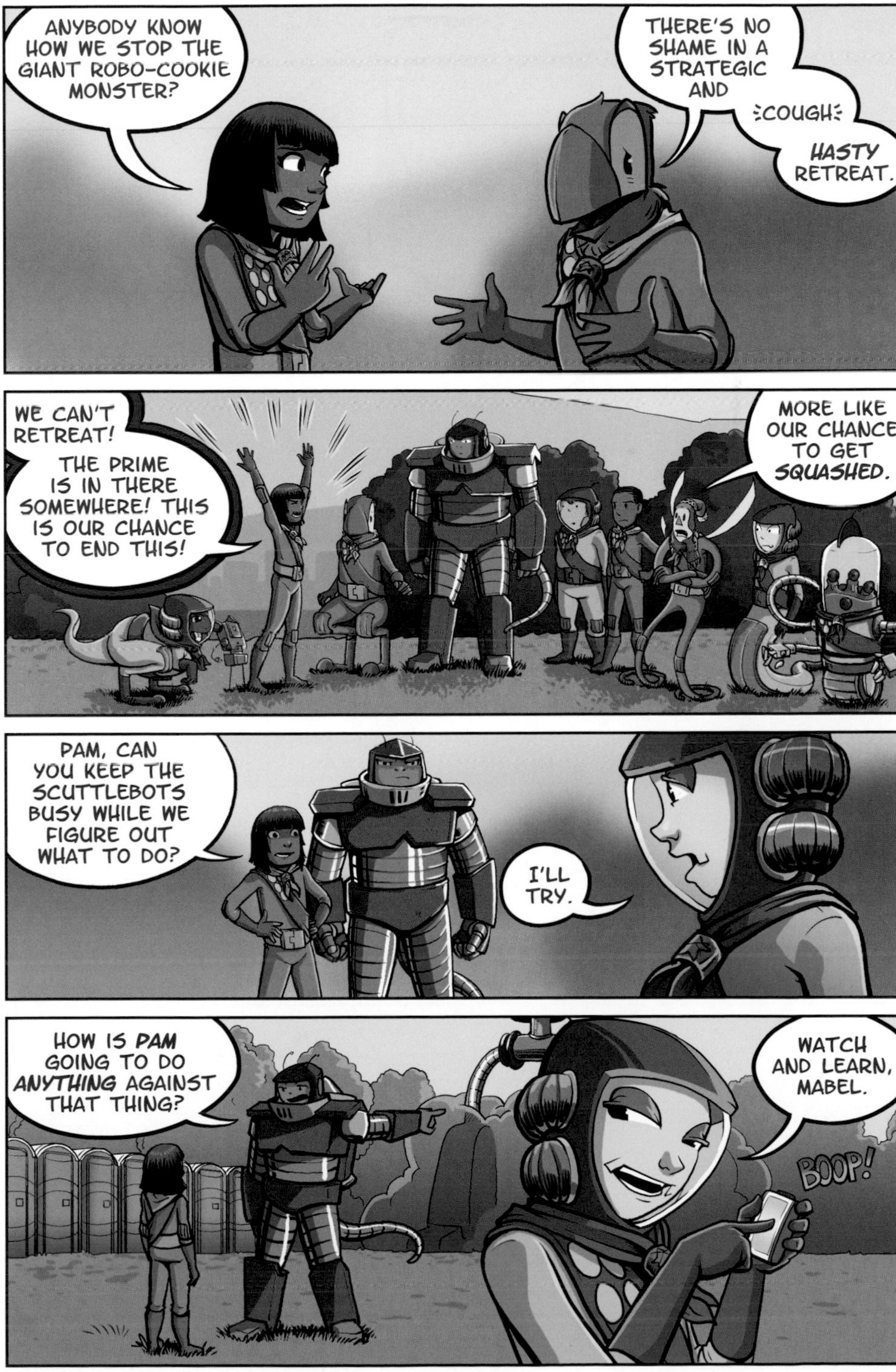

ANYBODY KNOW HOW WE STOP THE GIANT ROBO-COOKIE MONSTER?
THERE'S NO SHAME IN A STRATEGIC AND
COUGH
HASTY RETREAT.
WE CAN'T RETREAT!
THE PRIME IS IN THERE SOMEWHERE! THIS IS OUR CHANCE TO END THIS!
MORE LIKE OUR CHANCE TO GET SQUASHED.
PAM, CAN YOU KEEP THE SCUTTLEBOTS BUSY WHILE WE FIGURE OUT WHAT TO DO?
I'LL TRY.
HOW IS PAM GOING TO DO ANYTHING AGAINST THAT THING?
WATCH AND LEARN, MABEL.
BOOP!

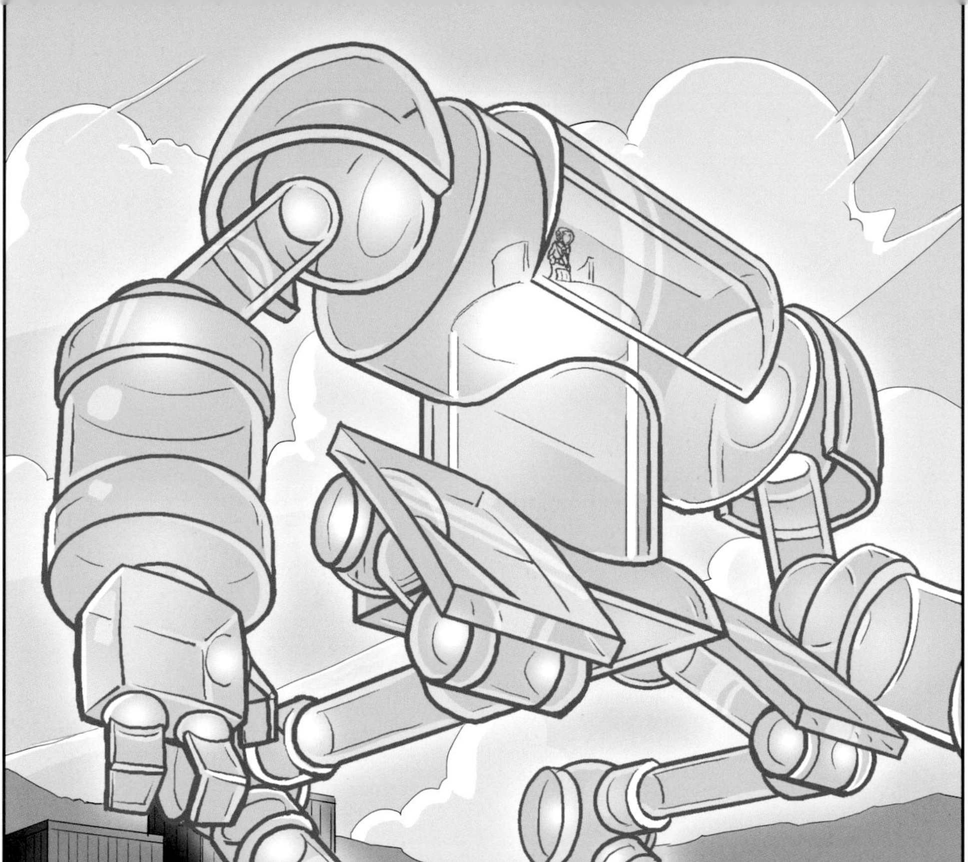

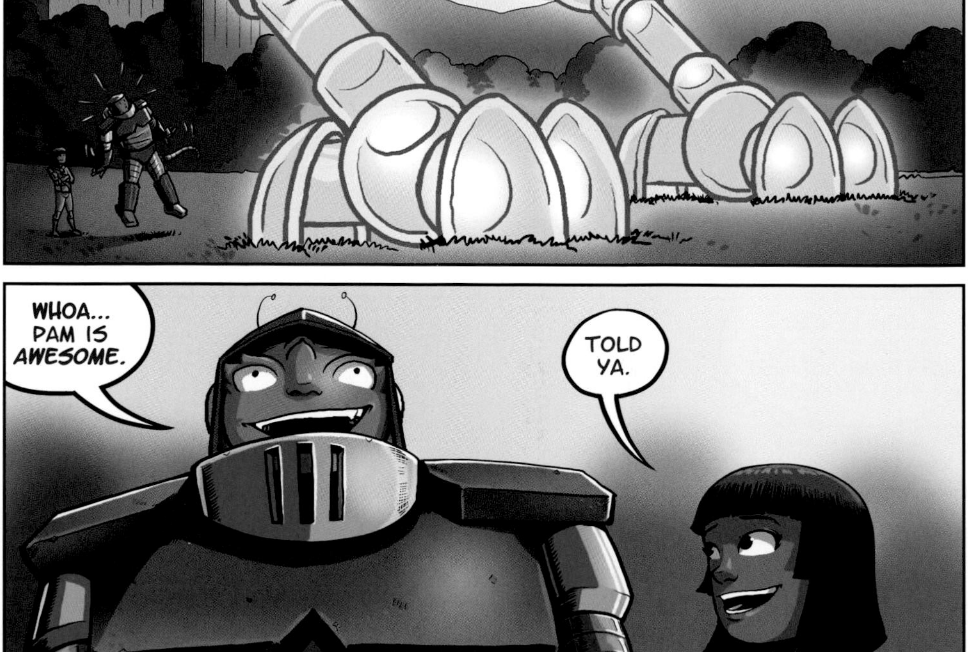
WHOA... PAM IS AWESOME.
TOLD YA.

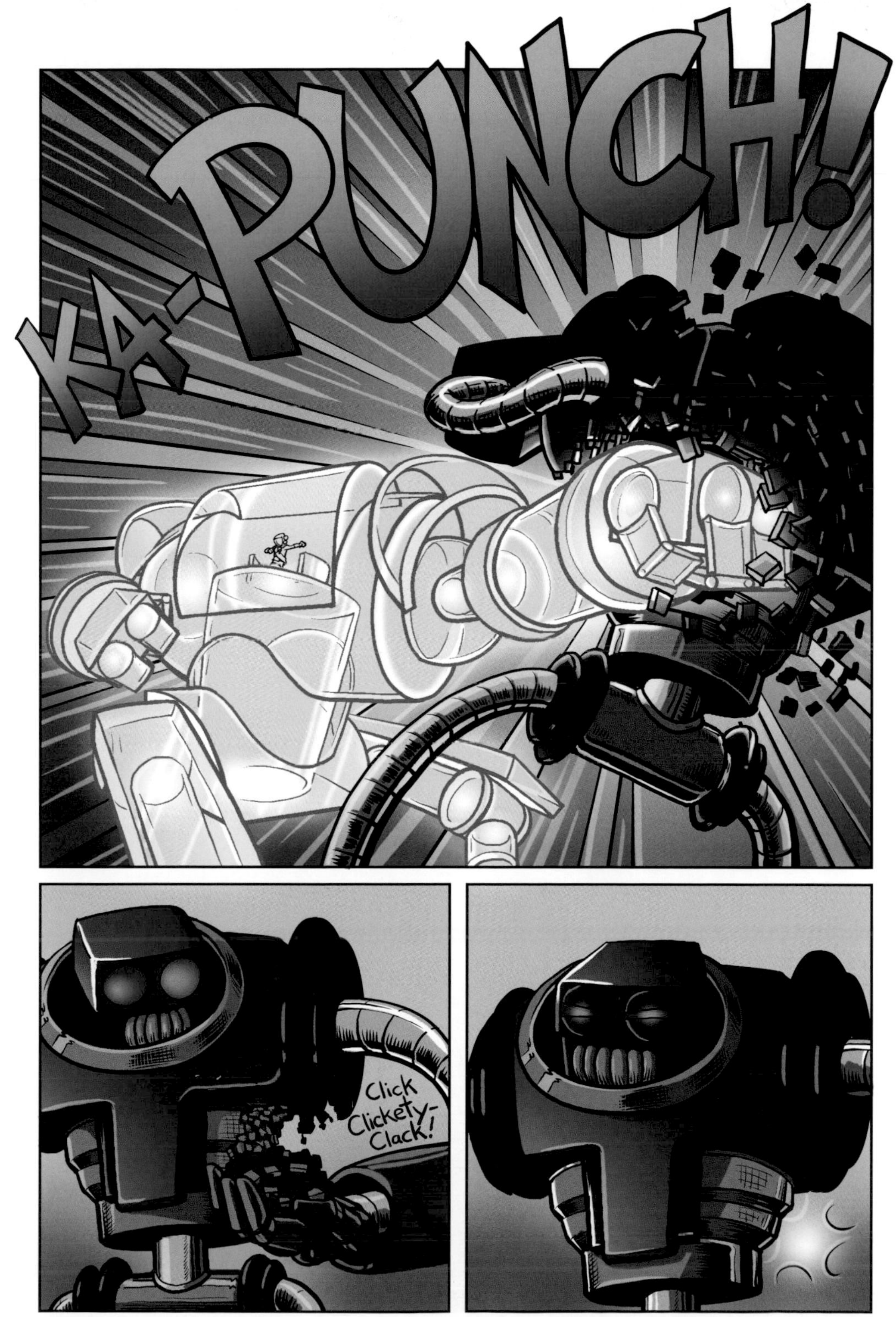
KA-PUNCH!
Click Clickety-Clack!

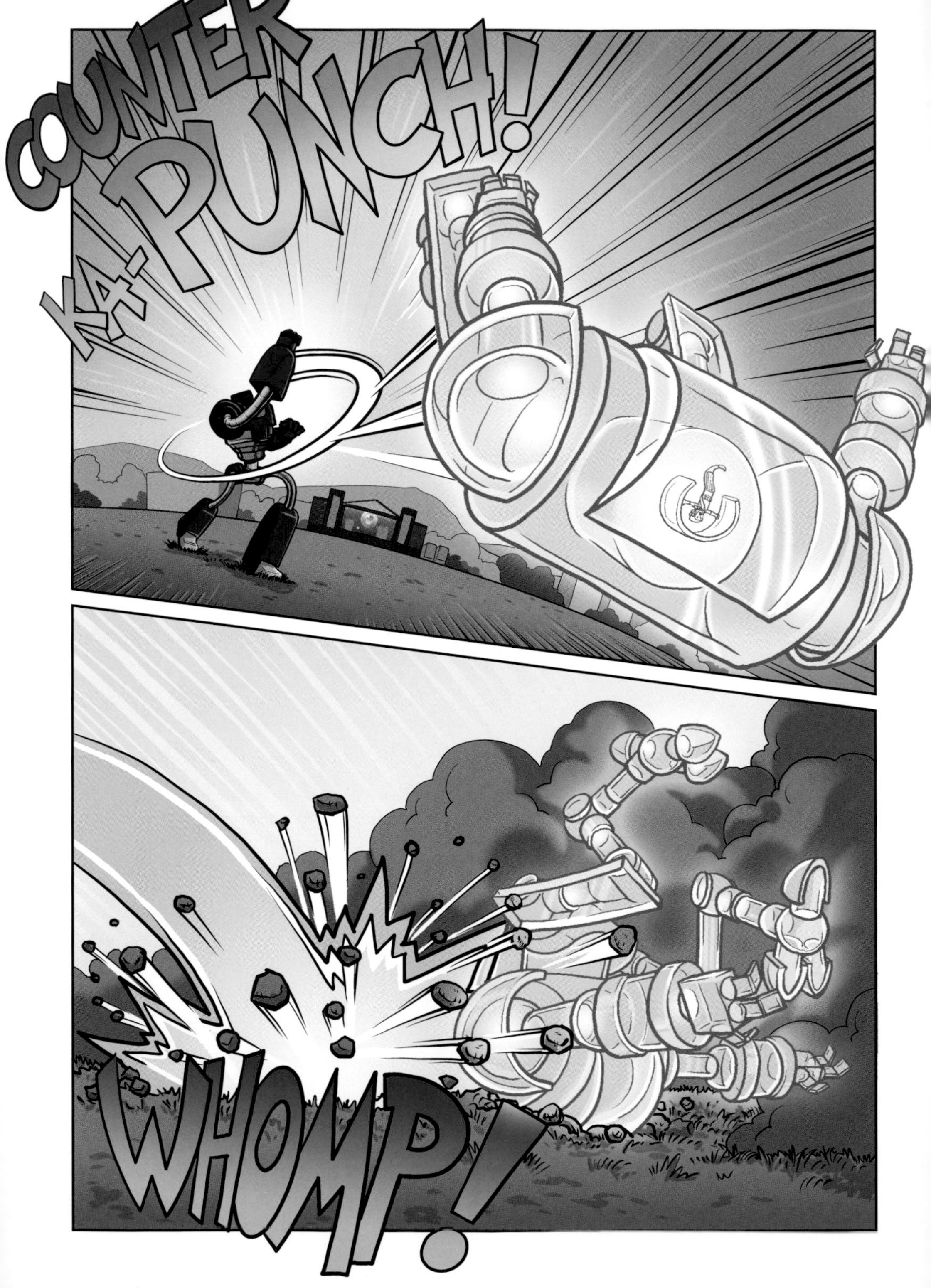
COUNTER KA-PUNCH!
WHOMP!

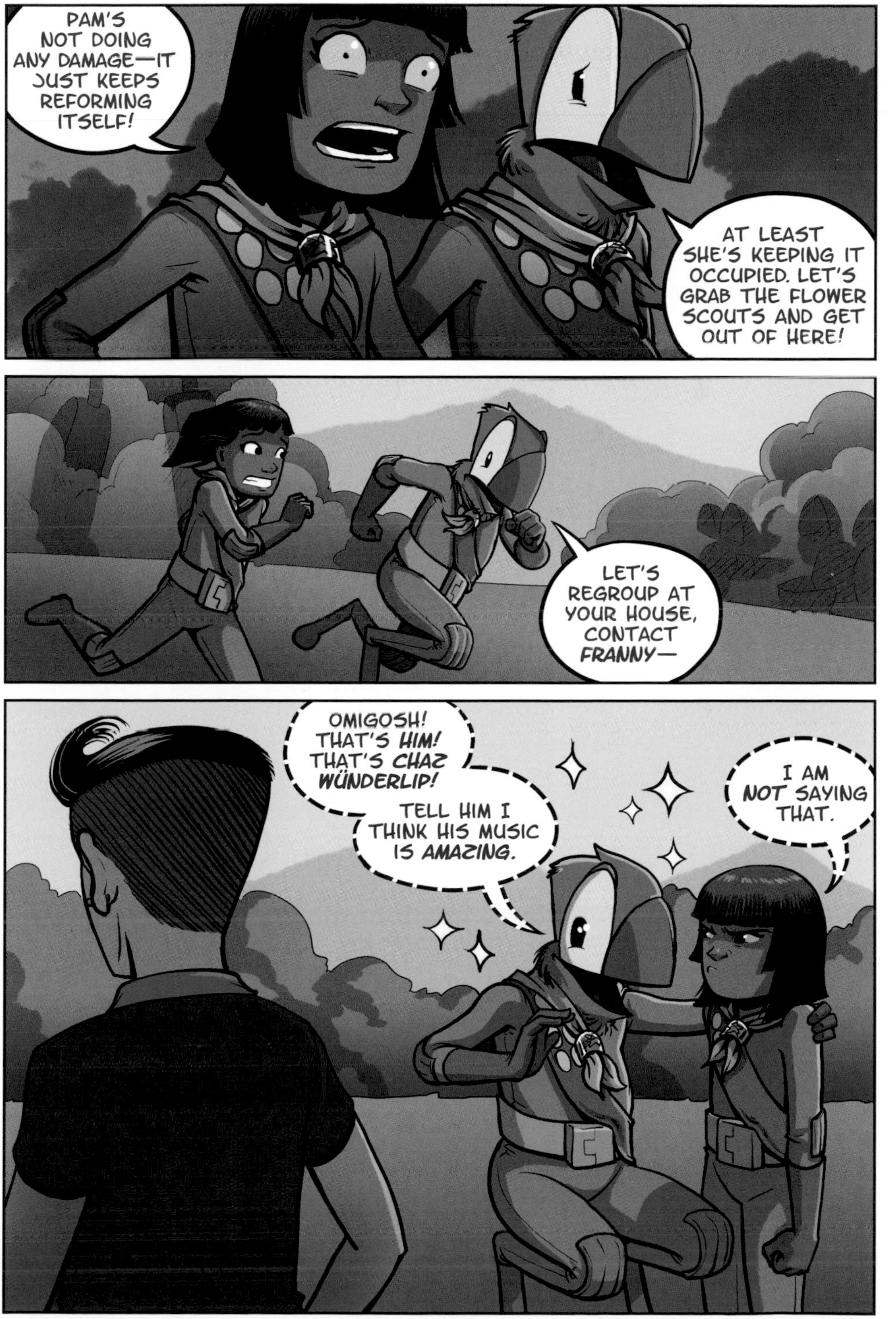
PAM'S NOT DOING ANY DAMAGE—IT JUST KEEPS REFORMING ITSELF!
AT LEAST SHE'S KEEPING IT OCCUPIED. LET'S GRAB THE FLOWER SCOUTS AND GET OUT OF HERE!
LET'S REGROUP AT YOUR HOUSE, CONTACT *FRANNY*—
OMIGOSH! THAT'S *HIM!* THAT'S *CHAZ WÜNDERLIP!*
TELL HIM I THINK HIS MUSIC IS *AMAZING.*
I AM *NOT* SAYING THAT.

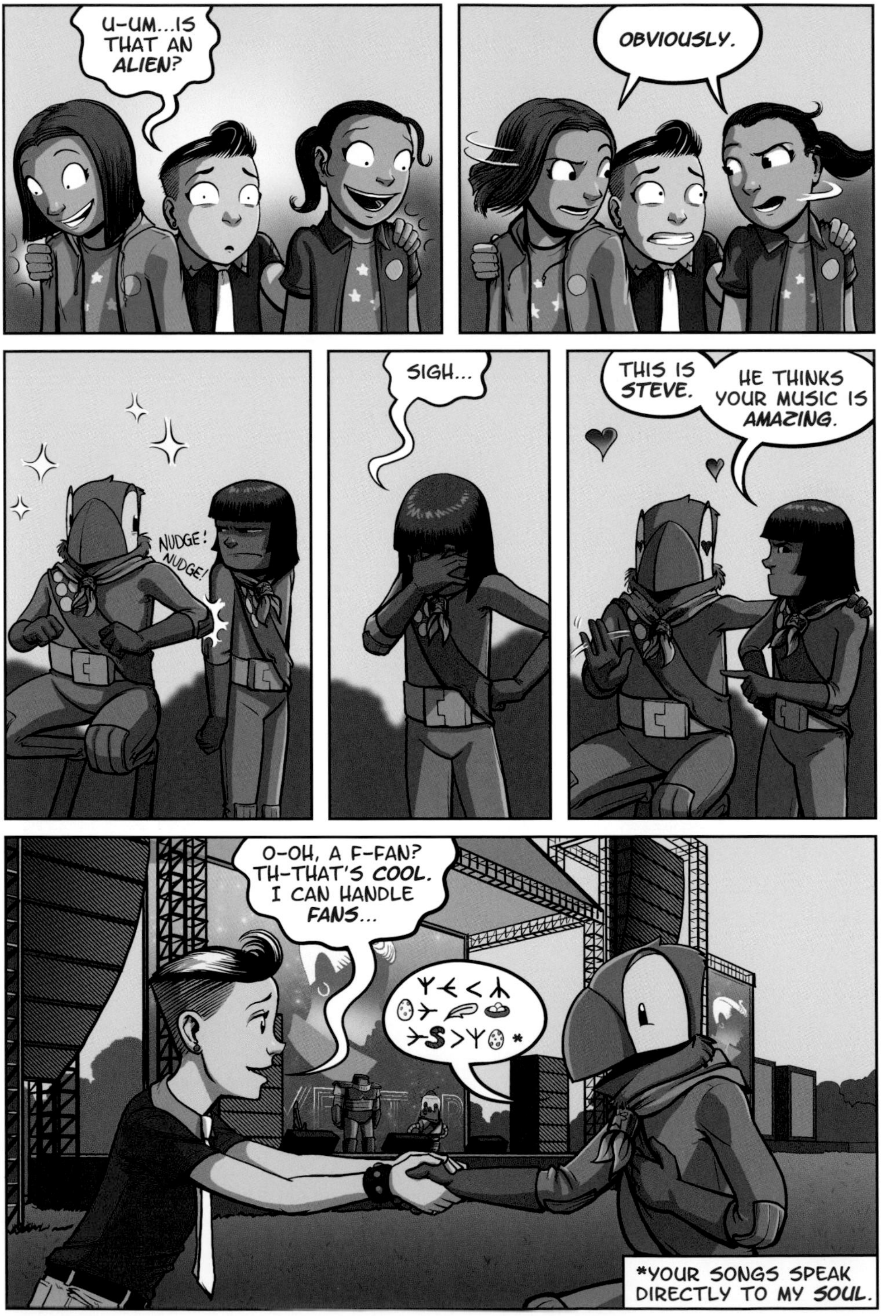
U-UM...IS THAT AN ALIEN?
OBVIOUSLY.
NUDGE! NUDGE!
SIGH...
THIS IS STEVE.
HE THINKS YOUR MUSIC IS AMAZING.
O-OH, A F-FAN? TH-THAT'S COOL. I CAN HANDLE FANS...
*YOUR SONGS SPEAK DIRECTLY TO MY SOUL.

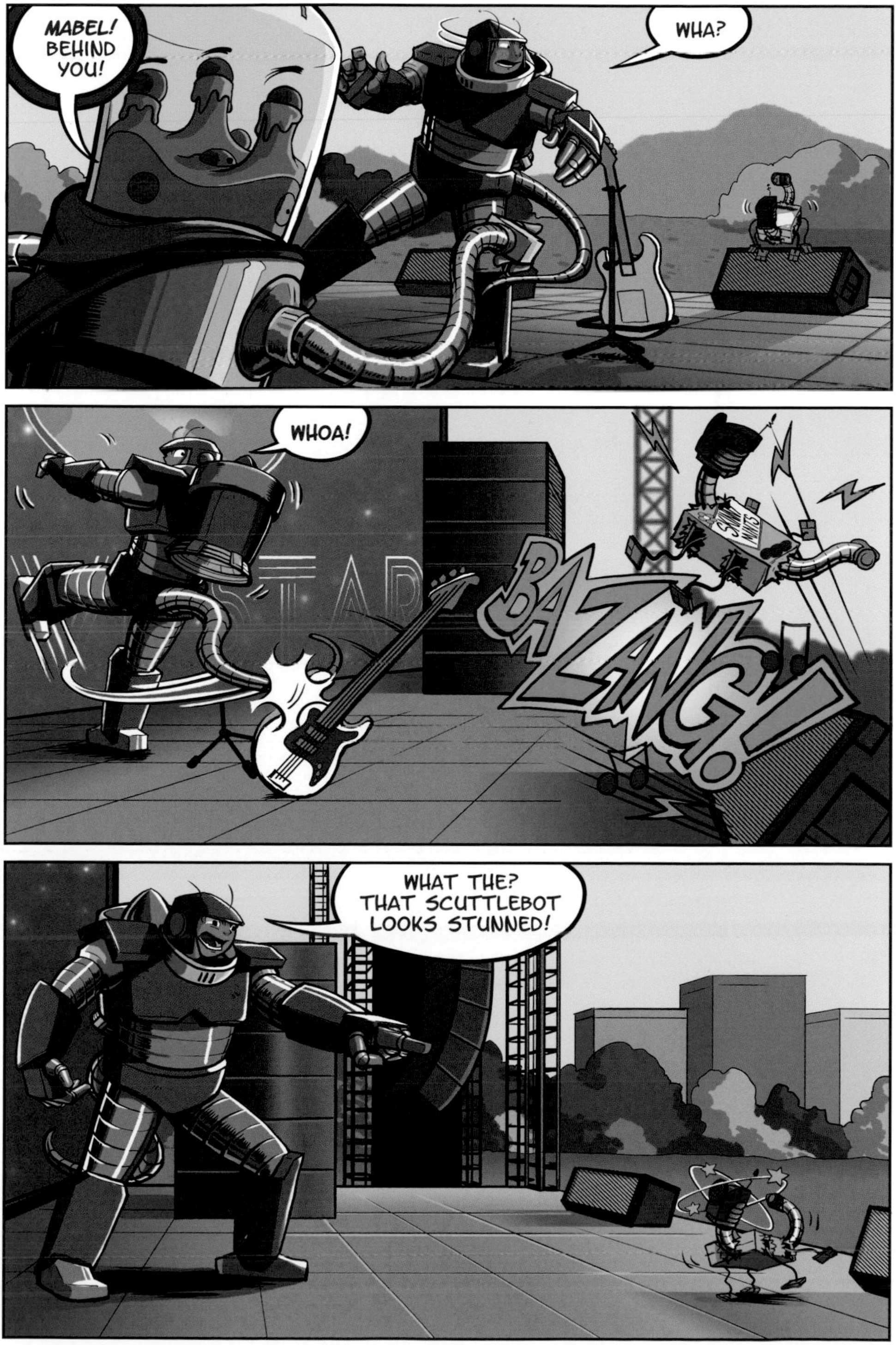
MABEL! BEHIND YOU!
WHA?
WHOA!
BAZANG!
WHAT THE? THAT SCUTTLEBOT LOOKS STUNNED!

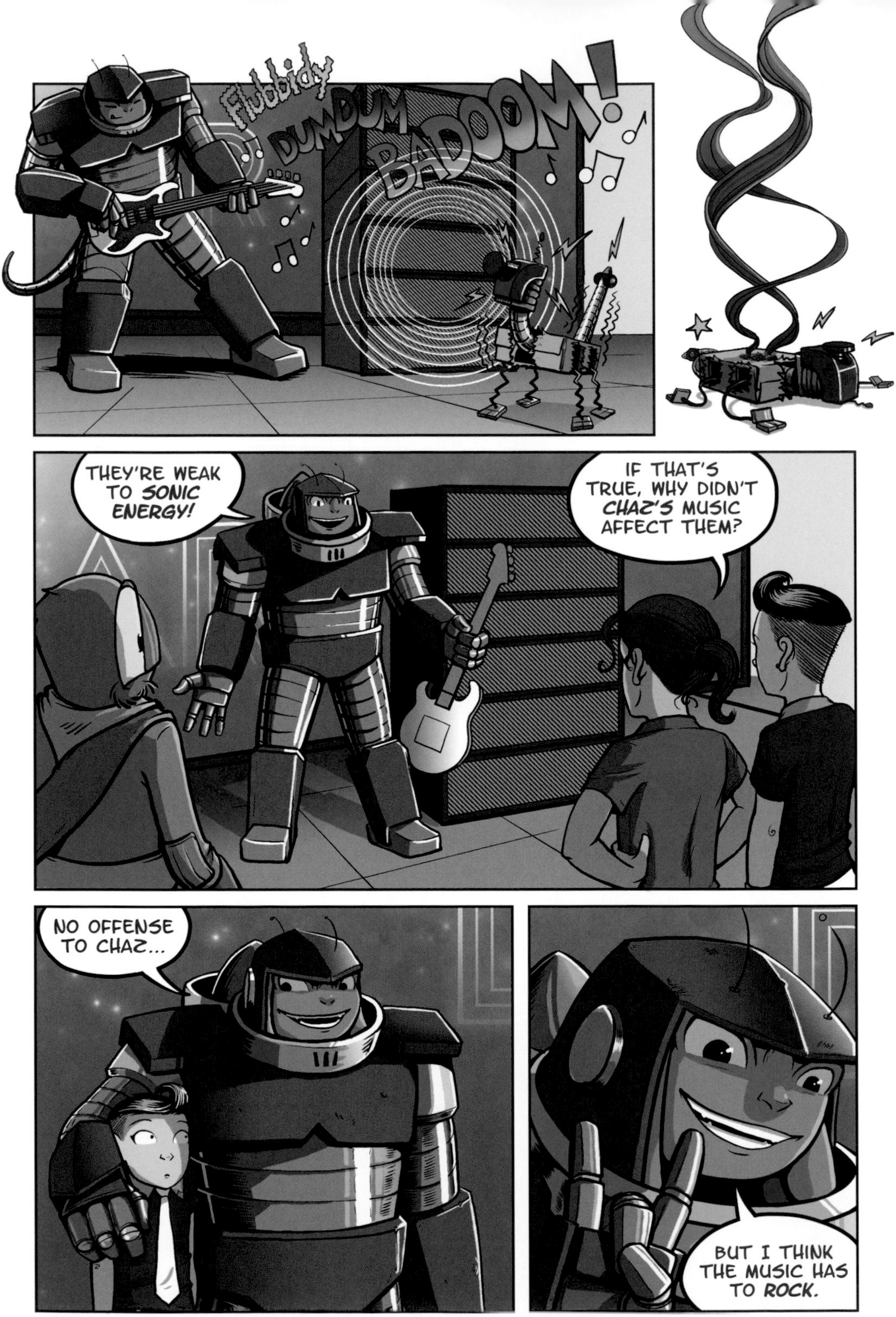
Flubbidy
DUMDUM
BADOOM!
THEY'RE WEAK TO SONIC ENERGY!
IF THAT'S TRUE, WHY DIDN'T CHAZ'S MUSIC AFFECT THEM?
NO OFFENSE TO CHAZ...
BUT I THINK THE MUSIC HAS TO ROCK.

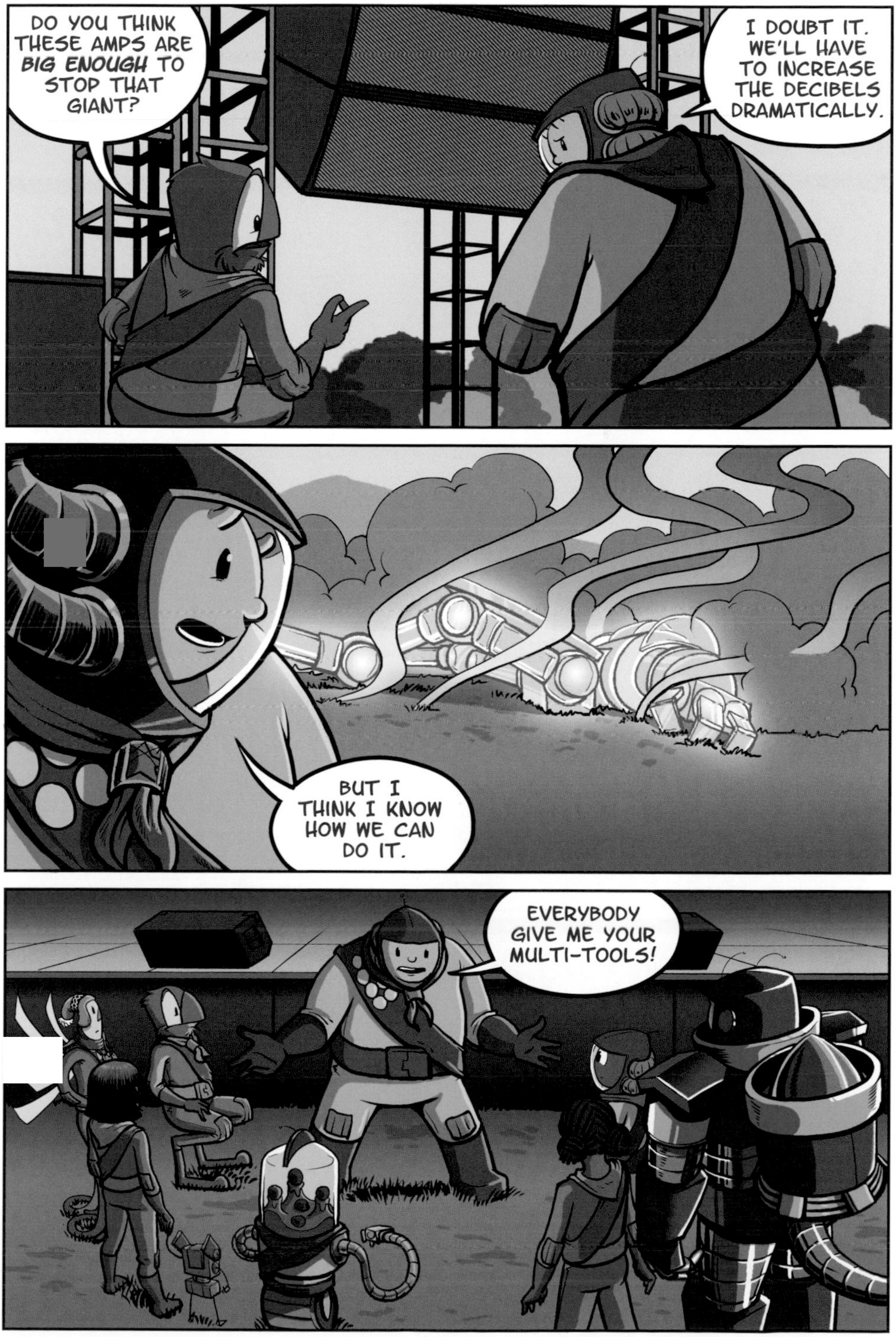
DO YOU THINK THESE AMPS ARE BIG ENOUGH TO STOP THAT GIANT?
I DOUBT IT. WE'LL HAVE TO INCREASE THE DECIBELS DRAMATICALLY.
BUT I THINK I KNOW HOW WE CAN DO IT.
EVERYBODY GIVE ME YOUR MULTI-TOOLS!

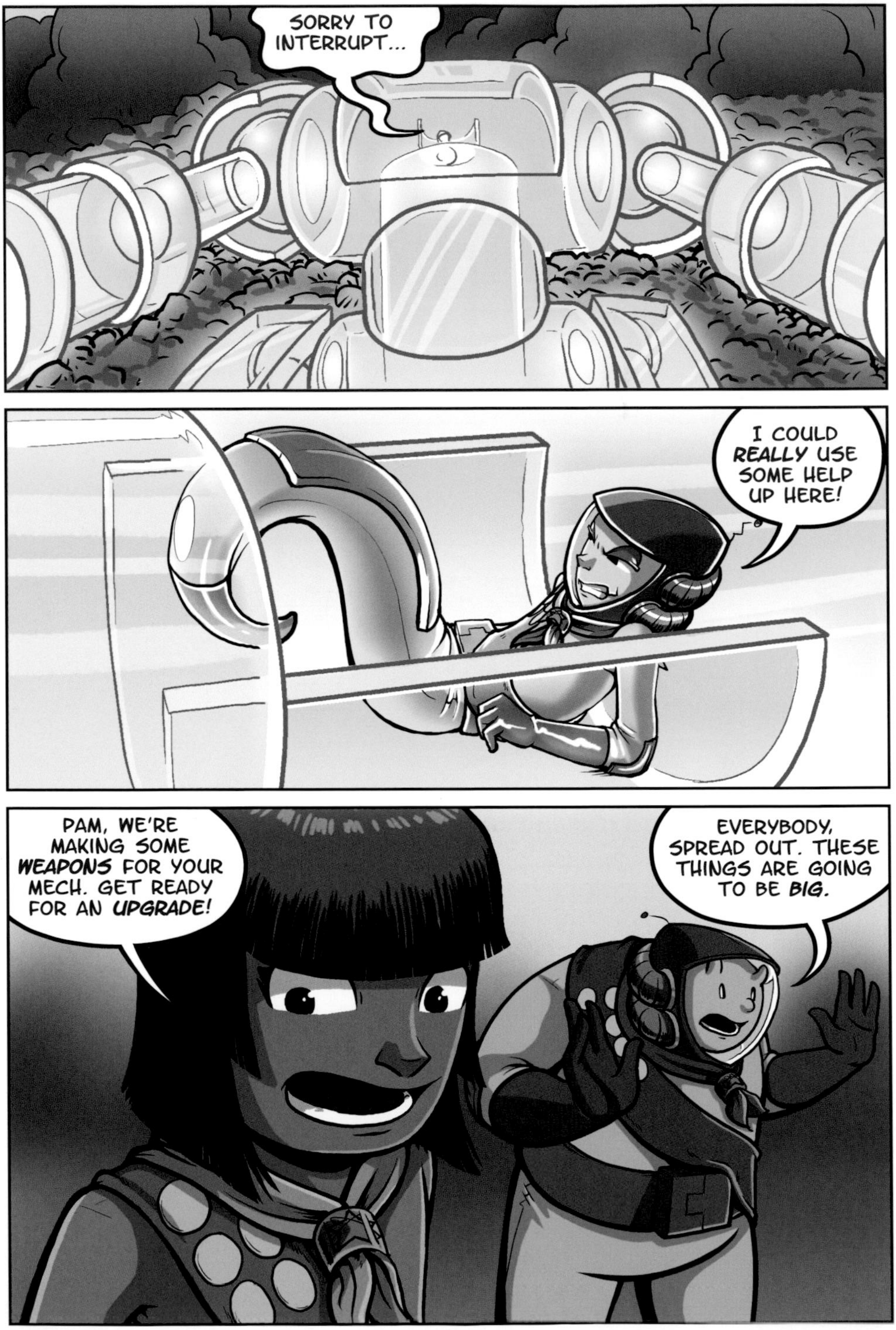
SORRY TO INTERRUPT...
I COULD REALLY USE SOME HELP UP HERE!
PAM, WE'RE MAKING SOME WEAPONS FOR YOUR MECH. GET READY FOR AN UPGRADE!
EVERYBODY, SPREAD OUT. THESE THINGS ARE GOING TO BE BIG.

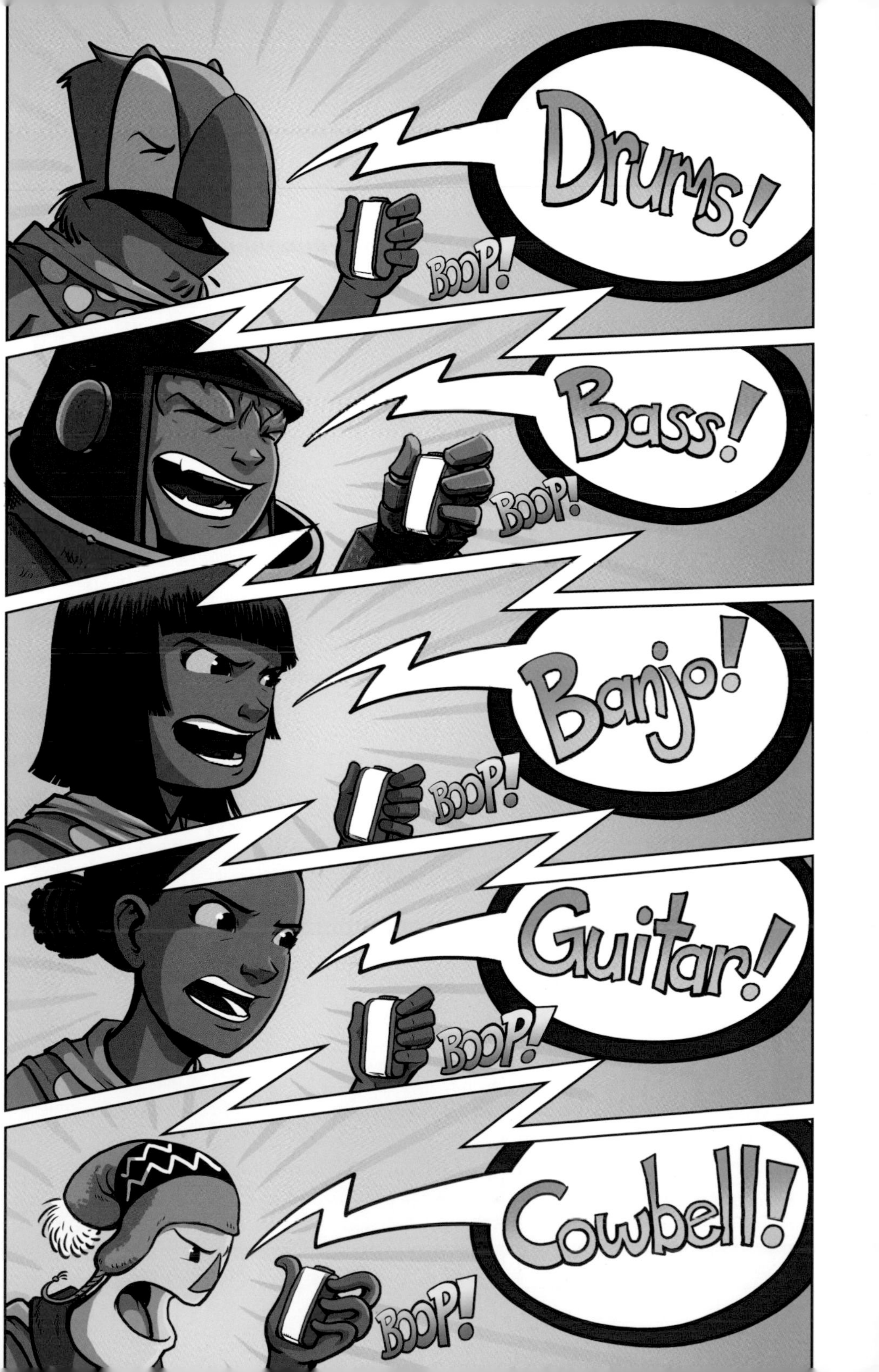
Drums!
BOOP!
Bass!
BOOP!
Banjo!
BOOP!
Guitar!
BOOP!
Cowbell!
BOOP!

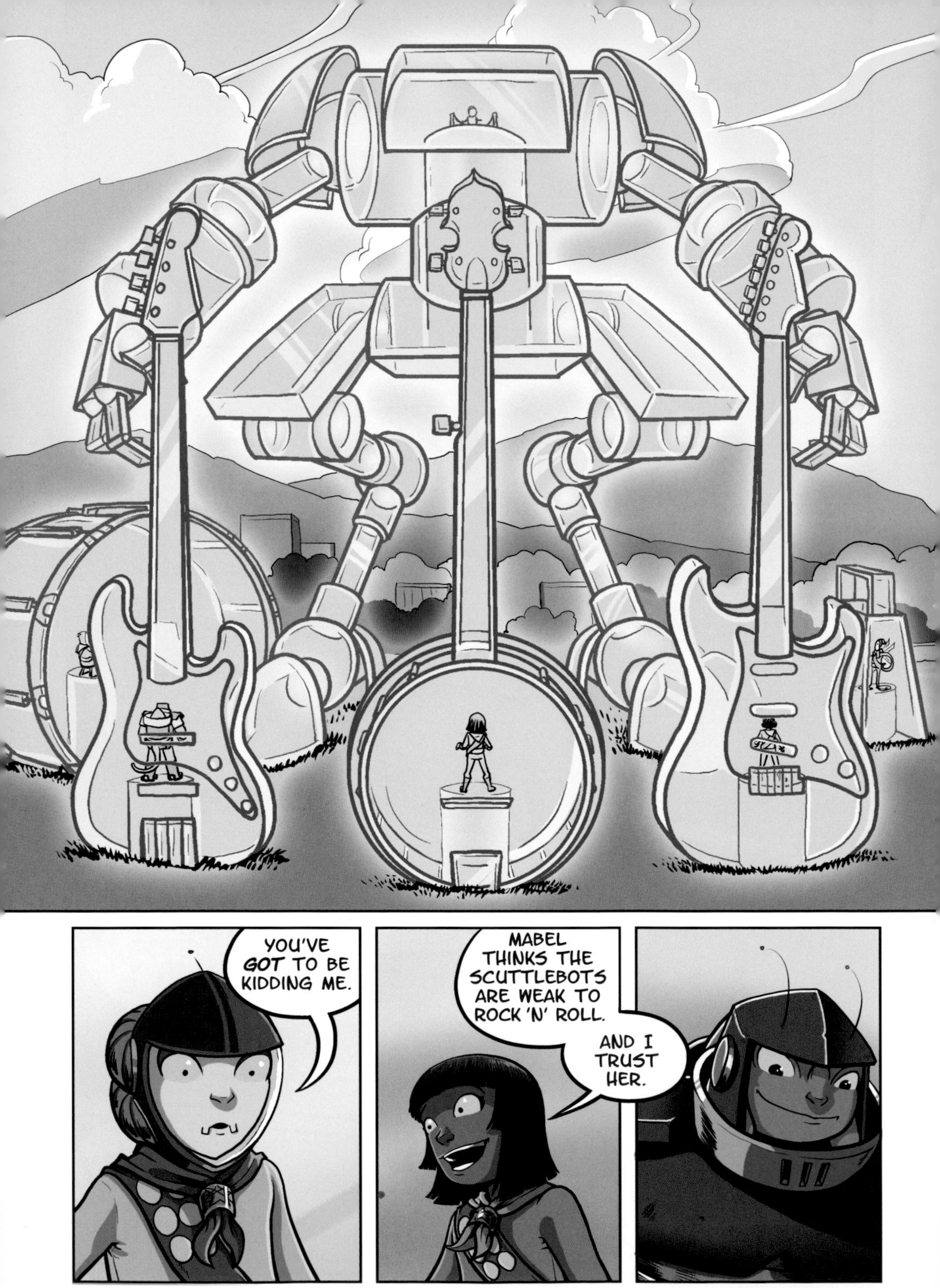
YOU'VE GOT TO BE KIDDING ME.
MABEL THINKS THE SCUTTLEBOTS ARE WEAK TO ROCK 'N' ROLL.
AND I TRUST HER.

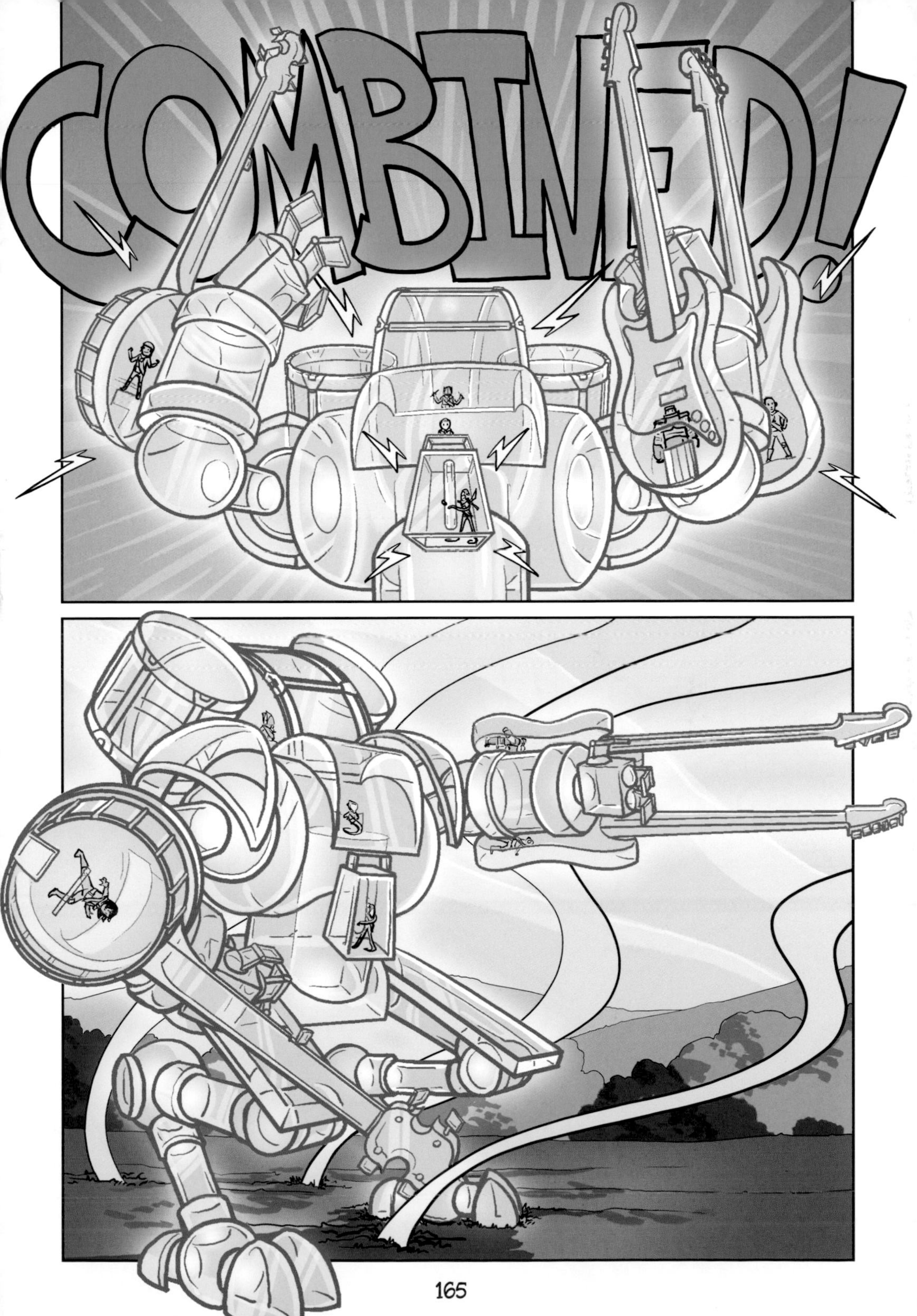
COMBINED!

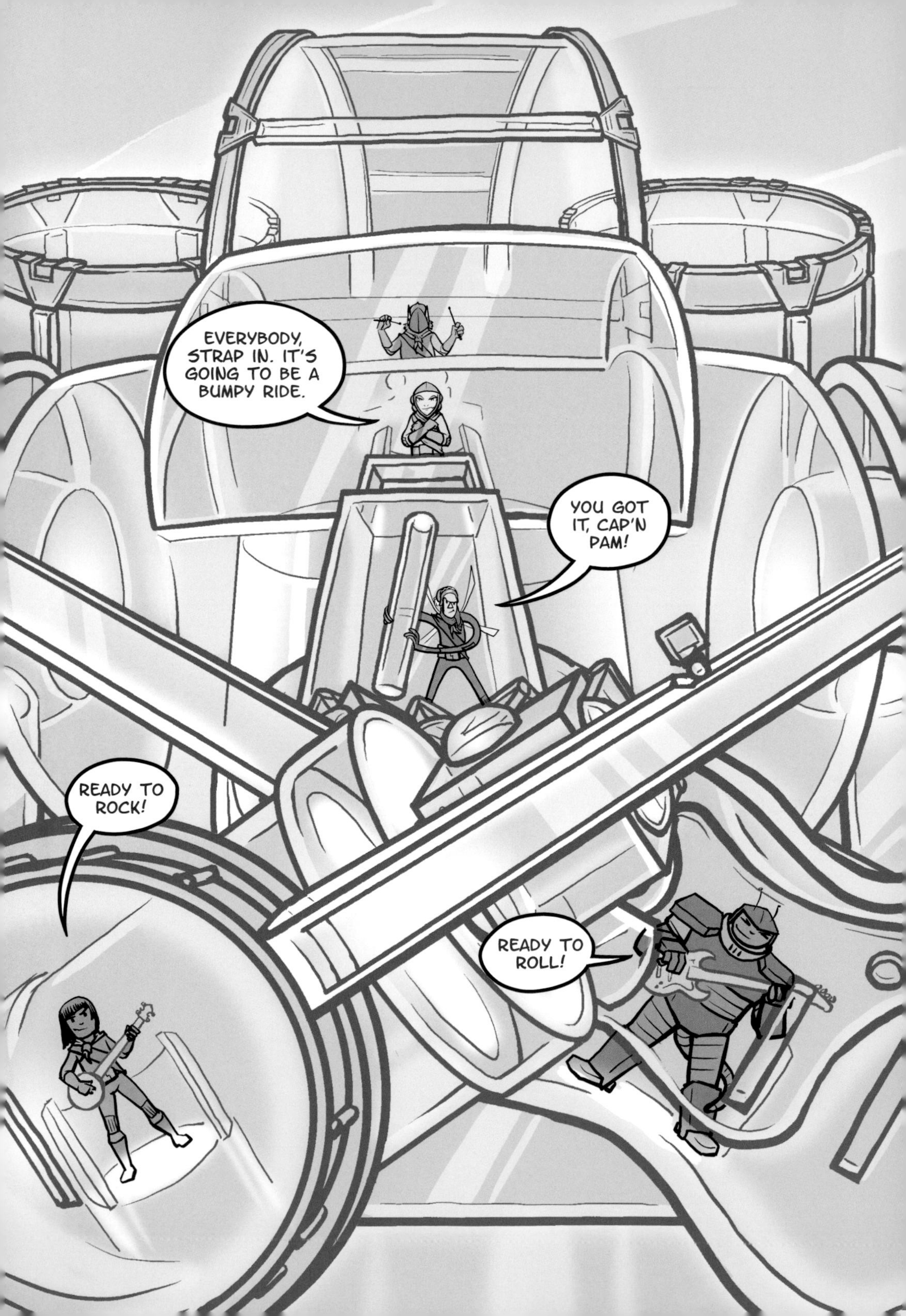
EVERYBODY, STRAP IN. IT'S GOING TO BE A BUMPY RIDE.
YOU GOT IT, CAP'N PAM!
READY TO ROCK!
READY TO ROLL!

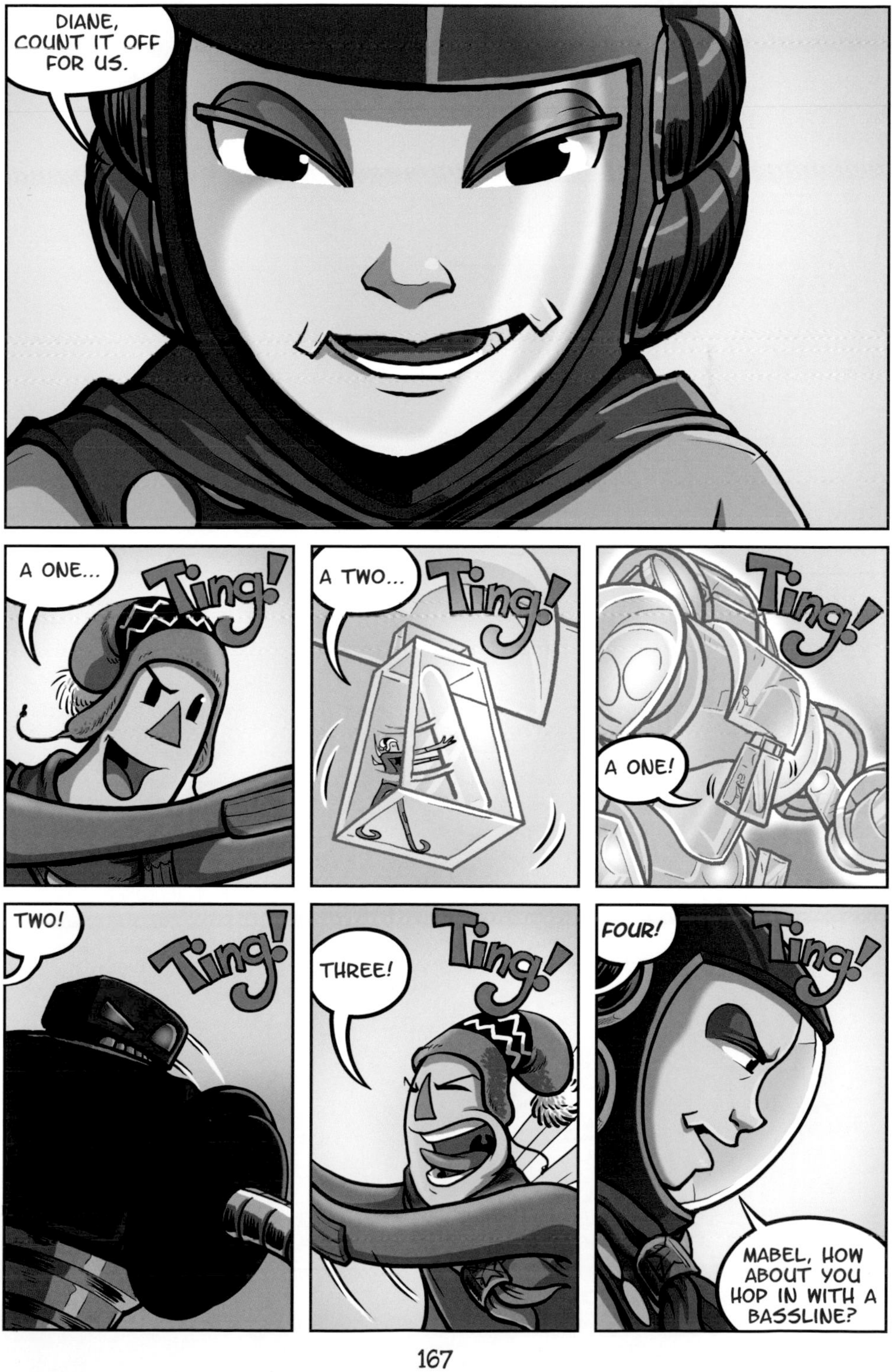
DIANE, COUNT IT OFF FOR US.
A ONE...
Ting!
A TWO...
Ting!
Ting!
A ONE!
TWO!
Ting!
THREE!
Ting!
FOUR!
Ting!
MABEL, HOW ABOUT YOU HOP IN WITH A BASSLINE?

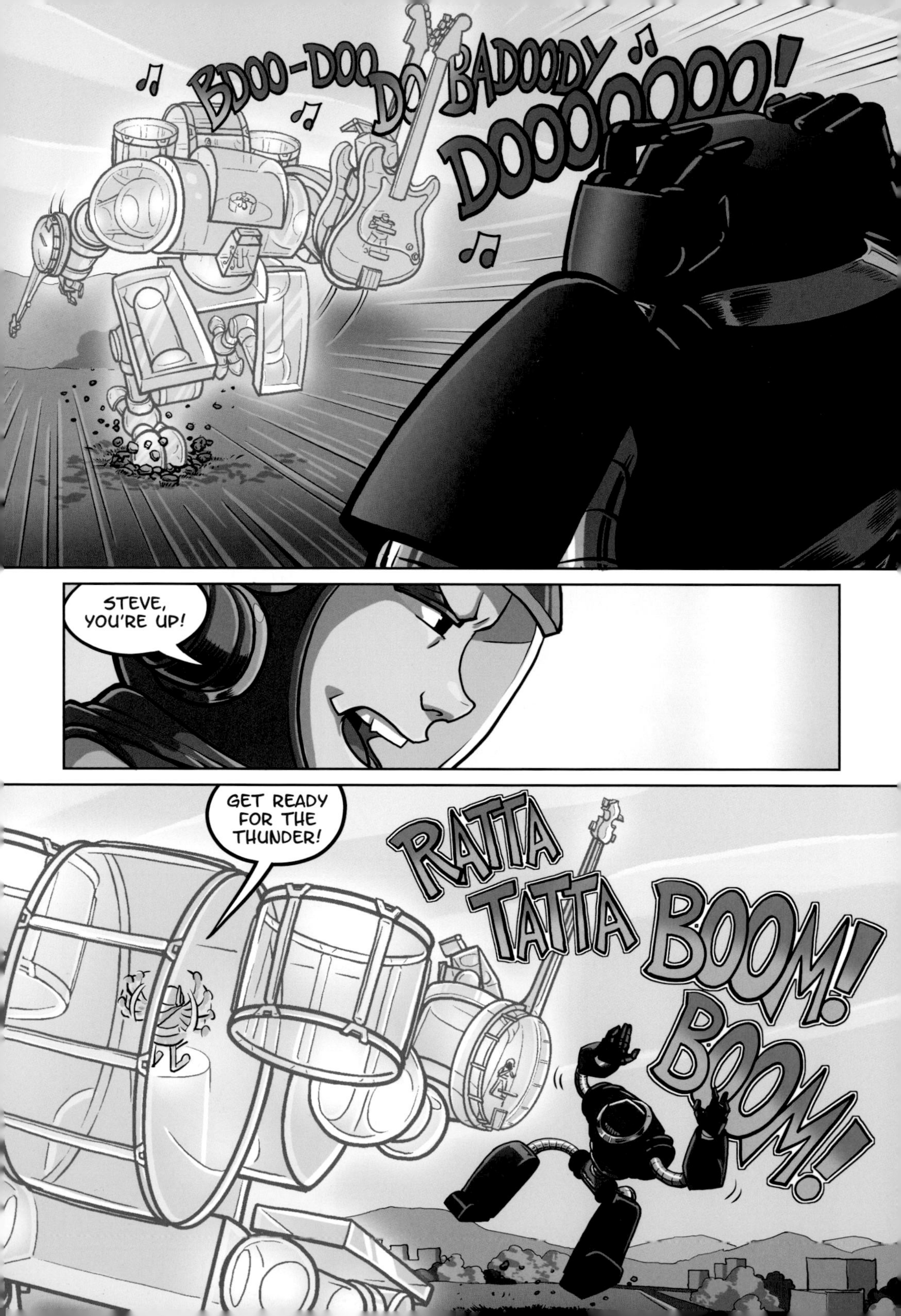

BDOO-DOO DO BADOODY DOOOOOOOO!
STEVE, YOU'RE UP!
GET READY FOR THE THUNDER!
RATTA TATTA BOOM! BOOM!

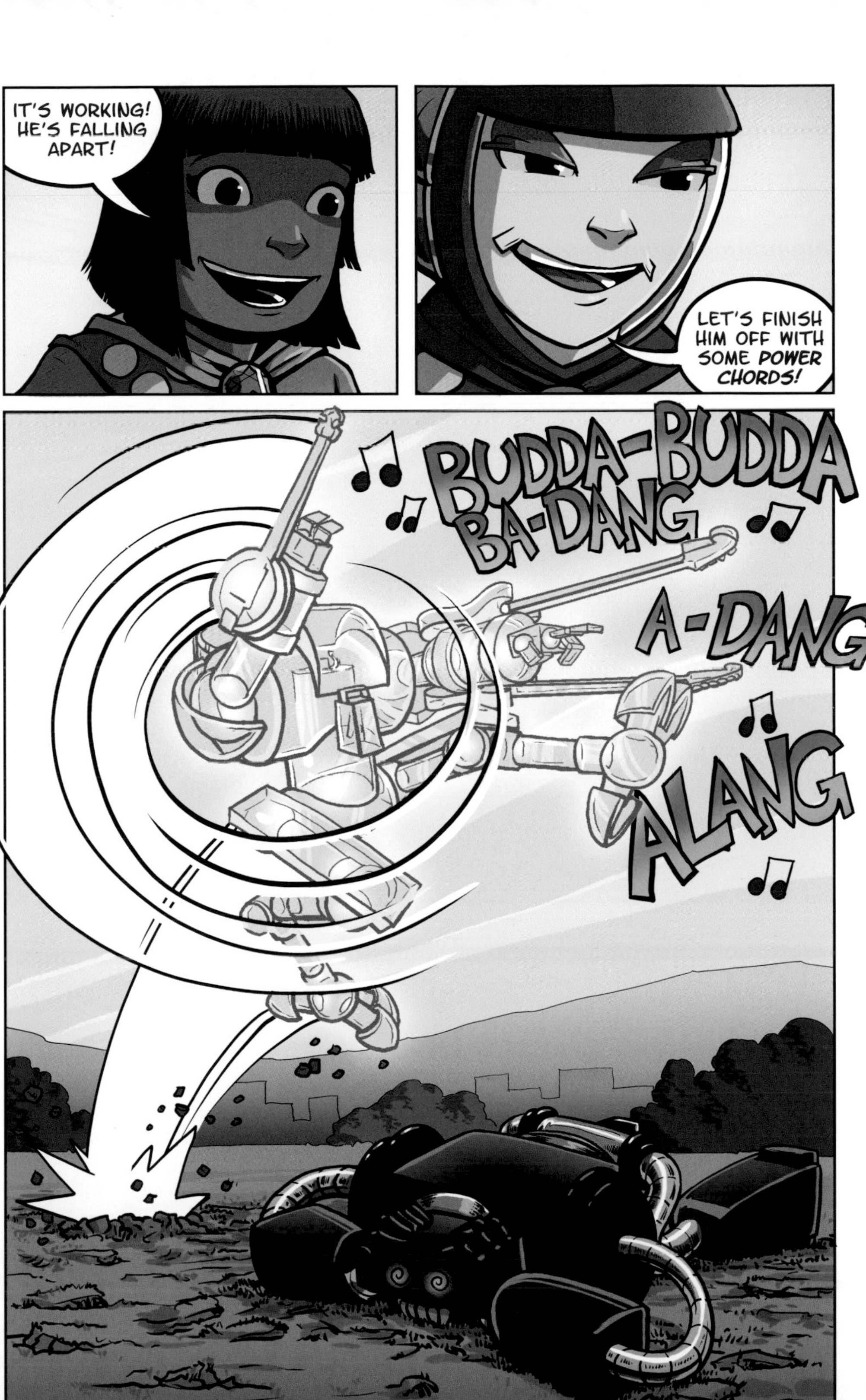
IT'S WORKING! HE'S FALLING APART!
LET'S FINISH HIM OFF WITH SOME POWER CHORDS!
BUDDA-BUDDA BA-DANG
A-DANG
ALANG

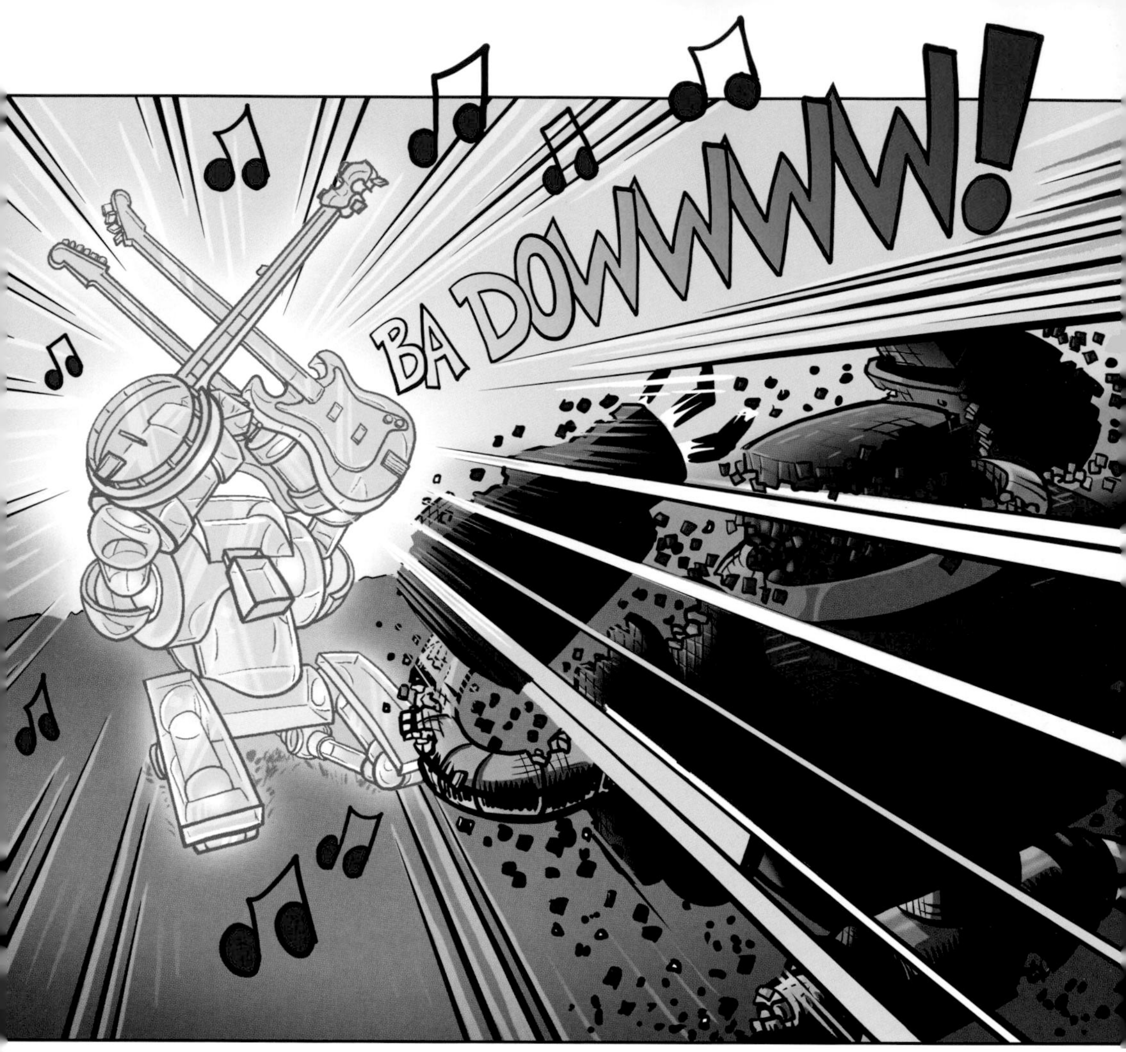
BA DOWWWWW!

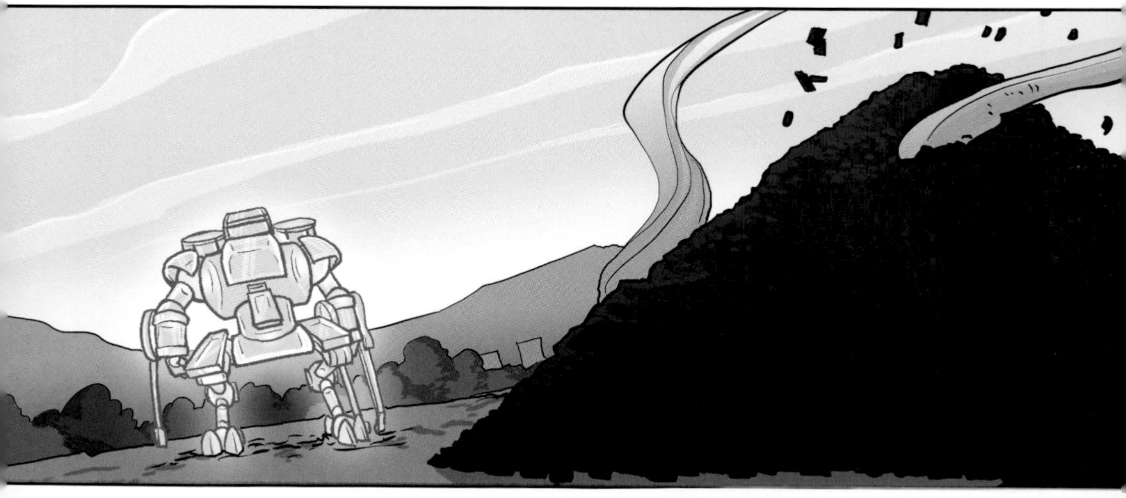

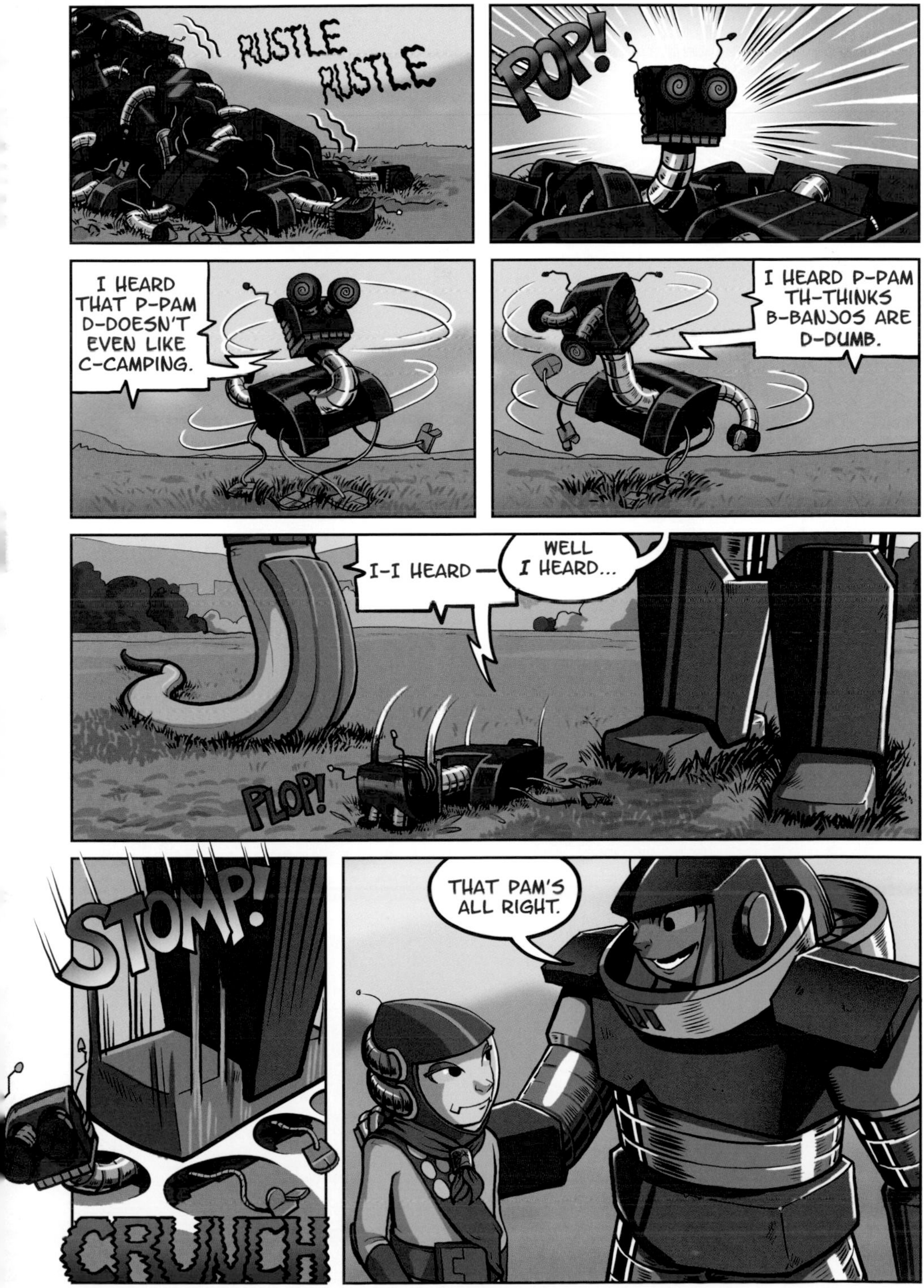
RUSTLE RUSTLE
POP!
I HEARD THAT P-PAM D-DOESN'T EVEN LIKE C-CAMPING.
I HEARD P-PAM TH-THINKS B-BANJOS ARE D-DUMB.
I-I HEARD—
WELL I HEARD...
PLOP!
STOMP!
CRUNCH
THAT PAM'S ALL RIGHT.

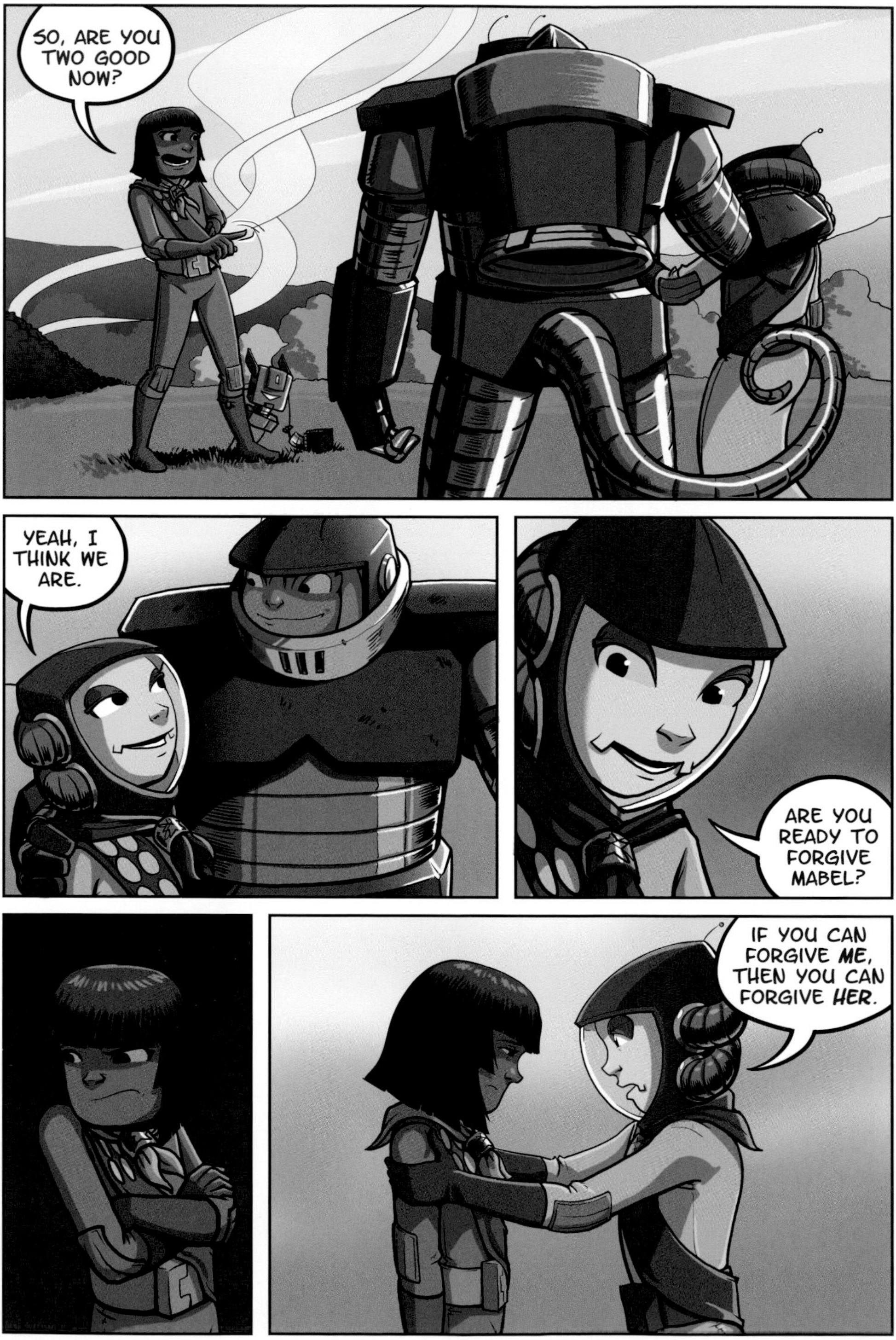
SO, ARE YOU TWO GOOD NOW?
YEAH, I THINK WE ARE.
ARE YOU READY TO FORGIVE MABEL?
IF YOU CAN FORGIVE **ME**, THEN YOU CAN FORGIVE **HER**.

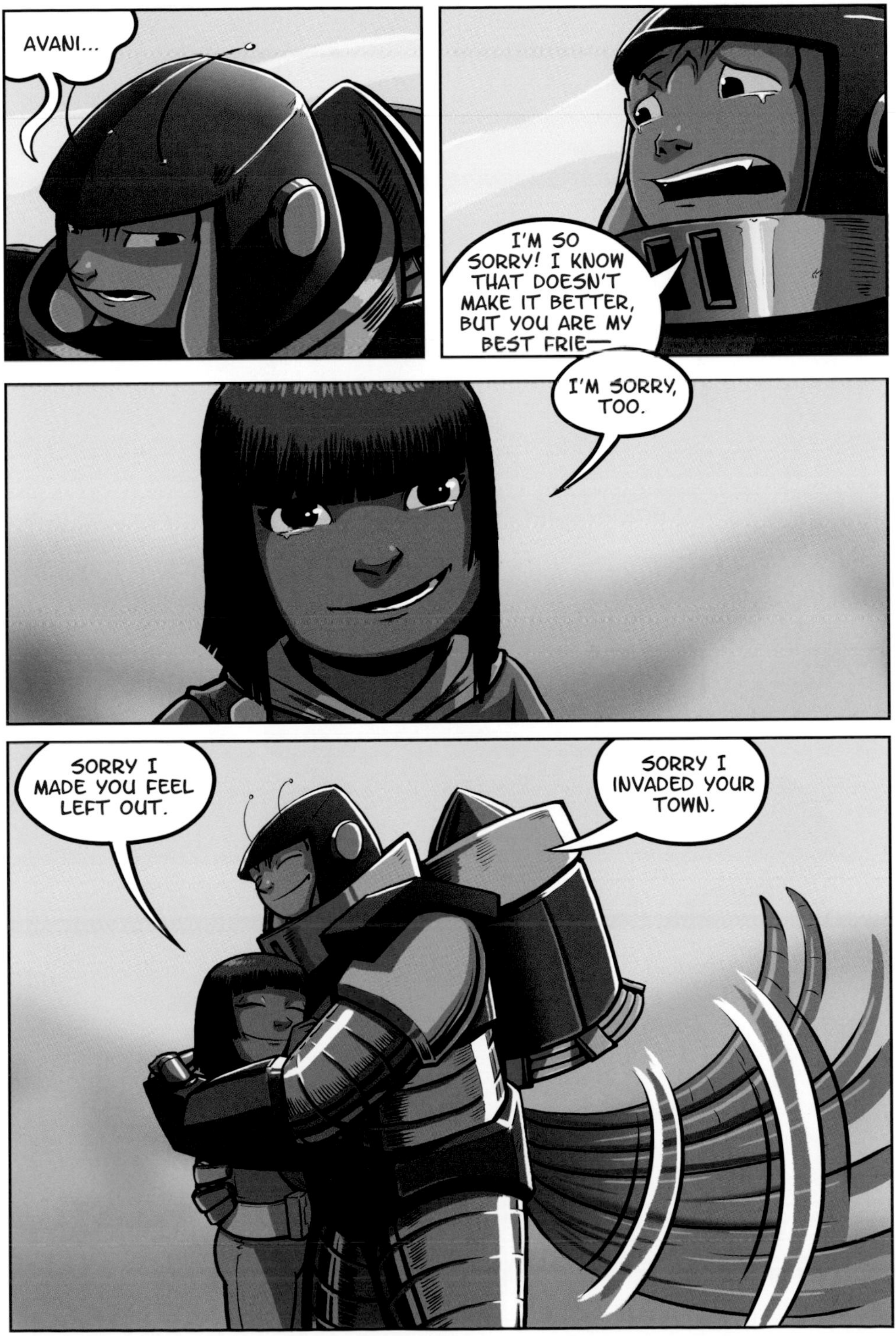
AVANI...
I'M SO SORRY! I KNOW THAT DOESN'T MAKE IT BETTER, BUT YOU ARE MY BEST FRIE—
I'M SORRY, TOO.
SORRY I MADE YOU FEEL LEFT OUT.
SORRY I INVADED YOUR TOWN.

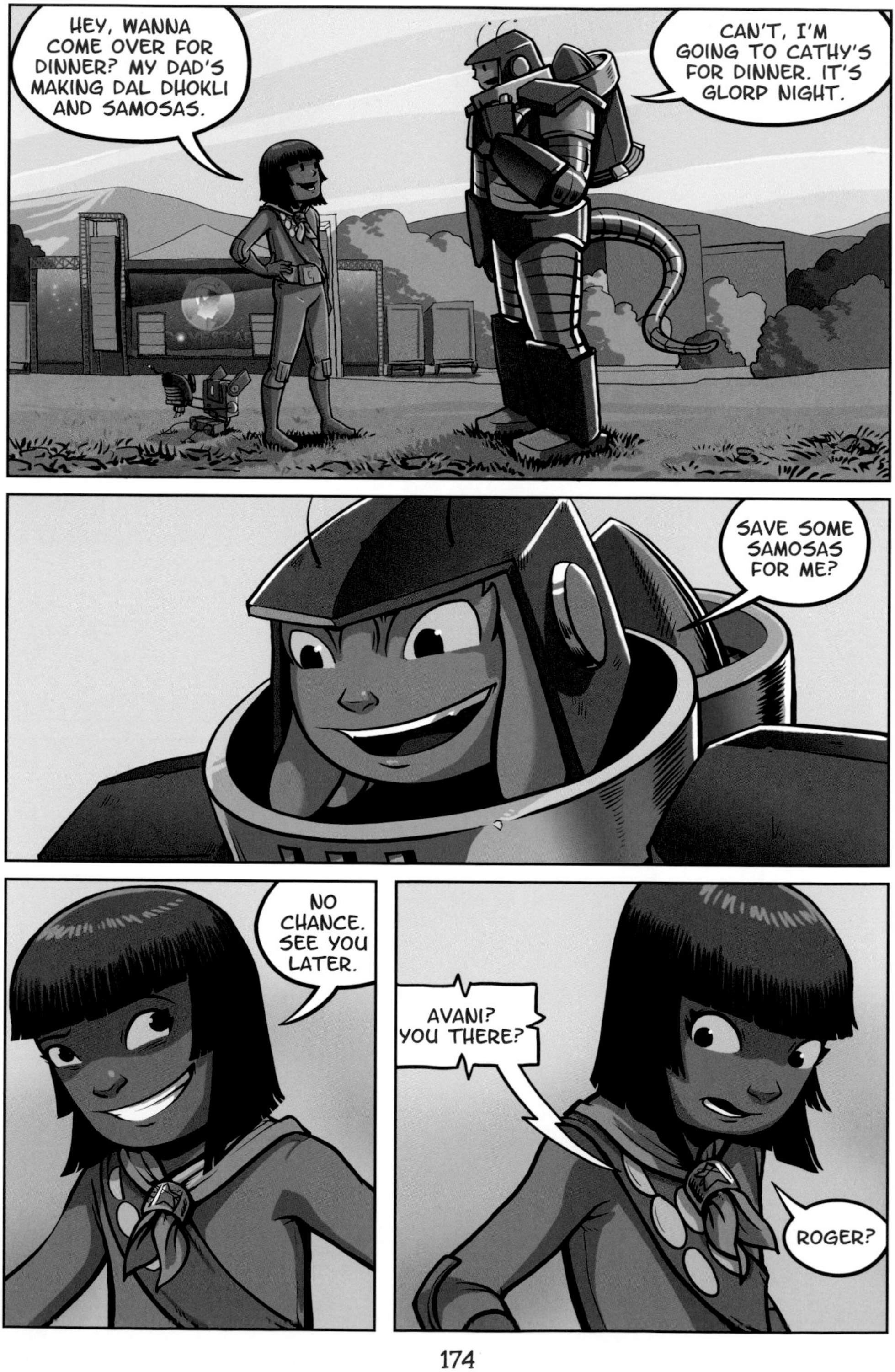
HEY, WANNA COME OVER FOR DINNER? MY DAD'S MAKING DAL DHOKLI AND SAMOSAS.
CAN'T, I'M GOING TO CATHY'S FOR DINNER. IT'S GLORP NIGHT.
SAVE SOME SAMOSAS FOR ME?
NO CHANCE. SEE YOU LATER.
AVANI? YOU THERE?
ROGER?

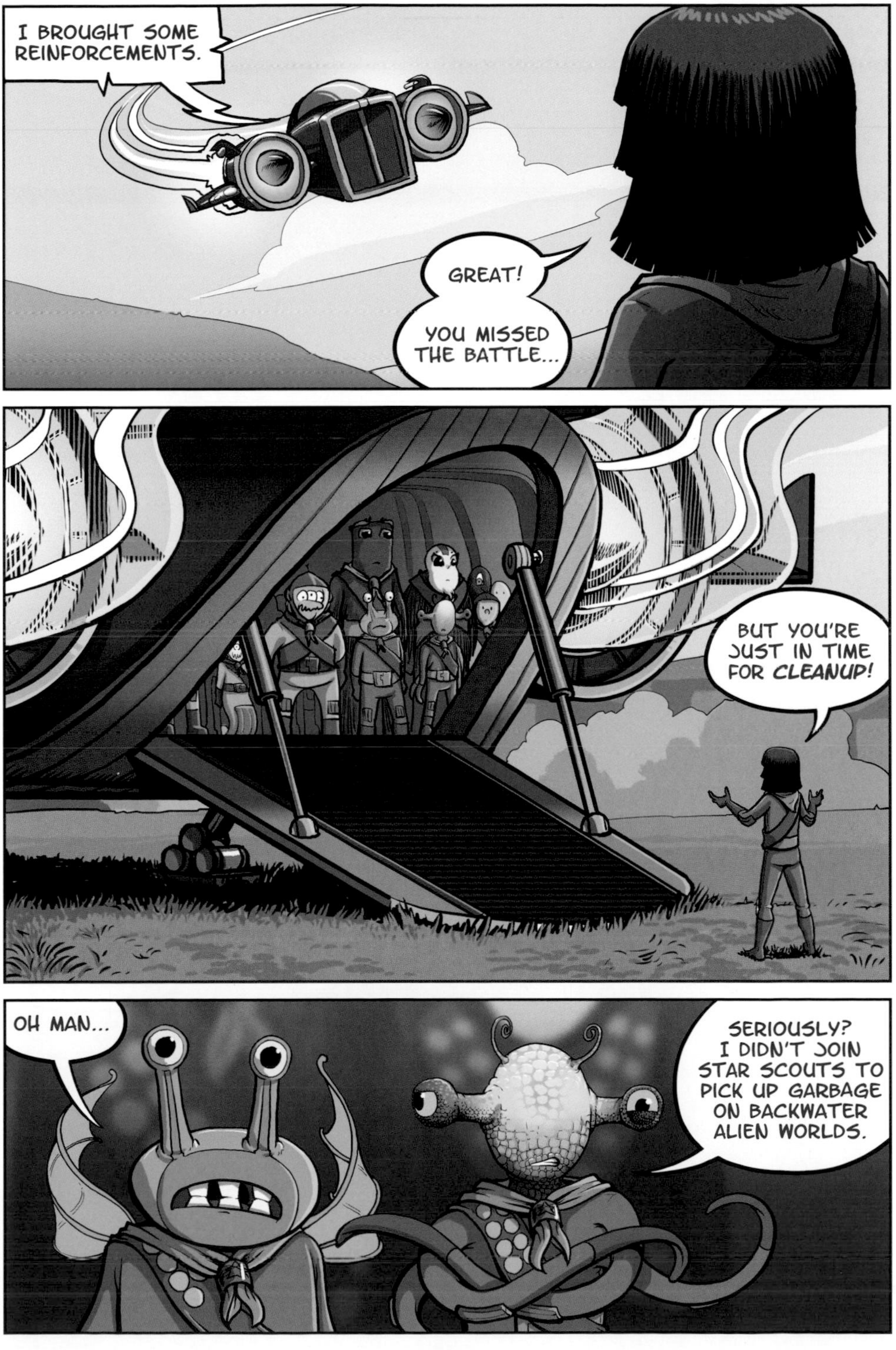

I BROUGHT SOME REINFORCEMENTS.
GREAT!
YOU MISSED THE BATTLE...
BUT YOU'RE JUST IN TIME FOR CLEANUP!
OH MAN...
SERIOUSLY? I DIDN'T JOIN STAR SCOUTS TO PICK UP GARBAGE ON BACKWATER ALIEN WORLDS.

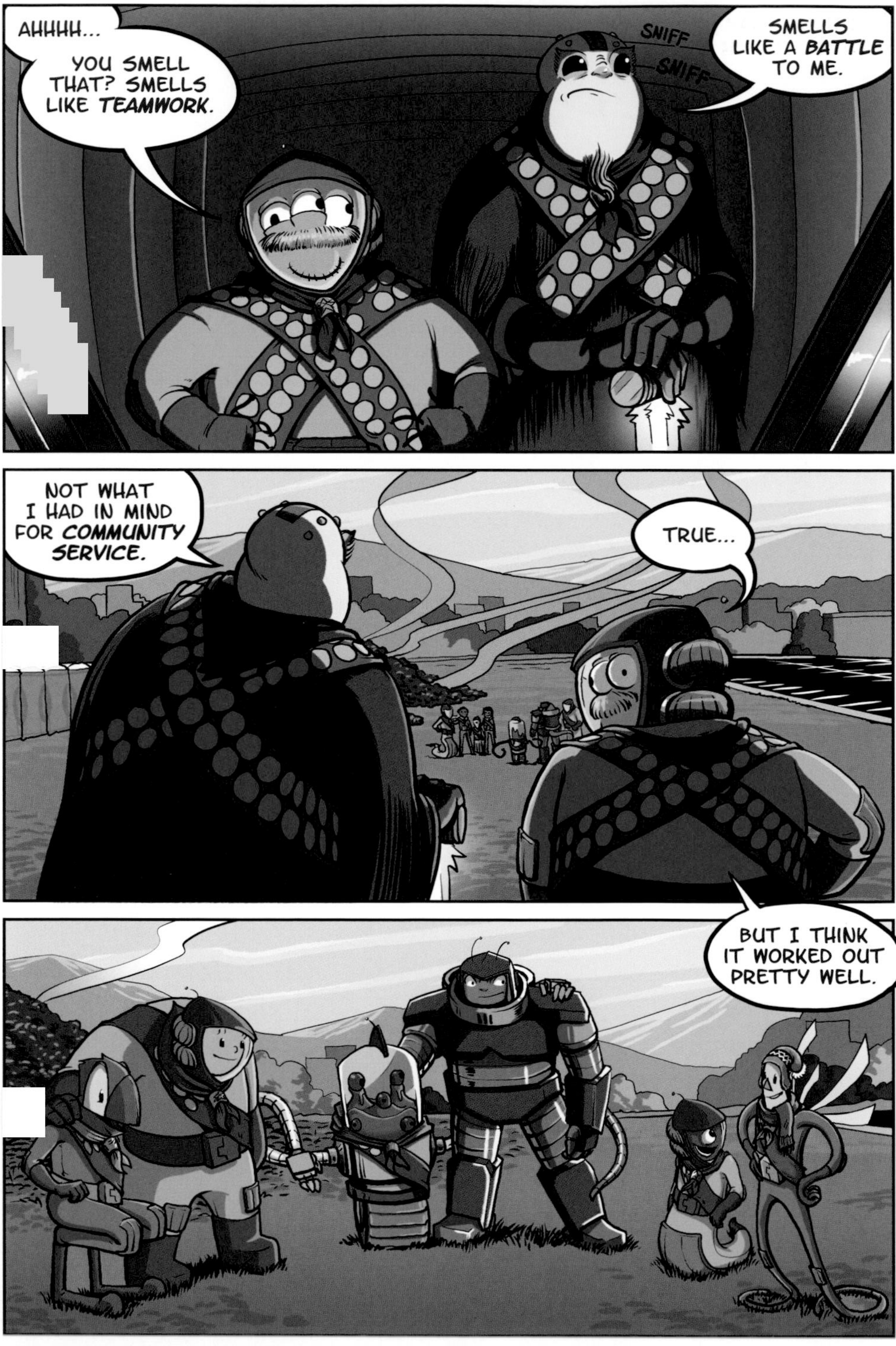
AHHHH...
YOU SMELL THAT? SMELLS LIKE *TEAMWORK*.
SNIFF
SNIFF
SMELLS LIKE A *BATTLE* TO ME.
NOT WHAT I HAD IN MIND FOR *COMMUNITY SERVICE*.
TRUE...
BUT I THINK IT WORKED OUT PRETTY WELL.

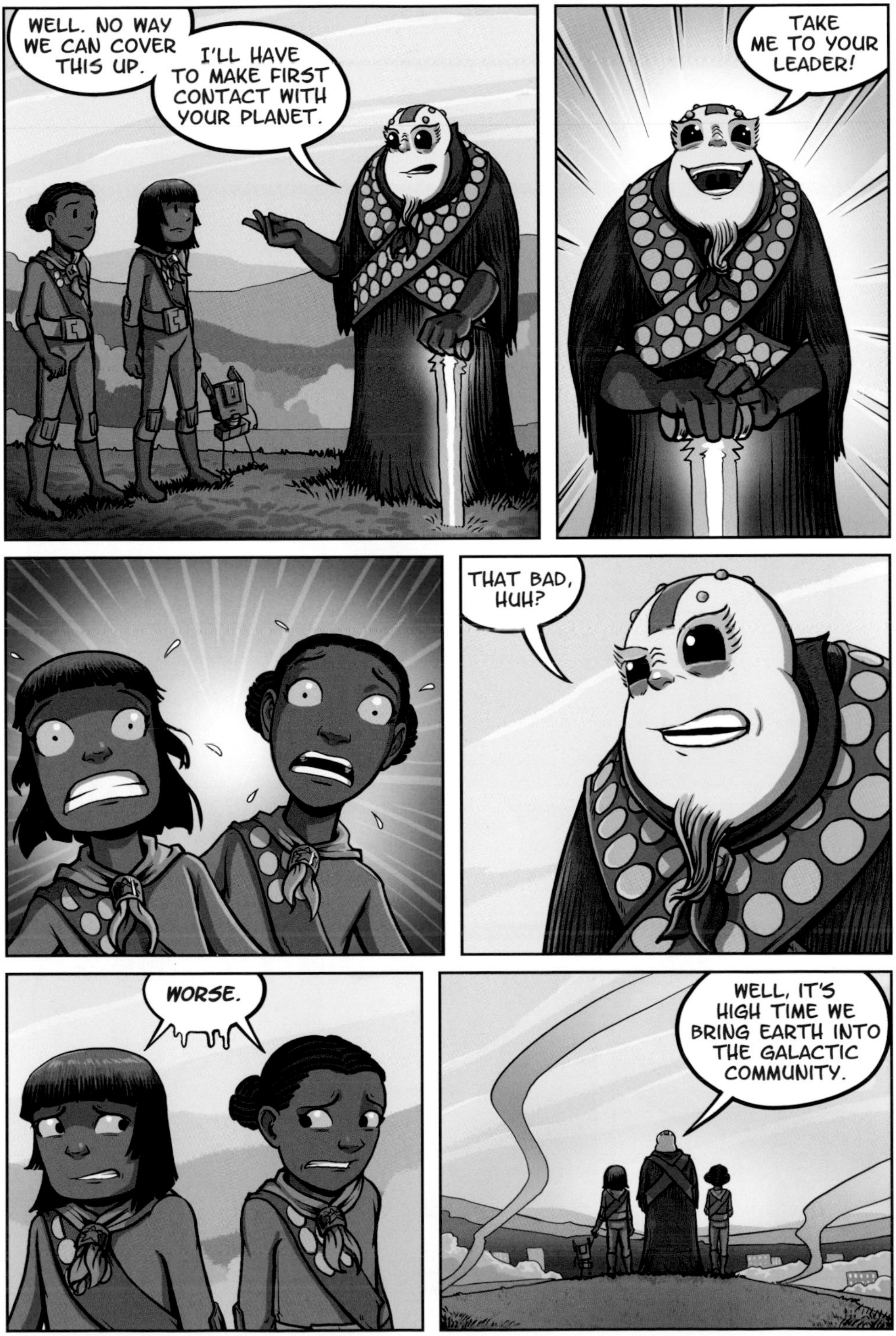
WELL. NO WAY WE CAN COVER THIS UP.
I'LL HAVE TO MAKE FIRST CONTACT WITH YOUR PLANET.
TAKE ME TO YOUR LEADER!
THAT BAD, HUH?
WORSE.
WELL, IT'S HIGH TIME WE BRING EARTH INTO THE GALACTIC COMMUNITY.

THIRTY YEARS LATER.

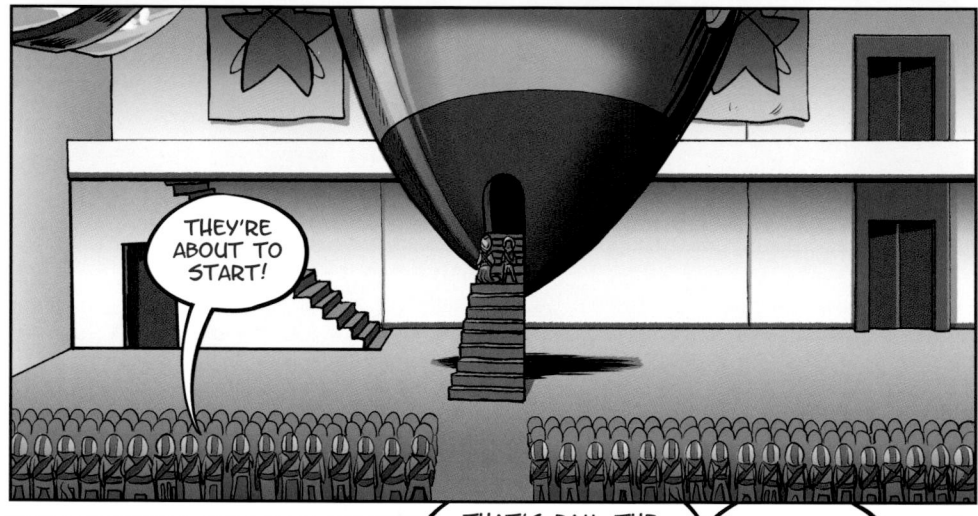

THEY'RE ABOUT TO START!

WHO'S THAT COMING DOWN THE STAIRS?

THAT'S PAM, THE *MASTER SCOUT.* SHE'S EARNED *EVERY BADGE* IN STAR SCOUTS.

EVEN THE ONES BANNED FOR SAFETY CONCERNS.

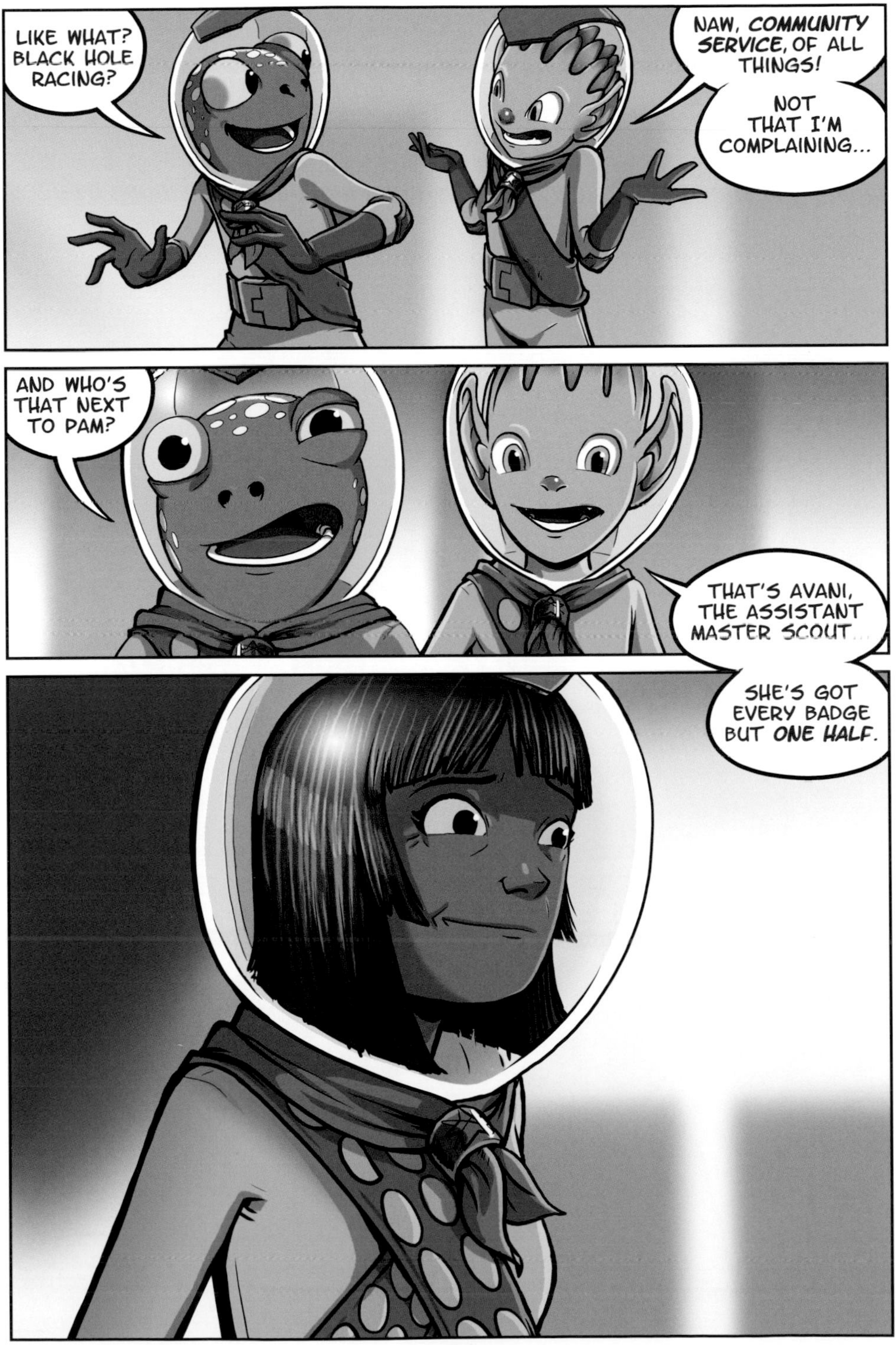
LIKE WHAT? BLACK HOLE RACING?
NAW, COMMUNITY SERVICE, OF ALL THINGS!
NOT THAT I'M COMPLAINING...
AND WHO'S THAT NEXT TO PAM?
THAT'S AVANI, THE ASSISTANT MASTER SCOUT...
SHE'S GOT EVERY BADGE BUT ONE HALF.

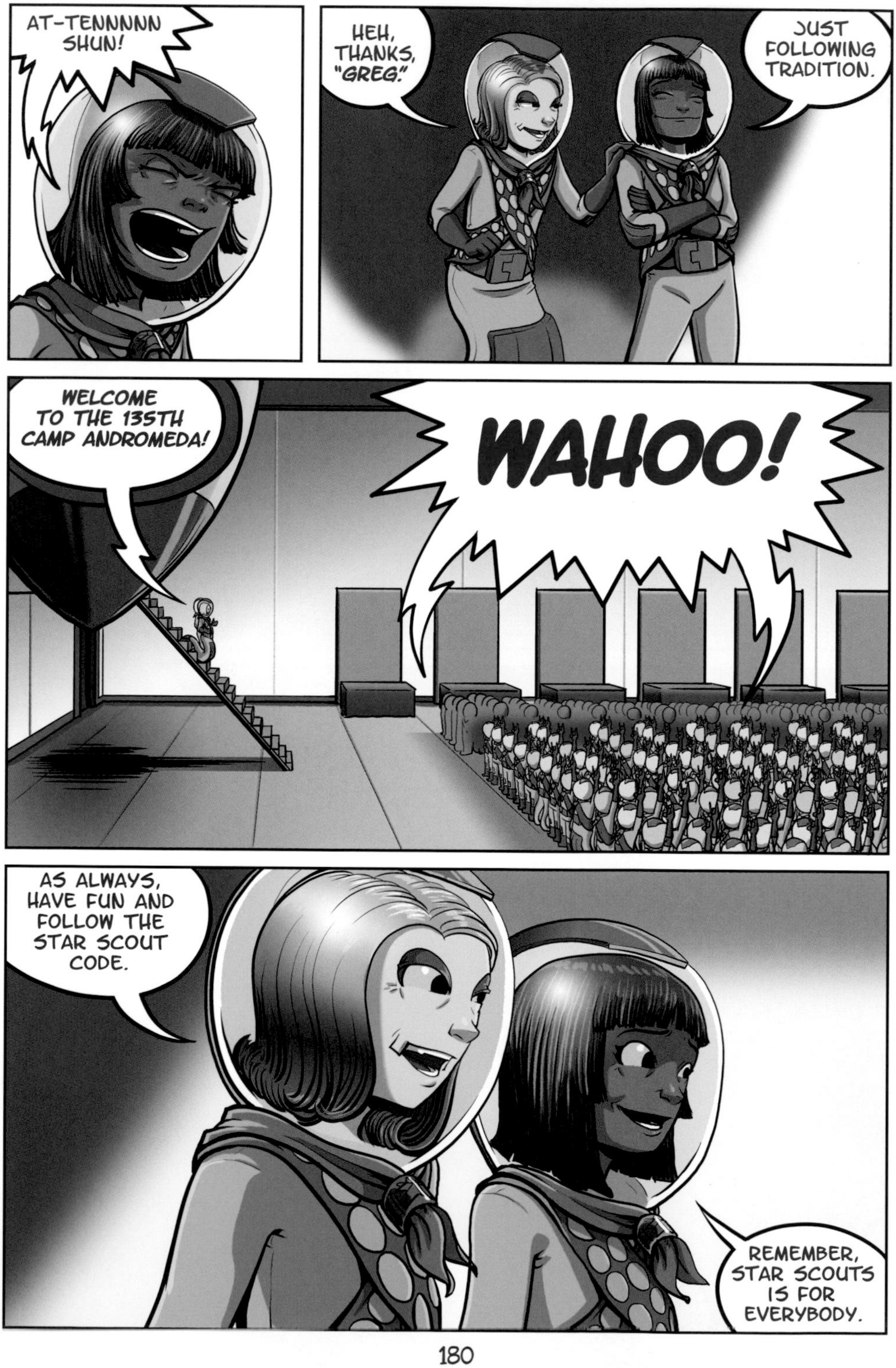
AT-TENNNNN SHUN!
HEH, THANKS, "GREG."
JUST FOLLOWING TRADITION.
WELCOME TO THE 135TH CAMP ANDROMEDA!
WAHOO!
AS ALWAYS, HAVE FUN AND FOLLOW THE STAR SCOUT CODE.
REMEMBER, STAR SCOUTS IS FOR EVERYBODY.

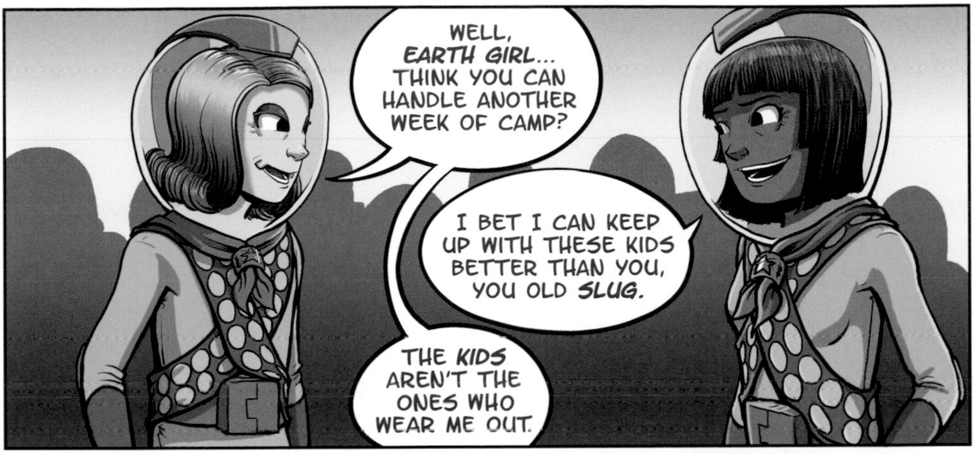
WELL, EARTH GIRL... THINK YOU CAN HANDLE ANOTHER WEEK OF CAMP?
I BET I CAN KEEP UP WITH THESE KIDS BETTER THAN YOU, YOU OLD SLUG.
THE KIDS AREN'T THE ONES WHO WEAR ME OUT.
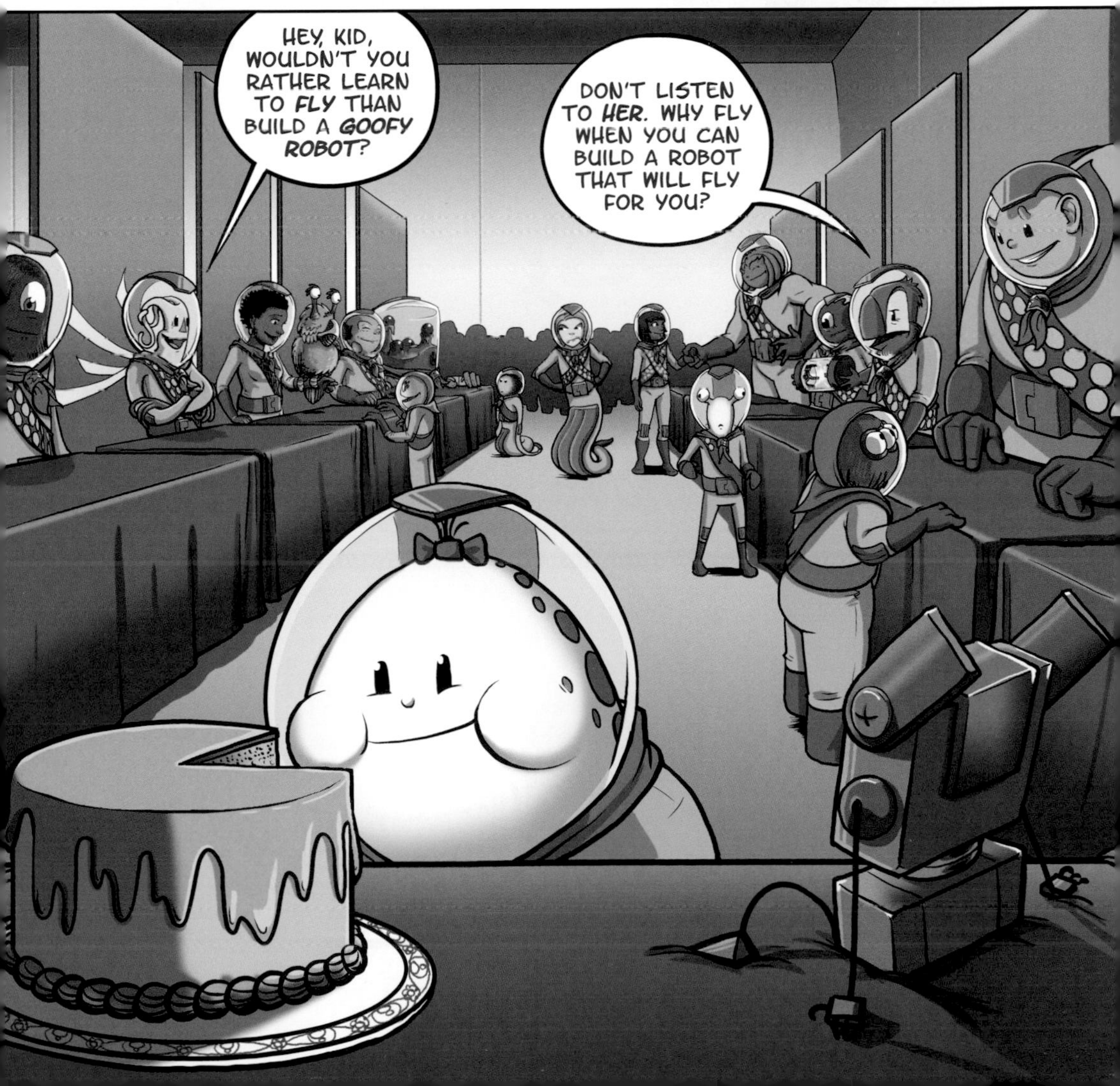
HEY, KID, WOULDN'T YOU RATHER LEARN TO FLY THAN BUILD A GOOFY ROBOT?
DON'T LISTEN TO HER. WHY FLY WHEN YOU CAN BUILD A ROBOT THAT WILL FLY FOR YOU?

THE MAKING OF STAR SCOUTS: THE INVASION OF THE SCUTTLEBOTS!

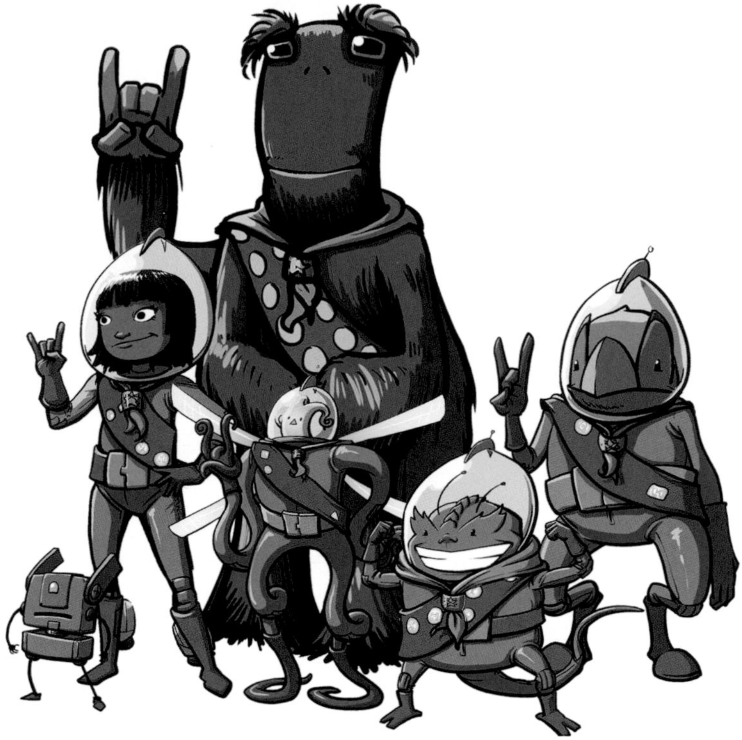

THESE ARE THE ORIGINAL CHARACTER DESIGNS I MADE WHEN I STARTED WORKING ON STAR SCOUTS. A LOT OF THE FINAL CHARACTER DESIGNS STAYED PRETTY CLOSE TO THESE EARLY CONCEPTS. LUNCHBOX AND CATHY ARE ALMOST EXACTLY THE SAME. THE CHARACTER WHO CHANGED THE MOST WAS MABEL.

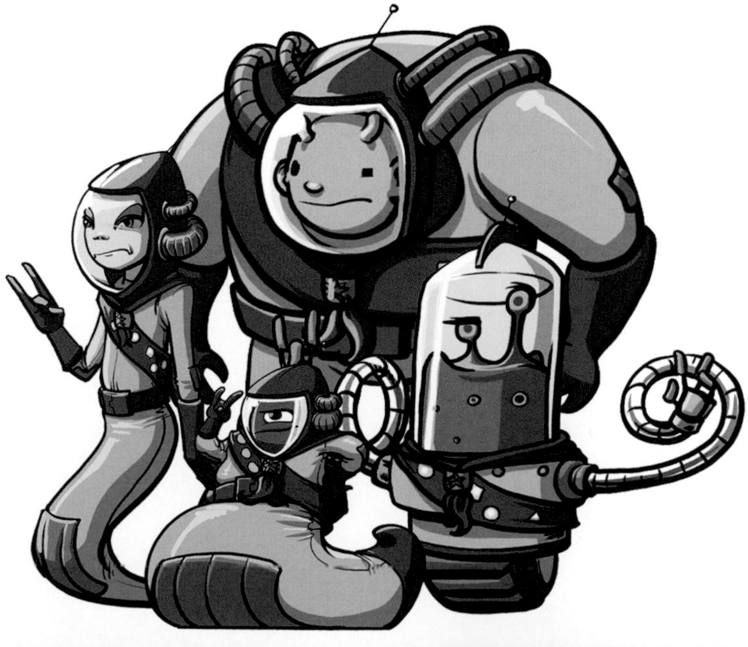

WHEN I STARTED PITCHING STAR SCOUTS TO PUBLISHERS, A FEW OF THEM TOLD ME THEY THOUGHT MABEL WAS TOO ALIEN LOOKING. I WENT BACK TO THE DRAWING BOARD AND GAVE HER SOME MORE "HUMAN" TRAITS, LIKE HAIR AND BIGGER EYES.

I WANTED TO KEEP MABEL SMALL, BECAUSE I'D ALWAYS THOUGHT OF HER AS THIS AGGRESSIVE BALL OF ENERGY THAT WOULD ONE DAY BECOME A GIANT WARRIOR. ONE OF MY FRIENDS POINTED OUT THAT IT WOULD BE EASIER FOR MABEL AND AVANI TO INTERACT IF THEY WERE ROUGHLY THE SAME SIZE, SO I WENT BACK TO THE DRAWING BOARD AGAIN.

IN THIS VERSION, I MADE MABEL TALLER AND GAVE HER LONGER HAIR, THINKING IT WOULD BE FUN TO DRAW IT SWINGING AROUND WHEN SHE WAS IN MOTION. BUT I QUICKLY REALIZED IT WOULDN'T WORK WITH THE STAR SCOUT HELMET.

IN THE FINAL VERSION, I SHORTENED MABEL'S HAIR AND GAVE HER BACK HER TAIL.

ONE OF MY FAVORITE THINGS TO DO IN STAR SCOUTS WAS DRAWING RANDOM FUNNY ALIENS IN THE BACKGROUND. AFTER A WHILE, IT WAS HARD TO COME UP WITH NEW IDEAS, SO I'D ASK MY KIDS TO HELP OUT.

DRAWN BY GUS, AGE 5

DRAWN BY HANK, AGE 7

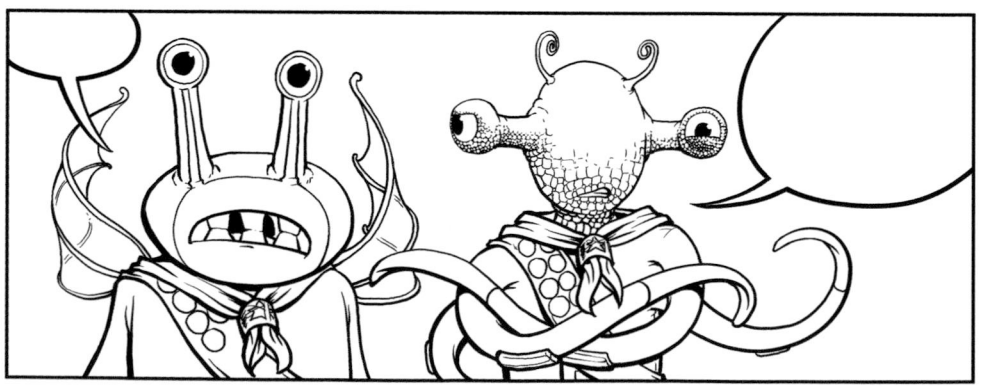

DRAWN BY MIKE, AGE 38

THANKS!

This book would not have been possible without the love and support of my wife and kids. Making comics is a labor of love, full of long workdays, missed deadlines (sorry, Robyn!), and gobs of self-doubt. Whenever I felt overwhelmed and wondered aloud whether these books are even any good, my family has always been there to say "yes." For the last four years, they have cheered me on every time I finished a page.

All 534 of them.

First Second

Copyright © 2019 Mike Lawrence
Published by First Second
First Second is an imprint of Roaring Brook Press,
a division of Holtzbrinck Publishing Holdings Limited Partnership
120 Broadway, New York, NY 10271

Don't miss your next favorite book from First Second! For the latest updates go to
firstsecondnewsletter.com and sign up for our enewsletter.

Library of Congress Control Number: 2018953667
ISBN: 978-1-250-19109-0

Our books may be purchased in bulk for promotional, educational,
or business use. Please contact your local bookseller or the Macmillan
Corporate and Premium Sales Department at (800) 221-7945 ext. 5442
or by email at MacmillanSpecialMarkets@macmillan.com.

First edition, 2019
Edited by Robyn Chapman
Series design by Danielle Ceccolini
Cover design by Andrew Arnold
Interior book design by Ellen Lindner
Color by Norm Grock
Printed in China by 1010 Printing International Limited, North Point, Hong Kong

Drawn digitally in Clip Studio Paint and colored in Photoshop. Lettered with Blambot fonts.

10 9 8 7 6 5 4 3 2 1